It's About Your
HUSBAND

It's About Your
HUSBAND

———❤———

LAUREN LIPTON

NEW YORK   BOSTON

5 Spot
Hachette Book Group USA
237 Park Avenue
New York, NY 10017

Visit our Web site at www.5-spot.com

5 Spot is an imprint of Grand Central Publishing.
The 5 Spot name and logo is a trademark of Hachette Book Group USA, Inc.

Printed in the United States of America

First Edition: October 2006
10 9 8 7 6 5 4

Library of Congress Cataloging-in-Publication Data
Lipton, Lauren, 1966–
    It's about your husband / Lauren Lipton. — 1st ed.
        p.   cm.
    ISBN 978-0-446-69784-2
    1. New York (N.Y.) — Fiction.   I. Title.
    PS3612.I68I88   2006
    813'.6—dc22
                                                    2006006880

Book design by Charles Sutherland

To David
For world enough and time

Acknowledgments

I am indebted to my early readers, whose suggestions, large and small, were invaluable: Christy Fletcher, Danelle McCafferty, Caroline Novak, Failey Patrick, Liz Queler, Lee Slonimsky, Nora Slonimsky, Sandra Waugh, my fellow workshop participants at the Writers' Voice, and, above all, Carol Goodman.

Naomi Henderson, chief executive of RIVA Market Research in Bethesda, Maryland, answered questions about focus-group moderators. San Diego attorney Cathryn Campbell offered insight into the California divorce process. Lynn Gonsor-Anvari supplied some choice business jargon, as did articles in the *New York Times*. John Stuart Wildman provided the details of acting and voice-over work. I am solely responsible for any errors or omissions in, or embellishments to, any of this information.

Clare McHugh, editor of *In Style Weddings*, was supportive, as were editors Joanne Lipman, Amy Stevens, Jeff Grocott, and Jonathan Dahl at the *Wall Street Journal*. Ken Wells of the *Journal*, Bob Christie of Dow Jones, and David Cay Johnston of the *New York Times* were generous with publishing and marketing advice.

Thank you to Laura Langlie, my agent, for your soft-spoken wisdom; and to the gifted Melanie Murray, for your inspired editing. Also at Warner Books, thank you to Brigid Pearson, Tareth Mitch, Michael Carr, Charles Sutherland, the effervescent Elly Weisenberg, and the amazing Amy Einhorn. Thank you also to Tooraj Kavoussi at TK Public Relations.

Everyone needs a person she can count on absolutely. I am lucky for my father, Lew Lipton, who has always been there with kindness, encouragement, and advice.

And as for David and James, I am blessed to have you both. Thank you for teaching me the meaning of life.

It's About Your
HUSBAND

ONE

Val is not herself today.

It isn't like her to be so subdued. She doesn't call to me as I make my way up the carved marble staircase, its edges worn smooth by generations of arrivals and departures. She doesn't wave me over once I reach the top of the stairs and wrestle through the crowd, elbowing past Wednesday-afternoon revelers raising their glasses to celebrate the end of another workday. She doesn't look up after I get myself a beer and approach her table, or offer any comment as I stand, dumbfounded, before the remarkable structure she has created. Here, in the mezzanine bar at Grand Central, with only a few square inches of table to work with, Val has erected a tower of shopping bags representing nearly every one of New York's best *B*'s (Bendel's, Barneys, Bergdorf's . . .). I'm ashamed to say, in my own state of mentally unstable not-quite-myselfness, this is the only unusual thing I notice.

Shopping. There's something else I won't be doing for a while.

I take a deep breath and put on the happiest happy-hour smile I can muster. "Look at you!" I chirp, holding my beer glass in a death grip, shoehorning myself into the three-inch gap between the empty chair and the edge of her table, goggling at the bags while using my free hand to push them out of my way. I poke a Burberry back from the edge of the table, where it threatens to drop into my lap, but that only makes the rest of the pile teeter precariously. I clamp down on the Boyd's of Madison at the top and struggle to shift my chair to one side without spilling beer on myself. Val makes no effort to help.

"If you wouldn't mind," I say, "could you help me move this stuff, just the tiniest—oh, my goodness!"

Val is crying.

No. Not crying—sobbing. Tears skid down her flushed cheeks to her jawbone and pause at the abyss a moment before splashing into her untouched cocktail. She's got mascara running down her wrist onto the sleeve of her pink cardigan, her demure blond pageboy is all mussed, and she's groping around in her pink quilted Chanel chain purse, perhaps for a tissue.

"What is it? You poor thing!" I'm no longer thinking about shopping bags and am halfway to forgetting why I've been feeling so sorry for myself. Until this moment it hadn't occurred to me that Val could get this upset about anything. Her tears are as unsettling as anything else I've dealt with over the past few days. "What's wrong? What's the matter? This isn't about me, is it? Because, really, I'll be all right."

She can't possibly be crying over me. Heaven knows I'm upset—rootless, loveless, and unexpectedly jobless. But Val is distraught. Trembling and pale, with a red, brimming gaze that, at last, she turns on me. "My husband is . . ." she clears her throat. "He's . . . ahem . . ." She takes a bracing swig of her pink parasol drink, sets it back down, and folds her hands on the table. "My husband is cheating," she says. "Again."

Her delivery—calculated, with a pause for emphasis after each word—makes it seem as if she were accusing me. It might be that all at once she looks more incensed than heartbroken, or maybe it's the way she's staring me dead in the eye. "Again," she repeats icily, and it's as if I were the other woman, here to confess all and beg forgiveness for coming between Val and her husband. That's when something dawns on me. Several somethings. One, Val is a vintage-clothing connoisseur who would no sooner patronize any of these *B*-stores than she

would cry like a baby in the middle of Grand Central Terminal on an early-May afternoon. Two, Val only wears black.
Three, demure? Blond? Pageboy?

And there's one very last little something.

Val doesn't have a husband.

It's a joke. Val doesn't take anything seriously. It's a joke,
right? Val's here to buy me a consolation drink to distract me
during my time of crisis, and this is just another diversionary
tactic. It's typical Val behavior, but it's freaking me out. "You're
not acting like yourself, and you're scaring me." I try to say it
jovially, as if I'm in no way about to start crying myself.

But instead of erupting into laughter and pointing to a hidden camera, Val just covers her face and sobs some more.

Her commitment is impressive. Still, how long will the show
go on? I've got jangled-enough nerves already, having spent
two hours in a Midtown unemployment office at a mandatory
New York State Department of Labor group-orientation lec-
ture: "Job-Hunting Tools for the Twenty-first Century."
("Does everyone here know what the Internet is?") After that,
I got all turned around coming over to Grand Central, first
walking four long blocks west, only to end up on a desolate,
trash-strewn stretch of Eleventh Avenue, leaving only two
thousand nine hundred ninety-nine and two-tenths of a mile
between me and my former life in Los Angeles—all right, the
San Fernando Valley—before realizing I should have been
heading east the whole time.

All this probably explains why she figures it out first.

"Oh, perfect. This is just great." She lifts her head, sniffles,
and dabs under each eye with her tissue. "You want *Val*."

Later I'll regret not having paid more attention to this
moment.

I won't have, though, and that's too bad. It might have been
an early clue that perhaps I'm unfit for the new career that's

about to fall into my lap. What was it they just said at the unemployment office? Our experience is our toolbox, with our
skills as the tools? Well, it seems I've locked my observational
skills into my toolbox and left it on a street corner somewhere.
Since relocating to New York five weeks ago for a fancy focus-
group moderator position at Hayes Heeley Market Research,
and up until getting "restructured" right out of that very same
position two days ago, I worked, went for coffee, and had
lunch with Valerie Benjamin nearly every day. After this much
concentrated time in her company I know what she looks like
down to the last eyelash. I know her taste in men, clothing,
and cocktails, her life's philosophy, and her family background.

I know she has an identical twin.

In fact, one of Val's favorite conversational pastimes is
counting the many ways her sister is spoiled and selfish, sharing stories of behavior so abysmal I always find myself grateful to be an only child. I know Victoria doesn't work, and that
she is married to a commercial real-estate broker named Steve.
Five years ago, minutes before her three-hundred-guest *New
York Times*-approved wedding at their parents' estate in Greenwich, Connecticut, Vickie got so overwrought that she screamed
a string of obscenities at Val, then fell weeping onto her bed
and refused to get up. Val was beginning to think she'd have
to give Vickie a slap—and, considering the scene to which she
was being subjected, was looking forward to it the tiniest little
bit—when Vickie snapped out of it abruptly on her own,
splashed some cold water on her face, and an hour later was
flitting happily around her reception without so much as an
apology to Val.

Right now, though, with Vickie here before me, bawling, I
only feel bad for her. "I am so sorry. I did think you were Val.
You must get that all the time."

"Constantly." Through her tears, Vickie sounds sarcastic. I'm this close to excusing myself and slinking away when Val, the genuine article, materializes at the top of the staircase.

I wave her over. Saved!

Now, in my own defense, I am preoccupied today. But Vickie is right; who could mix up these two? Yes, they have the same rosy cheeks, the same gray eyes, matching stewardess noses with the same smattering of freckles across the bridge. But Vickie wears a wedding ring, the Junior League hairdo, and sensible Ferragamo flats. And here's Val, my friend and, until Monday afternoon, office colleague. Ecstatically single, with an unruly electric-red downtown crop, deliberately smudgy eyeliner, vintage sixties go-go boots, and a mod little miniskirt in which it's pretty clear Vickie wouldn't be caught dead. Vickie: Greenwich. Val: Greenwich Village.

"Iris! And Vickie?" Val, too, looks perplexed.

"Val, it was the strangest coincidence." Life is looking better already. I provide a quick recap of the past five minutes while Vickie grudgingly clears two inches of space for her sister. Val's black vinyl skirt makes a squeaky noise as she sits down.

"It's not that strange," she says. "Manhattan is just a big small town. People bump into each other all the time. It can be a real pain."

"Believe me, if I'd known I'd bump into you here, I never would have come," Vickie retorts.

"Now, now, Vickie-poo, I wasn't talking about you. Tell me, Iris, is there a walk of shame in the San Fernando Valley?"

I lean closer, grazing my chin on the corner of a shopping bag. "Walk of shame? You mean Walk of Fame?"

"Walk of shame. When you go back with someone to his apartment and then, on your way home the next morning, run into one of your mother's ladies-who-lunch chums, who can tell you're blatantly wearing an outfit from the night before."

Vickie eyes Val's hemline. "Sort of like you're doing now?"

"I'll have you know, this is *not* a walk of shame. This is office attire," Val snaps. "I'm simply explaining to Iris that New York is a small town."

"Technically there's no walk of shame in the Valley." I say it quickly, sensing an argument about to happen.

"So, then, what were you wearing the first night you stayed over at Teddy's place?" Val asks me. "And what did you wear home?"

I scrutinize my glass of Rolling Rock. Had I thought to get something in a bottle, with a paper label, I could now make myself busy peeling it off.

"Come on, Iris. Don't tell me you wore his old sweatpants; that's a hundred times more shameful—a fashion faux pas."

"I just sort of never left." I'm blushing. "I just kind of stayed."

Both twins stare at me.

"Never mind." I take a drink. "Where I come from, people scurry out to the curb when no one's watching, dive into their cars, and speed home."

"There you go," says Val. "Another difference between the coasts. In New York, everybody walks at least one walk of shame. Now that you're living here, it's only a matter of time."

"Well, I've never done any such thing," Vickie says.

Val peers at her in a way that suggests her sister's presence has only now sunk in. "Why are you here, anyway? Don't they have bars in Yorkville?"

"I'm waiting for a train. And I do not live in Yorkville. Third and Eighty-fifth is Yorkville. Lexington and Eighty-fifth is the Upper East Side."

"Whatever you say."

"I know what I'm talking about, Val. My husband works in real estate. . . ." Vickie starts crying again. I look to Val for a cue, but she only rolls her eyes. Vickie sniffles loudly. "I can't believe he's cheating on me!"

Val doesn't react. She rakes her hand through her hair, which was black the last time I saw her, Monday afternoon. "Like it?" she asks me. "I got it done last night. I was considering something really light, maybe pink, maybe platinum, but then I thought—"

"Excuse me!" Vickie shouts.

Val sighs. "All right, Iris, here's the story. My sister suffers from seasonal suspicion disorder. Every six months, usually spring and fall, she decides hubby Steve is cheating on her, then retaliates by spending his money on new clothes."

"That's just mean!" Vickie swipes at her tears again with her tissue.

"It's true," says Val. "Remember the time you found the lipstick on his shirt, flipped out, and then realized it was your own lipstick?"

"It was Bobbi Brown Number Four! That could have been anybody's lipstick! Every woman in America has a tube!"

Val stops tapping her right index finger softly but insistently on the top of our table long enough to wave over a waitress and order drinks for herself and me. Then she gestures at Vickie. "And another—what is that, strawberry daiquiri?"

"Virgin," Vickie says.

Val rolls her eyes again. The waitress goes off to the bar. Val pulls out a cigarette and holds it in her mouth, unlit.

"No smoking," hisses Vickie.

"No shit," hisses Val.

This day keeps getting stranger and stranger. There are still hours to go before it's over, and I'm stuck with the only twins in history who lack that supernatural love bond everyone always goes on about.

Vickie does have a point, though. At my former marketing company in Brentwood, I once had to round up women for a focus group on makeup. A few days later, I watched from the observation room as one participant waxed rhapsodic about the MAC lip pencil in "Spice," and the universally flattering lipstick Bobbi Brown Number Four. "I have that, too!" said another, producing a tube from her Coach bag. The rest nodded knowingly and dug around in their purses until there were half a dozen Number Fours on the conference table. Afterward, I stopped in Sherman Oaks and picked up a tube. It was right on the way home, since Teddy and I had just bought our house in Studio City.

At least I still have that lipstick.

"This time there's no question," Vickie continues. "He's taken up jogging. At the crack of dawn." She gives us a look like, "See?"

"Pandora's Box." From above my head, the waitress places a drink in front of Val, who lunges at it.

"Virgin." The waitress sets down Vickie's daiquiri.

"Draft." She hands me a beer. I guzzle the remains of my first and give her the empty glass.

Vickie takes a dainty sip of her daiquiri. "My husband has gone on a fitness kick. At least, that's what he would have me believe. Men are such dogs."

"You're making absolutely no sense." Val seems to be speaking directly to her cocktail.

"This is a person who hasn't done any sport sweatier than golf since his squash days at Yale. Then three weeks ago, out of nowhere, he decides it's time to get in shape."

"He *was* looking a little soft around the middle," Val interjects. Vickie responds with one of what I have already come to recognize as her patented I'm-going-to-shove-my-shoe-down-your-throat-if-you-don't-shut-up looks. Val shuts up.

"And since then he's been getting up every weekday at six forty-five, dragging the poor dog out of his little bed, supposedly to go jogging in the park. Except that can't be where he's going. When he gets home, he's never even sweaty, and neither is the dog."

"I didn't think dogs got sweaty. Don't they, like . . ." What a lightweight. I'm four sips into my second Rolling Rock and already starting to slur my speech. "Like, drool or whatever it's called?" Forgotten the word. Better stop drinking now or I'm going to do something stupid. Such as, I don't know, relocate three thousand miles from home, to a noisy, grimy, indifferent city, in order to be laid off.

"Pant!" Val starts to giggle.

"That's it, pant." I can't help laughing myself. It's all too absurd.

"Hey," says Val, "maybe the dog's the one straying."

I should keep out of it. I should. I can't. "Dogs are such dogs."

"No!" Val howls. "Dogs are such men!"

"Oh, forget it!" Vickie starts crying again, with gusto. "This is why I never see you, Val. This is why I hate to tell you anything personal. You have no idea the stress I'm under right now. No idea!" She struggles to free herself from her chair, which is wedged between our table and the back of the woman behind her, and pulls an overnight bag I hadn't noticed before out from under her seat. "I'll wait for my train on the platform."

I realize how heartless I've been acting. Val must feel equally bad, because she grabs her sister's mascara-and-cashmere–covered wrist. "Where are you going?" She sounds contrite.

"To Greenwich," Vickie says. "I want Mother and Daddy."

"Don't you think you ought to stick around here and—Iris, how do you say it?—work on your marriage?"

"Work on your marriage," I repeat somberly.

"No." Vickie starts to gather up the rest of her packages. Not an easy feat, since the lot of them is taking up as much cubic footage as my entire apartment. The couple at the table next to us ducks to avoid being B-headed by a Bloomingdale's Big Brown Bag. "I should hire myself a detective to catch him in the act, and then use the evidence to stick him for a big, fat divorce settlement."

I could tell her, because I know, that she's oversimplifying things. In the no-fault-community-property-divorce state of California, for example, your assets get divided right down the middle, regardless of who did what to whom, unless you were cynical enough to draw up a prenuptial agreement. I could tell her, but I keep my mouth shut.

"Here's a plan!" Val pipes up. "While you're gone, want me to keep an eye on him? I could follow him around and see where he goes. I could be your scheming lookalike hiding in the bushes!"

"That's brilliant, Val. He'll never notice you. Make sure you wear that exact outfit."

Maybe Val hasn't been exaggerating about her twin. Whether or not Steve is the cad Vickie seems to think he is, he can't have it easy being married to her. Still, I have a real problem with cheaters. I know exactly what infidelity can do to a person.

Then it comes to me in a Joan of Arc moment, like a celestial omen from Grand Central's soaring signs-of-the-zodiac ceiling. I have no job and nothing to do. I have no social life. I barely have a love life. I have exactly one friend in this city: Val. And I'm broke. "Vickie!" I practically shout. "Hire me to do it!"

In the weeks to come, the foolishness of this idea will become so clear I'll wonder why some sort of actual winged messenger didn't appear—to grab me and smack some sense into
me. At the moment, with a little alcohol in my system, and a
thousand commuters bustling to and fro on the floor below,
I'm picturing myself in an office with a frosted-glass door,
smartly dressed in a suit (peplum, shoulder pads, brooch), feet
up on my circa 1945 standard-issue metal desk, answering my
old-fashioned dial phone: "Iris Hedge, dogcatcher." For some
reason, the image is in black-and-white.

Val, too, seems to have caught the fever. "Iris would be perfect! See how unobtrusive she is? She looks exactly like every
other woman in America! She could follow him around all
day, and he'd never notice."

"She's right," I add. "Just tell me when to come over in the
morning. In one day, you'll know whether he's telling the truth
or not."

Vickie wrinkles her nose. "How?"

"Come on. Think about it." Val is Hayes Heeley's youth ex-
pert, specializing in focus groups for teenagers. Right now she
is using exactly the same casually jolly voice I've heard her use
while passing around samples of pimple cream to a roomful of
sulky eighth-grade goths. "She waits for him to come out of
the building. She follows behind him on his, you know, morning rounds. If he *is* going running, then she'll just get in her
workout for the day. If he's not, you'll have your answer, once
and for all."

An incomprehensible message, the departure of the
something-o'clock train to Staticville on track mumble,
crackles over Grand Central's public address system. Vickie
consults her Rolex. "That's my train."

"I have to go, too." With no small amount of difficulty, Val
pushes back her chair. "You don't mind cutting this short, do

you, Iris? I'm meeting someone. He's a musician. Really cute. We met on the subway."

"You did *not*." Vickie looks horrified. "He could be anyone! What do you know about him?"

"That he gets on at Fourteenth Street and has great tattoos," Val says. "And his name is Ian, or Liam—something. Anyway I only just met him this morning."

"Oh, my god! And you're going out with him already? Don't you know no man will ever marry you if you aren't at least a little hard to get?"

"I have no intention of being hard to get," Val says.

I'm only half paying attention. I'm swaying slightly from the beer, looking past the twins at the magnificent four-sided brass clock at the top of the Grand Central information booth. "Five thirty-six," it reads. I'm thinking, *But Val,* you *invited* me *to happy hour.* I'm thinking I didn't get to talk about my day.

Val and Vickie stand up and eye each other warily: opponents trying to get away with not shaking hands after the big grudge match. In the end, Val avoids the issue by patting her sister's shopping bags instead of her sister. "Say hi to Mom and Dad."

"Okay." Vickie turns to me. "Take care."

"Yes, right. You, too." No spy assignment. So much for my new calling.

"I'll talk to you soon," Val promises me as she (thank goodness) settles the bill, and we all descend the stairs into the crowd, and the opposite twins head back to their opposite lives. For a moment I linger in the middle of the terminal, wondering what to do with myself, and am hit with the irrational urge to return to the bar, blow my future unemployment money on booze, and spend the night having gymnastic sex with a stranger off the six fifteen. Simultaneously, I am aware that what the evening really has in store for me is leftover sesame noodles from Szechuan Palace and, if the gods are smiling, a movie on TV I haven't already seen. I wonder if I'll have to cancel the cable.

"Iris!"

It's Vickie, hurrying back over from the doorway to track fourteen, shopping-bag handles looped over every inch of both of her arms. She glances nervously back toward the platform. The train must be close to leaving. "Go ahead," she calls over the din of the crowd. "Tomorrow morning. The address is Twelve Seventy-five Lexington, between Eighty-fifth and Eighty-sixth. He always leaves by seven sharp. You can hide across the street and follow him." She waits, tapping her foot the way Val, impatient for drinks, was tapping her finger on our table earlier. "Okay?"

Sure, except I've never met her husband and have no idea what he looks like. "Can you give me a physical description?" I'm so busy being pleased with myself at "physical description" that when Vickie shifts her bags, works a hand into her purse, extracts a credit card, and holds it up to my face, it takes me a moment to understand she's showing me her husband's postage-stamp–size antifraud mug shot on the front. "Steven Sokolov," the card says. I lean forward and study Steve's tiny face: brown hair, brown eyes—your basic aging frat boy.

Vickie slides the card back into her purse, readjusts her packages, and starts back toward the train.

"Wait!"

She whirls back around, looking agitated.

"Height? Weight? Clothing? Unusual birthmarks?" I don't want her to miss the train, but, according to the New York State Department of Labor, it's important to gather the correct equipment for my job toolbox.

Vickie edges backward. "About five eleven, one-eighty. No birthmarks. Shirt, shorts—you know, jogging attire. He'll be with a Parson Russell terrier. It's really, really time for me to go." She backs up a few more steps toward the platform doorway.

"Wait! What's a Parson Russell terrier?"

"For heaven's sake. A Jack Russell terrier. Same thing. All right?"

"Got it. Do you want me to call you afterward, or . . . ?"

She rips off a piece of the striped Bendel's bag, again reaches into her purse, pulls out a Tiffany pen, scribbles a 917 cell phone number on the back of the piece of bag, and practically throws it at me. I'm impressed at Vickie's ability to manage this cumbersome array of possessions while simultaneously walking in reverse and making me feel as if she's my superior. "What's your fee?"

"What?"

"Your fee. What you charge."

My fee? Good question. She's about to break into a run, so it might be smart to pin her down first. What would one charge for this kind of service?

"We'll talk about it later!" Vickie shouts, and runs for the train.

Cognitive dissonance. That's the official psychological term for what happens when you find yourself in a situation that completely contradicts the situation you were expecting, and your brain refuses to accept it.

For instance, you're in Grand Central to meet a friend, and get her mixed up with her twin sister.

Or, on your birthday, at the out-of-the-way restaurant where your sweetheart has taken you for a quiet dinner for two, you bump into someone you know: your boss, or a friend you made in the Blue Jay cabin at Camp Sequoia when you were eleven. Your eyes take in this out-of-context character, and your brain thinks, *Pat Sweeney at La Ventana the same night as us? Small world!* In walks someone else. *Aunt Rose, too? Spooky!* Only in the face of overwhelming evidence— like fifty people jumping out and yelling, "Surprise!"—does your brain finally make the connection.

Or maybe, in the middle of an otherwise ordinary day, you're somewhere arbitrary—perhaps in a parking lot, walking back to the car after an appointment. Someone you love, someone you trust more than anyone, could be no more than a few feet away in an illicit embrace. But you're not expecting to see this person, so the scene doesn't register, and you walk on by. Cognitive dissonance is just another way of saying it takes some time to come to terms when a person you thought you knew turns out to be somebody else entirely. My mother once felt moved to describe it, "Just as Mother Nature hates a vacuum, human nature hates a discrepancy."

This is what I ponder on my long walk home from happy hour. Any other day I would have taken a taxi without a second thought, but my new econo-life has me spending a lot of time—the one thing I suddenly have in abundance—performing what my "friend" Kevin would call cost-benefit analysis. Let's see. A cab from Grand Central to my brownstone at Seventy-sixth and Columbus equals about what I make an hour, based on my new state-subsidized paycheck—about an eighth of what I was bringing in at Hayes Heeley. There's the subway, but ten subway rides not taken equals one meal—two if I stretch the leftovers. Over the past two days everything but my rent has begun to seem a frivolous waste of resources. Truthfully, my rent has always seemed a frivolous waste of resources, but Val assures me that after enough time in New York it feels normal to spend half your take-home pay on a

"cozy" studio with a parked-cars view and a kitchen renovated in seventies reject materials.

Michelle, my erstwhile boss and head of the qualitative-
research department at Hayes Heeley, promised to send a
check for two weeks' severance in a week or two, and I've got
six months of medical insurance, which seemed pretty good at
first, considering I wasn't there that long. ("Guilt money," Val
called it when I told her. "You should have cried. They would
have started throwing hundred-dollar bills at you.") I can also
count on twenty-six weeks on the dole while searching for a
new job. I'm certain I'll land one before the money runs out.
Fairly certain.

The truth is, we responsible career-girl types know we're
supposed to have a cushion of savings, equal to six months'
salary, specifically earmarked for times like these. I remember
back in high school reading that savvy financial tip in *Cosmopolitan*, along with the more interesting advice about how
to attract a man at the office by ever so subtly crossing and re-
crossing your panty-hosed legs: "The faint whisper of nylon
on nylon will drive him wild!"

I never imagined I'd end up in a time like this.

"My roots are here. In Los Angeles," I tried to explain to
Michelle Heeley, after she phoned me at my old firm in Brentwood one day out of nowhere with what she called "a once-
in-a-lifetime career opportunity." Despite my protests, she
insisted on flying me to New York for an interview. "I couldn't
think of leaving," I told her again in person a week later. "My
whole life is in California."

Michelle wouldn't take no for an answer, ticking off argu-
ments on fingers laden with gems so large they looked edible.
"It's time you moved out of recruiting. It's a dead end." She
paused to move the clasp of her necklace from her throat to
the back of her neck. "You'd have a much better future as a

focus-group moderator. And as you know, no firm offers a better pedigree than Hayes Heeley."

Michelle was right: I did want something more. For seven years, I'd been slogging through data banks of names and numbers and making phone calls. Hello, Kimberly Anne Smith? Are you between the ages of twenty-five and thirty-four? Do you purchase mass-market cosmetics? Would you describe yourself as having dry, oily, or combination skin? Dry, you say? Would you like to take part in a two-hour discussion about moisturizer?

I took the job and moved, telling myself it would help my career and make me rich at the same time.

On my way to Midtown the first day, I pulled a wad of bills from the ATM, paid for a MetroCard for the subway, a taxi after I couldn't decipher the subway map, a cup of coffee, a bagel, a copy of the *New York Post*, a box of Band-Aids to protect me from my new pumps, and a few other assorted sundries. By the time I arrived at the office, I'd spent every last cent. Val calls this the ten-bucks-a-block rule, and until now I've coped by stopping every ten blocks at the ATM—a strategy that, clearly, will no longer work.

I meditate on all this for thirty blocks, up Madison Avenue, through Central Park, and on up Columbus. It keeps my mind off both the developing blister on my left heel and the nagging little voice in my head insisting the real reason I took the position was, in fact, to run away from my life. Shush, I tell it. Following Vickie's husband will keep me occupied until I can figure out what to do next.

I'm in the front hallway of my brownstone, about to unlock my mailbox, when I hear the phone start to ring inside my first-floor apartment. I have time only to grab a FedEx envelope addressed to me off the table in the foyer before bursting through my apartment door and catching the phone on the fourth ring, just as the machine is about to pick up. Maybe it's Val; her date canceled and now she can come over. Bad girl, Iris, that's unsportsmanlike. Maybe Kevin, my friend-with-benefits? I wasn't expecting to hear from him until tomorrow night but could use the company, not to mention the benefits.

"It's me," a woman says.

There's no one in the room, but I glance around anyway: Somebody, help! No luck. I frisbee the FedEx envelope onto my bed, bend to remove my belligerent shoe, limp across the hardwood floor into the two-foot-by-three-foot bathroom to rummage under the doll-size sink. "Joy," I say into the receiver. The two beers have done nothing for my verbal skills, even with a thirty-block walk to help sober me up, but on the one or two occasions a year when I accidentally answer one of my mother's phone calls, she does most of the talking anyway.

"You're in psychic pain," she says.

I locate a Band-Aid, put it on, and straighten up, examining the tiny crinkles under my eyes in the five-by-seven mirror over my bathroom sink. It occurs to me that I haven't seen myself completely since moving here, except reflected in the odd shop window.

"I'm sensing negative energy," Joy continues. "What are you doing in New York? I called your house, and Teddy said you'd moved out."

I'm going to kill him. My estranged husband, aspiring voice-over artist, eternal pursuer of the big break that never materializes, can barely remember to bring home a carton of milk, take out the garbage, or pay the water bill. He spent the month before I left camping out on a succession of actor-friends' sofas and twice had to call me because he'd forgotten at whose place he was scheduled to stay when. Now, having settled back into our house, he's efficient enough not only to recall where to find the address book but also to accurately relay my new contact information to Joy.

I back out of the bathroom and into the main apartment, where my bedroom furniture, after years of having its own space to itself, now rubs joinery with my living room furniture: The queen-size bed in which Teddy and I slept is next to the overstuffed armchair we'd squish into to read the *Los Angeles Times*; my nightstand, in its current dual role as nightstand/ mail table, sits on the rug that was our favorite living-room spot for eating pizza and watching movies. I sit on the bed next to the FedEx envelope and suddenly realize what it is: the court document saying my divorce is on track and will be final in six months, unless one of us tells our lawyer otherwise. I pull on the tab to split open the cardboard sleeve and peek in at the paper on top: "Interlocutory Decree," it affirms in fancy, legal-document lettering. "It's been a strange few months," is all I can think of to say to my mother.

"The candle told me. I came through the meditation room just now and found that the purple taper had wilted. The mid-day sun must have been unbearable. It's in its holder, slumped over onto the offering table. I thought, *It's trying to tell me something.*"

"Probably," I say. "Something like 'Please, close the curtains.'"

"Iris, the rest of the candles were fine. Only this one had wilted. It is purple, purple as in irises. It symbolizes awareness. I sense that you are bowed under a psychic burden. Perhaps you'd like me to send you an awareness candle?"

On the street there's a sudden commotion of honking horns. I hold the receiver between my ear and shoulder, open the window, and look out to see two women in business suits, screaming at each other: "It's mine!" "I had it first!" They have unearthed a cache of discarded clothing from one of a dozen black plastic garbage bags heaped on the sidewalk and are blocking the street, playing tug-of-war with what appears to be a men's blazer, each holding a sleeve.

I feel it coming on: the tidal wave of loneliness and desolation that not even happy hour and flippant banter and an amusing potential new career can stave off. And I'm tired. Exhausted, honestly. Ready to cry and then sleep for a hundred years. It's been like this since I got to New York: I feel as if I'm handling things, and then get blindsided by a sadness so deep and wide I could drown in it.

I'm certainly in no mood for Joy. I'll call her some other time, I tell her.

We both know full well I won't, but she lets my excuse go by. "Namaste, then, Iris. That is a yogic word meaning, 'I honor the divine energy within you.' "

But even after I hang up and set the alarm for my early wake-up call and crawl into bed with a take-out carton and the remote, I'm up for most of the night listening to the swoosh of passing traffic, keening sirens, people outside my window on their way home from restaurants and friends' apartments. Thinking, too. A little about tomorrow's assignment, a lot more about my money problems. But mostly reliving a scene that has haunted me far too often. It's an overcast February day in the San Fernando Valley. Fog-shrouded sun shines into my burning eyes. I'm desperate to protect myself from the glare and bury my face in the crook of my arm. *What if I had kept it there? What if I hadn't looked up?* I wonder as the hours tick by. *What would life be like now?*

As with so many nights, it's the last thing I remember thinking before finally falling asleep.

TWO

When the alarm rings at the dawn's early light, I get out of bed, wash my face, consider what a real spy would wear for the morning's errand, and, for perhaps the first time in my life, feel thankful for my inconspicuousness. Val is right: I do look like every other woman in America—at least, every other woman in my demographic subgroup. This is not low self-esteem but an objective fact. According to research, the average college-educated, thirty-to-thirty-five-year-old white female is five feet four and a size eight, at 140 pounds, with brown hair past her shoulders, and brown eyes. That is me except that, perhaps as compensation for a too-round face, a pasty complexion, short legs, and a tendency to blush at the slightest provocation, I got genetically lucky in the dress-size lottery. Usually I'm about twenty pounds lighter than the average. Right now the divorce diet—the continually nervous stomach and utter lack of appetite brought on by my split with Teddy—has left me twenty-five pounds lighter.

As a corollary to this first point, despite what Val said yesterday about my getting in my morning workout, I do not work out. I have taken my share of spinning classes and all that and eventually will need to start going more often. For now my feeling is, if you don't have to, why?

Finally, freshman year at Pomona, my friend Audrey started a contest among some of the girls in our dorm. She called it T-shirt hunting, and the object was, the first time you slept with somebody, you had to steal one of his shirts as proof. Immature, yes, but the game evolved into a fiercely fought dorm-wide competition. In the end, I scored somewhere on the low side. I amassed more shirts than Evie, who majored in organic chemistry and had plenty of it with her lab partner, Doug Amato; she met him the first week of school, married him the week after graduation, and is now a mom in Palmdale. And far fewer than Jadey, who majored in art history and, last any of us heard, was bartending in the Turks and Caicos Islands. As for Audrey, she vanished quickly, but her influence remained. It's embarrassing, but for years after graduation I kept stealing men's shirts out of habit.

This is all a very long way of saying that, as a corollary to points one through three, my choice of workout clothes this morning is limited to a single pair of sweatpants and a collection of ancient, stolen T-shirts. I can't have gotten more than an hour or so of sleep, but after drinking three cups of coffee and slipping into my chic sportswear ensemble, I'm remarkably upbeat. Maybe it's the idea of embarking on a new adventure, but I'm full of energy and ready to unearth what Mr. Steven Sokolov is doing behind his wife's back. I secretly suspect he's up to no good and won't be jogging today. So I'm bringing my wallet and keys and my sunglasses for comfort, and a windbreaker in case it's cold. I gather everything together and scamper out my apartment door—right into the bicycle my downstairs neighbor, who lives directly beneath me in what he probably calls the garden apartment but which is really the basement apartment, keeps chained to the hallway staircase. One of these days someone's going to trip over that thing and break a bone, and with my luck, that someone will be me. It does seem that the bike lies in wait for me: Every outfit I own, including, now, my sweatpants, has a track of grease on the leg.

No matter. I continue out the front door of my building, down the steps of the front stoop and toward the park, a few yards behind the woman in clogs and overalls who comes over twice a day to walk the building's dogs.

I smile at her and step around her and her four charges.

"Rocky, *down!*" she bellows at one, a pug, who lunges at my ankles and begins to lick them as if they'd been rubbed with steak juice. To me she says, "Beautiful day!" She pulls on the pug's leash. "He seems to like you."

I try to discourage the pug without actually shoving him away with my foot. "Might I ask a question?" I address the dog lady. "Can you please tell me what a Jack Russell terrier looks like? I'm pretty sure I know, but—"

"Sure." She points toward the end of the block, where a small white dog with pointy tan ears has its leg lifted beside a sidewalk planter. "Right there. They're all the rage these days. I don't recommend them as city dogs, in case you're in the market. They're way too energetic for apartment living, but what do people know? Most owners just buy for looks."

I thank her, disengage myself from the marauding pug, and walk to the corner. It *is* a beautiful day. Spring, Val tells me, is the most perfect time of year in New York for weather. The streets are quiet, and the air is cool and fresh. The sun has begun to break up the long shadows reaching across Columbus Avenue. A taxi driver notices me on the corner and starts to pull over, but I have planned for time to walk across Central Park. Stroll, even. It's still only six forty, a full twenty minutes before Steve is due out of his building with the Jack Russell terrier. I walk down a block of single-family brownstones with sleeping cats in the windows and potted hyacinths on the stoops, cross Central Park West, and step through an entrance in the park's stone wall.

Inside, there's a party going on. I wouldn't have thought this many people would be in the park so early, but the whole place is humming with New Yorkers taking advantage of the soft spring morning. There's a line of moms pushing baby strollers, skipping, bending, waving first one arm and then the other, as part of a group exercise class. Bicyclists dart single-file through the traffic on the park drive. I cut across the Great Lawn, which has been mowed into broad, dewy silver-green stripes, and wonder for the first time if the locals might be speaking the truth. Maybe this city *is* the center of the universe. The thought that I, Iris Hedge from the San Fernando Valley, am right here in the middle of it is at once so exhilarating that I stand still, breathing the heady perfume of daffodils and taxi exhaust. If life were a musical, this would be the moment where I'd rip off my "Three Stages of Tequila" T-shirt (Corey Najerian, sophomore year) to reveal a sequined leotard, and then burst into song.

Indulging in this New York moment, however, winds up not taking a New York moment, or even a New York minute, but a New York five minutes, which, it turns out, is just as long as it is everywhere else. By the time I emerge from the park near the Metropolitan Museum it's one minute to seven and I am still quite a few blocks from Vickie's building. I sprint like a lunatic across Fifth Avenue, up five blocks and over three to Lexington, my wallet in my windbreaker pocket pounding against my chest, the keys in my sweatpants pocket jingling, my sunglasses bouncing around on my nose. I'm all the more a spectacle here on the staid, wealthy Upper East Side, where the few people out on the street appear less hurried than people do everywhere else in New York. Since the Upper East Siders have obviously made it, they must have nowhere more pressing to get to.

By the time I screech to a stop in front of Vickie's building it's five minutes after seven. I am thoroughly winded, not to mention thoroughly panicked, thinking I have missed Steve and have metamorphosed in a matter of days from level-headed marketing professional into utter incompetent, when out of the building emerges the man himself. Brown hair, brown eyes, mid-thirties, six-footish, running clothes, zippy little tan-and-white dog; the life-size version of the photo on Vickie's credit card. He also has the exact look I've been expecting: that "I'm entitled" look. I've seen it a million times. If he lived in Southern California, he'd be one of those BMW reptiles who honk the horn behind you on the freeway off-ramp—Wake up! Go!—before the light has turned green. He'd be the one who, in a ten-mile afternoon traffic jam on the Santa Monica Freeway, would drive along the right shoulder and then, at the last possible instant, cut back in front of everyone else obediently waiting their turn in the blinding sun to creep ahead a few more inches. Here in New York, he must walk down the sidewalk shouting into his cell phone. I hate him already, just on principle.

Steve says something to the doorman, stops to untangle the dog (it has already managed to wrap its leash several times, maypole-style, around one of the brass awning supports in front of the building), and then stands there on the sidewalk, bouncing up and down a little on his toes, preparing for liftoff. For my part, I am so astonished to see my prey in the flesh, no more than ten feet away, that I, too, stop in the middle of the sidewalk, no doubt with my mouth open, and most definitely in his direct line of vision. To make matters worse, there's little else to attract his attention: Aside from Steve, me, the dog, and the doorman, there are maybe half a dozen people on the street, most of them descending into the subway station. Whoever wrote that song about the city that never sleeps must not have lived in this neighborhood; otherwise he would have come up with the far more accurate "the city that doesn't get out of the house until ten."

That is, nobody does but Vickie's husband, who seems

wide-awake and alert and, sure enough, looks right at me—
Great! Brilliant work, Iris!—and then looks away. There's no
flash of recognition, no "Aha! I know my wife sent you to spy
on me!" Nothing. Why should there be? He has no idea who
I am or why I am here. I am filled with glee at not having bun-
gled this too badly so far.

Steve bounces once or twice more before walking right past
me down Lexington to the end of the block, in the direction
from which I came. The moment he seems far enough away, I
step up to the doorman, tilt my head to one side, and smile—
the very picture, I hope, of neighborly innocence. "Excuse
me?"

"Miss?" He touches his cap.

"Is that Steve I see down there, with the little dog?" I gesture toward the corner.

"Mister Steve, yes," the doorman affirms.

"Thought so." I beam at him. He touches his cap again and
steps back into the building. Then, as surreptitiously as possible, I follow Steve across Lexington and over to Park Avenue,
where he turns north.

This part goes quite well. My existence didn't register with
Steve in the first place, so he doesn't notice me trailing him half
a block behind. He doesn't once glance back, just strides up
the sidewalk, the skittery Jack Russell beside him leaping and
nipping at its leash. Steve is behaving as if he's headed to an
important appointment. There's no pausing to admire the
tulips in full bloom, planted in rows, running red and yellow
down the center of Park Avenue, or the polished, landed-
gentry indifference of the apartment buildings lining either
side. No slowing down to avoid getting sprayed by a mainte-
nance man hosing down the sidewalk. (You could never get
away with wasting that much water in California.) I have to
trot to keep up with him.

But as the blocks go by, my original buoyancy gives way to stomach-twisting tension. What if Vickie is right? What if I have to break it to her that her husband is having an affair? I imagine telephoning Vickie this afternoon and informing her that Steve entered the lovely red-brick apartment house at Park and Eighty-seventh and left, whistling, forty-five minutes later, or was greeted at the door of a graceful single-family town house on Eighty-eighth by a woman wearing nothing but a triple strand of pearls and a smile. Will Vickie be devastated at the betrayal? Will she take it out on me? Will she collapse and end up in the emergency room?

It isn't until Steve makes a second left, toward Central Park, that my stomach begins to unknot: Steve could just be going for a run. The answer reveals itself minutes later when he crosses Fifth Avenue to the East Side entrance to the Central Park Reservoir, which even I know is the most popular place to jog in the city. He stops and stretches his arms over his head. Then he takes off at full speed.

Really. It's like one of those car commercials: zero to sixty in five seconds. With no time for a sigh of relief, I take off after him, scaling the steps to the reservoir, dodging between the silent, focused runners as he hits his stride on the narrow gravel track. Within moments my heart is threatening to explode. My wallet is whapping against me, and my sunglasses are back to sliding around precariously on my sweaty face. Note to self: Next time, leave this stuff at home. If you live that long.

I try to take a few cleansing breaths. Joy used to swear by this technique, but I never gave it much shrift until Michelle insisted I do it during my Hayes Heeley training. "It's to relax the body and keep your nerves from getting the better of you," she said, and I must admit, it works. I believe someone, possibly an instructor from a long-ago spinning class, also told me once that proper breathing makes strenuous exercise easier. I can't seem to get any air at all, though; while my heart may explode, my lungs may *im*plode. I struggle to turn my focus outside myself. The trees, the sky, the *jingle-jingle* of my keys harmonizing with the *skrish-skrish* of my nylon windbreaker, the morning sun on my face, the distance between Steve and me growing by the second.

He must know there's someone following him. Otherwise, why would he be moving this fast? He's practically a blur. How can I keep up when I'm about to pass out? If I do pass out, will someone stop to help, or will I be trampled by the pack of runners behind me?

Steve rounds the top corner of the reservoir. I can't be sure, but he appears to stumble for a few steps, as if trying to slow down. For a fraction of an instant, he glances backward, over his left shoulder. And a moment later, he veers to the right—and runs right off the edge of the track.

The move looks deliberate, although the embankment here on the northeast end of the reservoir has got to be fifteen feet high. I watch him and the Jack Russell leap over the edge, as if off the side of a building, and moments later spot them at the bottom, crashing through the trees in the direction of the West Side tennis courts. The whole incident takes no more than twenty seconds.

Now my heart really is going to detonate. In the quiet I hear it thrashing around in time with my serrated inhale-exhale and my staccato thoughts: *Steve suspected something. Saw me. Must have. Catch up!*

I muster every last bit of energy and run harder, the reservoir a blue haze on my left, the morning air scalding my lungs, my thigh muscles congealing like cement.

By the time I get to Steve's jumping-off spot, he's nowhere to be seen. I'm left at the edge of the track, doubled over and wheezing, still scanning the view below for some sign of him or the dog. I straighten back up, intending to jump down the side of the embankment after him, but my legs refuse to obey. So much for the mind-body connection Joy likes to talk about: The only place my body wants to go is back to bed.

———————

"What do you mean, you lost him?"

A shower and a catnap later, I'm feeling somewhat better. Still, there's a cramp in my side that won't go away. My calves are throbbing. I've already downed four aspirin and am thinking of trying a more potent pain reliever, like ibuprofen or a bottle of scotch.

I had assumed that after a home-cooked meal and a good night's sleep in Connecticut, Vickie would realize she'd been acting crazy. I figured she'd be ready to forget the whole thing, to come home and resume spending her husband's money. Not so.

"I couldn't keep up," I say. "He is amazingly fast."

Vickie snorts. "That's a laugh."

"It's the truth. Surprisingly, your dog handled it quite well."

"Just tell me what happened." Vickie isn't crying today, and she isn't interested in niceties. I relate the events of the morning, leaving out my tardy arrival at her building but including the part about her husband hurling himself down the reservoir embankment as if the IRS were after him.

Vickie cuts me off. "Is he cheating or not?"

"I don't know." That, too, is the truth. I have no idea. If he was simply out for a jog, why did he seem to be trying to throw me off his trail? On the other hand, if he is cheating, why go to so much trouble to fake a workout, especially with his wife out of town?

"Was he gawking at other women? He slobbers over anyone who passes by."

"Not that I noticed." He certainly didn't look at *me* twice. Really, he couldn't possibly have known I was following him.

Vickie half growls, half sighs. I picture her on the other end of the line, ready to throw herself on the floor in a tantrum.

"If you want, I can try again tomorrow." How, I can't imagine, unless someone can replace my entire cardiovascular and musculoskeletal systems with bionic parts. Not to worry—Vickie won't take me up on my bluff.

"Fine," she agrees.

"Really?"

"I said fine."

All right, fine. I'll think of something. It's not as if I had anything else to do. It's sad that Vickie doesn't have a better way to occupy her time. Though she hasn't asked, I let her know she owes me seventy-five dollars for today's work.

"How did you come up with *that*?"

"It's based on fifty dollars an hour." I decided on this figure after much deliberation. It's nothing compared to my Hayes Heeley salary, but with no experience in detective work, it hardly seems fair to charge more.

"Seventy-five dollars? How long could it have taken to follow him ten blocks?"

I explain that it took thirty minutes to get over to her side of town, fifteen for actual surveillance, and forty-five to hobble home. Vickie argues that she had been thinking more along the lines of what she pays her cleaning lady and, furthermore, that she shouldn't have to pay for travel time. She offers fifteen dollars an hour. As soon as I agree I want to slap myself.

After we hang up I call Joan in Human Resources at Hayes Heeley to ask when to expect my severance check. ("Month," she answers absently, perhaps interrupted at a critical moment

in her computer solitaire game.) Then I ask to be transferred
to Val's extension. I get Val's voice mail and leave a message
offering details of my assignment in exchange for details about
her date. After that, I use up another ten minutes dropping off
my laundry at the wash-and-fold around the corner. Then,
well, what do unemployed people do all day? Should I watch
the soaps or get on the Internet to find work? I compromise,
turn on the TV, and log on to my computer.

Here's a quiz for a focus group: Which of these selections in
my mailbox is not junk e-mail?

A. "DEBT FREE IN MINUTES!"
B. "XXX three-way action!"
C. "End female impotence!"
D. "Bliss Blitz From Joy!"

Those who chose D would be the ones getting my mother's
newsletter. Who else but my mother, finding herself divorced
after two decades of marriage, could pick up and leave the city
she'd grown up in and start an entirely new life? Once a yoga-
doing, herbal-tea–drinking, alfalfa-sprout–eating Southern
California mom, she is now, fifteen years later, remarried and
a cottage industry, a guru with a Web site and newsletter, who
dispenses nuggets of goddess wisdom to women she's never
met from a six-thousand-square-foot Arizona hacienda.

TO: Friends
FROM: Joy
SUBJ: Lost love? Lost career?

Dishearteningly enough, my own new status as a woman
lacking a job and a husband makes me just the type who

would come to Joy in search of easy answers. I never asked Joy to send me "Bliss Blitz." I usually delete it without opening it. But this week's subject line is speaking directly to me.

Dearest Goddesses:

If there is one thing in life we can count on, it's that few things truly turn out as we've planned. Dreams can die, relationships wither and the plans we made can shift and change. Don't despair! If we are able to embrace our disappointment, we can weather the storm and then emerge into the sunshine, a phoenix-goddess, reborn.

My mother, the Scottsdale goddess, goes on to outline a re-birthing ceremony in which any woman struggling with a set-back should form a "sacred circle" of close girlfriends around a plastic kiddie pool. She who wishes rebirth steps into the pool, and her friends pour water over her head "as a symbol of spiritual cleansing." Just before I hit the Delete button, I set up my mailbox to begin auto-forwarding each week's "Bliss Blitz" to Val. She's always complaining that her mother is emotionally repressed. Maybe she'll see that a little repres-sion can be a good thing.

"You've got mail!" my computer announces.

The newly arrived e-mail to which it's referring reads more like an interoffice memo than a personal note:

TO: Iris Hedge
FROM: Kevin Asgard
SUBJ: Agenda

Tonight actionable for me; call to arrange synch-up.

I call Kevin's hotel room. He answers halfway through the first ring. "That was fast."

"I was online."

"Job-hunting on the Internet? Bad ROI."

"ROI?"

"Return on investment. You're better off utilizing your existing contacts." It appears he's trying to tell me I'd be smarter to ask people I know to help me find work. But there's also a wink in his voice. "Unless you were really having Internet sex."

"You're more than enough man for me." I say it teasingly but am in fact sincere.

"So," he goes on. "Cabernet or zin? And is ten too late?"

"Don't bother bringing wine. Teddy has all the wineglasses, and I don't know where the movers packed the corkscrew. And why ten?"

"I want to go upstairs to the fitness center first."

"No problem. Go ahead." Here's something nice about being unemployed: I can sleep in. No, wait a minute. "You know what, I have to be up early tomorrow." And that's when I have my first clever idea in days. "Kevin, would you please do me a favor?"

"Name it," he says.

"Skip the gym tonight. You can go running at the reservoir in the morning."

THREE

The alarm goes off at six. Kevin opens one eye and croaks, "Let's streamline our time allocation and wait for him in the park instead of at his building." In English: Let's shave off fifteen minutes so Kevin can sleep more.

I've been staring at the ceiling for an hour, having been wrenched awake by the alarm of a weatherbeaten Cutlass Supreme parked under my first-floor window—the kind of alarm that cycles several times through *whoop, whoop, whoop, eeeop, eeeop, eeeop, aaaa, aaaa, aaaa, aaaa, oooooeee, oooooeee, oooooeee, oooooeee,* until it finally wears itself out. By now fully conscious, I slide out of bed and shuffle to the kitchen for a glass of water. This must cause a considerable racket, because my basement-dwelling neighbor, as he so often does, immediately begins pounding on his ceiling with some sort of blunt object, perhaps the butt of a rifle. So by the time Kevin starts trying to negotiate with me, I'm pitiless. "Come on, get up. I don't want him to get away again."

"Iris, the most effective solution is generally the simplest. Odds are, he'll do exactly the same thing today as he did yesterday."

"How do you know? Is this business-consultant logic?"

"Yes. Plus, I'm jet-lagged," he mumbles, right before I pull the sheets off him.

Meet Kevin Asgard, the ultimate no-fuss fling. Kevin is from California; he and I have known each other since high school and, up until the week before I moved, were nothing more than platonic friends. Now we have a deal: We see each other once or twice a month when he comes to New York on business; then he flies back to his home in Newport Beach, no strings attached. It's the ideal setup. I never want a serious relationship again; Kevin is about as commitment-phobic as a man can get. And though he's hardly my soul mate, he is easygoing and game for anything, which is why he finally rousts himself from my bed and accompanies me to the Central Park Reservoir, as promised, because I myself am not up to this "enterprise," as he would put it.

Besides, Joy is the one who believes in soul mates; that love between two people is a mystic, inexplicable connection of spirits. I can hardly think about it without gagging.

"I don't understand where you get so much energy," I tell Kevin. Earlier sleepiness long since forgotten, he is doing lunges, leaning into the spear-point–topped iron fence that divides the running track from the water. The sun glints off the golden hairs on his legs. The track is just a few feet wide, and it's not the best place for him to be warming up; a runner in a leopard-print bra has to hop over the back of his foot as she goes by. Still, she gives him not a dirty look but a "Hi, there, handsome" grin. So that's one of a hundred reasons Kevin will never be anything but a fling. He is so much better-looking than I am that if I had any real claim on him, I would be continually insecure.

Kevin stretches his arms behind him, narrowly missing a ponytailed runner, who emits a small squeak but doesn't slow down. "Sorry!" Kevin calls after her. She turns back to answer, and her face softens. She keeps looking back at him as long as she possibly can.

Kevin says to me, "It's a win-win. If I didn't work out, I'd be out of shape and the top of my head would blow off."

"Isn't that funny. My head would blow off if I *did* work out. Yesterday I exerted myself for ten minutes; now look at me."

I knew I should have tried the scotch. My calves are so stiff, I'm limping with both feet. The cramp I was feeling yesterday has honed itself into a knifelike pain on one side of my waist, my right breast is sore from its wallet beating, and, for whatever reason, under the "Caesars Palace" logo on the back of today's T-shirt, one I poached six years ago from Gregg Singer, who spent every other weekend in Las Vegas, my left shoulder is aching. And I thought I was in good shape because I can walk thirty blocks. Ha.

Something gets Kevin's attention. He tilts his head slightly toward an approaching runner. "That him?"

It isn't. "The one we're looking for is about this tall, brown hair, with a Jack Russell terrier."

Kevin surveys the blue water of the reservoir. Hundreds of seagulls have congregated on the narrow bridge of land that juts out into the lake. I can never understand how they locate their mates in those big crowds, but evidently, to seagulls, all seagulls don't look exactly alike.

Right then he appears: Speedy Steve and his sidekick, Wonder Dog, approaching the reservoir's lower track. Not the one up here by the fence, with the view of the water, but the horse trail through the woods below us. I grab Kevin by the shirt. But just as I'm spinning Kevin around, Steve stops abruptly. Still on the lower track, he stoops to tie one of his shoelaces. Maybe it's nervous energy, but before thinking it through, I shriek, "Steve!"

It comes out ten times louder than I intended. Steve starts a little as he looks up. I duck behind Kevin and clamp my lips shut to keep from laughing. "*That's* him," I mutter.

Steve takes off for real.

This time I give Kevin a push. "He's getting away!"

As Steve rounds a bend ahead of us, Kevin sprints down the embankment.

Back at home, I shower, drink more coffee, and straighten up the apartment—not hard, since the bed takes up about a third of the floor space. My apartment is a coffin-shaped studio on the "parlor floor" of what must have been a gracious brownstone house back in the eighteen-hundreds. It's not without its charms, such as a real fireplace and Victorian woodwork. And although the rent costs more than my monthly mortgage did in California, things could have been much worse. Val says her place has no closets, so she keeps her vintage wardrobe in boxes behind the sofa. Instead of a kitchen, the stove, sink, and fridge are in a nook behind the front door. One time, Val says, she had Thanksgiving over there and had to stuff the turkey on a card table in the hall outside her apartment. Her neighbors just walked around her without looking twice.

I wonder how Kevin's mission is going. The way we've set it up, he'll give chase until Steve gets to where he's going, and will either call me on his cell phone or return here with a full report. It's been half an hour already with no call, and I'm beginning to think Steve caught Kevin following him and invited him up to his mistress's house for some XXX three-way action. But if there's one thing I know about Kevin, he lacks the patience to juggle more than one woman at a time.

I e-mail a few friends from California, updating them on my employment status but assuring them everything will be all right. When Kevin still hasn't called, I walk to the corner to pick up yesterday's laundry before I run out of cash completely and have to abandon my clothes forever in wash-and-fold purgatory. On the way home, I nearly collide with a woman who walks up to me, touches my arm, and sings out, "Well, *hello*, there!" She's in her early twenties, pert and petite, with a messenger bag under her arm. "How are things going?"

I say hello equally enthusiastically while I try to place her. Someone in this city recognizes me! It would be a shame to have to admit I have no idea who she is.

"Do you mind if I ask you a question? Who cuts your hair?"

I shift the laundry sack onto my hip. Of course! I've heard of this happening: A woman in New York stopping a stranger for a salon recommendation. I wish I could help, I tell her, but my stylist is in Encino, California.

"California! That's far for a haircut!"

I set down the laundry bag. Out of nowhere a lump has set up camp in my throat.

"But it's your lucky day." She whips out a coupon book. "Rapture Salon, just over on Broadway, has a special deal for special new clients like you—seven haircuts for the price of six when you buy one of our VIP styling packages. We also do color, corrective color, highlights, lowlights, baliage, and Japanese straightening."

My cell phone rings. Actually, because I have never figured out how to switch it to a normal ring, it plays "La Cucaracha." Usually this annoys me, but right now I couldn't be happier to hear it. I should have known she was trying to sell me something. "Hello, *Kevin*!" I sing into the phone, hauling up the laundry bag and glowering at my nonacquaintance.

"I'll be at your place in a few minutes," Kevin says.

Brownstone etiquette: Usually, when a visitor you're expecting rings the outside bell, you buzz him in through the intercom and wait for him to get to your apartment door. In this case, I am already at the front entrance of the building. When Kevin comes up the front steps, sweaty and enigmatic, I pounce on him: "Tell me!"

"Let's do a walk-and-talk," he says, sounding serious. My stomach begins to reknot itself. My first assignment, and I've just busted someone. Or, rather, the person to whom I've "outsourced" the assignment has just busted someone. I may have to beg Kevin to help me break the bad news to Vickie.

Yet even after we've turned onto Columbus and walked two blocks up to the Natural History Museum, I still can't get anything out of him. Kevin is not a man who follows anyone else's agenda. He doesn't like to be pushed. First he has to stop at a deli for a bottle of Gatorade. Then he has to dig out the correct change. All the while I'm grinding my teeth, trying not to say anything. It's only when we're in the little park around the planetarium, below the enormous glassed-in atrium with the models of Saturn and Venus and Jupiter, that he fixes me with a grave expression.

"Come on, Kevin. Is it awful? A hooker?" I'm rigid with anxiety. "A *man*?"

"He went running."

There must be a hidden meaning in this phrase. "Running as in . . . ?"

"As in running. He ran around the reservoir—"

"Aha, like yesterday!" Except on the lower track. This has got to be significant.

"—and then, by the tennis courts, got onto the park road and went down and around the park and back to his building. A good five miles."

"Twelve Seventy-five Lexington. That's the building? Big white monstrosity by the subway entrance?"

"Green awning."

That's the one. "Nothing unusual at all?"

"Nothing. He was one hundred percent aboveboard."

I sink onto a bench in relief. Kevin finishes his sports drink and drills the bottle overhand into a metal wastebasket several feet away. Makes it. A passing couple gawks.

"Tourists," Kevin says.

"How can you tell?"

"You just can."

The couple huddles together on the tree-lined pathway. The man fumbles with his fanny pack and pulls out a New York guidebook while his companion studies her acrylic nails, which resemble ten squared-off, French-manicured miniature kitchen spatulas. He says something to her and points at a page in the book. Kevin and I watch as he approaches us, looks at me, then at Kevin, then at me, and finally says to Kevin, "We're pretty near the World Trade Center, right?"

"Not really." Kevin finds the correct chapter in the guidebook and points the couple toward the subway station on Central Park West. The woman waves at Kevin as they wander off.

Kevin shakes his head. "You know they're going to end up in Inwood."

"Why did he ask you and not me? You don't live here." For some reason I'm insulted. On the other hand, I couldn't have told the couple how to get downtown and am eager to get back to the Steve story. "You're sure about Steve? You kept up with him the whole time?"

"Based on what I saw today, you can tell your client not to worry; there's no negative change agent in her interpersonal enterprise." Kevin plunks down next to me and stretches luxuriously. Even though he's all sweaty, I would have no problem ravishing him right this minute. If Vickie's marriage is intact, that's one less divorce in the world, one less couple quibbling over who gets the dishes and who gets the TV and whose books are whose, not to mention who keeps which friends. The dirty little secret about divorce is that once your paired-off friends hear of your marital problems, a good number stop inviting you places and returning your calls. They must be worried about catching the discord virus.

When my divorce is final, most of our couple-friends will wind up allying with Teddy. This already depresses me. I'm not the one with the spotty employment record and the little-kid habits, leaving my socks on the hamper instead of in the hamper. "What. Is. So. Hard. About. Opening. The. Hamper?" I once screamed at Teddy, just before throwing his sweaty gray sports socks in his face. I regretted the outburst instantly. Teddy had stood there in his purple-and-yellow Lakers basketball shorts, just taking it. Until that moment I hadn't realized I had the capacity for that kind of cruelty. I'm glad Vickie's marriage isn't in trouble. Nobody should have to find out just how much ugliness she has buried inside herself.

FOUR

If I was relieved that Steve wasn't cheating, I was completely unprepared for Vickie's reaction. I thought she'd be reassured and grateful. All she said was, "How much do I owe you?" Yesterday an envelope arrived in the mail with a check for forty-five dollars. Val says Vickie returned to New York the day after I called, took a taxi straight from Grand Central to Tourneau on East Fifty-seventh, traded in her Rolex for a Cartier, and charged the difference on Steve's American Express.

"In other words, life is back to normal." Val punches a button on the arm of her adjustable massaging chair. It's been just under a week since our incomplete happy hour, and when I called to ask if she wanted to try again, she said she had time only for a quick post-work chat at the nail salon around the corner from Hayes Heeley. While she gets a pedicure, I stand to the side, out of the way of the woman crouching at her feet. "The water's getting cold," Val announces loudly, rolling her eyes at me and lowering her voice to a level the pedicurist can still hear. "I never come to these cheapo nail mills, but I was desperate. I made last-minute plans to see Declan later, the bass player from the subway. Turns out he has a bit of a foot fetish! What are you doing tonight?"

I'm doing nothing. Val, who's truly like no one else I've ever met, must think I'm the dullest person on earth. How can I compete, with my unexciting, unemployed, unchic existence? Val always has a fun tale to tell, and her love life—make that sex life—is straight out of a madcap women's novel. By the end of my second day at Hayes Heeley she'd already told me that once, for a Yankees fan she was sleeping with (only she didn't phrase it quite that way), she'd gone to J. Sisters for a custom bikini wax in the shape of an interlocking NY, then broken up with him before it could grow back. During the same conversation she'd also revealed that the intensity and frequency of her orgasms had improved dramatically since she'd turned thirty. "How old are you?" she had asked. Thirty-three, I told her. She said, "So you already know." Val dates men she meets on the subway, goes to nightclubs that open after midnight, and never, ever plans to be tied down. And she's effortlessly stylish. Today she's gone easy on the eyeliner but penciled in a beauty mark. She's combined black flip-flops with a black pleated kilt and a black Peter Pan–collared blouse for a quirky twisted-schoolgirl effect. I am wearing ChapStick, a light blue cotton tank top, and an old denim skirt I bought before my marriage to Teddy.

The pedicurist fishes Val's left foot out of the water and squirts pink liquid on her toes. Val holds out a black satin bag. "I brought my own tools. There's a cuticle-pusher in there." She says to me, "Aren't you getting a pedicure?"

"Not in the budget," I sigh.

"That's ridiculous." Val sinks deeper into her massaging chair. "It costs nothing. And what, you're going to do your nails yourself?"

That's the other thing. Even before I got laid off I couldn't keep up with Val financially. Despite her arty Greenwich Village thrift-shop persona, she'll never have to choose between getting her toenails tended and buying groceries. Even her fauxhemian apartment is subsidized by Daddy.

I pick up a bottle of polish from the display and roll it around in my palm. "When you first moved here, did you feel invisible?"

Val props an elbow on the arm of the chair and rests her

head sideways in her hand, anchoring a strand of Hawaiian-Punch hair behind her ear along the way.

"I was on the sidewalk just now, with people coming at me in all directions, people passing by with inches to spare, not one of them making eye contact, and I realized how profoundly separate each of us is. Have you ever felt that? There's something about New York that underscores the loneliness of the human condition in a way other places don't. Where I come from you can be by yourself in a car all day without speaking to a single other human being, and it doesn't feel half as isolating."

Val isn't listening. She's watching an enormously pregnant woman weave her way between manicure stands, at times rotating sideways to get through, to reach the other, empty pedicure throne.

"Hiya, stranger! Is this the hot new after-work hangout?" The woman hauls herself into the chair. I recognize her as Carmen Riggio, another Hayes Heeley staffer.

Val smiles unenthusiastically. "Hi, Carmen."

"How are you?" I add. Carmen works a few doors down from my former office.

"Ready to burst!" Carmen pats her belly. "I figure, might as well have nice toes while I can still see them, barely. Mind if I eat?"

"Not at all," Val says, like she does mind.

Another pedicurist steps over to fill Carmen's foot basin with water. Carmen takes a banana from her bag and devours it in four bites. "You can't believe how ravenous pregnancy makes you. Also, you have to pee every five minutes. Meanwhile, we're touring day-care places, trying to get on the wait lists, realizing we should have started looking three years before conception!" She hitches up the legs of her stretchy black maternity pants, and the second pedicurist swabs polish from her toes and says something in her language to Val's pedicurist. I imagine the two as friends outside work, riding the subway home together once they've logged their ten daily hours hunching over strangers' feet for three-dollar tips. Carmen catches my eye. "I heard you got downsized. Have you found anything else?"

"You won't believe what she's been doing." Val splays her toes so her pedicurist can weave cotton between them. "Detective work!"

"Really?"

My "no" is drowned out by Val, who's already recounting my ill-fated experience with Steve.

"So he wasn't cheating. That's nice to hear," Carmen says when Val is finished.

"I'm just glad it's over. I need to start my real job hunt. If you hear of someone who needs a freelance moderator, I'm available. I can file, write reports, anything within reason."

"What would you call not within reason?" Carmen inquires.

"I don't know." I watch another customer come into the salon. "Bringing the boss coffee? It's too close to my waitress days."

"You were a waitress?" Val asks.

"In college. I was awful. Every few months I'd accidentally dump a customer's plate in his lap. It's scary how few skills I really have."

"I bet I *could* get you a quick freelance gig," says Carmen as her pedicurist props her foot on a roll of paper towels to better pumice her heel. "I have a friend who's in a bind right now, and it seems right up your alley—"

"Where does she work?" I interrupt.

"At Shafran, Leonard and Stout. Should I call her? Of course I should. Give me a moment." I spin my mental Rolodex, but the name Shafran, Leonard and Stout means nothing. Carmen finds her cell phone, presses a few buttons, and holds it to her ear. "Linda, great news. I think I've just found someone who can solve your problem. Incredible, right? I'm with a girl from my office, Iris, who just got laid off."

"Tell her it was a fluke," I whisper. "I'd never been laid off until—"

Carmen waves me away. "...detective. No joke! My friend's sister? Iris followed her husband around last week. Isn't that funny? I'll ask." She looks at me. "What kind of money are we talking about?"

"Um," I say. "Commensurate with my experience? I have ten years."

"I'll let you two work it out."

Carmen passes me the phone, and I say hello to Linda, who skips the greeting and jumps right into the business part of the conversation: "You'd be willing to do this on such short notice? Because I've got a bit of a situation here. A total mess, more like it." There's a weird, whining quality to Linda's voice.

"I'd love to help if I can."

"Well, Carmen seems to think you're the answer to my prayers. You work evenings, I assume?"

"For after-hours focus groups? Sure. What kind of research does Shafran, Leonard and Stout do?"

"We're an interior-design firm."

I've never heard of an interior-design firm that does its own market research, but certainly there's a first time for everything.

"I need someone right away. Maybe Carmen told you. Things have reached desperation level. It's all gone horribly, horribly awry. All I wanted to know was whether he was the cheating kind."

Exactly what kind of work are we talking about here? asks the nagging little voice inside my head.

"I didn't think it through or I wouldn't have gotten myself into this mess. I would *never* stoop so low as to *plan out* something this sleazy. Can you imagine? It was a whim. A stupid whim. Let's get that perfectly clear. And now, what a mess. Are you cute?"

My heart starts to head south into my shoes. Carmen offers no assistance; she's regaling a yawning Val with the details of her pregnancy-related sciatica: "like someone grabbed a nerve in my leg and sliced it with a knife!" The pedicurists are deep in their own conversation.

"This isn't about a job in market research?"

"What? No, it's about my husband, Elliot."

Linda's story unfolds quickly. For weeks her husband's behavior had been most peculiar. He'd arrive home each night, and then after dinner, immediately disappear into the bedroom to get onto the computer. Linda would come in, and he'd jump up from the computer and stand in front of the screen with a funny look on his face. Still Linda thought nothing of all this until one Saturday afternoon last month, when she went to sign on to her gourmet cooking chat room, only to find a name she'd never heard of in the rectangle on the signing-on page.

"Icarus. That was the name. I thought, *Who is Icarus?*"

"Icarus is a character in Greek mythology. The sun melted his wax wings and he—"

"Right, right, whatever. I meant, why was there a strange signing-on name on our computer? Finally, finally, I realize this is an account Elliot made up, probably to pick up women. For all I know he's got a girlfriend with a Greek name, too—Guinevere or Ophelia or what have you." I have the craziest desire to swat Linda's mosquito voice away from my ear.

On discovering that her husband of eleven years had a secret Internet identity, Linda naturally became obsessed with knowing more. But instead of asking him to explain, she decided to catch him in the act. She made up her own fake identity, and a few nights later, while he was in the bedroom on the big computer, she was in the living room on her laptop, using her new name to send him a provocative instant message. When he didn't answer, she bombarded him with messages until he finally took the bait, and pretty soon they were instant-messaging back and forth. "Naturally he didn't know it was me. He thought Sexy Lexy—that's my made-up name—had spotted him once in a chat room or something."

"Why would you do this?" I lean against a wall. The nail polish fumes are going to my head.

"To see if he's cheating on me. Which he now is, with me. Well, almost is. He's never seen Sexy Lexy, obviously, so no, nothing has happened physically. But it's a deeply *emotional* relationship. Deeply emotional. He's online every night telling Sexy Lexy how he regrets not having done more with his life, how he's never been to Egypt or learned to hang-glide, and all your typical midlife-crisis baloney. He has no idea he's talking to his own wife."

There's no break in the conversation, so I can't ask Linda why she doesn't just tell him.

"I should tell him. I know; it's awful. I just *really* wanted to see if he would cheat on me. But up until last Thursday he never came on to Sexy Lexy. Never." She stops for the first breath I've heard her take.

"What happened last Thursday?"

"Thursday is when I decided to ratchet things up a notch and so was like, 'Why don't we meet in person?' "

I would laugh if I could. The world's most hapless soap opera character couldn't concoct a more harebrained scheme. Have I really understood this correctly? "You've set up a rendezvous with your own husband, hoping to catch him cheating on you with a fictitious woman you invented?"

Carmen, having caught this last bit of the conversation, widens her eyes and bounces in her chair as wildly as a pregnant woman getting a pedicure can, touching her index finger to her nose—the charades gesture for "You've got it!"

"Right. It's this Friday night. What would it cost to have you go in my place? Just to show up, pretend that you're Sexy Lexy, and see what happens from there?"

I'm no longer blaming the nail polish for my light-headedness. The problem, I believe, is that I'm being asked to pose as someone who would willingly call herself Sexy Lexy—and, no doubt, to fend off the advances of an amorous husband. I don't need to stoop to this sort of thing. I am sorry, I tell Linda, but I'm trained in market research and that's where my interest lies.

Carmen waves her hands frantically. I ask Linda to excuse me for a moment, and rest the phone against my leg.

Carmen says, "Don't tell me you're turning her down. You're perfect for this!"

"Linda's loaded. She'd probably pay you twice whatever Vickie did," Val adds for good measure.

The phone, with Linda's voice trapped inside, buzzes against my leg. I crush it harder against the denim of my skirt.

"Just help her," Carmen implores. "She deserves to know the truth!"

"Beggars can't be choosers," Val says.

It becomes clear that saying no is really not an option. I don't have enough friends in this city to risk offending anybody, and—Val said it—I'm in no position to turn down work.

I return the phone to my ear. "I charge fifty dollars an hour, plus cab fare."

Carmen pantomimes a cheer. Val ascends from her throne and walks stiff-legged to the drying area in her paper pedicure shoes. Linda, on the phone, asks me to come to her

office Thursday so she can tell me everything I need to know.
There's more?

"By the way, you wouldn't happen to be a redhead, would
you?"

"No," I say. "I wouldn't."

"You're probably not a double-D cup, either. But not to
worry. Both can be arranged."

———————

I awake the next morning with a mission. I've said it myself:
It's time to find a real job. Admittedly, this is easier said than
done. I can't just pick up the phone and call my former boss,
Pat Sweeney, even though I left on good terms. Much as I
would like to return to California, I have no desire to crawl
back, explaining that my dream career in New York didn't
work out any better than my marriage did. I can just see Pat,
with his goatee and square-framed spectacles and ironic sympathy: "Poor Iris. It seems you *couldn't* make it there." I don't
have enough for plane fare in the first place. And even if I did,
where would I live, now that Teddy and two of his acting-class
buddies have taken over my house? Evie Amato, my friend
from college, the one who got married right after graduation,
says I could stay in Palmdale with her and Doug and their
three kids, Chadwicke, Fairchild, and Sinclair. It's a sweet
offer, but I'd sooner sleep in the back of my car. Not that I have
a car anymore.

So it seems staying in Manhattan is my only choice until I
can scrape up enough money to go home on my own terms,
and I suppose the sooner I accept that, the better. I do sort-of
know three freelance moderators in this area, and I spend the
morning calling each to remind her who I am. Each says
she'll keep me in mind for the future, but none asks me in for
an interview.

Having "utilized" every last one of my "existing contacts," as Kevin would put it, I shower, dry my hair straight, put on some mascara and ChapStick, and locate on the Internet the addresses of two dozen other local freelance moderators. I update my résumé and print it out to take to the copy shop on Broadway, to have it reproduced on nice résumé paper. At the end of my block, I catch my reflection in the window of the gourmet kitchen-gadgets store on the corner and note that forty seconds in the sticky summer-is-coming humidity already has my hair back to its not-curly-enough-to-be-curly-but-not-straight-enough-to-be-straight natural state. Also, there's bicycle chain grease on my left calf.

By the time I've walked the four blocks to Photo/Copy Express, my forehead is dripping with sweat. I fan myself with the résumé folder while the clerk, with jangling jewelry and an unflatteringly tight top, twirls, then inspects, a strand of her hair, which is orange at the ends and dark brown at the roots, as if she's growing out last year's highlights. On my way in I noticed that Rapture Salon is two doors down from this place. The salon has a sign in its window saying "We Specialize in Corrective Color." That woman who accosted me by the wash-and-fold should be looking for customers a little closer to home.

The clerk examines my résumé sullenly and takes it back to a copy machine. I mop my face with an old deli napkin from my bag.

When she turns back around, she breaks into a huge grin. "Hey, you!" she squeals, tossing her hair and all but skipping back to the counter. Who is this girl, Dr. Jekyll with a dye job?

"Hi!" I respond, then blush. She's not talking to me but to whoever is in line behind me. To camouflage my mortification, I get busy digging into my wallet.

"Not with your blond bombshell today?" the clerk says

over my head. I hold out my credit card. She accepts it wordlessly.

"*You* are the bombshell," answers a male voice.

The clerk titters. If she had a parasol and a hoop skirt, she'd be Scarlett O'Hara at the Wilkes family barbecue. Remembering me, she silently relinquishes my résumés and a credit slip. I sign it, and she plucks her pen out of my fingers.

"May I have the receipt, please?"

"What can I do for you today?" she says over my head.

"The receipt, please?"

"It's in the bag."

"It's right there." I point at the register.

She tears off the receipt and makes a big show of holding it out to me.

Part of me wants to climb over the counter and slap her. I pull the receipt out of her hand. Before I can stop it, the other part of me says automatically, "Have a nice day."

Arrgh! Supremely irritated by now, I turn and plow right into the man behind me. I am about to yelp, "Sorry," but what comes out of my mouth instead is a surprised gasp.

This person looks so familiar!

Why? I think. *Who? Where have I—?*

A split second later, something clicks in my brain and I'm opening my mouth and exclaiming, "It's *you!*"

And one more split second after that, something else clicks in my brain and I understand, clear as the face before me, that I've said too much.

FIVE

Caught in the act of patronizing an Upper West Side copy shop by a woman he's never met, Vickie's husband looks exactly as you'd imagine he would: as if he's drawing a complete blank. He turns around to glance over his shoulder; seeing no one else behind him, he turns back to give me a long, slow, exceedingly nerve-racking once-over. "I beg your pardon?"

I, meanwhile, have clapped my hand over my mouth while trying to muddle through my cognitive dissonance. Why is Steve here? Why isn't he at the reservoir in his running clothes? He must be having an affair! With this counter clerk! "My mistake," I gasp out. "I thought you were someone else." I wish he'd stop staring.

After what seems like several hours, he shrugs. "No problem." He gives me one last look, then steps past me up to the counter to speak to the clerk. "How are you today, um . . ."

"Mona," she tells him.

"Now I remember. How are you, Mona?"

He's having an affair with the counter clerk and doesn't even know her name!

The haze in my brain begins to dissipate. That seems unlikely. Besides, Mona, with her two-tone hair and too-tight top, can't possibly be Steve's mistress. Surely he could do better.

The smart thing to do now would be to bolt out of the store before Steve connects me with Vickie. But my leaving quickly would imply I had a shred of common sense. "Then why *are* you here?" I blurt out instead.

Now he's staring like I'm one of those lost souls who mutter in the subway, and my face is ten degrees hotter than it already was. I rush to the door and yank it open.

"Can you believe the rudeness?" I hear the clerk say as the door closes behind me. I dash up the sidewalk and race-walk back to my apartment so intently that a blister rises up underneath my sandal strap.

When I call Kevin to tell him about seeing Steve, he seems to think it's no big deal. "What is the critical issue here?"

I've got plenty of issues. What is Steve up to? Do I tell Vickie I saw her husband acting suspiciously? Who's the blond bombshell? Why was he on the Upper West Side? And why a copy shop? "You're trying to tell me a real estate executive wouldn't have his secretary do his copying at the office?"

"He could have been getting photos developed."

"You don't think he'd own a digital camera?"

"Do you own a digital camera?"

"No, but he's got money. Besides, this place is nowhere near his neighborhood."

"So it's near his office. Or a building his company manages. You did say he was in commercial real estate—maybe he was showing property nearby."

"Maybe he's cheating on his wife."

"You have no actionable proof of that."

"Kevin. Come on. 'Where's the blond bombshell?' "

"What makes you think she wasn't referring to—what's her name again?"

"Who, Vickie?" The thought hadn't occurred to me. Would anyone call Vickie a blond bombshell? A cute blond, sure. But a bombshell? "It's too odd a coincidence, then. What are the chances that I would randomly bump into Vickie's husband?"

"People bump into each other in New York all the time."

"Right, right. It's just a big small town."

_____

The next day, over a breakfast of Cheerios and my next-to-last Diet Coke, I write a cover letter for my résumé. I explain that I'm hoping to build up a client list by apprenticing with an established moderator and that I have a decade of experience in qualitative research, including five years as a recruiter at PKS Associates in Brentwood, California. But how to account for only a few weeks at the famed Hayes Heeley Market Research, New York? I can't come up with an answer, so I decide not to mention it at all. I print out individual letters tailored to each of the two dozen firms I've dug up. I'll stuff everything into envelopes later; there's a far more pressing problem to tackle first. I finish the last flat remains of my soda and leave for my meeting with Linda.

On the way out, I brush up against my neighbor's bike for the umpteenth time.

That's it. Someone needs to tell him he's being inconsiderate. I march one flight down to his subterranean lair, miss the last step in my haste, and land with a thud at the bottom of the stairs, bashing my tailbone in the process. Ouch, ouch, ouch!

At the crash, a barking begins behind the door: "*Woowoowoowoowoo!*"

My downstairs neighbor has a dog? You'd think a man so averse to noise would have opted for a nice, quiet boa constrictor or tank of piranhas.

The doors in my building are impressive: solid oak, nine feet high. Backside throbbing, heart pounding, I knock.

"*Woowoowoowoowoo!*"

I knock harder.

"Who is it?"

"Your neighbor!"

From inside, the clicking and thwacking of a dead bolt being disengaged. The door swings open four inches until it reaches the end of the safety chain. My neighbor is in his mid-forties and cue-ball bald; his head appears to have been buffed to a mellow patina with scalp polish and a soft cloth. On a chain around his neck, a diamond peace sign clicks against a gold cross and a pair of military-style dog tags. He looks at me.

"Hi. I'm Iris, from upstairs."

From inside the apartment the dog barks again: "*Woowoowoowoowoo!*"

"I'm not sure if you're aware of this, but—"

"*Woowoowoowoowoo!*"

"It's come to my attention that—"

"*Woowoowoowoowoo!*"

Despite what I suspect he would have me believe, my neighbor's expression does not appear to be genuinely apologetic.

"*Woowoowoowoowoo!*"

"Pardon me, doll, but as you can see, the baby's crying. Perhaps some other time." He smiles tightly and shuts the door.

Linda sits, dwarfed behind a massive desk. There's a rectangular carafe of icewater to her left and, to her right, a sinister, spidery alien life form disguised as an orchid. Otherwise the desk is bare. There is none of the comforting flotsam of office life—not a scrap of paper, photograph, or pushpin. She unfolds her spindly arms and pulls from a drawer a folder of printed-out instant messages and e-mails. She passes it to me—the written record of Sexy Lexy's and Icarus's relationship. "For background," she says, fixing me with her intense, white-gray eyes.

I open the folder to skim the first line of the first note, and slap it shut again, red-faced. "I'll read these when I get home," I promise, anticipating a long evening ahead of me.

She next removes a pencil and a graph pad from the drawer and instructs me to take notes. I scribble madly to keep up with her instructions: I'm to meet Icarus/Elliot at the bar at the Hotel Royal in Midtown, have a drink, flirt a little. If he tries anything, I am to excuse myself and call Linda, who will be here at her office, blocks away, ready to trip-trap over in her high heels and confront him.

I look up from the pad. "You're sure you want to do that? If it were me, I wouldn't want a public scene."

"If he's cheating, he deserves a scene." Linda jiggles one pointy-pump–shod foot and looks pointedly at my graph pad. I dutifully make a notation. "Next, your appearance. Sexy Lexy has red hair. I trust you're comfortable with disguises. Buy a hair color you like at the drugstore and put it on my bill. Get the semipermanent kind and it'll wash out in a week." She appraises my chest. "You're certainly no Playboy bunny, so you'll have to stuff your bra. Good. You'll be less tempted to take your clothes off."

Back at my apartment I call Val at her office.

"You have no idea what it's been like around here," she starts in right after we exchange hellos, her words nearly drowned out by what sounds like a mile-long procession of fire sirens passing seventeen stories below her office. When the noise fades, she continues, "Michelle is suddenly sending me all over the country. She just told me I have to leave Sunday to run groups in Minneapolis, St. Louis, and Tampa. Three second-tier cities in three days. I just joined an Internet dating service and have dates lined up for Monday and Tuesday that now I'll be forced to cancel."

"What happened to Declan?"

"Declan wore out his welcome." That's the extent of Val's explanation. "You're lucky not to be working, Iris. If I'd known how demanding this field was when I got into it, how far it would cut into my social life, I would have gone into jewelry design."

There's no use, really, in trying to explain to Val the true meaning of the word "lucky." "You wouldn't happen to own an auburn wig, would you?" I ask instead, going over the highlights of my assignment tomorrow night.

Val does own a wig, she confirms. It's blue.

I sigh. "I was afraid of this. I have to color my hair."

"No, Iris, you should be glad. Your hair just begs for some drama. I'd give you the number of my salon, but there's a four-month waiting list."

I explain that I'll be doing it myself.

Val gasps. "You're not going to a salon?"

"She didn't offer." I collect the morning's dishes and lay them on the mustard Formica countertop in the kitchen, between the avocado refrigerator and the sink with the cold-water tap that reads "hot" and the hot-water tap that reads "cold." "Do you think you could come over and help me? I'll use semipermanent color, but it would help to have someone supervising." It also would be nice to have company.

"Can't. I'm going out tonight. But since you're a dye virgin, I could pick out a color for you on the way home from work and send it over. I'll loan you something to wear, too. Nobody's going to believe Sexy Lexy in that denim skirt."

I blush. My entire wardrobe does seem mysteriously off-kilter: dresses all too short or too long, beachy, anachronistic skirts, blouses with freakish buttons, pants of the wrong cut or fabric or both. I'd been planning to wear a sleeveless navy linen shift bought right before the move, which looked chic to me at the time, and a pair of four-month-old slingbacks that suddenly have heels of entirely the wrong height and shape.

"I'll throw in some chicken cutlets, too," Val continues.

My phone makes a beeping noise.

"All I ask is that it's not too big a change, Val. Promise me."

My phone beeps again.

"Is that your call-waiting?"

"Beep," goes the phone. It's hard to believe that two people simultaneously want to speak to me. "So, nothing drastic."

"Have fun," Val says. "Don't sleep with Linda's husband unless you want to."

She clicks off before I can explain that I have no intention of sleeping with Linda's husband or anyone else's, or ask Val why she's sending me food. I switch over to the second line and say hello.

"Iris?"

It seems I haven't had enough recent practice operating the call-waiting, because it's still Val on the line. "What did you mean by 'chicken cutlets'?"

"It's Vickie."

Oops.

"Steve's at it again," she says. "I need you to follow him tomorrow morning. You're not busy, are you?"

There's something to that old saw about how in New York you can get anything delivered, anytime. At eleven o'clock Thursday night, a scruffy, marijuana-scented bicycle messenger arrives with a battered Louis Vuitton garment bag and a box of haircolor in the shade Val has chosen especially for me: Scarlet Sunset.

I reach for the phone, to call Linda and back out. Then I stop. I need the money. I can't back out. And, it already being past my bedtime, I'm too tired to walk over to the drugstore for some other, barely detectable color—called, say, "Infrared." Truth be told, I'm not all that concerned. In my former working life I observed countless hair-care focus groups, and one of the most common complaints is that hair color is never as vibrant in real life as it is in the package photo. Besides, it will wash out soon enough. I set the box aside to unzip the garment bag. Inside is one of those slip-girdles designed to hold you in under a clingy dress. The actual dress must have slid off the hanger and fallen into the bottom of the bag. I feel around inside, and my hand brushes against something clammy. I yank it back, suppressing a shriek, and zip the bag open all the way. Two glistening, flesh-colored blobs tumble out, slap-slapping softly onto the floor.

I bend down and poke at one; it jiggles gently. I pick it up. It's half-moon shaped, made of some kind of space-age polymer with the pliant surface of a slab of raw meat crossed with the rubbery heft of a water balloon. And then I understand, not just that these must be what Val meant by "chicken cutlets," but also what they're for. I reach under my shirt, stuff one cutlet into each side of my bra, and then stand on the toilet and lean out over the sink to view them in the bathroom mirror.

Amazing. I've never minded being small-breasted, but my 34-Bs have become nothing less than awe-inspiring. I spend the next fifteen minutes trying on every last bra, camisole, and tank top I own, balancing in front of the bathroom mirror, sticking out my chest at various angles, and staring down into my own cleavage. I snap out of my self-worship only after my downstairs neighbor, out of nowhere, starts another round of percussion practice on his ceiling. Bang! Bang! Bang!

I pull the cutlets back out of my bra and toss them onto my bed, open the hair color box, put on the plastic gloves, pour vial B into bottle A, shake well, and get to work. It's simple: You squirt the dye onto dry hair, let it fester for thirty minutes, and then rinse it out. Since I'll be sacrificing a T-shirt to the cause, I choose one of Teddy's but still try to protect it from spills while gingerly squeezing overlapping stripes of goo into my hair. Once I've painted every last strand and molded the entire mass into a gloppy spiral on top of my head, I set the digital clock on my microwave to "timer only," punch in thirty minutes, *beep-beep-beep-beep*, and "start," *beep*. Then I hit the speaker button on my phone, ready to collect my first un-employment check.

The routine supposedly works like this: Once a week during your allotted time on the dole, you call a special number, where a recording welcomes you to the New York State Department of Labor's self-service phone line and asks for your personal identification number. You press a few buttons, and a few days later the check arrives in the mail. It's pretty simple, aside from one thing: I've been calling all week during business hours and haven't gotten through. It seems the line has been in use by untold scores of other downtrodden New Yorkers calling in for their checks. So my new plan is, do it after hours! Surely all those other unemployed people are asleep or dead drunk by now.

Wrong. It's the same routine as always: I dial, get a busy signal, hang up, hit redial, get a busy signal, hang up, and so on. I finally get through, but it's so frustrating that when the microwave timer goes off—*beeeeep!*—I don't hear it. It's only after I hang up in relief, absentmindedly scratch an itch on my head, and come into contact with the slimy mess up there that I realize I've been engrossed in my phone-calling for much, much longer than thirty minutes, and when I dash into the bathroom (admittedly an easy two steps from where I've been sitting), it is as bad as you might expect.

The Beauty Parlor Massacre. Scarlet Sunset glistening like congealing blood in my hair, my scalp stained fuchsia. I bolt into the shower and rinse frantically. Crimson water swirls into the drain. Maybe it won't be that bad, I try to reassure myself during the interminable two-minute conditioning phase.

But after blow-drying and styling and forced objectivity, the truth is, it's that bad. Scarlet Sunset falls somewhere on the red spectrum between "strawberry Jell-O" and "traffic light." And then my stomach jumps as I remember the one thing I forgot to double-check. I dig the dye-covered box out of the trash. "Permanent haircolor," it says.

"I said subtle!" I wail into my phone. "Now I'm Raggedy Ann's punk-rock love child!"

Val laughs. "Subtlety gets you nowhere in New York."

SIX

That's not Steve. That's not Steve, either. Neither is that one. He's not Steve, nor is he; no; no; no. Not that one, either. The first few weeks after my move to Manhattan I navigated the city in a constant state of sensory overload. Honking horns, thundering delivery trucks, barking dogs, screeching toddlers, singing drunks. Groaning cranes hauling steel beams high into the sky, jackhammers biting through sidewalks, and backhoes ripping up chunks of street. The random intermittent scream of emergency sirens. People everywhere, overheard gossip, public foreplay, subway drummers, drunken singing. Garlic and stale beer and raw fish, the cloying piña colada smell of the taxicab air freshener. A trick wind gusting up from a sidewalk grate as a subway train passes beneath, and farther below, under the asphalt and cement and bedrock, the pounding pulse of the city, like the heartbeat of a malevolent giant. I felt drained and manic at the same time, unable to sleep or think.

Not Steve; no; no; that one doesn't even look like Steve; no; no; no.

But you have to adapt quickly or you'll lose your mind. One day, on Sixth Avenue, I found I was able to resist the skyscrapers' magnetic pull, the compulsion to gawk up every few steps to catch a glimpse of the people inside. A few days later, I realized I could focus enough on the subway map to no longer find myself on the train east to Queens when I'd meant to take it west to Times Square, and as people passed by I could become thoroughly focused on the smallest of details, such as the limitless diversity of the human earlobe. I've learned to filter out the stimuli and concentrate only on the task at hand. Not Steve; no; no; not Steve; nope; this one has cute shoes; that one has a cute baby; not Steve; not Steve; no; did that cyclist just laugh at my hair? I can think all of these thoughts at once while standing for another morning in Central Park, this time poised on in-line roller skates, vetting the passersby, waiting for one of them to be Vickie's husband.

I fight back a yawn. I was up much too late last night fixating on my hair.

Vickie admits she still has nothing concrete to back up her continuing suspicions. There's been no smudge of lipstick, her own or anyone else's, on Steve's collar, no unexplained charges on his American Express. She doesn't know about the thing she should be suspicious of, the "bombshell" episode in the copy shop. I haven't told her. Kevin says I wasn't on assignment for her when it happened and am under no obligation to give away information for free.

"Only someone living with infidelity would understand the pain of my existence right now," Vickie told me yesterday. I did not try to explain how very, very much I do know about the pain. I listened when she described how Steve seemed more distant, distracted, and snappish than usual. And his morning workouts, she said, were getting longer. She was still sure this was when he was finding time to cheat. Could I follow him once more?

I agreed, vowing to myself that this was the last time, knowing I wouldn't catch Steve doing anything but exercising. With Kevin not in town to help, I spent last night "strategizing" between hair-related panic attacks, and the Rollerblade idea came to me. I also finally realized the benefit of waiting for Steve on my side of the park, at the tennis courts, to give myself a head start. Sure enough, after about fifteen minutes of surveillance, he emerges from a trail a few feet ahead of me. Just like clockwork.

He looks the same as usual, except where's the dog? Is the absence significant? I remind myself to mention it to Vickie, then push off and begin skating furiously to keep up with him. This all begins on an uphill. I bought the inline skates a few years ago on a whim and haven't used them a dozen times, and I'm in no better shape than I was last week. Within a minute I am sweating and gulping for air, cursing my unemployed state. I could be skating on the beach path in Santa Monica right now if I hadn't put the entire country between it and me.

I lean into the hill, curling my hands into fists and clenching my jaw and stumbling over a rough place in the pavement, hanging in the balance between upright and facedown, before steadying myself and dragging myself forward. At last the hill levels out, and I turn my attention back to Steve, who's about twenty feet ahead and doesn't seem to be in agony of any kind. Actually, he looks good. I hadn't noticed he's in much better shape than Vickie and Val give him credit for. I feel like a pervert, ogling Vickie's husband, but it's hard not to. He's lean and light on his feet, with just the right amount of muscle—not gym-bulky but nicely toned. Most of the other men are overdressed in shiny, expensive workout wear, with headphones and heart-rate monitors. Steve's only gadget is a runner's watch, and he's in plain gray athletic shorts, a well-worn navy-blue T-shirt, and battered running shoes without socks. He doesn't seem Vickie's type. I'd have imagined her with someone who wore his wealth obviously.

This train of thought gets me up a second, much longer hill that starts near the bottom end of the reservoir and doesn't crest for a good quarter mile. This time, when it switches abruptly to down, I push off as hard as I can, just to get some air on my face. Suddenly I'm rolling forward at a healthy clip, fast approaching Steve on the right edge of the road and gaining speed by the second. He may have established a nice lead early on, but he's no match for me now that I'm moving at what feels like eighty—no, ninety; no, a hundred—miles an hour. I'm sleep deprived. My reaction time is impaired. If I fall, I'm going to die, or at least break every bone in my body.

I try not to panic; it will make everything worse. I try flexing my left foot to drag my skate brake on the pavement, but the motion throws me off balance. I move my feet apart, hoping it'll slow me down, but all that happens is, I pick up more speed and am now doing the splits. Okay, I'm officially panicking. The wind whistles in my ears, and the road's a flash under my feet, and I'm about to barrel into a clump of pedestrians in the crosswalk just ahead, scattering them like bowling pins.

I take the only way out I can think of: I aim for Steve's back, extend my arms in front of me, and squeeze my eyes shut.

"Oof!" Steve grunts as I slam into him. My eyes fly open in time to see him sail over the curb—one of those slow-motion moments of clarity when you can foretell exactly what is coming next but are powerless to stop it. I'm right behind him, airborne. The two of us clatter to the ground in a bone-shattering heap. My teeth snap together as we hit.

Yet it's not as gruesome as it could have been. Steve has managed to land on a patch of grass at the side of the road. He's conscious, isn't screaming, and doesn't appear to be bleeding. Of course, he still has a 115-pound, Rollerblade-wearing human projectile on top of him.

"Oh! Oh! Oh! I am so sorry!" I struggle to disentangle myself, clipping him in the shin with my skate. I flinch when I feel myself kick him and, in flinching, whack him on the shoulder with my wrist. "Sorry! Sorry! I'm so sorry!" I'm eventually able to crawl off him, but not before knocking the front of my skull against the back of his.

My sunglasses have flown from my face and landed on top of a discarded watermelon rind. I crawl to them, put them on, and repeat, in case he hasn't heard, how sincerely sorry I am.

Steve struggles to his feet, brushing bits of grass off his green-stained knees. I have never been so embarrassed. I have never been so petrified, either. Why did I have to crash into an Upper East Sider? I can only imagine what the next words out of his mouth will be.

"Are you all right?" He reaches to help me up. "Are you hurt?"

I stand unsteadily and inventory my body parts. No broken bones, it seems; the jury's still out on the surface wounds. "Are you?"

He examines a raw spot on his right knee, gingerly massages his right wrist. "Not too much."

"It's all my fault. I feel terrible." I do. Not so much sorry, truthfully, as furious at myself. I've just made the stupid mistake every driver in California knows never to make: admitting responsibility for the accident. I also feel a surge of tears rushing toward shore. Could he just publicly berate me already and get it over with? I bug my eyes out in that genius way people do to try and keep themselves from crying.

But he's not looking at my eyes.

"My word!" he says.

In the excitement I had forgotten. I instinctively touch my hair, knowing how it must look: garish and brassy, like Val's.

Val.

Steve's sister-in-law.

I'm done for. He's going to link me to Val, and then to Vickie, and have me thrown in bungling-detective jail.

"Have I seen you somewhere?"

In the time between his asking the question and my coming up with a good answer, it seems a thousand New Yorkers whiz past with bikes and skates and jogging strollers. I can't let him think about this for too long. Otherwise he's sure to figure out he's seen me *everywhere:* in front of his building, in the park, in line at Photo/Copy Express.

I lean down and clutch my right shin, wail loudly, and crumple back onto the grass. The ploy is reasonably convincing. There's a cut there that truly does hurt. "Owww!"

Steve sprints away.

My stomach lurches. This is not my day. I'm going to have to get up and keep following him, and also do it without his realizing it. But Steve is just hurrying to a snack cart a few yards away. He returns with two plastic bottles of Poland Spring and a wad of paper towels. He kneels down and hands me a bottle. Then he opens the other and pours water on the paper towels. "Let's see your leg."

I yank it away.

"Let me see," he repeats sternly.

I extend my leg tentatively toward him. Maybe if I do what he tells me, he won't reprimand me in the middle of Central Park.

He dabs at my wound.

"Ow! Stop it!"

He pours more water on my leg. "Hang in there."

"What do you think you're doing?"

"Do you want it to get infected?" More dabbing.

"Owww!" It really stings.

"If I were your dad, I'd say, 'Don't be a baby! Pain builds character!' "

My eyes burn at Steve's unexpected invocation of my father. I rub away the unshed tears. "Would you let me go?"

He stops his triage and sits up straight. He has a faint

white scar under his chin and laugh lines at the corners of his eyes. His runner's watch is still in stopwatch mode, the electronic numbers transforming and retransforming, unreadable. "Sorry. I know that hurt, but it had to be done. Take off your sunglasses."

"Excuse me?"

"Glasses. Take them off. You might have a concussion. I should check your pupils."

A trickle of sweat runs down my neck. "I do not have a concussion."

"But *I* might, and if I do it's your fault. So take off your sunglasses, please, and look at *my* pupils."

What if he does have a concussion? Could he die in his sleep from it? Forget that I'd be responsible for taking another person's life; Vickie would never let me hear the end of it.

I clench the sunglasses in one sweaty palm, lean forward, and look intently into Steve's pupils.

They don't seem to be dilated, but I'm no doctor.

He gazes back into mine. "Do you feel faint or shaky?"

The thing is, I do feel that way.

Steve's eyes are liquid brown with flecks of green and gold and something else, too.

There's a spark. A flare of the combustible element men give off when they're attracted to someone. To my horror, I feel my body sending the same spark toward him. It crackles in the space between us, uncontrollable. Dangerous.

He moves his face in closer.

I can't think. I can't move. I can barely so much as breathe, waiting for what I know will come next. *He's going to kiss me,* I think wildly, with equal parts dread and excitement. *He's really going to kiss me.*

It's that magically charged first-kiss moment, when you're longing with every last nerve, *Please, let this happen,* and it happens, his lips brushing yours softly, that tentative dance of desire and hesitation, until you give in, melt into him, and he folds you into his arms. . . .

No, no, no. God, no.

Steve doesn't kiss me. What I meant was, it's like that other kind of moment where the man is about to kiss you but then realizes that if he tries anything, you're going to punch him in the stomach and call the cops.

He pulls back. "Nothing there."

It takes me a moment to understand that he's talking about my pupils.

Just for a flash, I'm disappointed. Right away the disappointment gives way to disgust, then outrage. Steve isn't some stranger I happened to crash into! He's Vickie's husband! How dare he!

I stand, pull the bottom of my sweatpants back down over my aching leg, and test my center of gravity on the Rollerblades. I'm pretty sure I can make it home without passing out. I pull a few dollars from my pocket and hold the money out to him. "For the water."

"Keep it." His tone is as frosty as mine.

I should insist more vehemently, force the money on him, but instead return it to my pocket. Hey, I'm unemployed. Every little bit helps.

"Maybe I'll see you around," he says.

I may not be a professional private eye. I may not be a good amateur private eye. I suspect, though, that the first rule in the handbook has got to be, don't let your client's husband try to seduce you.

"I don't think so," I say as I find an unsteady balance and skate painfully away.

SEVEN

Hi, Vickie? You won't believe this, but I bumped into Steve today. Literally. During the stakeout. Yes, crashed right into him. On Rollerblades. He may need his head examined. No, I mean that literally, too. Cheating? Still couldn't say, although talking to him I got the strangest feeling he was trying to . . ."

Vickie needs to know what happened this morning. She needs to know right away, but I can't face her, not in person and not over the phone.

I open my laptop and bring up a blank e-mail.

TO: Vickie Benjamin Sokolov
FROM: Iris Hedge
SUBJ: Steve

The screen watches, blank and impatient, as I fidget in my seat, stretch my arms, try to work a kink out of my neck, and succeed only in reminding myself of the extent of my Rollerblade injuries: skinned knee, sore back, and bruises in places I didn't know could bruise. I drop the stretching and survey my apartment. Spotless. That pillow could use plumping, though, the one on the side of the bed that used to be Teddy's. Should I do something with myself? I've got Linda's assignment tonight. Should I tweeze my eyebrows? Give myself a clay masque? Take off the faded nail polish I've been wearing since before I got laid off? Stare at my hair and cry? No—mail my résumés. I stuff and seal the two dozen envelopes, slip on my sandals, and limp off to the Columbus Avenue post office. Forty minutes later I return to the computer.

TO: Vickie Benjamin Sokolov
FROM: Iris Hedge
SUBJ: Steve

But it's pointless to go further until I remove that nail polish. Regrettably, I appear to be out of cotton balls, which necessitates another side trip, this time to Duane Reade. It does not escape me that in my former life I knowingly fed the marketing machine that lays all this pressure on women.

My face is plastered with clay, and I'm in the middle of obliterating the offending polish, when the phone rings.

"Well?"

I should have written that memo.

"Well?"

"Vickie," I say carefully, through the drying masque that has left me barely able to move my lips, "have you spoken to Steve today?"

"To his secretary. He was on his way into a meeting. You sound funny. Are you lisping?" In the background on Vickie's end of the line, a teakettle shrills.

"Did his secretary mention how he was feeling?"

"No, why?"

"She didn't say he seemed hurt, or anything?"

"No! Iris, what happened?"

"Nothing. I thought I saw him limping a little when he was running, but I guess not. Anyway, not to worry. He's fine."

The whistling grows deafening; Vickie must be walking toward the stove. "Okay," she says as the noise cuts off abruptly. "You're telling me yet again that he just went running."

"That's it." I prepare myself. Vickie's going to fire me, the way I imagine she must dismiss anyone who doesn't deliver exactly what she wants: the cleaning lady whose hospital corners aren't up to par, the facialist whose hot towel isn't quite hot enough. She wants me to catch Steve cheating, and I am simply unable to do so.

It will be a relief. There's something cheap and sordid about this spying business, and I'm not just talking about what Vickie pays me. After this assignment for Linda is over I'm going to hang up the chicken cutlets, retire the Rollerblades, and concentrate on getting my dignity back. "Vickie." My face is a lakebed of cracked mud. "Have you considered couples counseling?"

"I would never trust my marriage to a total stranger."

I go to the bathroom, dampen one of my wedding washcloths, and scrape some of the masque away from my mouth. "Even so, it's probably time you and I parted ways. I'm sure you can find far better uses for your money." *The pittance you tossed my way, that is.*

"I guess you're right," she admits in a small voice. "Let me know what I owe you."

And just like that, my time in Vickie's employ comes to a merciful end.

Val says the bar Linda has chosen for the Sexy Lexy–Icarus rendezvous, at the Hotel Royal on Forty-fifth Street, is years past its peak, but it's still plenty intimidating to me. Nearly every wall is mirrored, lending the place the disorienting ambience of a carnival fun house, and its clientele is made up of the kind of people who spent junior high school tormenting the smart kids. It's as if someone had tossed me into the chichole to teach me to swim. "Sorry!" I squeak after planting the wrongly shaped heel of my slingback onto the instep of an actual woman—not the reflection I'd assumed her to be—while groping my way into the long, narrow room. The woman confides something mean-seeming to her equally flawless friend. I blush and continue on my path toward the bar, nearly colliding with the trashy, half-naked redhead with the skinned knee, who's marching straight toward me. Good Lord! That *is* me, stuffed and trussed into the black "slip" Val sent over. It took a careful search of Val's garment bag before I realized that this, the lone article of clothing within, *was* the dress: A cross between a corset and a slip girdle, on top it's little more than a glorified bra, out of which, I fear, a cutlet may fly at any moment.

The bar is three deep with exquisite creatures ordering neon-colored cocktails that look to have been synthesized in a lab. I want to order a beer but don't want to be laughed out onto the street.

"Pandora's Box, please," I tell the bartender, remembering the name of the drink Val ordered at Grand Central.

"You don't want that. The Pandora's Box is so last month. For you, a Wallflower: Stoli, Galliano, extract of Jamaican ortanique, which is a cross between a tangerine and an orange, garnished with a dandelion blossom not yet gone to seed." I walk away with a fifteen-dollar cocktail the color of a highway safety cone. It doesn't taste half bad, though the dandelion sprig keeps tickling my ear.

Now what? The blind-date concept is completely foreign to me. Probably I should handle this like market research: Hayes Heeley has asked me to study ways to make male customers feel more comfortable in pretentious watering holes. Okay. I search the crowd for Elliot, who has told Sexy Lexy he's six feet tall, with brown hair, blue eyes, and an athletic build, but,

Linda tells me, is really five ten on a good day, with thinning
hair and the beginnings of a pinot grigio belly.

A man standing to my left, holding not an electric-orange
technodrink but a plain glass of red wine, returns my gaze with
an almost imperceptible nod.

Bingo. Now for introductions and rapport building. I un-
cross my arms over my artificially boosted breasts and walk
over to stand next to him, smiling my warmest moderator
smile. "Hello, there!" I switch my Wallflower to my left hand,
surreptitiously try to dry the right one on Val's dress as I tug it
down over my thighs, and execute a perfect moderator hand-
shake: neither too brief nor too lingering, firm without being
overbearing. "You've been waiting awhile!"

He appraises me quizzically. "What makes you say so?"

I motion toward his glass. "Half empty."

His grin reveals an unexpected dimple in his left cheek.
Linda gave Icarus short shrift. He may not be Hotel Royal perfect, but he's real-life attractive, with a slightly rumpled suit, a
touch of gray at the temples, and glasses like my favorite socio-
cultural anthropology professor at Pomona. "Don't you mean
half full?"

"Definitely not! That's something my mother—" Iris, stop!
Your mother would, but Sexy Lexy's might not. Let's do the
introductions. And whatever you do, don't call him Elliot.
"Hi, Icarus, I'm Sexy Lexy." Saying the name makes my
cheeks burn. "But you can call me, um, Lexy." I pull at Val's
dress, which is creeping up my legs again. My right breast
slides back a fraction of an inch into my armpit.

"Pleased to meet you, Lexy. But who's Icarus?"

Oh, great. "You mean you're not Icarus?"

"Sorry to disappoint."

I dissolve into giddy laughter. "I thought you were my
date!"

He laughs, too. "I'm Frank Hudson and try never to fly too close to the sun."

I cover my face with my hands. He pats me on the right shoulder. As I'm plotting an escape into the crowd, someone else taps my left shoulder.

The tapper—five feet ten, brown hair—clears his throat. "Did you just call him Icarus? Because Icarus, th-that's me." Icarus shakes my hand damply. His eyes dart around the room. Compared to him, I am the picture of composure.

"That's my cue," says Frank. "I enjoyed meeting you, Lexy." He flashes his dimple again and walks off with one last, bemused over-the-shoulder glance.

My real date stands stiffly. Other than homing in for a nanosecond on my cleavage, he doesn't seem much of a Casanova. His shoulders are hunched, an ink stain dots the bottom corner of his shirt pocket, and his tie is askew. I want to straighten it and tell him to mind his posture. He stammers something about the subway being slow, and then we both look at each other. I should say something, but what? When you've read a man's e-mail description of his recurring nightmare about falling from the Empire State Building in his boxer shorts, it's hard to discuss the weather. And while that was probably as risqué as Icarus's revelations went, I can't say the same for his wife. Last week Linda, as Sexy Lexy, e-mailed him a disturbingly insipid erotic fantasy involving a bathtub full of chocolate sauce.

This man thinks I wrote it.

"Hey!" His face brightens. "Looks like you've finished your drink. How about something else from the bar? A ginseng martini? That's your favorite, right?"

"Shot of tequila."

Elliot looks nonplussed but goes off to fetch it. When he returns I drink the shot down with a triumphant shiver and ask something innocuous about his day. Soon the ice is broken and Elliot is talking about a recalcitrant client who won't pay her bills, and the new restaurant where he had lunch last week, and the Vermont summer camp he attended as a boy, and his feelings about the mayor. I lean against a mirror, debating another shot. Haven't had tequila for years, come to think of it, and why not? My college friend Jadey used to claim the stuff made her hallucinate, and my other one, Audrey, once drank nine margaritas and passed out for eighteen hours, but right now it's providing me with a surprising streak of empathy for Linda's husband. The poor man must be desperate for a woman to listen to him. I ask a waitress for a second shot— *¡más tequila, por favor!*—and drink it; the wisdom of the ages courses through my veins. I pull Val's dress back down over my thighs.

". . . and sure enough, the stock tanked, as I'd been warning all along." Elliot nods his head in satisfaction at a story well told. He's absolutely harmless. Dull, yes, but harmless.

"It always happens that way, doesn't it?" I'm beginning to have a hard time concentrating. My head feels funny, and I'm finding it a challenge to stand in heels. I should go. I don't think Linda has any cheating to worry about. I look forward to telling her she's got one of the good guys.

"That's right." Elliot moves closer to me. "It always happens that way."

I move away. My brain sloshes from side to side.

Elliot takes a second step forward, puts both hands on my shoulders, and puckers up. Before I have a chance to react, he crushes me to him and plants a big, sloppy kiss on me.

"Mmmmmm!" I try to struggle free. My left cutlet wedges itself under the band of my bra top. The right one moves farther back under my arm. Elliot tries to work his tongue between my clamped lips. "MMMM!" I shove him away and wipe my mouth. "What do you think you're doing?" I yell.

"L-Lexy!" Elliot stammers. "I'm sorry!"

"You should be!"

"I am! I've never done anything like this before, and I thought . . ."

"You thought wrong!" I'm sincerely angry. My evening has just gone from an easy fifty dollars an hour to a hard fifty dollars an hour. I'll have to call Linda, wait until she arrives, and be exhibit A in a noisy scene in front of all these self-impressed neon-drink drinkers. "Ooooh! Why'd you have to *do* that?" I stomp my foot.

With that, my left cutlet breaks free of my bra top and oozes down, down, down under my dress. Under a looser garment it might not have stopped until it hit the floor. But restrained by Val's slip-girdle, the cutlet succeeds only in scoring itself a few inches of freedom. I sneak a look into a mirror at my lopsided chest and prod the new bulge over my lower left ribs.

Elliot doesn't notice. He just looks miserable. "You've been coming on so strong these last few weeks. I thought it's what you wanted. My wife is going to kill me!"

It is then, as I resist the temptation to reach down the front of my outfit and straighten out my breasts, that I realize I can't watch this marriage, ridiculous as it is, crumble over a stupid kiss that's as much Linda's fault as Elliot's. What is she doing, trying to entrap the man into cheating on her? Who does he think he is, pulling a stunt like this?

I pull myself up to my full five-feet-four-with-three-inch-heels, as morally outraged as a woman wearing lingerie in public can be. "You're *married*?"

Elliot raises his arms and drops them against his sides in a gesture of defeat.

"Shame on you, Icarus! I am not that kind of girl! I've never been with a married man and am not about to start now!" Another tequila has found its way into my possession. I toss it back ferociously. A term from my college days floats into my head: the death shot. That's what Jadey and Audrey used to call the shot that put you over the edge from pleasantly tipsy to staggering, slobbering drunk. With zero inhibitions left, I stick my hand into my top and reposition my wayward cutlet. Elliot's eyes look about to pop out right into his drink. "And how would your wife feel," I go on, "knowing you were here with me? And you, spending all those nights on the computer, telling me your innermost secrets? For shame! You should be sharing those secrets with your wife! That's what you do when you're married! You share your hopes and dreams with the person you're married to! Not with a complete stranger! Hey, you, mind your own business!" I direct that last bit to a woman in hot pants and gladiator sandals gawking at me over her cocktail.

Elliot's hands are actually shaking. He puts them in his pockets and drops his head and promises never to do anything like this again.

"You'd better not. Cheating is wrong! You go home to your wife, cancel that e-mail account, and start honoring your marriage vows!"

I wouldn't say Elliot runs screaming for the exit, but I can say he's gone before I can sort out what has just happened. All I know is, my heart is pounding and the room is whirling and I need to sit down without delay. There—there's a stool up at the bar. I totter up to it. "Can I sit? I mean, is that open? I mean empty?" I inquire of the person nearest the stool, a man in khakis holding a business book. I put one hand over each breast to check that they're still positioned correctly and push them both closer together. Whoopsie. Hands off the cutlets. "I'm Sexy," I inform the man. "I mean Lexy."

He straightens the collar of his polo shirt and lays *The Wall Street Journal Complete Real Estate Investing Guidebook* facedown on the bar. The letters swim before my eyes. "I'm Joe. By all means, sit."

Accepting his offer may be harder than it looks. The stool seems to have reproduced itself while I wasn't watching. There are now two overlapping stools. I'm no fool. Clearly one is real and one is a mirage, but which is which? I swipe out my hand and strike it on the stool closest to me. Got it, that's the real one. But when I go to sit, it does a sly feint to the left. I miss it by an inch and have to catch myself on the edge of the bar, barely avoiding ending up sprawled on the floor with Val's dress bunched up around my neck. I should probably go home, but then I wouldn't get to share my triumph.

"Joe!" I scramble, finally, onto the stool and slam my hands down on the bar. "You, like, wouldn't believe what just happened. I just saved someone's marriage! Hey, you aren't married, are ya? 'Cause if y'are, whatcha doin' in a hotel?"

Joe hooks his thumbs into his pants pockets. He's the male version of me—the usual me, not the current me—unremarkably dressed, average-looking, though he does have exceptionally white teeth. "I'm not married. What are *you* doing in a hotel? You from around here?"

"I'm new in town from Losh Angelesh." Is that me slurring?

"New in town, huh? Well, I live in Connecticut but work here in the city. I just bought a new Land Rover. I've got a summer place right on the beach. Maybe you'd like to go with me sometime. I'm an endodontist. Harvard Dental School."

It's funny how New Yorkers from Ivy League schools always want you to hear all about their educational credentials within five minutes of meeting you. Why did I start talking to this person? What was it I wanted to tell him? Something about marriage, if memory serves.

"Well." I slip back down off the stool and grip the bar for support. "I got married on the beach. It was shupposhed to be the two of us barefoot at shunshet, reciting poetry, all romantic. Ha! Guessh what, Joe? It was freezing. The guests were all shivered up together, and the wind blew off my veil. Whoosh! Right into the ocean. Teddy shaid we'd laugh about it on our twenty-fifth annivershary, and now we'll never have a twenty-fifth annivershary, sho I'll never laugh about it!"

Joe blinks his two sets of eyes.

"I'm shtill married, Joe. Why do I like tell everybody I'm divorshed when I'm shtill married? Know what, Joe? Maybe I should call Teddy! Maybe I should call him right now!"

Joe is dumbstruck. He's holding a glass with a paper cocktail napkin stuck to the bottom. Something momentous is about to happen. Joe knows it, and I know it, and the napkin knows it. Teddy is going to send for me to come back to Studio City. Maybe Joe will hail a cab to take me to the airport. He'll give the driver the fare and say, "Take this woman back where she belongs." Before the cab drives off he'll press the napkin into my hand as a memento. Years from now Teddy and I will show our grandchildren the napkin, which I will have carefully preserved between the acid-free pages of an archival-quality scrapbook, and we'll raise a glass to the compassionate stranger who helped us find each other again all those years ago.

Joe removes the napkin from the bottom of his glass and scrawls something on it. He gives it to me. "If you ever feel like going out."

The napkin has no name, only a phone number. I tuck it into the recesses of my bag, knowing full well it will never again see the light of day, and grope slowly toward the door. I stumble out into the warm May evening, and the door closes, leaving behind a fleeting puff of cool air. I lean against the

front wall of the Hotel Royal and manage to dial my old home
number on my cell phone.

"Hah!" hollers a happy male voice. A happy male voice
with a Texas-sounding accent, so that I must assume he means
"hi."

"I'm like looking for Teddy." Thanks to all that tequila, it
takes some work to get the words out.

The happy Texan drawls, "Ah-ris?"

"Ish Teddy there?" It's hard to be sure over the din of the
city, but . . . have I called in the middle of a party? At *my*
house?

"Ah-ris, what tahm is it out there?"

"Dunno. Can I just shpeak to Teddy?"

"This *is* Teddy, Ah-ris."

"Oh, Teddy . . ." I trail off. Groups of New Yorkers walk
past me in twos and threes. A man and a woman, arms around
each other's waists, look me over and continue down the sidewalk. I try to identify the distinctly festive sounds on Teddy's
end of the line: the thud-thud of music on the stereo, shouts of
laughter, a whir that could be a blender. "You're having a
party?"

"A barbecue, here at the ranch, yes ma'am." Teddy remains
stubbornly in character.

"Teddy, can I, like, ashk you a quesshion?"

"Sure thing, ma'am."

"I was wondering . . ." But what? What do I want to ask,
and what am I hoping to hear? The rush of Teddy's blender
whirls with the clatter of the city until it's impossible to separate one from the other. "What is there to celebrate?" I shout
into the whirling.

But the last word comes out "shellebrate," and I hang up
without waiting for Teddy's answer.

Someone, somewhere, won't stop playing that song.

Over and over, the same few maddening chords: "La-la-la la-LA! La-la-la la-LA! Yaah-dah yah-dah yah-dah YAH." It won't stop. It'll play for a while, cut off abruptly, and then, after an all-too-brief period of quiet, start up again from the beginning: "La-la-la la-LA! La-la-la la-LA!"

Moaning, I maneuver myself from my back onto my stomach and pull the bedcovers over my head. After a spell, the music stops. I lie with my face buried in a pillow that is mysteriously, repulsively, cold and damp, and savor the silence. Perhaps this time the music has stopped for good.

"La-la-la la-LA! La-la-la la-LA!"

"Teddy, please." I believe I am talking. It doesn't sound much like me, but I'm thinking, *Teddy, please turn it down,* and hearing somebody croak those words as I think them, so I believe the croak must be mine.

But wait; Teddy isn't here; he's in California. And "La-la-la la-LA!"—could that possibly be "La cu-ca-ra-CHA!"? I force open one eye and pull back a corner of sheet. My cell phone is tweeting away on the nightstand/mail table. Oh, no—could I possibly have forgotten to call Linda? No, I vaguely remember telephoning her a few minutes ago. Or a few hours ago. What time *is* it?

"La cu-ca-ra-CHA! La cu-ca-ra-CHA!"

The act of reaching for the phone, grasping it, snapping it open, and speaking into it seems slightly less taxing than listening to it make that unholy racket for one more instant.

Vickie is on the other end, brimming with excitement. "Iris! Iris! Where are you? This is it! You need to get over to Eighty-second and Columbus right away!"

I do not. I need to sleep. I hang up the phone.

It starts to cucaracha again. This time I hit the answer button and don't even bother to say hello. Why won't this woman leave me alone?

"Steve just left the apartment," Vickie continues, as if there has been no pause in the conversation. "He says he's got a meeting at one of the buildings his company manages. It's right in your neighborhood! But you've got to go now!"

"Go away. I'm asleep." I'm still wearing my watch. I concentrate on its face until the hands swim into focus. "It's three a.m."

"What are you talking about? It's three o'clock in the afternoon. What are you doing asleep? I need you, Iris! Don't do this to me! You've got to follow him!"

I pull the covers back over my head. "No more spying. Go away." There. That should do the trick. I wait for Vickie's good-bye.

Vickie's first sniffle is only a decibel or two above the threshold of human hearing. The second, third, fourth, and fifth get progressively louder. Then the weeping commences, quietly at first but escalating rapidly into a symphonic crescendo of boo-hoos. "I should have known," she sobs. "You've never taken me seriously. You're just like Val!"

I consider a weak joke about how, at the moment, I am more like Val than Vickie can possibly imagine: in bed with a debilitating hangover. Under the safety of the covers I open both eyes for the first time. That's what the cold, wet thing is: a hand towel. I put it across my forehead last night just before passing out.

Vickie allows her weeping a moment's pause. "Do you know what Val said last time I tried to talk about Steve's cheating? She said, 'Isn't it a little late in the season for this? All the good spring handbags are already sold out.'"

I slide from the bed onto the floor, slipping out from under the covers inch by inch, a snake reluctantly shedding its most beloved skin, and crawl to the bathroom, stopping every foot or two to hold the phone back up to my ear from where I'm scraping it along the floor. "You probably heard Steve wrong." I sound slightly less croaky. "He can't be having a meeting. It's the weekend."

"That's what I've been saying! What is wrong with you?"

I maneuver myself into a standing position and consult the bathroom mirror.

"Did I just hear you gasp? Do you get it now? He can't possibly be having a business meeting today. It's Saturday. That's why I must know if he really is at that building."

I wasn't gasping for the reason Vickie thinks. My hair! I'm a freak! I'll never land a real job looking like this! And my face! The towel's tone-on-tone monogram, which Teddy's mother insisted we had to have, has left in my forehead a temporary indentation of Teddy's and my intertwining initials.

Will it really take four months to get a salon appointment? Will my Department of Labor paycheck cover what it will cost to return my hair to its natural state of drabness?

"Fine," I tell Vickie. "You get fifteen minutes. That's all. I'll leave here in five minutes and go up to Columbus and Eighty-second, and whatever I can observe in fifteen minutes is what you get. Not sixteen minutes. Not fifteen minutes and thirty seconds. After fifteen minutes I will come home and call you. Then, no matter what, I am going back to bed."

"Great. Now, what you'll want to look for is—"

I rub the monogram on my forehead. "I'm not finished. My fee just went up. I get a hundred dollars an hour, with a one-hour minimum, whether I work the whole hour or not. Plus all expenses. Travel, snacks, wigs, disguises, cosmetic surgery, whatever."

Vickie, for once, doesn't argue.

Swaddled in sweatpants, shielded by sunglasses, I make my way north to Columbus and Eighty-second. Vickie isn't sure exactly which building on the corner Steve claims to be visiting, or if his company even manages anything in that area. She's instructed me to look for his company's sign by each building's main door. Despite my sorry state and that I'm not expecting to find a sign, I spot one right away: a small, rectangular brass plaque that reads "Empire Property Management," on the five-story building on the intersection's northeast corner. I cross to the building on the northwest corner. It's a similar turn-of-last-century brick low-rise, a few stories of apartments above a ground-floor business. This building's bottom floor is a Spanish-language church. I could use a little help from a higher power simply to keep me standing for the allotted time. I duck into the side doorway and stare across the street. So Steve's company manages a building at Columbus and Eighty-second. He's still not going to show up. I check my watch: fourteen minutes to go.

As I'm leaning against the church's faded-orange–painted steel door, massaging my temples, a low, black car pulls up to the curb in front of the building I'm watching across the street. A young woman emerges. She struts up to the ground-floor door, rings the bell, and looks into a small porthole at her eye level. From the inside, someone opens the door. After she disappears through it, I take a couple of steps closer to the curb and, from behind the pole of a street lamp, try to figure out what kind of business this might be. It looks like a Prohibition-era speakeasy. There's no identifying sign of any kind, and its windows are blacked out. Something about it gives me the creeps. I check my watch again: twelve minutes and fifteen seconds until I can leave.

Across the street, the door opens again and two beautifully

dressed women emerge. We could almost be different species, these women and I. They are coiffed, polished, pampered, *cared for.* They're laughing, all glossed lips and white teeth. When was the last time I laughed with such abandon?

Another woman, passing them from the opposite direction, approaches the door. On her arm hangs what even at fifty paces I can identify as this season's wait-listed Gucci handbag, one of several styles Val must have rightly described to Vickie as already sold out. The woman reaches out with what is surely a manicured, bejeweled hand to ring the doorbell. The door remains shut. She rings again and presses her nose against the porthole, shading her eyes to see inside more clearly. She taps on the glass with a fingernail and presses her hands together, entreating. The door stays shut. After another round or two of pretty-please pantomiming, she gives up and walks away, glancing behind her, it seems, to see if anyone has witnessed her humiliation. What kind of business *is* this?

Seven minutes until I can go home. My ears are ringing. My skull is throbbing. My skin feels a size too small. My eyeballs feel a size too large, pushing up against their sockets. Four boys skateboard past me. The rush and clatter sets my stomach to churning, and I lean back into the dank doorway of Iglesia Sangre de Cristo, closing my eyes.

A passing car honks its horn. I jump and open my eyes, disoriented. Could I have lost consciousness for an instant? Incredibly, according to my watch, three minutes have gone by. I'm falling asleep standing up. Time to go home. Vickie won't know if I leave four minutes early. I step out of the doorway with one last, reflexive look across the street.

The porthole-door opens, and out comes Steve.

My heart pounds. I shrink back into the church doorway and cover my telltale hair with my hands. Steve doesn't look across the street. He gives a jaunty salute to the person on the other side of the door—just a standard, uniformed doorman—saunters to the corner, and summons a taxi coming down Columbus. The yellow car pulls over, and Steve slides into the backseat, pulling the door shut. The lighted roof sign goes dark, and the cab drives away. I watch the taxi's taillights until it turns left toward the park and out of my sight.

Did that really just happen?

Wretched physical state momentarily forgotten, I cross the street. The porthole-door has closed again, and the blacked-out windows give nothing away. Dare I ring the bell? I peek into the porthole and jump back with a squeak; the doorman's face is inches away on the other side of the glass.

But my watch says Vickie's time is up, and I say it's time to go home. There's a wet hand towel there with my name on it.

EIGHT

Saturday, six p.m.:

"Really." Linda has lost her buzz. I almost feel sorry for her. It's as if by assuring her again that nothing happened, that her husband didn't make a single inappropriate remark, didn't so much as lay a finger on me—by telling a little white lie for the good of her marriage—I've pulled out her wings. "Are you positive? You sounded a little out of it when you called last night. Don't get me wrong; it's good he didn't, but I thought he would."

I switch the phone to my other ear. "But he didn't. And what you did is called entrapment, and it's illegal." Is this true, or something I heard a cop say on the soaps? "More than that, it's immoral. You shouldn't be trying to lure Elliot into an affair. Don't try anything like that again."

"All right, all right, I won't."

"Good. I'll send you my bill. What's your real e-mail address?"

Sunday, eleven a.m.:

"He's absolutely up to something." This time it's Vickie making a follow-up call. "I asked him how his meeting went. He said, 'Well.' I said, 'Well, how?' He said, 'Just well.' Six times I asked, and all I could get was, 'Well.' Do you see how evasive he is?"

"I told you yesterday. He was exactly where he said he would be." I'm afraid I sound thoroughly unsympathetic. After this many tries at catching Steve doing something, even I have to agree with Kevin that there's simply nothing to go by. *Except for that zap between the two of you,* my little voice whispers.

I flip on the television with the sound on mute. There's an advertisement for a correspondence trade school. I should write down the number, look into getting my diploma in computer repair or medical billing. No, I've got to be more optimistic. I just mailed my résumés. I could start getting interview calls in a matter of days.

"I don't care. You said he got into the cab around three forty. Well, he didn't get home until after five. What took so long is what I want to know. It doesn't take an hour and a half to get across town. And what *was* that place, anyway? Why didn't you go in and find out?"

"Listen to me. Stop. Get hold of yourself. Give it up."

"I want you to go back and find out what he was doing in that building."

"No."

"He's cheating on me, Iris. Okay, maybe he is going jogging in the mornings. And okay, maybe he did have a business meeting yesterday, and maybe he does have a golf game today. But somehow, some way, my husband is finding time to be with another woman. I need to know who, when, where, and how often. If that means having you follow him night and day, so be it. If it means you have to bug his office, tap his phones, interrogate his secretary, whatever, do it. I have to know the truth!" Predictably, Vickie is crying.

I am unmoved. Bug his office and tap his phones? What does she think I am, a CIA operative?

"Iris, I'm pregnant."

I turn off the television.

"I'm about fifteen weeks along. I'm due in November. Maybe Val told you already."

I sit on the edge of my bed. "She didn't say anything."

"I'm not surprised. She couldn't care less what's going on in my life."

Upset though I am that Val didn't share this bit of information—and that since I left Hayes Heeley she doesn't seem to care much about what's going on in my life, either—I feel compelled to defend her honor. "We haven't had much time to talk lately. Michelle's been keeping her pretty busy at work." That's what I'll tell myself, anyway.

"Since when does Val not have time to gossip about me?"

Good point, I think. "Congratulations on your pregnancy. It's wonderful. You're happy, right?"

"It's what I've always wanted," Vickie answers. "I only wish I knew what was going on with my marriage. Now I hope it makes sense why I've been acting this way."

It explains a lot. But I can't spy on Steve. He's seen me. He's talked to me. He knows me, sort of. I don't plan ever to admit any of this to Vickie, however. "Perhaps you should hire a professional detective. Someone with experience."

"I looked into it. Don't take this the wrong way, but it costs a fortune. There are surveillance fees, videotaping fees, mileage fees, retainers. It would be fine if my husband didn't pay all my bills, but he notices if I go too far over budget." She laughs half-heartedly. "That leaves you. You're the only one who can help."

"What would you want me to do, exactly?"

"Follow him as much as you can. His schedule is totally unpredictable, but whenever he tells me he's going somewhere specific, I'll call you, and you can run over to the place he says he's going, and wait for him."

I'm envisioning a hellish existence in which I literally am at Vickie's beck and call, my phone ringing at all hours, Vickie capriciously dispatching me to various points in the city.

Vickie has read my mind. "That would only be a few times a week, at most. Usually he doesn't tell me anything. When you're not following him, you could maybe revisit some of the places you've seen him, like that building, and see if there's anything you missed."

Vickie and Steve are bringing a child into the world—a child who deserves parents who don't lie to each other, whose life isn't torn apart by divorce. If Vickie and Steve split, better now, before their child can suffer permanent damage. I can do this. I *want* to do this. It's the right thing. I'll recolor my hair back to brown. Steve knows me as a redhead, not as a brunette who looks just like every other woman in America. I'll recolor my hair and wear sunglasses, and hide behind a magazine or something, and Steve will never know I'm there. I'll ask Vickie for a few hundred dollars up front, for expenses.

"I'll do it!" I feel noble and heroic. "I won't let you down!"

"Thank you, Iris. I've been married to my husband for almost six years. It's about time I found out who he is," Vickie says. "You don't think I'm crazy, do you?"

It's the oddest thing. At least for this moment, Vickie doesn't seem crazy in the least.

———————

"Of course we take walk-in appointments," the receptionist at Rapture Salon assures me Monday morning. "And we specialize in corrective color, too." He waves breezily at the sign in the window.

I pretend not to have seen it already. "That's what I'm here for."

Half an hour later I'm in consultation with Charles, the colorist, who asks what I would like today. Brown, I tell him. He asks me to describe my hair color as a child. Brown, I tell him. He asks what shade of brown: Caramel? Chocolate? Chestnut? I tell him, just plain old brown. He covers my hair with a towel to determine the undertones in my complexion. He speaks of luminous brown, moonlit brown, the color I was born to have, the ideal version of my genuine self. I succumb to his poetry and nod yes, yes, and lean back into a stream of warm water as an assistant massages almond-scented shampoo into my scalp and brings me the new issue of *Vogue*. I sigh and read and float away on a cloud of happiness.

When the fog lifts, my hair is the grayish-beige of a pair of faded khaki pants.

"Moonlit brown," Charles announces. He lifts a few strands to demonstrate that he has woven in face-framing highlights in ecru and wheat.

I didn't think it existed, but apparently it does: a hair color that makes Scarlet Sunset seem flattering. At least that shade contrasted with my complexion. With this it's hard to tell where my pallor ends and my hair begins. I take surreptitious calming breaths. Charles presses his palms together as if in prayer and looks at me with nothing short of reverence. On my way out, the receptionist says, "May I interest you in one of our VIP packages?"

I next go two doors down to Photo/Copy Express, to see if I can get something out of the counter clerk. A craggy, sour-looking man mopes behind the counter. When I ask for Mona, he says she's on break and won't be back for half an hour. In that case, I tell him, I'm here to pick up photos for someone but unfortunately don't have the claim stub.

He sighs. "Who?"

"Steve Sokolov." I take two more calming breaths as he riffles through the photo packets in a drawer behind him. Please let there be photos. Please let there be photos that provide a clue to something.

"No Sokolov."

"Did I say photos? I meant copies."

He shuffles back to the stacks of copy projects and looks through them. "Nothing for Sokolov."

"Maybe it's filed under 'Steve.' "

He doesn't look. "Nope."

I leave the copy shop and walk to the cheap-gift emporium on the next block, the one that sells faux-wood–handled umbrellas and gold-tone watches and packages of men's boxer shorts, and buy myself a five-dollar Yankees baseball cap, which I wear out of the store.

I return to the copy shop to find Dr. Jekyll leaning against the cash register, chatting on a cell phone. I wait until she's finished with her conversation. Then I channel my inner moderator and ask if she has seen Steve Sokolov lately.

"Who?" She's already started dialing her phone for the next call.

"Steve Sokolov? About this tall, brown hair, brown eyes?"

"I don't know a Steve Whoever-you-said. Yo, Nancy!" she says into her phone. I sigh a suffering sigh and slip out the door.

In the afternoon I check my e-mail. No responses from any of the companies to which I've sent résumés, only the typical insulting spam and the latest installment of "Bliss Blitz from Joy!"

Why I open it, I have no idea.

TO: Friends
FROM: Joy
SUBJ: When mind over matter isn't enough

Dearest Goddesses:

Sometimes, it takes more than spiritual faith and ritual to heal a wounded soul. If positive thinking and meditation have only brought you so far, it may be time to take more practical steps toward fulfillment. Bliss Bits from Joy!, my new line of tools and totems, has been developed by me to help guide your spiritual practice to its next level.

Come see them, and meet me, at the New Age Expo in August. More
details coming soon!

I can't recall how it started, but whenever Teddy and I got
pizza delivered in Studio City, he liked to order it pretending
he was Joy. He'd sit on a sofa cushion on the rug that's now
in my apartment, feet bare, legs crossed in the lotus position.
Then he'd blink serenely and affect the twinkly goddess voice
Joy adopted after she and my dad divorced. When the pizza
guy answered the phone, Teddy would trill, "One large, and
please be sure the sausage and mushrooms are blended har-
moniously."

I never shared with Teddy the whole story about Joy. He
must have assumed that my animosity toward her was typical
mother-daughter growing pains. He simply saw the humor in
her life philosophy, cobbled together from a little Buddhism
here, a little Wicca there, with pinches of New Agey earth-
mother/Eastern wisdom/yoga/meditation/mysticism. My problem with Joy's spiritual mumbo jumbo is that it's inexcusably
forgiving. You do something terrible, but you're not terrible.
You're wounded from past traumas, or your chakras are out
of balance, or there's a blockage in your mind-body energy
flow. You're not selfish; you're someone who gives and gives
to everyone else and now must feed your own soul. You're a
good person who's done a bad thing.

I think if you do bad things, you are by definition a bad
person.

"Was Joy this bizarre even when your dad was alive?"
Teddy once asked.

"We had no idea," I told him.

NINE

On Tuesday morning I walk up to Columbus and Eighty-second, gather my courage, and ring the bell next to the speakeasy door. Behind the porthole window the guard is an unsympathetic monolith. I knock twice and wait. He stares straight through me. I call, "I need to ask you something!" and finally get a response: a definitive shake-of-the-head no. I shrink away and tiptoe into the dry-cleaning establishment next door, praying the guard isn't tracking my movements.

The dry-cleaner knows nothing about the place with the blacked-out windows. Nor does the newsstand cashier next door to him. The psychiatrist's office receptionist, futon salesman, and antique-furniture-and-cheese shop owner speculate that the place is a day spa, photographer's studio, and tropical-fish store, respectively. The manager of Farber's Hardware, across the street by the storefront church, is sure it's a gambling den or a money-laundering operation. Why doesn't he tell the police? I ask him. He answers, "Ain't bothering nobody."

Across the street, a fashionable, attractive woman is coming up the block. I dart out of the hardware store and take advantage of a hole in the traffic to cross against the light. I reach the woman as she's about to ring the speakeasy bell. "Would you mind telling me what's in there?"

She looks at my sweatpants and sneakers, my khaki hair tucked up under a counterfeit Yankees cap. "If you have to ask . . ." She lets the rest of the sentence dangle.

I walk home.

I'm approaching the steps of my brownstone, hat in hand,

when my downstairs neighbor comes out of the building lugging a hard-sided travel case that looks constructed of quilted aluminum foil. Seeing me on the staircase, he stops and clucks his tongue.

I reach into my sweatpants pocket for my door key. Behind my neighbor, the dog lady emerges from the building, pulling a bag of bone-shaped biscuits from the front pocket of her overalls and handing out one each to the dogs whose leashes are tethered to her ample waist: two matching poodles, a big, dim-witted Lab, and Rocky the pug, who looks as if he wants to lick my ankles again. The door clicks shut behind her.

"See you soon, Simon," the dog lady says to my neighbor.

"Lord help me, Rina, tell me I'm hallucinating. This is Iris. She lives in One-F, above me." He eyes my hair. "Oh, dear. Dear, dear."

"I know, I know." *Now, go away,* I will him telepathically.

"It's all wrong for her," Simon announces to Rina, who departs with the dogs. Simon sets down his box on the stone landing and, with one hand under my chin and the other on the top of my head, tips my face backward until I'm staring straight up at him. He's tall, at least six feet four, and my neck threatens to snap in two.

He releases me from his grasp. "Do yourself a favor, kitten. Don't go back to whoever cut it like this."

I clap the hat back onto my head and climb the rest of the steps, overcome with beauty shame. But hold on. I haven't changed my style or gotten a haircut since I moved here. What's wrong with the way I wear my hair? It's perfectly ... oh. Generic. "You weren't talking about the color?"

"Color?" He squints. "Now that you mention it, it could be more flattering." He picks up his box and continues down the stairs. I go inside and check my phone messages to see if I've gotten any response to my résumés. No luck.

When Vickie calls for a progress report, I trowel on the phony enthusiasm: nothing yet, but I'm going to keep trying! "I want you to follow him tomorrow morning," she says. "When he leaves for work, after he's come back from jogging and dropped off the dog and taken his shower." She instructs me to be outside her building by eight thirty sharp so I'm there when he leaves around ten minutes to nine. "And don't be obtrusive," she says in her bossy Vickie voice.

On Wednesday I yet again miscalculate the time it takes to get to the East Side, and arrive across the street from Vickie's apartment house promptly at 8:38, yet again promising myself to do better next time. Still, with twelve minutes to spare I have time to buy a newspaper for disguise, and there's a deli right behind me. I dart in for a *Daily News* and stake out a spot near the subway station, with the paper held up so all that's showing is the cover—headlined "LIAR!" above the face of a man I don't recognize—and my sunglasses and baseball cap above it. I'm dying to find out who the liar is, but train my laser vision back across the street at Vickie's building, a nondescript, early 1960s white-brick rectangle with its name printed in white script on its awning: "Merit House." A green and orange grocery truck pulls up and double-parks in front of the entrance, obstructing my view. I step farther down the street so I can peer around it, and watch the doorman point the deliveryman toward the building's service door. Eight minutes until Steve comes out. I stare idly up and down Lexington, longing for a cup of—

Is that Steve? Up there on Eighty-sixth, about to board the crosstown bus?

I stuff the newspaper under my arm, run for the corner, and look helplessly across the street. It is Steve. How did he get to the bus stop without my seeing him? Can I make it across Eighty-sixth, against the light, before the bus pulls away? I step off the curb—and into the path of an oncoming car. I can see the whites of the driver's eyes. I jump back on the curb in time to see the bus pull away. I run after it on my side of the street, pacing it for a long block until it roars out of sight. I call Vickie when I return home to tell her, with slightly less cheeriness than yesterday, that it seems I've struck out yet again. She does not sound pleased.

But two hours later she calls back. Steve has told her offhandedly that he's leaving the office tomorrow at twelve thirty to show some retail space. "That means," she says, "you can wait for him in front of the Empire Property Management offices, and then, when you see him come out, follow him."

"I can try."

"Good, because if you don't get something soon, I'm firing you."

No one calls about my résumé.

By noon Thursday I'm seated on the granite rim of an enormous water sculpture in front of a forty-story office building at Fifty-fifth and Sixth, watching for Steve to emerge. Vickie didn't mention that the building would be half a block long, with two entrances separated by a good dozen car lengths, one on the building's east corner and one on its west corner. Each of those entrances has three sets of revolving doors. And it's lunchtime; each door is in constant rotation. Trying to simultaneously monitor every human being whirling out feels like watching a six-way tennis match in hyperspeed. To make matters worse, though I remembered my baseball hat, in my rush to get down here on time I forgot my sunglasses. For almost two hours I wait and watch anyway, until my neck aches from swiveling, my head aches from squinting, and the rest of me aches from sitting. No doubt Steve slipped out of one entrance while I was keeping an eye on the other. I haul myself to my feet and walk home. My answering machine light remains stubbornly off.

"It wasn't the brightest idea." Vickie makes it sound as if it were mine. "His schedule changes constantly. By nine most mornings, he's already reshuffled half a dozen appointments. The only constant thing about him is this jogging. You're absolutely sure he's just jogging, Iris?"

At bedtime Thursday I resolve to take Friday off. I'll use the day to follow up with marketing firms right after I sleep in and watch *Guiding Light*. Naturally, my little voice has to put in its two cents, keeping me from falling asleep with its whispery scolding. At one thirty I sit up in bed and call Kevin. "Where are you?"

"In the Denver airport, waiting to board. Where are you?"

"In bed."

"What are you wearing?"

"Some other time. Kevin, can you remind me again what Steve did when you followed him?"

"Sure. He started out on the trail below the reservoir. Ran past the tennis courts. Cut over to the park road. Went around the park back to the reservoir, stretched at the stretching area, then back to his building. I think he was working on his sprints."

"What stretching area? You never said anything about a stretching area."

"I did," Kevin says.

"Kevin!" I wail. "The stretching area could be the key to the whole mystery, and you didn't even mention it!"

"Mystery? There's no mystery. There's no data lost here. He went running and afterward spent thirty seconds stretching his hamstrings."

I groan, dive backward onto my pillow, and stare up at the

ceiling. It's a dramatic twelve feet high, the only thing about
my apartment you could legitimately call spacious. "Where
did he do this purported stretching?"

"At the south end of the reservoir, those benches by the
stone boathouse, where everybody stretches after they run.
You're not still following him, are you?"

———————

Early Friday morning I dress quickly in my sweatpants and
sneakers and pull my beige hair into a ponytail through the
back of my cap.

Bang! Bang! Bang! The sound of Simon's banging vibrates
up through my feet.

I jump up on my hardwood floor, thudding down on flat
feet. For good measure I do it eleven more times. Take that!

There's a knock on my door.

I freeze in the preparing-to-jump position.

"I know you're in there!"

I slide on the chain and slowly open the door. Simon is there
with his metal box. I touch the cap to be sure it's still securely
on my head. Simon raises an eyebrow but says nothing. It's a
small blessing.

"*Woowoowoowoowoo!*" The sound is coming from somewhere near our ankles. I look down to find a black pug.

Rocky. I should have recognized that bark when I knocked
on Simon's door last week. It figures Rocky would belong to
my downstairs neighbor. An obnoxious dog for an obnoxious
human.

Simon reaches his right hand through the space between the
door and the doorjamb. There's a leash looped around his
wrist. "Sweetie, I need a favor. I've got to go to work, and Rina
is out sick today. Could you find it in your heart to walk him,
just this once?" He pauses. "Where are you off to?"

"The park." I'm planning to wait for Steve at the stretching area and make sure there's nothing else Kevin didn't tell me.

"Perfect! Rocky here loves a good walk in the park." He slips his hand out of the red leather leash and holds it out to me.

I study Simon's dog. Bulgy eyes, smooshed nose, barrel body, folds of skin in odd places, pig tail, toothpick legs, claw feet like the ones on my great-aunt Zinnia's dining room chairs. He jingles his engraved, heart-shaped silver name tag against the buckle of his red leather collar. I would help out, I tell Simon, except that I have some business to do in the park.

"Perfect! Rocky has to do some business of his own."

I hate to admit it, but having Rocky with me might help me blend in better. Everybody walks dogs in Central Park. I would certainly be less conspicuous by the reservoir if I had one, too. Besides, I can't waste any more time arguing with Simon. I tell him, just this once.

"Hooray! Kitten, you're a lifesaver." Simon slips me a set of spare keys. "So you can let Rocky back inside." He hands me a wad of plastic bags. (What are those for—oh.)

Fifteen minutes and one revolting baggie break later, Simon's pug and I approach the stone staircase below the boathouse, at the south end of the reservoir, watching die-hard runners climb the stairs to the stretching area. Die-hard because it's dark and warm, and the threat of rain is heavy in the air. If Steve has checked the weather, he may well stay home. My stomach ties itself up into a bow. Will Vickie pay me if Steve never shows up anywhere? Why did Michelle Heeley have to lay me off? Why hasn't anyone responded to my résumé?

My thoughts are interrupted by an explosion of barking and a sharp yank at the leash in my hand. For a creature the size of my microwave oven, Rocky is surprisingly powerful. I return to reality in time to keep the pug from taking a flying leap at a woman strolling by.

"Bad dog!" I reel him back toward me. He sprawls on the staircase landing and grimaces. The woman looks ready to shoot me. No wonder Rocky is agitated: She's walking, at the end of a green rhinestone leash, an enormous, fluffy gray cat.

I apologize and start to hustle Rocky up the stairs. We've got to get to the stretching area!

But Rocky, the little beast, leaps back up and makes another lunge for the cat. This time the cat gives it right back. It is exactly like in cartoons when two fighting characters become a whirling cyclone with exclamation points and little puffs of dust. Worse, this cat is as brash as a street-corner thug and is as big as Rocky. The cat's owner helps out by contributing a series of colorful expletives. Meanwhile I am helpless with fright: Simon's dog is about to be eaten!

This is exactly the point at which Steve arrives. As a detective, it's not my shining moment. As Rocky's temporary guardian, I don't care. When he looks toward the commotion, I catch his eye.

He does a double take.

"Help!"

He sprints up the steps to meet me on the landing and takes Rocky's leash from me. "Here, boy," he calls sternly.

The woman continues to curse, and the cartoon cat-on-dog whirlwind roils, but somehow, Steve manages to haul Rocky out of the fray. Rocky barks a few more times but trots back to us and once again slumps onto the landing. I'd swear the cat is smirking.

"No dogs at the reservoir!" the woman screams at me before stomping off.

Guess what? She's right. there at the top of the stairs a green-and-white Parks Department sign, one I haven't noticed during my past two outings, quite clearly prohibits dogs (and strollers, skates, skateboards, tricycles, and bicycles) on the reservoir track. It reminds me that again Steve doesn't have his dog with him.

Steve hands me Rocky's leash. "What do you do, wait in the park for me to rescue you?"

"Right. I'm following you around." I hope I've infused that with a credible amount of irony. "All joking aside, thank you."

"Anytime." He crouches down and pats Rocky's softball-size head. Rocky sticks out his tongue to sample Steve's left running shoe. "Nice pug."

"He's my neighbor's." For some reason Steve needs to know I would never own a gargoyle with a heart-shaped ID tag.

Steve gives Rocky a slow-motion fake punch to the jaw, the way one might a favorite nephew, and straightens back up. He lifts a dry corner of his shirt to mop his face. I try not to notice the sliver of skin his gesture exposes, and instead glance down at Rocky, whom I find gnawing noisily on one of his dining-room-chair paws. Fighting a fit of giggles, I look back up.

Steve catches my eye, looking close to laughter himself. "Next time I'd put my money on the cat," he says.

"Who walks a cat on a leash?"

"One time I saw a rabbit on a leash. Another time on the subway, a lady had a ferret in her purse. She was feeding it an everything bagel."

Before I can stop myself, I laugh.

Steve looks me over for, as seems to be his habit, several moments too long.

I pull the cap lower on my forehead.

Steve says, "I told you this last time, but I'm positive we've met before."

I'm desperate to change the subject. I'll even point out my hideousness, if that's what it takes. "I'm surprised you recognize me at all with the different hair," I mutter.

"Well, you're hard not to notice. Which is why I feel sure I know you from somewhere."

I think: Upper reservoir track, two weeks ago, perhaps? Photo/Copy Express? Lexington Avenue, across from your building?

"I doubt it. I just moved here."

"You did? From where?"

"Studio City, California."

"Hmm. I don't know anyone from there."

If only he would stop looking at me. I steal a peek at my filthy sneakers, then at my grubby sweatpants, and then, because if I consider my appearance any longer I may die from the humiliation, turn my attention back to Rocky, who's now chomping on a stick. Are there pesticides on that thing? Can dogs die of splinter ingestion? I reach down to take the stick away. Rocky growls ferociously.

Steve continues, "Perhaps I've met you through my line of work."

Not unless you're really a claims processor at the Department of Labor, I think, and then say, "I'm kind of between jobs."

He nods. "I've had to cut back myself."

"You're not working?"

"Working, but shorter hours." He tilts his head to the left, pauses, then gingerly braces his right hand against his right cheek and pushes. "I needed time to"—the vertebrae in his neck make faint popping sounds—"get my affairs in order." He repeats the spinal adjustment on the left side.

Get his affairs in order—did he phrase it that way on purpose? It comes to me, watching his hands, that he's not wearing a wedding ring. Is that important? Or is he one of those married men who don't wear the ring? I'll have to remember to ask Vickie. And where is the dog? It's missing yet again.

Steve smiles down at me.

And zap!

It's the sensation from last time, only stronger—a current of raw energy hitting me with a shock like my apartment buzzer going off unexpectedly.

"Your friend's dog looks thirsty," he says. "Come with me. I'll buy him some water. It's part of our tradition."

Another zap. BZZZZT! There's someone at the door!

Iris, you idiot. This is Vickie's husband. He is either an innocent man who loves his wife, or a sociopath who's betraying his wife. That zap you felt? Pure physical revulsion.

"I think I'll go home and get Rocky some water there." I tug on Rocky's leash and say formally, "Thank you again, Steve."

Steve stares at me.

And it's clear I've made a catastrophic mistake.

TEN

I take in Steve's body language: arms crossed, back rigid. Even Rocky seems to sense that something momentous is happening, because he stops what he was doing—rooting in the dirt with his nose—and fixes us with his rheumy eyes.

"If I don't know *your* name," Steve says slowly, "how is it you know mine?"

I may faint.

"Sit down." Steve points to a stair. "Now."

I obey. So does Rocky.

Steve remains standing. "I want to know what is going on. Do not even think about lying. Who are you, and why are you stalking me?"

My brain gropes frantically for an idea, any idea, even a stupid, nonsensical idea. I play with the string of my sweatpants. "You told me your name was Steve. Just the other day."

"Strike one."

I can't do this. "I guessed."

"Strike two."

"It's not as if Steve is an unusual name. I could just as easily have said Mike or Dave. Scott. Mark or, you know, Matthew, Luke, or John."

"Strike three. Now the truth."

Like an evil spirit leaving my body, the urge to fight evaporates. I don't want to be a detective anymore. Surely there are easier ways to make a living. And technically I'm not even making a living. "All right, here's the truth. I've been following you, not stalking you. My name is Iris. Iris Hedge. I'm sort of a detective. I was hired a few weeks ago by"—my voice cracks—"your wife."

Steve starts to laugh.

It isn't a happy laugh—more a rusty, off-balance caw. It's the sort of laugh people laugh when life has become so awful there's nothing left to do. "Haaaa! Ha! Ha! Haaaaaaa!" Finally, he stops and sits on the step below me. When he speaks, I have to strain to hear him. "You've spoken with her."

"Well, yes, sure." I reach down for Rocky. He's surprisingly soft, and his head fits nicely in my palm. I pat him, and he leans against my calf.

Steve's face is drained of color. "My wife," he says, "is crazy."

This time it's my turn for the life-is-ridiculous laugh.

Steve must read my concurrence between the lines, because he relaxes his posture slightly. Still, his skin remains ashen. "What did she hire you to do, exactly?"

"I can't tell you that."

"It's either me now or my lawyer later."

It's the word "lawyer" that does it. I crumble instantly. "She hired me to check up on you to see if you're doing what you say you're doing." The words are practically jumping over themselves to get out of my mouth. "I guess she doesn't think you are. You aren't going to tell her about this, are you?" Right, sure. He's going to go home tonight and keep this little mishap to himself. Vickie will have my head.

"What, exactly, doesn't she think I'm doing?"

I'm trying to keep it vague. "What you say you're doing."

"Which is *what*?"

"Let's put it this way. She wonders if you truly are, you know, to be trusted."

"When have I ever given her any indication that I'm not trustworthy? Did you ask her that?"

I'm dying to say, "Why would she trust you?" Instead I fix him with what I hope is a steely grimace. Under the tough act, I'm ready to cry.

"And—Iris, is it?—what have you been telling my wife?"

"The truth. I haven't caught you doing anything, you know, wrong. Anything untrustworthy."

"Well, well. Not doing anything wrong. What a disappointment that has to be."

"I said I haven't caught you doing anything wrong. I didn't say you weren't doing anything wrong." As a matter of fact, he's just now provided me with plenty to be suspicious about. The mysterious disappearing Jack Russell terrier, the missing wedding ring, and the line about getting his affairs in order, for starters. But that's for him and Vickie to work out now.

Steve shakes his head, hard. "That woman owes me a big apology, considering the way she's treated me. But she has no sense of duty to anyone but herself. So that leaves you to clean up this mess. And though I'd rather never see your face again, you're to meet me here in the park Monday afternoon, two o'clock sharp, by the statue of Daniel Webster. I'm choosing that location because it's near my lawyer's office. If you don't show up, I can walk straight there and discuss with him what we can prosecute the two of you for. Do I make myself clear?"

My face is on fire. "As far as today, though, should I, um, tell her about this, or do you want to?"

"Don't you dare breathe a word of this to her. Do you understand? As far as you're concerned, nothing unusual happened today. You saw me running in Central Park; that's it. And in case you were planning to follow me to work, too, don't bother. I'll be there, as always, making money that will go straight to her, as always. She can call me there herself if she doesn't believe me. She knows the number."

I'm surprisingly calm as I cross the black and tan diamond-patterned terrazzo floor in the lobby of Vickie's building, past spiny plants in silvery pots, give my name at the front desk, and wait twelve centuries as the doorman dials upstairs and stands with the desk phone to his ear. Though he's got the receiver, I can hear Vickie's line ringing and ringing. What's taking her so long? She knows I'm coming; I called first. I look out the lobby windows. The morning's clouds have broken up, and in the building's private garden two babysitters socialize while a boy and a girl nearby chase after a big yellow ball.

"Hector!" A grandfatherly man steps up next to me, lays a tennis racquet on the desk, and reaches across to clap the doorman on the shoulder. "Can you do something about this weather, Hector? It's sweltering!"

It's seventy-seven degrees. I read it on a digital billboard clock on the way over.

"Wait till August, eh, Hector?" the man goes on. "Hell on Earth. That's why God made the Hamptons, Hector, right?"

"Miss Iris to see you," Hector says into the phone. He replaces the receiver and gives me the nod to go up.

Apartment 12-C, Chez Sokolov, is at the end of a long corridor with beige-on-beige carpet and wallpaper and a lineup of indistinguishable doors. Vickie answers my knock casually dressed in a pressed pink oxford shirt—untucked, perhaps to accommodate her slightly thicker middle—chinos, and driving moccasins. When she sees my hair, she lets out a little scream.

My stomach lurches. The woman has no compassion. When she hears what happened this morning, she's going to tear me to pieces.

She composes herself. "I still don't see why you had to deliver your bill to me in person."

"I have a matter to discuss. May I come in?" I try to step into the apartment. She blocks me with one hand flat against my chest, looks up and down the empty corridor, and stage-whispers, "Promise me he won't catch you here. I have no idea where he is. I haven't heard from him all day."

"Why are you whispering?" I stage-whisper back. "I told you. He's at the office, at his desk."

"How can you know that? Did you follow him?" she asks in her normal voice.

"No." I know because he told me after I blew my cover. "I called there pretending to be a client," I lie, "and his secretary told me he was there but tied up in phone meetings for the rest of the afternoon. May I come in?"

Vickie seems appeased but doesn't remove her hand from my chest. "This is a shoe-free home. Before you enter, would you?"

I silently curse Vickie and wrestle off my decrepit sneakers, balancing first on one sweaty foot, then on the other. I didn't think to wear socks, so I cross my right foot behind my left to hide my unpolished toes, and fix my eyes jealously on Vickie's pristine moccasins.

"They're just-for-the-house shoes. I don't even wear them to take the garbage down the hall," she explains. "You never know what kind of slime you're stepping in out there. We wipe the dog's feet when he comes in."

"Where is the dog, by the way?" I'm still wondering why Steve was Jack Russell terrier-less again this morning.

"He's at his playgroup." Vickie leads me into the living room and demonstrates that one can see the East River if one stands to the left of the sofa, tilts one's head, and squints. But the apartment's truly notable feature, besides that I could easily fit three of mine into it, is its disarray. The living room walls are bare except for the nails that must have held the framed photos and artwork now stacked on the dining table; at the top of the stack is a gauzy black-and-white portrait of Vickie in her wedding dress. Drop cloths cover the china cabinet and dining chairs, and a rolled-up carpet leans into a corner. Vickie makes a face. "Remodeling. What a nightmare." She walks to the dining area and extends her arms like a game-show prize presenter in a sparkly gown. "We're putting a wall here and a door over there and making this space Steve's study. We need the second bedroom back for the nursery." Her words echo off the bare walls. "We should have bought a three-bedroom right from the start. Isn't that what you would have done? Better to grow into an apartment than out of it."

I could live happily in just the space allotted to the china cabinet.

"Where was I?" Vickie looks around the apartment. "He used to eat away at the corner of the sofa whenever I left the house."

Steve?

"Separation anxiety, the vet said. Now I drop him at this place on York after lunch and pick him up at five. It's an all–Parson Russell facility, so he's around others like himself. You should see the change in his attitude. Plus, he takes a little doggie Prozac."

Right. The dog. Maybe I just misheard her when she said Steve always takes it running.

She sits on a striped brocade wing chair and gives me one of those "make yourself comfortable" hostess nods. Easy to be magnanimous when you're the one in the position of power, wearing the shoes. I alight on the edge of the matching sofa and tuck my feet under the dust ruffle. Out of the blue, I'm hungry. I was too rushed to eat before I went to find Steve in Central Park, and too nervous afterward. You'd think Vickie would offer me a cookie or something—at least, before she finds out why I'm here.

"So . . ." She claps her hands together, indicating that the social part of our meeting is over.

My heart pounds. From the pocket of my sweatpants I pull a slightly rumpled, folded square of paper—my six-hundred-dollar bill for one full week of fruitless detective work. I give it to Vickie, knowing that the odds of seeing any of that money are only slightly greater than the odds of getting a call from Michelle Heeley begging me to come back at twice my former salary. "What I wanted to tell you is, I'm resigning."

Vickie frowns at me. "What for?"

I tuck my toes more deeply under the dust ruffle. "It just isn't working out. I'm not giving you what you want. I thought we could settle the bill and call it even." I wait for Vickie to go get her purse. She doesn't.

"Well," she sighs. "You said you saw him in the park this morning, just jogging as always. But did you notice anything unusual? Think back. Surely there's something, maybe something tiny, but important."

"Not really." I can't wait, can't wait, to get out of here.

Vickie looks disappointed. It becomes clear at this moment that tossing her some tidbit of information might be my one shot at getting paid. I can't repeat Steve's "getting my affairs in order" line because she'd wonder how I'd come to hear it. But I could tell her what I saw. "Actually there was one thing. Didn't you say he always runs with the dog?"

"Yes, right. He does."

"Because the dog hasn't always been with him. He wasn't there today."

"Snooky wasn't with him?" She looks shocked. I am shocked, too—that the Steve I sort-of know would own a dog named Snooky. "But I saw the two of them come back in this morning. If the dog wasn't jogging, where could Steve possibly—no!" Vickie claps her hand over her mouth, then continues talking through it, a note of hysteria creeping into her voice. "You don't think that while he works out he's— oh, my God—leaving my precious Snooky at some slut's apartment?"

"No, no, no, no." It seems far-fetched, even to my overblown imagination. "I assume he just tied him to a fence somewhere."

"Tied Snooky to a fence? Alone? So any weirdo could walk by and kidnap him? Oh, my God!"

"Not that, then. But I'll bet there is a simple and perfectly reasonable explanation."

"Which I won't ever find out, Iris, because you're quitting on me! My husband's a cheater *and* a dog-neglecter and I'll never know the truth! Oh, my *God*!" She bends forward at the waist and buries her face in her hands. My stomach roils as I imagine what might happen to me if, despite having sworn me to secrecy, Steve comes home tonight and tells Vickie all about his and my little surprise meeting. *You can't think that way,* I tell myself. *You'll give yourself an ulcer.*

After a while Vickie raises her head and takes a breath. "Oh, God," she whimpers. "I feel sick." Truly, she doesn't look so good. Her eternally rosy cheeks are as pale as Steve's face was this morning. "Is there more? There's more, I know it. You tell me, right now."

Maybe I'll keep the part about the missing wedding ring to myself. What if she gets so upset she loses the baby? "That's it, really."

Vickie's mouth droops. The sun shining in through the windows highlights faint purple shadows under her eyes and minuscule cracks in the concealer she's used to cover them. She rubs an invisible smudge off one of her tastefully short, whisper-pink manicured nails. "I wish," she says in a weary monotone, "there was someone to tell husbands how to treat their wives."

I'm heavyhearted as I leave. Somewhere under my general feeling of failure I should be happy to be free of Vickie, but there's little to be pleased about. My stupid gamble didn't even pay off; she claimed to have no cash on hand, so I fear I'll never see a cent of the money she owes me. I still have no real job prospects. And I have to meet Steve Monday. Will he go easy on me or have me arrested?

But the walk home through the park is a nice distraction. It's turned into a dazzling day, bright and breezy. Suspended above the treetops are a few clouds so sublime in their puffy whiteness they appear to have been placed there by a decorator. The yellowy-green buds of early spring have given way to mature leaves and lush emerald lawns dotted with clover. White butterflies flutter past as I walk. Deep inside the park, the streets are closed to traffic, and the noise of the city is a world away. Beyond the treetops a coronet of skyscrapers stands out against the brilliant blue sky. I cross to the West Side but find myself walking past my exit and turning south toward the baseball diamonds near Tavern on the Green. Two teams are playing a game, getting a head start on the weekend. I climb into the bleachers in the shade of an oak tree and watch and listen to the men alternately encourage and heckle each other in English and Spanish. They remind me of Teddy—unaffected by society's insistence that people work on a spring afternoon this glorious.

"A walk's as good as a run, baby; a walk's as good as a run!" someone calls to his teammate at bat, but the batter sends the ball soaring in a high arc. His team whoops as the player rounds third base and slides into home plate, joyously, gracefully, as if his entire life has been a series of choices and decisions and random events all leading up to this moment, and he didn't know it until now.

At home I find a message on my machine. Could this be an interview call? I hold my breath and push the button.

"Namaste!" Joy's voice floats into the room. "Just calling about the New Age Expo!"

I exhale, press "Skip," and dial Val, who hasn't called me, despite having been back from her trip for two days. "Why didn't you tell me Vickie was pregnant?"

"Didn't I? I thought I did."

"No, Val, you didn't."

"Well, she only told me a couple of weeks ago. I guess she was waiting until she got out of the first semester."

"Trimester."

"Whatever," Val says. "Is this why you called?"

I explain that I'm no longer working for Vickie, expecting Val to ask for details. She launches into an exhaustive account of her last four dates, in two days, with four different men.

I stare up into my storage loft, a four-foot-high balcony-style crawl space in my apartment, above the kitchen and bathroom. The realtor who showed me the apartment said the loft was for sleeping. "You see? You put your mattress there," she called up to me, "and free up thirty square feet in your living area." I looked down at her from behind the balcony railing several feet above her head, accessible only by a rickety ladder. At twenty-three, sleeping in a loft would have been an adventure. At thirty-three it would be life-threatening. And I could see that this tiny apartment wouldn't hold all the possessions I'd brought from California. "I'll use the loft for storage," I told her. Then I wrote her a check.

As Val continues her monologue, I find myself thinking, *I*

really should look for that corkscrew. And before I know it I'm
hunched over in the loft, holding the phone to my ear and
using a fork to pick the tape off a moving box labeled "Kitch."
Yet there's nothing in it from my former kitchen. I find the
crushed, powdery remains of a dried rose from my wedding
bouquet, and several framed photographs wrapped in layers of
moving paper: Photographs of Teddy and me visiting his
mother in La Jolla, hugging each other in front of the polar
bears at the San Diego Zoo. One of my mother and father in
the late seventies, on someone's sailboat in Newport Beach. In
the photo my mother is every inch the hippie in bell-bottom
cords and a crinkly cotton tunic embroidered with flowers and
mushrooms; my father, in his white canvas hat, blue oxford
shirt, and slacks, plays the uptight-establishment role. It seems
obvious now, looking at them, that they were unsuited for
each other, but they were young and happy that day. They
didn't know their marriage would end, or how, or that less
than a year after it did, my dad would die in an ambulance on
its way to West Valley Hospital, clutching his heart.

". . . which reminds me." Val appears to have come to the
end of her dating chronicles. "You need to get back out there
yourself. Go out with some fresh meat. Sure, you have Kevin,
but that's, what, once a month?"

I pull out a small, heart-shaped bed pillow with a circular
stain where Teddy once rested a cup of coffee. "I don't want
to get back out there. I'm through with love."

"I'm talking about cheap, meaningless sex," Val corrects
me. "Who said anything about love?"

ELEVEN

On Monday at a quarter to two, I enter the park directly across the street from the Dakota, the ornate, turreted apartment building where John Lennon lived and in front of which, years ago, he was gunned down. Fans still come to cry at the John Lennon memorial in a clearing right inside the park. On this warm, damp afternoon, this is where I end up myself, lost. "Do you know where the Daniel Webster statue is?" I ask a woman at a card table, who's hawking CDs of herself reading her own Lennon-inspired poetry. Behind her a man sinks to his knees to lay a plastic-wrapped rose on a sun-shaped tile mosaic with the word "Imagine" in its center.

The CD seller wipes sweat off her face. "I'm from Cincinnati."

Eventually I find the statue, half-hidden behind an over-grown shrub. Daniel Webster stands cast in bronze, hand-over-heart, on a pedestal inscribed "Liberty and Union, Now and Forever, One and Inseparable." Though it may put me at odds with 99 percent of the people in this country, I prefer this memorial, with this slogan, to "Imagine," which sounds like something Joy might say. ("Joy, I lost my job, my four kids are sick, and there's nothing to eat. What should I do?" "Imagine.")

He isn't here. By my watch it's now two on the dot; could it possibly be slow? Did Steve decide to skip the meeting and take his grievances straight to his lawyer? I pace around Daniel Webster and his enveloping shrub. There's no sympathy on the statue's unsmiling nineteenth-century face.

At four minutes past, Steve walks up wearing a tan poplin

suit over a pressed shirt and an expensive-looking tie. I don't know why I thought he'd be in workout clothes. I feel slovenly in my usual sweatpants and tee.

"Sorry to be late," he says. "Let's walk."

He doesn't sound furious. Thrown off, I follow him up a small incline and then down a grassy slope that ends at the edge of Central Park Lake. It's the one you always see in movies, the lake in which swans float by in pairs and lovers row each other around in boats—and where hapless joggers discover bloated corpses in the reeds. In starts the voice in my head: *He's going to cut off your arms and legs and throw you in!*

Steve motions toward a shaded bench. "It'll be cooler here."

I take one end. He takes the other. We survey the lake. Ducks drift watchfully, waiting for someone to toss in picnic leftovers or a piece of soft pretzel. It won't be long before someone comes and sits between us, thinking we don't know each other.

Finally he speaks. "As you might imagine, I've been under a great deal of pressure lately. I was extremely angry on Friday, and I probably overreacted."

"That's an understatement." Bad, Iris. Not very neutral of you. "But I do apologize."

"You mean you're sorry you got caught."

"That, too." I'm still fretting that he may have told Vickie, though I suspect that if he had, I would have heard from her by now.

He lets escape another one of those cackling laughs. "I take it you're new at detective work? You don't seem to have been doing it long."

"It's a more complicated job than you'd think." Is this a trick? Why isn't he shouting? He's again observing me so intently I want to cover my face with my hands. I also really,

really wish I'd worn anything but these sweatpants. And what I wouldn't give for dignified, respectable hair I didn't have to stuff under a Yankees hat.

"Why are you doing it?"

"I told you before. I'm between jobs. I need the money."

"You'd have to be desperate to want to work for an insane woman. Have you known her long?"

"Just a few weeks. And for what it's worth, I do agree that Vickie can be demanding." Something registers on Steve's face. An emotion I can't decipher. Recognition? Irritation? Surprise? Offense? What might have triggered it? "I shouldn't have said that," I add hastily. There's no sense upsetting Steve further when he's considering a lawsuit. "It's not my place to judge her behavior. A better way to put it would be that Vickie knows what she wants. In a way I admire that about her. Don't you?"

Steve stares at me.

"Well, don't you?"

After a long pause, Steve says, "Iris, where is my dear wife Vickie at this very moment?"

"I assume, home in Yorkville. Sorry—Upper East Side. Why, did she tell you she was going to her parents' house? Somewhere else?" Is this a crucial piece of information I'm supposed to have known?

Steve is somehow frowning and smiling simultaneously. It's eerie. "No," he says. "No, Vickie didn't tell me anything."

A child comes near. A little boy, about three, with luminous, long-lashed brown eyes and close-cut hair shining gold in the sun. He's carrying a bag to the edge of the lake, turning back every few steps to locate a thin woman wearing a huge, floppy-brim hat on a bench a length or two from ours. The woman waves to the boy.

"Do you have any kids, Iris?"

"Oh, no."

Steve's expression turns definitively to a frown. "Don't you like them?"

"Very much." I'd planned to have children with Teddy. The new plan is that on my thirty-fifth birthday, I'm heading for the sperm bank. Too bad life isn't a soap opera, so I could seduce Kevin, get pregnant, and have his baby without ever telling him.

"Are you married?"

I don't answer, because I have no intention of losing control of this conversation, and the way to maintain control is to keep the talk about Steve, not about me. That's Hayes Heeley Market Research moderator training 101.

"No boyfriend?"

"That's none of your business."

To my surprise, he moves across the bench to sit closer to me. "You're right. It was out of line." He stays like that, his left leg millimeters from my right leg, for a split second, until something like *This woman works for my wife* must register in his mind and he moves away.

I can still feel the closeness of his body.

"You said Friday Vickie doesn't trust me. Doesn't trust me about what?"

Could this man be more audacious? "Why don't you ask her?" To illustrate my point I slide farther away from him on the bench. "I resigned. I can't keep spying on you now."

The little boy has arrived at the water's edge. He takes a handful of bread from his bag and casts the pieces every which way into the water. Ducks swim over, singly, then in pairs, then in threes and fours, until there are two dozen at the boy's feet, paddling, quacking, and gobbling. The child seems overwhelmed and looks about to run back to his mother. Instead, he calls toward the park bench, "Mama! I'm the boss of these ducks!"

Steve smiles at me. He has just-full-enough lips and the smallest chip in his left front tooth. I wonder how he got it and—the thought pops out before I can squelch it—whether I could feel it if we were to kiss. Of course I hate myself for thinking it.

"If you've resigned, that must mean you're a free agent," he says.

BZZZZT! Zap!

What is happening to me? I slide all the way over to the end of the bench. The armrest digs into my side. "Whatever it is you're assuming, Steve, you're dead wrong. You're lucky I'm not working for Vickie anymore, or I'd have to tell her you're not as angelic as you claim to be." My leg slips off the edge. I recover my balance and stand up to leave.

Steve goes back to watching the little boy.

"Are we done here?"

"Not quite," he answers. "Do you have any experience with divorce, Iris?"

I watch him suspiciously. "Some."

"You must have noticed, then, that newly divorced people are off-center. Their judgment goes awry. One minute they're full of hope about the future, and the next they're wishing they could go back to being married, if only to avoid the pain of change. Their emotions lie in ruins. Worst of all, they can't help but spread that feeling to anyone around them. Especially their children. Have you noticed that, Iris?"

It's uncanny how well he's just summed up my own feelings. "What's your point?"

He turns to face me. "Just thinking out loud."

I feel bad for speaking rudely, and silly standing up. I sit back down on the bench at the maximum distance from Steve and play with the end of my khaki ponytail. Among the thoughts now keeping me up at night is whether I can recolor my hair one more time without it falling out. I can only imagine what Simon would have to say about that.

I drop the ponytail; Steve is watching me as if he wants me to say something. He's going to set his lawyer on me. I just know it. "Not so long ago I worked for a woman just looking for a reason to split from her husband." It's a bald appeal to his humane side. "She wanted proof he was a bad guy. I could have told her he was, and it wouldn't have been entirely untrue. And despite that, all I could think about was saving their marriage."

"So what did you do?"

"Shamed both of them into being nicer to each other."

Steve chuckles. Then he says, seriously, "I'm sorry she is so unhappy." It's not clear whether he means Linda or Vickie.

It dawns on me that all Vickie truly wants is for Steve to be nicer to her. Unlike Linda, she's desperate for proof that he isn't the cheating kind. She wants him to feel closer to her, to tell her about his day without her having to drag it out of him. She wants him to pay as much attention to her as he pays his clients. She wants him to talk to her, well, the way he talks to me.

The tiny seed of an idea begins to germinate.

I recall Kevin's words: The most effective solution is generally the simplest.

The more I think about it, the better the idea seems.

You can't do this, my little voice warns. *You can't save anyone's marriage. It's none of your business and not your place. And it's dishonest. And you're repeating slogans to yourself in business jargon.*

I could use the money, I tell it.

That's disgusting, it retorts.

I'm unemployed. We're unemployed. Don't be so judgmental. I'm not trying to take advantage of anyone. I can help these people.

No, you can't.

Steve stands up. "I've got an appointment. I need to get going."

I feel a sudden chill. "You're not going to your lawyer's office, are you? You're not going to tell Vickie? She doesn't know, not unless you told her. I didn't say anything. You told me not to, and I didn't."

He brushes a leaf off the shoulder of his jacket. "Don't worry about it. I didn't tell her. You're off the hook. Sorry again for yelling at you the other day."

Then it's now or never. "I have a proposition for you."

Steve stops walking.

"A business proposition. I want to make your marriage better."

He laughs. At me.

"I'm serious. I can teach you how to be a better husband."

"Oh, really?" The laugh lines deepen at the corners of his eyes. "Is that so?"

"Hear me out. You just said yourself you're afraid of getting divorced."

"That's not quite how I put it."

"That's what you meant, though. You're afraid of getting divorced, and you know Vickie doesn't want a divorce—not now, especially. You refuse to see a therapist, and you clearly have something to hide."

Mirth and disbelief dance a pas de deux in Steve's gold-flecked eyes. "What happened to being innocent until proven guilty?"

"Quit the coy act, Steve. This will be good for Vickie, and you, too. I can tell you exactly what she wants from you. What I'd do is get her to tell me all the ways she wishes you would change. Then you and I could set up times to talk on the phone, let's say, once a week. I'd pass her pointers along to you, you behave better, and voilà, your relationship is saved. All for one hundred dollars a session. In cash."

Steve shakes his head, disbelieving. "You're saying you want to deceive Vickie, basically by working as a double agent."

"I wouldn't phrase it like that, but I suppose so."

"And how would you get her to tell you all of these personal secrets? Are you two friends?"

"Not really, no." His attitude, his insufferable arrogance, are again beginning to get to me. "But that's what I'm trained to do. In my real career, that is. I know how to get people to share their innermost thoughts."

Steve appears unconvinced. He checks his watch. "I have to be somewhere. I'd help you if I could, but trust me on this—I am not the one to be listening in on Vickie's complaints."

I seem to be channeling Val, or Michelle Heeley, because I don't plan on letting him say no. I grab his sleeve. "That's the lamest excuse I've ever heard. You can do your best to help the person you're supposed to love. Or you can be someone who lets a perfectly good marriage—all right, a troubled marriage, but, still, a marriage—fall apart . . ." I'm choking up. "Fall apart through sheer inertia and stupidity. . . ." The end of my speech gets swallowed up in a strangled sob that seems to belong to someone else, not me.

I let go of Steve's sleeve. The ducks are disbanding now; the little boy has used up his bread. His mother is beckoning him back from the water's edge. "Let's go see Daddy!" she calls out. The boy gallops back to her.

"You win, Iris," Steve says quietly. "Maybe I can help save Vickie's marriage."

"It's *your* marriage, too," I correct him, struggling to regain a shred of my authority.

"I'm willing to coach Vickie on being a better wife."

Unbelievable. Un-be-leev-a-ble. "You think Vickie needs relationship pointers?"

"Everyone could use relationship pointers, Iris."

That stops me for a moment. If someone had given me relationship pointers, would Teddy and I still be together?

"And you think you're qualified to be a . . . a wife coach?"

"Provided Vickie is willing to listen. But I have parameters. I don't want this to drag on beyond one or two sessions. I will answer no specific questions regarding my behavior—where I go, what I do, how I feel. I will not promise to act on any of Vickie's complaints."

"This is outrageous!"

"These are my terms. You and I meet in person, not over the phone—"

"I guess that makes sense. She might be checking your phone bills," I think aloud, then shut myself up before he changes his mind.

"—on mornings convenient to my schedule. Wednesday works for me, over by the boathouse, same place I saw you last time, at around the same time. And should this plan backfire—"

"It won't."

Steve sighs. "I wouldn't be too sure of that, Iris. If it does, you remember, it was your idea."

He is right; a lot could go wrong. Even if my plan works perfectly, I'll be fraternizing with the enemy. And I'll be deceiving Vickie—assuming I can persuade her to be my friend. I'll be pressuring her to change her ways without any such promise from her husband. And I'll be doing this during time I should be spending job hunting. I should feel terrible and shameful and devious.

But you know something?

I feel better than I have in weeks.

TWELVE

At noontime on Fifth Avenue, sparkles of sunlight bounce up from the white sidewalks and ricochet off the mirror surface of the boutique windows, turning the people passing by into formless, indiscriminate blobs. So I don't notice Vickie until she's nearly on top of me. From the look on her face, she's hardly thrilled to see me after my abrupt resignation. Still, she must not completely hate me. She's here, isn't she?

"That Yankees hat doesn't hide your hair, you know," she says, smoothing her pink ladybug–embroidered skirt.

I blush and pull the brim down farther anyway, remind myself that sometimes good deeds take great effort, and force a light, positive tone. "I'm glad you could make it. I don't have a lot of friends in New York, really."

"I had an errand to do here anyway." She leads me up the sidewalk to Bergdorf Goodman, where a uniformed doorman whisks us through an impossibly heavy revolving door. It's hushed and cool inside. I follow Vickie across the floor, longing for every beautiful object on display: the burnished leather bag, the glittering bracelet, the mohair scarf as feathery as cotton candy. The store is already starting to show autumn merchandise, and my throat constricts with homesickness. Two falls ago Teddy and I spent every Friday night in front of our fireplace, drinking wine and watching the flames, without needing to say anything to each other. The fireplace was one of the best features of our otherwise mundane bungalow in the flats north of Ventura Boulevard. With no money we'd had to spruce up the house ourselves. Teddy had stripped and re-painted the mantel, and I'd tackled the bougainvillea on the chimney—hours on a ladder, taming the overgrown vines with shears and gardening tape, paying no mind to the barbed-wire thorns hidden among its orange blossoms.

We take the escalator down to the beauty level. "How are things going?" I ask, watching our reflections in the mirrored walls.

"The same. No thanks to you."

My confidence starts to falter as she threads her way between the crowded cosmetics counters, leaving me to trail along behind. Yesterday this seemed such a good idea. I'd be better off focusing on getting the money she owes me from last week.

We arrive at a small display case. "The Elixir," the sign reads. The saleswoman behind the counter looks up from addressing a stack of postcards. "Mrs. Sokolov, how nice to see you. What would you like today?"

Vickie returns her smile. "*Et toi,* Alouette. Just the usual."

Alouette has a good thirty years on Vickie. I can't help feeling that if the world were in its right and natural order, their roles would be reversed; Vickie would be addressing Alouette respectfully by title and last name.

"My pleasure." Alouette sets a diminutive square box on the counter. "The Elixir." Her pronunciation makes it obvious that both words are capitalized. "The Eye Elixir as well?"

"*Oui.*"

Alouette brings out another small box. "Anything else?"

Vickie removes a Bergdorf's charge card from her Louis Vuitton wallet. "*C'est tout* for *aujourd'hui.*"

"Very well. Your total today is four hundred thirty-seven dollars and seventy-eight cents."

Vickie looks unmoved. As for me, I have to bite the insides of my cheeks to keep from shattering the Bergdorf's calm. Four hundred thirty-seven dollars and seventy-eight cents!

Alouette eyes me. "You have lovely skin." She indicates my baseball cap. "You take good care of it, I see, keeping out of the sun."

"Oh, thanks," I stammer. "I think it's pasty. And I normally wouldn't wear the hat but—"

"Porcelain, dear, not pasty. Have you experienced The Elixir?"

"I, no. . . ."

Alouette purses her lacquered lips. She reaches under the counter and sets a large pastel box onto the counter. Nestled inside are half a dozen lotions and potions, each, in its glass container, a perfect miniature of its full-size counterpart displayed on Alouette's backlit shelves. Based on what Vickie has just paid for her two one-ounce jars, this box of samples represents a queen's ransom in beauty products.

Alouette slides the box into a tissue-lined shopping bag. "For you. Try, see if you like, and then, if you wish, come back. My card is inside." When she gives me the lavender bag, I feel like stuffing it under my shirt to make it harder for her to grab back when she realizes she's wasted her samples on an unemployed woman. But Alouette just smiles.

Riding back up the escalator, I rummage happily through my shopping bag. "Look at all this, Vickie! I can't wait to use The Eye Elixir. I've started noticing these crinkles . . ."

Vickie scowls, and it's clear she has no desire to talk beauty products, and zero interest in being my friend. It's too ironic. If I weren't trying to salvage her relationship, she'd be the last person I'd choose to spend time with.

We arrive at the main level. Vickie heads for the door.

"I talked to Steve on Friday."

Vickie stops.

"I didn't want to tell you before. I was in Central Park, waiting to follow him, and he noticed me."

Her jaw drops.

"He doesn't know I was spying. He just came up to me out of the blue and started chatting. He has no idea I was working for you." I'll be amazed if she believes me.

"He started chatting with you out of the blue?"

"That's right." Even *I* don't believe me.

"That dog! He's hitting on you!"

Fighting back a twinge of shame, I assure Vickie nothing could be further from the truth. Steve and I struck up a casual conversation, that's all. I resigned on Friday because I knew I could no longer follow him. But what I've realized, I tell her, is that I might be able to spy on him in a different way. Vickie looks dubious as I explain how, if she were to rehire me at my standard rate, I could engineer ways to keep running into Steve and find out more about why he's so unhappy at home.

"He said he's unhappy at home?"

"He mentioned wishing you two got along better." A confession: By now I can't recall whether he said this or not. But it's just one more half-truth piled on top of all these others: "I get the sense Steve might consider me a friendly acquaintance he can confide in. Let's say once or twice more—like, how about, tomorrow and one day next week—I were to 'accidentally' cross his path in the park after his jog. I really feel I could get him to open up and reveal some intimate thoughts."

Vickie narrows her eyes at "intimate" but recovers quickly. "And you believe you can somehow do this without letting on that his wife is paying you for it?"

I'd like to tell her to quit with the attitude; I'm doing this for her own good. "Leave it to me. He'll have no idea what we're up to."

I can hardly believe it, but by the time we leave the store, Vickie is convinced. Sure, she says. Bump into him in the park accidentally-on-purpose. Find out why he's so unhappy at home. She flags down a taxi and waits for the elderly couple inside to pay their fare and inch out onto the sidewalk, while I steel myself for the twenty-block walk back to my apartment. Almost as an afterthought, Vickie removes an envelope from her purse and gives it to me. "This is for last week."

I practically take her hand off as I grab for the money. "Thanks," I say. "And you won't regret this new plan, either."

"I hope not," she says. Then—story of my life—she steps into the cab, leaving me alone in the city.

————

There are three messages on my machine when I get home. Three messages! They've got to be about my résumé. I hit the button without so much as taking the time to put down the Bergdorf's bag.

"Namaste! It's your mother. I'm concerned that you're never home, Iris. I know you've embarked on an exciting new journey, but I remind you to take time each day to rekindle your sense of Irisness."

She's too much to take. *Sense of Irisness?* Let's move on to message two, shall we?

"Hey, it's Teddy."

Teddy called? Why? Does he want me back? Is something wrong? I imagine various scenarios until I've missed most of the message, but tune in again in time to hear all that I need to.

". . . tax thing from the state," he concludes. "Anyway give me a call." Then, in a pompous newscaster's voice, "Thank you and good night."

Tax thing? Tax thing? But I paid our taxes! Deep breaths. I can't deal with this now. Now the third message really has to be for a job interview. Come on, job interview!

But it's Joy again, promising to call tonight at eight.

I spend the remainder of the afternoon calling the marketing companies I've sent my résumé to—a task I had vowed to complete on Friday. In each case, I'm reassured that my résumé is on file. After dinner à la Kellogg's, I unplug my phone as a preemptive strike against Joy and lie on my bed staring at the ceiling. Somehow, while wondering whether I can really pull off this business between Vickie and Steve, agonizing over how much I might owe in back taxes, and despairing over ever saving enough money to get back to California, I fall asleep.

I'm shocked awake, who knows how much later, in the middle of a dream in which I've moved back into my childhood home in Encino. In the dream, someone is pounding on the door and yelling my name. I open the door. Steve is standing at the far end of a long stretch of asphalt, silhouetted against light so dazzling it's painful. I cover my eyes with my hands. "Open up!" he demands. "Open up!"

I awake to realize that Kevin is banging on my apartment door.

I stumble out of bed and open up. "What are you doing here?" Stupid with sleep, I have to prop myself against the doorjamb for balance. Kevin gives me a quick kiss, squeezes past me into my apartment, thoughtfully scoots me back into position against the door frame, and studies me with a perplexed expression.

"Did you change something? You look different."

"Not a thing." I stumble back out of the doorway and drop back onto my bed, trying to clear the dream from my memory.

It was a last-minute trip, Kevin explains; he called from JFK but the phone just rang and rang.

"I unplugged it." Never mind, though; Kevin's surprise appearance is opportune. I get him up to date on my dead-end job search, ask him how he thinks I should proceed, and leave him alone while I find us something to eat. "How about an overripe banana with Hershey's syrup?" I call from the kitchen. Kevin declines, but to a starving woman with bare cupboards the combination doesn't sound half bad, especially accompanied by the single bottle of beer I've been saving for a special occasion. I emerge from the kitchen dunking a banana slice in a pool of chocolate, the bowl balanced on my forearm, the beer bottle dangling by its neck from between my ring finger and pinky. I set the beer on the floor and sit down with the bowl on my lap.

Kevin looks up. "You had a game plan you thought was working. If you're getting pushback from these marketing firms, it's time for a paradigm shift."

My eyes alight on the phone cord snaking untidily across the floor. It's long past eight o'clock. I set aside the banana concoction and crawl over to plug the phone back in. As if it had been poised for the past several hours waiting for its big chance, it rings, interrupting Kevin in the middle of a sentence. Spooked, I grab the receiver and yelp hello.

"Hello," Vickie says.

Kevin shakes his head and flips open his cell phone.

"I'm surprised you're up this late," Vickie continues, and in the time it takes for me to ask myself, *If she thought I'd be sleeping then why did she call?* I realize it's not Vickie but Val.

"I have a surprise for you, Iris. Your passport to the exciting world of casual sex! I signed you up for Matemarket!"

Kevin is deep into his own conversation: ". . . architect a scalable fulfillment model while embedding an adaptive protocol into the transport infrastructure . . ."

I cup my hand over the receiver and hiss into it, "What are you talking about?"

"Matemarket! My Internet dating service. They're having a special offer—your first three months free!"

Kevin snaps his phone shut and returns it to his pocket.

"Do you have a photo of yourself we could download?"

"Val, I'm not interested." If it were possible to reach through the phone and shake her for emphasis, I would. "And this isn't a good time to talk. I'm busy with something."

"Ohhh. Sure thing. Call me tomorrow." She has such a one-track mind, you can just hear the *wink, wink, nudge, nudge.* I hang up.

Kevin says, "As I was saying, you'll need to realign your end-state vision."

I struggle to focus, but I'm infuriated at Val's meddling, and there's a sticky spot on the inside of my wrist. Chocolate sauce. I bring my arm up to my mouth to lick away the offending smudge. Something about the gesture makes Kevin reach for me.

I let him pull me close. I have on a pair of Teddy's old boxer shorts with one of those insubstantial ribbed cotton tank tops, the slightly sheer kind meant for sleeping in, and Kevin traces his finger across the outline of my breasts and murmurs, "No bra." I can feel his muscles trembling, the tension in his arms and back.

"I wasn't expecting visitors."

He pulls the top up and over my head.

"I'm not really in the mood." I'm thinking of a nice way to tell Val that if she doesn't get me off this Matemarket, I'm going to kill her.

Kevin slips his hand under the elastic waistband of my shorts. I'm about to push it away when he bends his head to kiss me, and my thoughts of Val and unemployment and bad dreams and Vickie and Steve and everything else give way to the soft, insistent pressure of Kevin's mouth. And as he slides his hand farther down under my boxer shorts, I find, quite unexpectedly, that my end-state vision has realigned itself with his.

THIRTEEN

Wednesday morning, after Kevin has left, I sleep later than usual. When I finally feel like getting up, it's past eleven. I dial Val at Hayes Heeley and recite the phrase I've practiced: "It's sweet of you to sign me up for your dating service, but as you know, I'm not ready to get involved in any way with men. For one thing, I'm still married."

"If you weren't ready to date, you'd be running back to Teddy to stop the divorce," Val insists. "Besides, it's too late. You're signed up. It's done. Now, do you have a photo on your computer we could download into your profile? Without a photo nobody will even consider you."

I look around my apartment. It's a mess: clothing from last night strewn everywhere, the sheet half-pulled from the bed and drooping onto the hardwood floor like a discarded evening gown. It's futile to argue with Val. I am aware of this. "Sorry, no photo."

"Not a problem. Come down to my place and I'll take one."

I start to collect clothing off the floor. "I don't want to meet men."

"Don't be ridiculous. You'll never find more of them in one place. It's so much fun."

I could never act the way Val does. I'm a stringent user of condoms who took to heart all that sex-education propaganda about how you're sleeping not only with the guy but with every person he's ever slept with. But I can see it will be easier for me if I just play along. Let Val sign me up for her service. I don't have to accept a single date.

"I'm doing something nice for you, Iris. The least you could do is be grateful."

Yes, right, grateful. "Thank you," I say mechanically.

It's the placebo effect—or a miracle. I may have been part of the health-and-beauty marketing machine, but I'm still not entirely immune to cosmetics company promises. After one night of The Eye Elixir, my eye crinkles seem slightly less crinkly. To be sure it's not a trick of the bathroom light, as I walk to the park for my first meeting with Steve I lift up my sunglasses and check again in the side-view mirror of a van parked along Central Park West, trying not to skew the results by squinting.

I shouldn't have pushed my luck. Even if The Elixir were working, who would notice? They'd be too busy pondering the way my taupe hair makes me look like a walking cadaver.

Steve has asked me to meet him at the stretching area, and I climb the stairs to find him resting on a bench. From a distance there's a melancholy quality to the way he's sitting, staring out, it appears, at nothing.

I greet him as I walk up, but he doesn't move. I repeat my greeting in a louder voice.

He looks at me as if he's never seen me before, then recovers. "There you are. I was starting to think you weren't coming."

It seems I'm two minutes late. I apologize and turn on my moderator persona. "But you used that extra time to think of some great, wonderful, fascinating ways to help your wife be the best wife she can be, right?"

Steve doesn't respond.

"But you're having a fantastic morning so far, right?"

"To be honest, this is one of the worst days I've had in a while."

This isn't going the way it's supposed to. Hayes Heeley says you should use the same handful of jokey "purposeful ice-breakers" as you lead participants into the two-way–mirrored interview room: "Hi, there, my name is Iris, and I'm here to make this the most fascinating two hours of your life!" By the time the person responds with a courtesy laugh, you're in the conference room showing him to his seat. Nowhere in my line of work is there room for anyone to have a bad day.

"I'm still not comfortable with this."

"Oh, no, you don't, Steve. You promised, and I promised Vickie, and now you have to keep your word."

"I made the promise under duress."

"Too bad." My stomach starts to twist itself into one of the macramé plant hangers my mother had in the kitchen when I was a kid.

"I'm curious, Iris. Why do you care so much? You and Vickie aren't friends; you said it yourself. What's in this for you?"

"I have my reasons."

"It's not the money, is it? Vickie had better not be paying you."

"Actually, she is. It would have seemed suspicious if I hadn't—"

"No. Under no circumstances are you to bill her for this. Whatever fee you two agreed on, I'll pay it myself."

"That doesn't make sense. It's your money, whether it comes from her wallet or yours."

"That's the way I want it."

So I agree to his terms and promise to stop charging Vickie, even though, I explain, my interest here isn't only financial. *Broke though I am,* I add silently. In my continuing quest for a real job I've just sent out another big batch of résumés. I now know that the mailman's name is Art and that he owns his own home in Queens. I can tell how much postage an envelope will require simply by balancing it in one hand. I've even applied this time for lowly recruiter positions. I haven't had the nerve to call Teddy back, but in my mind I hear him on the answering machine—"tax thing from the state"—and my stomach commences macraméing itself again.

"If it isn't just for money, then why?" Steve presses.

"I want to help Vickie. And you."

"But why?"

"I just do."

Steve must realize I'm not going to budge. "All right, let's get down to business," he sighs, and hands me a wad of cash.

On the way home I call Vickie to tell her I have some tidbits from her husband to share.

"So share." Couldn't she *try* to sound grateful?

"Sorry. I've got urgent business." I climb the steps to my brownstone. I feel the urgent need to get to work with the L'Oreal Medium Ash Brown I just bought. Vickie grumblingly agrees to live without my information until tomorrow morning. She's coming to my apartment. I make her promise not to act suspiciously around her husband tonight (Steve insisted I say that) and fantasize about taking her shoes.

Yes. I know that by subjecting my hair to a third round of coloring, I risk ending up bald. But Val has summoned me to her apartment tonight to take my Matemarket photo, and I want my old hair back. In my Barbie bathroom I set out the bottles and jars from the box of hair color, follow the instructions to the letter, and this time manage not to let the mixture sit too long. I gingerly rinse out the color, preparing myself should clumps of hair start coming off in my hands, but nothing bad happens, and when I'm finished, despite that my hair feels a bit like wool, there's the old me in the mirror.

Miracle of miracles.

Some music is in order. It's been a long time since I've felt like playing music, doing a little lip-synching with the hairbrush microphone, dancing, should the mood strike, around the room. What could be making me so happy? Is it being a brunette again? Is it that I've worn nothing but sweatpants for so long that the idea of dressing up, even if only to get my picture taken, is thrilling? Is it the tips I've extracted from Steve? All of the above?

I now know precisely where my box of CDs is in the storage loft, so I scramble up the wobbly ladder in my bare feet and terrycloth robe—if there were people beneath me, they'd be getting a major show—stuff my pockets with as many CDs as will fit, and scramble back down. Teddy may have gotten the house, our friends, and all the wineglasses, but I have the stereo. I wipe the dust off my CD player and turn the volume all the way up—

—and immediately back down a notch or two. How sobering is it that I've become too old for full-volume Madonna? (Alas, the movers must have packed the boxes with the CDs I actually listen to, the newer ones, down at the bottom, and the ones I've had for a million years at the top; I essentially have my entire musical youth stuffed into my bathrobe pockets.) So I'm singing and putting on makeup and have been having a great time for all of one minute when someone starts pounding on the door. I'm quite certain who.

I slide the chain lock into place, unbolt the dead bolt, click apart the bottom lock, and open the door. There's Simon in lounge pants and a sweater, the dog tags, and leather bedroom slippers.

"Okay! Okay! I'll turn it down!"

"No way!" Simon hollers. "Turn it up!"

Now I have to turn it down to make sure I heard right.

" 'Like a Virgin' is one of my personal anthems! May I borrow? I lost my tape at a party in nineteen eighty-nine. You'd think if you invited friends into your home, they wouldn't steal your music as party favors, but everyone was in a nasty phase back then, doing all that coke. I swear that's when my hair started to go. Speaking of"—he waves his hand toward me— "much better color. Somebody's face has a fresh coat of paint, too. Big date tonight?"

"If you must know, I'm getting my picture taken."

"Let me in," he orders.

I unhook the chain, and he steps into my living room and moves in closer.

"Hmm. What is that on your lips, Bobbi Brown Number Four? Nice on you for daytime, but for a photo not so much. Where's your beauty booty?"

I point into my bathroom, at the makeup bag balanced on the edge of the sink. He picks it up and inventories its contents: mascara, eyebrow tweezers, the worn-down nub of a drugstore concealer stick, the Bobbi Brown lipstick I wear five days a year, the ChapStick I wear the other 360, a pot of goopy lip gloss I have worn all of twice, and a used-once compact of candy-apple-red powder blush that was supposed to have given me a fresh-faced glow but only made my cheeks look as if they'd been attacked with a can of red spray paint.

"Lambie," Simon says, "where's your beauty drawer?"

"There isn't one." Unlike most women, I don't have a stash of gift-with-purchase samples. Unless you count my miniature trove of The Elixir, which Simon has just discovered in the medicine cabinet.

"How miraculous is this stuff? You've got to keep it in the

fridge, kitten, so it stays fresh longer. I use it by the gallon on my cuticles."

Good grief. Am I the only one in this city who isn't rolling in disposable income?

"Muffin," Simon continues, "you don't have a lot to work with here, but I can whip something up. You wouldn't possibly have a Q-tip, would you? Never mind. Be right back." He disappears down the stairs.

It's all so unfamiliar. The only time Californians see their neighbors is after an earthquake—a significant earthquake. Even then you converse only on the front lawn. I can't imagine any circumstance in which a virtual stranger would insinuate himself not just into my home but into my makeup bag, unless he had broken in to steal it.

"I'm back!" Simon calls as he springs up the staircase. "I know, I know, running with scissors. Don't put it on my permanent record. You don't mind if I bring a friend, do you? He insisted on following me up here."

I don't understand what Simon is talking about until I see he's holding scissors as well as a Q-tip, and that Rocky is snorting and wheezing up the stairs behind him. It's the first time I've crossed paths with the silly little animal in several days, and to my surprise, I'm happy to see him.

"Hello, Rock." I bend down to pet him. Rocky licks my ankles. "Is Rina feeling better?" I ask Simon.

"Rina. I hired that woman to wear Rocky out, and it's just not helping. I'm starting to put a hole in the ceiling, not to mention ruining my broom." Simon begins a detailed pantomime of grasping a vertical handle and jabbing it up above his head. "Don't tell me you haven't heard the pounding. I'm beside myself. Who knows what I'd do if I had a higher ceiling, like yours. I'd have to stand on a ladder. Honest to God, the banging-broom bit is the only thing that shuts him up."

"*Woowoowoowoowoo!*"

"Rocky, shush," I say. Rocky stops barking, settles obligingly onto my instep, and nibbles my bathrobe tie.

Simon stares at his dog. All at once I remember I'm half dressed and pull the robe extra tightly around me.

"Don't worry about it, honey; nothing I haven't seen before. Now, give me that lip gloss you have in there, and that blush. We'll need a little plate, too. Also a butter knife."

I'm genuinely curious about what he plans to do, so I get him what he needs and watch as he uses the knife to scoop a glob of the clear gloss onto the plate.

"Brawny," he orders, the way television surgeons say, "scalpel." I fetch a paper towel from the kitchen. He wipes the knife with TV-doctor precision, then digs out a chunk of blush and deposits it on top of the glob of gloss. Using the Q-tip, he blends the two together into a sheer, sparkly red.

He wipes my lips with a paper towel. "Now put this on."

I dab the mixture onto my lips.

"Kitten, for the love of God, it's not poison. And don't use that; it's too dainty." He plucks the Q-tip out of my hand and attacks my lips with his fingers. Amazingly, the color looks great, instantly transforming me from average Iris to foxy Iris.

"Where did you learn how to do this?"

Simon looks pleased. "In the military, if you believe it. Try it on your cheeks. Use your fingers." He pats his dog tags. "Fort Polk, Louisiana, early eighties. I used to glam up some of the girls before they went off base. There wasn't a lot to work with, so I learned to make do with what we had. Now, go ahead, kitten; try it."

I do as I'm told. What do you know? There's that fresh-faced glow I'd been aiming for.

"Not bad," Simon pronounces.

"Thanks so much." I mean it. "What a difference."

"Not so fast." Simon picks up the scissors. "That hair has got to go."

———————

Val's building in Greenwich Village is storybook charming: black-painted brick with white trim, authentic Federal-era iron star ornaments on its corners. Boxes of crimson geraniums grace each paned window. Behind the adorable facade, the place is crumbling. Val's buzzer doesn't work, and since I've forgotten my cell phone, I have to call her from an infectious-looking pay phone down the block. The booth is surrounded by garbage: empty beer bottles, dog feces, a half-eaten pizza. While I'm dialing, a wild-eyed man lurches by screaming, "You can't make me! You can't make me!"

When I return, Val is at the front door. "You're gorgeous!" she shouts as she leads me up flight after flight of stairs. "What happened?"

I'm feeling too good to let Val's backhanded compliment bother me. Simon's custom-blended makeup would have been enough, but he's also given me a hairstyle I would never have considered for myself: pixie short and tousled. I'm no longer a generic thirty-three-year-old; I am, as *Kitty* magazine might put it, a "doe-eyed gamine"—viewed in the right light and at the proper angle. I was so grateful, I sent Simon home with the Madonna CD.

"Who cut it?" Val unlocks her apartment door.

"My downstairs neighbor."

"You said he was a neurotic pain in the ass!"

"I was wrong. He's a hairdresser."

As proof of Simon's genius it takes Val just six tries to get a digital photo we both agree is suitable, and while she loads it onto her computer to send to Matemarket, I reposition a spiky purple blossom in the large flower arrangement on her coffee table.

"They're dahlias. Read the card." Val taps a command on the computer keyboard. "Guess who sent them."

I remove a small white card from among the dahlia stems: "Let's do it again." No signature. I have zero desire to know anything more.

"I sent them to myself!" Val crows. "Listen up, because you're going to start dating again and it's a trick you should know. Whenever I think I might bring someone new home, I have my florist put together a big bouquet with a card saying something suggestive. Just knowing there's someone else sending me flowers drives them insane with lust!" She clicks a last button. "Okay, your photo is downloaded. I just sent you your account name and password. Now"—she shuts off her computer—"let's go out."

We walk over to Bleecker Street. It's a warm night, and the bars and restaurants have spilled their tables out onto the sidewalks; people are drinking, laughing, and talking. I'm lost in my own thoughts, which at the moment all center on the mystery of Vickie's husband. I've witnessed for myself his erratic schedule, the copy-shop clerk asking about his blond bombshell." Yet despite it all, despite that I myself couldn't stand him the minute he walked out of his building that first morning, why does he seem a decent person? He's been nothing but kind to me. Even his outburst Friday seems justifiable. Who wouldn't be upset to find out his spouse had hired someone to watch his every move?

Val tugs on my sleeve. "I'm going to go talk to that guy eating the salad."

"Uh-huh," I answer.

Because my thoughts have unexpectedly led me to a different and unwelcome recollection, a moment in my life like a million other inconsequential moments—one my brain would surely have relegated instantly to some inaccessible corner, never to be retrieved again, had it not been for a fateful, and unforgettable, twist. I recall misty sunlight glaring off the white-stucco exterior of a Valley strip mall, the smell of damp eucalyptus, a familiar voice coaxing me out of a blindness I've foolishly imposed on myself. I recall a faltering, unseeing journey across patched asphalt as I cover my face to block the light, the voice calling, "That's dangerous, Iris. You'll get hurt if you don't open your eyes."

You have to open your eyes, I tell myself in my memory. *You're being reckless. It will hurt a little, but the alternative is far worse.* And so, because I am not reckless, I open my eyes to see where I'm going.

My world hasn't looked quite the same since.

FOURTEEN

I don't offer her a cookie.

The truth is, her very presence throws me off. Vickie seems out of context in my apartment, the way your grandma would seem at your Monday staff meeting, or the UN secretary-general would at your neighborhood block party. She takes in my four hundred square feet, and I'm sure she's thinking, *I didn't know Iris was so down-and-out.*

Still, I can't quite bring myself to confiscate her shoes. She sits regally in my armchair while I teeter on the garage sale footstool Teddy helped me refinish one weekend early in our marriage.

"Tell me everything." It's an order as always, but Vickie sounds less commanding than usual. She brushes back her bangs, a forced nonchalant gesture, and in doing so catches several strands in her gold charm bracelet. She inhales sharply and begins working on the tangle, holding her left wrist, the one with the bracelet, up near her ear so as not to pull her hair.

I start by reminding Vickie that her husband does not know I'm working for her. Steve simply thinks, I tell her, that he and I have struck up a casual friendship. I must be getting better at this. The lie rolls right out.

"Did he admit to cheating?"

"No, but—"

"Did you tell him he needs to be nicer to me?"

"He told me you need to be nicer to him."

Vickie's face goes two shades of pink. "Nicer to him? He wants *me* to be nicer to *him*?"

"That's what he said."

"Why should I be nicer to him if he's committing adultery? If you're such good friends now, why can't you find out if he's running around on me?"

Her mind-set is all wrong. "I thought we were here to save your marriage. The idea was to find out why he's unhappy at home."

"How can he be unhappy at home if he's never at home? Get him to answer that. Just come right out and ask him, 'Hey, Steve, are you cheating on your pregnant wife?' "

I'm starting to rethink my choice not to take her shoes. I stay quiet for a few moments, long enough for what sounds like several cars that have been idling under my window to finally roar away. "It doesn't work that way. When you run a focus group, the way you get people to talk about themselves is, first you build trust and then you get into the tough questions." Of course, Steve also said he wouldn't answer any questions.

"This isn't a focus group, Iris! All I want to know is, is he cheating or not?"

"Why don't *you* ask him?"

"As if he'd tell me."

"He won't tell me, either. Maybe if I could meet him more than a couple of times I could ask, but if I did it under these circumstances, his guard would go right back up. You hired me for my expertise, so why not let me do my job?" Another clump of idling traffic starts to gather under my window.

Vickie grips the arms of my comfy chair. "I did not hire you for your expertise! I hired you because you begged me to hire you. But I've had enough. I'm going to find someone else. This is just ridiculous."

It's probably not worth mentioning that I never begged. "Forget the money. You don't have to pay me anymore. The advice is on me." *Actually it's on your husband.* "And I was just about to tell you that men who are unhappy at home are also tempted to find someone else."

"Is that so."

"Yes, it is."

"Says who?"

This is starting to sound like a playground spat. What's next, a volley of "is not," "is too"?

Actually no. For perhaps the first time ever, I've got the last word. "Says your husband. He says when men feel unloved by their wives, that's when they start looking around. Sounds familiar, right? Now, do you want to hear the rest, or would you prefer to bury your head in the sand as what's left of your marriage disintegrates?"

For the next half hour I play back yesterday's conversation with Steve. I tell Vickie her husband thinks she should consider how much she criticizes him, because, he says, too much criticism is emasculating to a man. I tell her that according to Steve, if she'd try not to point out so many failings, he'd feel a lot more content and relaxed with her.

Vickie is so still, she barely appears to be breathing. When I'm finished speaking, she stays quiet a long time. Then: "He has never used the word 'emasculating'—ever."

"Maybe he doesn't feel comfortable saying it in front of you. But it's something he wishes you knew."

She rubs her eyes. "This is too strange. My husband is complaining about me to a perfect stranger."

"I think he just wants to tell somebody his side of the story."

"How am I supposed to do the things he says? It's impossible not to criticize him. Do you know how hard it is to watch him put dishes in the dishwasher? He throws them in there every which way. He never rinses them first. That's on a good day. Usually he leaves his coffee cup or ice cream bowl lying around until it drives me so crazy I do it for him. You can't possibly imagine how irritating that is."

"I can. To this day, my husband doesn't know how to put clothing in a hamper."

"You have a husband?" Vickie glances around the apartment, perhaps expecting one to pop out from his secret hiding place.

Should I be insulted at the way she emphasizes both the "you" and the "husband"? As if she sees me as nothing but a pathetic spinster whose sole purpose in life is to serve her needs? I sound huffy, defensive: "Is it so hard to believe?"

My window air-conditioning unit, which has been grinding laboriously in its efforts to keep the heat outside at bay, decides at this moment to take a break. The unexpected stillness makes my words even more emphatic. Vickie lowers her eyes. "Forgive me. I didn't mean it that way. I've just never heard you talk about being married. Why did you never mention it?"

"Because . . ." Because that would require me getting a word in edgewise. ". . . it isn't easy to talk about."

Vickie says softly, "I understand how you feel."

The sky, already gray, has grown darker. "You do?"

"Sure."

Never have I considered a scenario in which Vickie Benjamin Sokolov might be nice to me. It's simply too out of character to process. "It's not important anyway." I turn to take a long look out the window. There's the cause of all the traffic: a moving van double-parked in front of the building across the street. Burly men are loading it with bubble-wrapped mirrors, blanket-covered sofas, plants in cardboard boxes. I wonder to where the owner of these objects is lucky enough to be escaping.

Vickie says, "I can't imagine not being annoyed beyond

words at my husband ten times a day. Did he say how I was supposed to not bring up the dishwasher?"

He didn't, I tell her.

"How do you handle it with your husband, then?"

I shrug. "I filed for divorce."

Vickie gasps.

I did just joke about a scenario looming pretty large in her own life. "Maybe . . ." I want to make it up to her. "Steve and I set up another meeting next Wednesday. I figured you'd want me to. Maybe I could ask him about the dishwasher then."

"Would you?"

"Of course."

"Thank you in advance." She stands up to leave. "By the way, your new haircut is pretty on you. The color, too." She crosses to the door to let herself out, then stops and turns back around. "This was more interesting than I thought it would be," she says.

"Don't go quite yet." I get to my feet, too, and step toward the kitchen. "You look like you could use a cookie."

———

I could spend the rest of the day analyzing that strange scene, but there's work to do. In my e-mail this morning there was a welcome note from Matemarket reviewing the terms of my three-month free membership and going over the information included in my profile. This was the profile that Val had written for me—captioned "Just Moved to NYC, Ready for Fun!" For my screen name, Val has chosen NewGirl. I sign on to Matemarket intending to cancel my account immediately, but just as I'm about to push the button, an instant message springs up.

VixenNYC: Hey! You're on Matemarket! I'm signed on too! Check out your photo! Met anyone yet?

It's Val, probably on the site setting up her dates for next week. It might make more sense to play along until she loses interest in this latest amusing project and stops checking up on me. There can't be much harm in keeping my profile active for a few more days. Who's going to try to contact NewGirl based on a one-inch-by-one-inch photo and a few perfunctory statistics? She's indistinguishable from all the other women up for romantic adoption, hundreds of them, like lonely puppies in an electronic pet-shop window, peering out from their photos with smiles by turns wistful, hopeful, provocative, desperate. *Have you considered that the love you're seeking doesn't exist?* I want to tell them all. *Will you mind when the romantic candlelight dinners give way to takeout by the flicker of ESPN? And can you promise you're the woman you say you are?*

Outside, thunder, like the guttural growl of an earthquake, rolls through the city. A spatter of drops hits the screens of my two bay windows. I get up to close them, return to my computer, and call up my own Matemarket profile, scrolling down to the empty space that's there to hold my optional personal statement. "Describe who you are and what you're looking for," it invites. I reflect for a moment and type, *I don't know who I am anymore.*

The statement looks stark in its big white box. I can think of nothing else that might soften it, so I delete it entirely.

I can't trust those I love, I type, and then, because it seems the wrong thing to confess on a dating Web site, I delete that, too. I try *Everything I thought was true is false* and *I'm better off being alone for the rest of my life* and have to laugh at my own bleakness. Good thing I mean what I say about being alone. What man in his right mind would want to get involved with me?

The rain is coming down hard now, crashing against my windows like buckets of water hurled by angry weather gods. I delete what I've written and start typing:

> When I was seven, I decided I was going to marry my dad. He was my hero, always willing to play Barbies with me, and I liked the way he cut pears in horizontal circles, with a star-shaped cross-section of core at the center of each. My mother could never remember my doctor and orthodontist appointments, so my dad would leave his office to take me himself. I knew no one else would look out for me and keep me safe and love me no matter what. A few years later I'd gotten over the fact that my dad was taken and vowed to find someone just like him. And yet, when it was time to make my choice, I married a man just like my mother—irresponsible and distracted. The truth is I am not looking for a mate or even a date. I'm here because a woman I hardly know thinks I need to "get back out there." I've been out there and see no reason to go back. If we only get one chance at love, then I've already

That's as much as will fit in the box. I look my words over and imagine a stranger reading them and thinking what a peculiar, self-pitying person NewGirl must be. I press "Delete," and the box returns to its original emptiness. I sign off Matemarket, leaving only my original profile, the profile Val set up for me. "Just Moved to NYC, Ready for Fun!" it says, with one statistic: "Marital status: separated."

———

At Steve's request, we were again supposed to meet at his usual post-workout spot, the stretching area, for our second appointment, but I find him at the bottom of the stone staircase that leads up to it. "I keep forgetting there are no dogs allowed up there," he explains. The Jack Russell sniffs around at his feet.

"So you brought your dog after all this time. Where has he been? Vickie thinks you've been leaving him at your—" I cut myself off. I'm trying to honor Steve's unfair rules.

"How do you know about the dog?" Steve looks momentarily confused. "Ah, yes. Of course. From following me."

I try to greet the animal with a straight face. "Hi . . ." I drop my voice several notches, as one does before saying something humiliating. ". . . Snooky. Honestly, Steve, why would you do that? What living creature deserves a name like Snooky?"

I can tell even Steve finds the name ridiculous. "Vickie might call him Snooky. Between us, let's call him Jack Russell. Jack for short. Vickie does not need to know this."

I feel pleased to have correctly identified Steve as not a "Snooky" person. The dog appears pleased, too; he seems to prick up his pointy ears at his new name.

Steve continues, "Mind walking a bit? You'd think a five-mile run would wear this guy out, but it hasn't made a dent." True enough, the dog, frolicking on the end of his leash, doesn't seem a bit tired—more as if someone had just plugged him into the wall to recharge him.

I kneel to retie my sneaker, then straighten back up and brush off my hands on my sweatpants. "Let's go."

Ten minutes later, Steve has led me away from the reservoir to a wooded path called the Ramble, which Val once told me has long been a classic cruising spot for gay men. I can see why: It's shady and secluded, with lots of rocks to hide behind. Immediately another murder scene pops into my head: Steve strangles me with the dog's leash and tosses my body into the underbrush, where it remains undiscovered for days. Weeks. Who would miss me—Vickie? Val? Sure.

"Nice weather," I say, mostly to keep my mind off thoughts

of my corpse decomposing unattractively in a clump of poison ivy.

"Of course it is. It's only the first of June. By August it'll be hell on earth," Steve says from a few steps ahead of me on the narrow path. He stops to let Jack sniff at a tree. "Tell me about yourself, Iris. I don't know much about you, except you're having money problems and view yourself as the savior of Vickie's marriage."

"You mean your and Vickie's marriage."

"That's what I meant."

I hop over a stick. "We're supposed to be talking about you, not me."

"Why not? I think you're very interesting."

I put my hand up to smooth my new short hair, realize what I'm doing, and pull my hand away. I'm not on a date; I'm on assignment. I assume my no-nonsense moderator stance. "Vickie is confused about some of your advice."

Steve is about to answer when his right arm suddenly jerks in its socket. Jack has run up ahead and is straining at the end of his leash. Steve starts moving again. "What's she confused about?" he calls back.

"That no-criticism rule."

"It's not a rule. I only said when men feel criticized by their wives, they—"

"I get it. We both get it." I address his back as the three of us continue our amble through the Ramble. "But how is she supposed to not criticize you?"

"That's pretty much all she needs to do—not criticize. It's not hard."

"What about the dishes? When you even bother to do them, you put them in the dishwasher all jumbled together. And you don't rinse them."

He looks back over his shoulder at me and snickers.

"What's the punishment for that: jail time or a fine?" He sounds just like Teddy.

"That's not funny, Steve. Why can't you give her a break? Why can't you just do it her way, if it would make her happy? How hard is it to rinse out a coffee cup?"

"I told you this kind of conversation is off limits," Steve says. "These meetings aren't about my behavior; they're supposed to be about Vickie's behavior. Why does it matter so much anyway?"

"Because! It just . . ." Too late, I realize I've never thought out exactly why dishwasher etiquette is so important. "It just does."

To slap the smirk right off Steve's face would be unprofessional. Settle down, Iris. Act like a moderator. You'll get more out of him if you aren't confrontational. You can't get angry. I breathe for a moment, and when I start again my voice is calmer. "You really feel very strongly that you may not be able to change your ways. It sounds like you feel Vickie should make all the concessions."

"Not necessarily. But she's the one so unhappy she hired a spy."

"I'm not sure I understand. She's unhappy with you, but you feel *she* should change?"

"You can only change your own behavior, Iris. You can't change anyone else but yourself. And that's only if you want to change. Why are you looking at me like that?"

There is something vaguely Joy-like in the way he is speaking. I replace what must be a disapproving scowl with that moderator classic: the Mona Lisa smile.

He continues walking. "Besides, men are always the ones making concessions, because women are always the ones with the demands: 'Your track trophies are going in the basement.' 'I don't like your friends.' 'I never said I wanted a baby.'"

I stop short, grab the back of his shirt, and pull him around to face me. "What did you just say? Vickie doesn't want a baby?"

From behind us comes the faint shuffle of footsteps. Steve and I freeze, the way couples do when they've been caught bickering on the welcome mat on their way into a party. A handsome, shirtless man squeezes past us. He gives Steve an approving once-over before disappearing around a bend.

Steve and Vickie are fighting about starting a family?

"No other straight guy would tell you this, but we secretly think that's kind of flattering," Steve says once we're alone again. "Is that how you feel when men stare at you, or does it really make you feel like a piece of meat?"

If only Michelle Heeley were here to realize the mistake she made in laying me off. Imagine the job I could have done on the organic bubble bath launch for Lizzie B Cosmetics, a client toward which I harbored no animosity whatsoever, if I can stay poised during a conversation with a man I can barely stand. Steve probably uses this charming-banter routine all the time to win over his conquests. "You know, Steve, Vickie told me this pregnancy is all she's ever wanted. She was very clear about it. Why would she lie about something like that? Are you sure you heard her right?" He must think I'm pretty gullible, anyway, to fall for that kind of empty flattery. Men don't stare at me. I'm unobtrusive, remember?

Steve kicks at a root in the path.

"I can't imagine her saying she didn't want a baby."

He doesn't look at me. "Sorry."

"Then what did you mean by that?"

He doesn't answer.

I remember something Michelle used to say: If you stay quiet long enough, most people will eventually start talking again to fill the silence. I prepare to wait him out.

Steve blows air out of his cheeks, making a whistling sound.

Ahead of us, Jack appears to have finally run out of battery power and is dozing on his side in the middle of the trail. Even sleeping, his legs twitch.

"This is getting complicated." Steve kicks again at the root. "You know, I told you I'd meet with you once or twice, and this makes twice. I'd say you and I are square. I don't think we should do this anymore."

"Whatever makes you comfortable, Steve."

"Then this will be our last meeting. Deal?"

"If that's what you want." *Whatever made me think I could save someone's marriage?*

"I'd like to know why Vickie hired you in the first place, though."

I smile vaguely.

"I assume she thinks I'm having an affair."

"I see. Tell me how you came to that conclusion."

"Isn't that why wives hire private eyes?"

"Is it?"

"Are you trying to sound like a shrink?"

No, like a focus-group moderator. Turns out that while the Hayes Heeley method is all right for getting strangers to open up about bubble bath, in real, human discourse it sounds stilted and phony. "All right, then. Are you cheating on Vickie?"

I'm expecting the irate denial of a liar trying too hard. But Steve's voice is calm. "I can't answer that," is all he says.

Art the mailman is in the middle of the day's delivery, unlocking the bank of mailboxes in my front foyer with one of about ten thousand keys dangling from a ring the circumference of my thigh.

"For you." He hands me a stack of catalogs and junk mail. "How's job hunt?"

I make a face.

"I know. Economy not so good for everyone, right? Last guy who lives in your apartment, he lose his job, spend eighteen months looking. You think of moving to Jersey? It's cheaper out there."

"That's where I'll end up," I say mournfully. "In New Jersey, right next door to that guy who used to have my apartment. More likely, in New Jersey, sleeping on the sidewalk."

"Uh-uh. He doesn't move to Jersey." Art clanks shut the bank of mailboxes and locks it with his key. "He lands bigger job and buys a loft in SoHo."

Inside my apartment, I flip on *General Hospital* for background noise and settle into my chair to go through the mail, hoping that hidden among the junk I'll find a response from a potential employer. No such luck. But at least my Department of Labor check has arrived, so I'll be able to eat for another week, and there are no credit card bills today, only catalogs, which I can't help flipping through even though I'm in no position to buy anything.

Everything in Lands' End looks downright grandmotherly. I switch to J. Crew, but the bikinis, flip-flops, T-shirts, and shorts just blend together. Why do these clothes seem so pedestrian? There's not a thing in here worth going into debt for.

Vickie calls. I toss the catalogs into the recycle pile and tell her I've got a few things to report.

"I have news for you, too."

"You go first." I'm in no hurry to tell her I asked Steve the cheating question and blew my chance forever, because our meetings have come to an end. I can't tell her I'm disappointed that I won't be able to help her after all. That part is all for the best, I suppose. It isn't fair that Steve was willing to offer pointers but not take any himself.

"That's all right; you go," Vickie says.

Deferring to me? How refreshing—on any other day. "It's okay. You first."

"Thank you," Vickie replies. "Guess what? It worked! Your advice. His advice. About not criticizing him in any way! After I left your apartment last week, I thought, why not try it for twenty-four hours? I put a rubber band around my wrist, and every time I got the urge to criticize—and believe me, I got the urge a lot—I gave the rubber band a snap."

My heart leaps. My plan may actually have worked, in just two meetings?

"I've managed not to say one mean thing to Steve for six days straight," Vickie continues excitedly. "Can you believe it? It's got to be some kind of world record!"

I can't help but have the tiniest cynical thought. Was this some kind of scheme? Did Steve plan to use me to help to transform Vickie into a Stepford wife? *Think about it.* That's my little voice talking. *He said he would answer no questions and make no promises to change his own behavior. He only wanted Vickie to change hers.*

"And guess what else? This morning, before he left for work, he made me toast! And brought it to me in bed! Without being asked! And he put exactly the right amount of butter on it!"

I'll bet he did. It was part of his wife-coaching plan. Okay, so he changed his behavior slightly, just to keep her on track. He got me to tell her to act exactly as he wanted, and now, whenever she heels or rolls over on command, he's going to toss her a little treat. Soon the toast will turn into flowers and the flowers into jewelry, until he's got her so well trained she won't notice that the rewards have stopped.

"Now, he didn't put the plate into the dishwasher afterward, but still! He hasn't made toast since we were dating! So everything I said about why should I change? Forget it. I want more advice, and the sooner the better. Now, what was it you wanted to— Is that your call-waiting?"

Indeed it is. Saved by the bell. I say good-bye to Vickie and click over to the other line, thanking my lucky stars that I don't have to admit my failures until later.

As it turns out, I've simply traded one messy phone call for another.

"Praise be to Jee-sus!" my soon-to-be-ex shouts in a revivalist preacher's twang. "A miracle is in our midst! Our own Iris has answered the call! Brothers and sisters, I prevail upon each and every one of you not to follow the example set by sister Iris. I prevail upon you to *hear* the message. To *accept* the message. And most of all, brothers and sisters, to *respond* to the message."

"All right, enough. Just mail me the tax thing and I'll take care of it. Somehow."

Teddy chuckles. "Don't worry about that. I already forged your signature."

He forged my signature. That's just swell. I think about Vickie getting annoyed at Steve ten times a day. If it's really only ten, she's luckier than she realizes. I take a cleansing breath. "How much was the bill?"

"Bill? It was a refund. One thousand, two hundred sixty-three dollars and seventy-eight cents we overpaid last year. Amazing, right? I probably should have double-checked the numbers. Didn't you tell me to do that?"

I did tell him, as a matter of fact. But there's no need to dredge that up now. My imagination has already gone to work on the . . . please hold on while I do the math . . . six hundred thirty-one dollars and eighty-nine cents that comprises my half of this unexpected windfall. I'm saved! Saved, brothers and sisters! I want to jump up and down on my bed like a five-year-old. "When do we get the check?"

"I got it," he says. "That's what I was calling about."

No, wait; I want to bang my head against the wall. "Ted, you have my address. Write me a check for my half. Then send it. What's the big mystery?" I let the tirade fade out as Steve's voice echoes in my head like a bad soap-opera flashback in which the heroine relives a dire warning she's been given, even as she's doing the very thing she's been warned against: " 'Men just can't take constant criticism from their wives . . . wives . . . wives. . . . They withdraw . . . withdraw . . . withdraw. . . .' "

"Teddy, I was being harsh."

"No problema."

Steve must be overgeneralizing. Maybe some men get upset at criticism, but Teddy, off in his own little galaxy, has never paid attention to a thing I've said.

That's his way of coping, snipes my little voice.

"I'll pay you back soon, I promise," Teddy is explaining. "With interest."

"What did you just say?"

"I'd been needing a new demo CD. You know, to get voice-over work. I didn't have enough cash on hand, so I borrowed your half of the refund."

No. Please, no. Teddy hasn't borrowed my six hundred thirty-one dollars and eighty-nine cents—he has *embezzled* it. Sure, he'll try to pay it back. He'll try valiantly, but he'll never have enough cash of his own to spare. I want nothing more than to scream at him—in a most emasculating way.

Teddy must sense this. "Hey, it's an investment. And hey! How about that preacher character? Pretty good, don't you think?"

I pull the phone away from my ear and drop it silently onto the bed, letting Teddy chatter away into the empty room, imagining the walls moving closer and closer together, closing in on me until I'm trapped in here, in New York, forever.

FIFTEEN

The next day, when I go to check my e-mail, my mailbox is stuffed with come-on after come-on, so many that when I start to sort through them my computer crashes, and I have to restart it twice before I can tell what's going on. I've never seen anything like it.

"MEAT ME TONITE!"
"WANNA GET NASTY?"

And on and on and on. Do these hucksters have no shame? Then I look closer and realize this isn't junk e-mail at all. Not the usual kind. Mixed in with the pitches for discount amphetamines and requests for my bank account number from exiled Nigerian princes are a good fifty notes from Matemarket men. The notes go like this:

TO: NewGirl
FROM: Studmuffin
SUBJ: Yo cutie

Yo, check me out. If you like it we could hook up. Love Alex

and like this:

TO: NewGirl
FROM: IDigHotGirlz
SUBJ: Cum over 2 my place!!!

"Fifty responses? Not bad," Val says when I call her to complain. "The hot girlz one may not be your type, but how about that one who wants to see you naked?"

"Not naked. N-A-K-K-E-D. I can't date an illiterate."

"How many times do I have to explain this to you? Don't think about dating him." If Vickie's signature expression is "I'm going to shove my shoe down your throat," Val's is the exasperated eye roll, and I suspect she is executing a flawless example of it right now. "Think, *Could I spend one night with him? Could I meet him for one drink and see what happens?* Basically, is he decent-looking and breathing? If so, what's the big risk?"

"Val, spelling is very important. And I don't want to get involved with anybody even for half an hour. I probably won't like him, so I've just wasted half an hour. If I do like him, all of a sudden we're going on a second date and a third date, and then we're in a relationship and then we're moving in together and then we're married and then it all falls apart. And I'm hating myself because not only have I made a mess of my life yet again, I did it all for some man who can't spell 'naked.' "

"Would you just go out with someone, already? If you don't like the naked guy, pick another one. I'm not hanging up until you reply to one of those e-mails."

I scroll through more subject lines: SUBJ: Let's Party, SUBJ: I HAVE $$$, SUBJ: Blow me baby. I click open one that says simply SUBJ: Hi. The note is from someone named BuzzBuzz and consists of one line: Meet sometime?

Not exactly compelling, but inoffensive. "Fine, Val. I'm replying. What do people write in these things?"

" 'Dear so-and-so, I'm available . . .' When are you available?"

I stop typing. "Weekdays, weeknights, weekends."

"Not weekends. Never make a date for a weekend night."

"So I won't look desperate."

"It's not that. You don't want to be out with the bridge-and-tunnel crowd. That's what people from Manhattan call people from New Jersey, the Bronx, Brooklyn, Queens, Staten Island, the Westchester County suburbs, and certain unauthorized areas of Long Island. Every Friday and Saturday night the city is overrun with them. You see them outside clubs and bars those of us who actually live here got sick of weeks ago. Tell him Tuesday or Wednesday. Say your favorite bar is—"

"No bars."

"No bars?" Val sounds incredulous. "Then say you'll meet him for coffee or something."

I type.

"Sign it 'NewGirl.' Now send."

I click the Send button. The e-mail vanishes from the screen. "I did it."

"Finally," Val says.

After we hang up, I continue my massive delete-fest, which includes tossing, unopened, a "Special Edition" of my mother's newsletter (SUBJ: Mark Your Calendar! Joy at the New Age Expo!). But also in my e-mail, Kevin has sent an invitation to dinner next week. That's odd. The only time Kevin has ever taken me to dinner was just before I left L.A., the night during which, over chicken mole in Hollywood, he suggested that we take our years-old friendship "in a more proactive direction." Now he wants to speak with me "regarding a third-party proposal with significant future impact." *What does that mean?* I wonder, as I write the dinner date into my barren day planner.

Rather than dwell on it, I spend ninety minutes visiting the Web sites of every last marketing research outfit in the Tri-State area, on the slim chance that I might have missed one. In the process I stumble across a firm called the Christmas Company, with a president–chief executive named Sandy Christmas. The name is so strange I pull up her corporate biography, and when her photo appears I'm astounded. Sandy Christmas is Cassandra Krysakowski! Cassandra Krysakowski from PKS, who hired me right out of school as her assistant and left three years ago to form her own company. How could I have forgotten she was in New York? Cassandra loves me!

Sure enough, she takes my phone call immediately, tells me how happy she is to hear I've moved to the city, and suggests lunch at Undine's on Thursday. I write that into my datebook, too, not knowing what thrills me most: that there's someone in New York who has known me longer than five minutes, that she could easily hire me, or that she's going to buy me an expense-account meal at the city's restaurant-of-the-moment. That will be two meals out—in one week! My life is on an upward swing! I turn off the computer and call Val back to see if she wants to celebrate after work. Her voice mail says she's out in the field for the rest of the afternoon. She doesn't answer her cell phone, either. Maybe it's time to start making other friends. I think on it for all of ten seconds and then, before I can change my mind, dart out of my apartment and down one flight to the basement.

"Door's open, kitten!" Simon yells when I knock.

I step into his apartment. Simon is nowhere to be found. "Be with you in a second!" he calls from behind a doorway. How luxurious—he must have an actual bedroom. I stand in the living room, awaiting further instructions.

"Have a seat!" Simon calls from the beyond.

I recline into his leather Eames chair, put my feet up on the matching ottoman, and stare into the fireplace. It looks exactly like mine, except that instead of the remains of the one Presto Log I burned back in April, Simon has set up a display of religious candles, Mardi Gras beads, flowers, and oranges. It's so

endearing and whimsical I want to run right upstairs and put
a plant or something in my own fireplace.

"It's my hair shrine. I pray in front of it every morning.
Damn, sweetheart, that's one brilliant cut." Simon emerges
from behind the door and comes over to inspect my head.
Rocky trots out after him. I make a kiss-kiss noise to lure the
pug over for a pat, and then look at Simon. "If someone you'd
been sleeping with asked you to dinner to discuss a third-party
proposal, what do you think he'd be about to ask?"

"Threesome. But we're talking about you here? Marriage."

"Not a chance. Kevin is the least commitment-minded person I know. He won't even leave a toothbrush at my place.
That's the whole point of our relationship—no emotional in-
volvement. Besides, I still have a husband."

"Maybe he wants to propose a threesome with you and
your husband."

"Simon, stop. Want to go shopping with me?"

"When?"

"Now, I guess. I have a job interview next week and need
something nice to wear." I'll have to put it on a credit card.
It's stupid, I know, but if—no, make that *when*—Cassandra,
a.k.a. Sandy, offers me a job I'll be able to pay it off right away.

Simon swoops me into a hug. "At last! I'm so proud of you!
You're much better than those nasty old sweatpants! Why do
you wear those things all the time, anyway?"

"They've been matching my mood." My reply is barely au-
dible because he's got my face crushed into his left shoulder. I
try to free myself without seeming impolite. "Besides, everything in my closet is wrong. Somewhere between Studio City
and here it all became a decade out of date."

Simon nods knowingly. "Manhattan wardrobe spoilage.
Happens to everyone who moves here, except for the girls

from Paris and Tokyo. The only cure is to toss everything onto the sidewalk and start from scratch."

"Then you'll come with me?"

"I would love to, but I must perform an emergency updo downtown." He opens the door to what in my apartment is the kitchen, but in this case is an enviably spacious closet, and extracts his quilted metal box. He pats it. "I ought to get a red cross stenciled on this thing." I must look crestfallen, because he adds quickly, "Don't be a sad kitten. If you want me to drop by tomorrow afternoon you can model everything for me. I'll tell you what works and what doesn't. For company now, bring the Rock along. He's great in boutiques. The shopgirls go ape over him."

Rocky is lying on his back, all four paws in the air.

"Why not?" I tell Simon.

"That's my girl."

SIXTEEN

Rocky and I walk Simon to the corner, where he hails a cab. I put his spare keys in my purse, even though I suspect he will be back from his house call long before Rocky and I have expended my pent-up shopping energy. But no sooner do I set off down Columbus than Rocky swoons operatically onto the sidewalk. He's so exhausted, the pose suggests, he can't possibly make it another inch.

"He's thirsty," a giant, lumpy-faced man grunts from behind me. "You do know that if that animal isn't properly hydrated, he won't reach his full intellectual potential, don't you? You need to carry a collapsible water bowl at all times." He wipes his hands on his stained shirt and lumbers away. "There oughta be a law."

"You must be pleased with yourself," I whisper to Rocky as I haul him up and carry him under my arm, his legs scrabbling in the air, for two blocks until we reach a restaurant with outdoor tables set off from the sidewalk by a row of low planters. Gratefully I set him back down. He's got to weigh fifteen pounds.

"Adorable boy!" A fresh-faced blond waitress, who could have been teleported directly from an Iowa cornfield, seats me at a prime people-watching table next to the planters. She hands me a menu but speaks only to Rocky. "Are you thirsty? Are you thirsty? Are you? Look, we have our own doggie drinking fountain."

Running along one side of the building at Rocky's chest level is a narrow water trough, tiled with a mosaic of dog faces.

"Don't worry," the waitress informs Rocky. "We have a special system that circulates and triple-filters the water to get out all the nasties. It's cleaner than the water in Mommy's kitchen!"

I watch Rocky slurp at the trough, his curlicue tail twirling in delight, and long for an intelligent human with whom to discuss the new depths of absurdity to which this city seems to sink on a daily basis. That dog water probably *is* cleaner than the water out of my tap. I'm sure it never comes out looking brown.

Rocky jumps up—the trough must in fact contain the healing waters of Lourdes—and makes a beeline between the planters for a dog passing by on the sidewalk.

I'm learning, though. I've already thought to loop his leash around my chair leg. Rocky reaches the end of the line and slingshots back toward me like a furry tetherball.

"Ha!" I shout exultantly.

"*Woowoowoowoowoo!*" he protests.

"I'd know that bark anywhere," remarks the man walking the other dog.

I'd know that voice anywhere. It's too bad Val and Kevin aren't here to chant, "It's nothing but a big small town." Because the other dog is a Jack Russell terrier. And the man is Steve.

"Well, well, if it isn't Iris and Rocky. Are you two following me? Never mind; don't answer that. Mind if we join you?" Before I can utter a word, he squeezes through the planter-wall, drags over an empty chair, loops Jack's leash under its leg, and makes himself at home. So does Jack, after a brief skirmish with Rocky that seems mostly for show.

"And what are you doing here on our lovely Upper West Side?" The way Steve says it, you'd think it was his neighborhood and I was the one on the wrong side of town.

"I was just about to ask you the same thing."

He grins and scans the menu the now-vanished-back-to-Iowa waitress has left on the table. "Perhaps *I'm* stalking *you*."

"That's creepy and rude." The way I say it reminds me of the way I used to speak to Teddy when he'd do something like drink milk out of the carton. Maybe I did treat Teddy the way Vickie treats Steve. But I can understand what Vickie said about Steve and the dishwasher: How was I supposed to not get upset?

"I was teasing. I'm between appointments and have about an hour to kill. I was going to sit somewhere and read my paper. You know something, Iris? I've missed you. And I only just saw you yesterday. So how about a sandwich? My treat."

I can't get out of my head the suspicion that Steve is using me for something. Still, I haven't eaten for hours. It wouldn't be a bad idea to fuel up for shopping, especially on his dime. And deep down, so deep I never would admit it to anyone, ever, I'm glad he's shown up like this, on my side of town.

I stand up. "I have errands." I bend down to unhook Rocky's leash.

"Want some company?"

Yes, but not yours, Steve. "I'm going shopping."

"Clothes shopping?"

"I have a job interview."

"Good for you! When?"

"Next week. I'd better get going."

"Not to brag, Iris, but I'm a great shopper."

"How lucky for your wife."

He ignores my comment. "I don't even mind sitting on the little pink chair outside the dressing room. You should bring me along."

This is a first. No man has ever campaigned to accompany me shopping.

"I promise not to ask why you need another black skirt when you already have six in your closet."

That makes me laugh. "I do have six in my closet."

"Every woman does," he says. "Also black shoes. Let me guess. Ten pairs?"

"Eleven. Not one of them suitable for New York City. This friend of mine calls it—"

"Manhattan wardrobe spoilage."

"How do you know that?"

He opens his wallet and leaves a few bills on our unused table, then gets up and leads me out onto the sidewalk. "Didn't you get the handbook? I thought they passed it out to every new New Yorker. The one that explains how much to tip the grocery delivery man, and why there's always scaffolding going up somewhere, and the difference between Ray's Pizza, Famous Ray's Pizza, The Original Ray's Pizza, and Famous Original Ray's Pizza."

"And how to get a taxi in the rain?"

"No one knows how to get a taxi in the rain."

We go on like that, and before long he's led me eight blocks up to a spot I know well: Columbus and Eighty-second. As we near the speakeasy/white slavery den/whatever it is at the northeast corner, with its darkened windows and porthole-door, my heart starts to pound. What is he up to?

"I thought we were going shopping." I try to sound nonchalant.

Steve ties Jack Russell to a parking meter and approaches the porthole. I stick fast to my spot on the sidewalk. This would be an ideal time to bow out, take Rocky, and go do my shopping the proper way, that is, without Vickie's husband. I grab him back toward the curb. "Whatever this is, I don't want to go in."

"What's the matter? You've not heard of Rubicon?"

I've heard of Rubicon.

Everyone has heard of Rubicon.

Rubicon stocks only the most obscure, up-and-coming designers—no Ralphs or Calvins, no Pradas or de la Rentas. It's credited with launching dozens of the now famous and far more expensive labels Vickie undoubtedly has in her closet, and which would be in Val's except that she wears only vintage and doesn't have a closet. It's also located way downtown. Good try, Steve.

I give him my best "gotcha" look. "There is no Rubicon on the Upper West Side."

He bounces it right back to me. "There wasn't, until they opened this annex last fall."

Rubicon Annex! This unmarked door leads to Rubicon Annex? I live just blocks from the only branch of the boutique *Kitty* calls "Manhattan's, and therefore the world's, most selective," and for which there's no listed phone number or address? What a coincidence that it's in the same building Steve manages.

"This is Rubicon?"

"This is Rubicon."

"If it is, even more reason for me not to go in." To be sure he understands my point, I perform a satirical catwalk twirl in my outfit—not as bad as the sweatpants, but almost: my boring denim skirt. "Besides, I can't afford anything in there. And I'm not on the list."

Yes, Rubicon is so selective it also maintains a tightly controlled guest list, the way nightclubs do. You need to be on it just to get in the front door. How you get on the list is a tightly guarded secret, according to *Kitty*. Now I understand why that poor woman was left tapping on the glass. She must not have been on the list, either.

"You look fine. Anyone they let past the threshold does not get judged."

I shake my head.

He steps toward the bell.

"Don't."

"Iris," he says. "I *am* on the list."

I'm at a loss for words. "I can't just leave Rocky out here on the sidewalk."

He stops, his hand poised in the air. "Jack would reduce the place to shreds, but Rocky is welcome to come inside."

He's making this hard. If I can't exit gracefully, perhaps I should take better advantage of the situation. "All right. Let's say we do go in there. This can't be a friendly outing."

"I'll try to be as surly to you as possible."

"I mean, if I'm going to spend time with you, I want more tips for Vickie."

Steve drops his hand. "I told you I wasn't going to do that anymore."

"Come on, Steve. It would make her happy. Just get together with me a few more times. Do some more wife coaching. What's the matter?"

Steve's happy face is gone. He stands with his arms crossed over his chest, feet apart: partly defensive, partly defiant. "You wouldn't give me the time of day if it weren't for Vickie, would you?"

"That's right." I glare at him: What's *your* problem? "I wouldn't."

"Even if I were single and we just happened to meet?"

"Especially if you were single."

"Why not?"

You're a despicable, cheating lout; that's why not. "You're not my type."

"Couldn't we be friends?"

I look across the street to Iglesia Sangre de Cristo. That dingy door could use painting. "Steve, you and I aren't friends. We're never going to be friends. I'm proposing a business arrangement, and when that's over I don't plan on ever seeing you again. Do you understand?"

"You've made yourself clear." Steve's mouth smiles, though his eyes don't. "You don't expect me to continue paying you for these meetings, do you?"

"I don't need your money. I'm getting a real job. This interview I'm going on is just a formality. I'm practically hired already."

He looks unconvinced. And unhappy.

"Please, Steve. I wouldn't ask you to do this unless I thought it would help Vickie. And your coaching *is* helping. Vickie told me so yesterday. She said you've been so much better to her since she started being nicer to you."

"Really?" Steve rubs Rocky's stomach with his foot. "She said that?"

"I don't know what you're up to, Steve, and I can't say I approve, but Vickie seems to be happy. Don't you owe this to her?"

And at long last, Steve smiles for real, if a bit wanly. "You win." He steps up to the porthole. "If it's wife coaching you want, wife coaching you'll get. But I can't meet on Wednesday mornings anymore. I have somewhere I need to be. We'll have to do it Tuesdays instead."

"That's fine," I agree, wondering what exactly he could be doing Wednesday mornings.

"And I don't want you to tell Vickie we went shopping. Deal?"

Before I can answer, or reconsider, he rings the bell. The doorman nods gravely and lets us in.

The store, elegant and minimal with high ceilings and modern furniture, and library silent already, gets even quieter as Steve, Rocky, and I enter. The shoppers who have been browsing through racks of stunning clothes stop and look up to see who's come inside. It's like a kids' staring contest, where you try to get your best friend to blink before you do; nobody says a word, and every second seems an hour. That's how it feels inside this place, until a chilly-looking saleswoman spots us.

"Darling!" She rushes over, heels tapping on the hardwood floor, satiny black hair swinging back and forth, throws her arms open to embrace Steve, and kisses him on both cheeks. Not air kisses; full lip-to-face contact. It's a greeting I'd find intrusive. Steve doesn't seem to mind a bit.

"I've brought in a friend. She's new in town, from California, so go easy on her." He guides me forward. "Iris, this is Ilona. Ilona, Iris. Iris has a very important interview coming up, and she could benefit from your help."

"Welcome to New York, Iris, and to Rubicon. I'm at your service." Ilona sandwiches my hand in both of hers—a protective, motherly gesture, even though she's no older than I am. I watch her. How did she and Steve come to be so chummy? Is she his mistress? Would he bring me in here if she were?

"May I take your dog?" she asks.

Steve nods at me, and another equally chic salesgirl glides over with a biscuit, which she uses to lure the pug into a back room. Rocky follows obligingly, and I try not to imagine having to tell Simon I inadvertently turned his dog over to a cult of animal vivisectionists fronting as Manhattan's boutique of boutiques. If so much as one *"woo"* comes out of that back room, I promise myself, I'll kick down the door.

"Chantal will look after him. Would either of you care for a drink?"

"No, thanks," I answer immediately.

"None for me," Steve replies. "I've still got a full day ahead."

"Our Mr. Responsible." Ilona leans over and presses her cheek against his.

Steve pats Ilona's shoulder and takes an infinitesimal step back. "You're sure you don't want something, Iris?"

"There's bubbly in the back fridge. We should celebrate," Ilona says. "It's been a while since darling Steve has brought a woman in here. Not counting Jessica. Right, Steve?"

Jessica? I whip my head around to stare at Steve. He gives Ilona a hard look—the kind that communicates to the recipient, stop talking immediately. Ilona must interpret it that way, too, because without missing a beat, she turns to me. "Let's choose you some clothes. You say you have an interview?"

I've been expecting her to act catty or snobbish. Do I trust her? I don't suppose I have much choice. Steve is standing between me and the door, and the other cult members have spirited away Simon's dog.

I begin guardedly, "It's more of a lunch. But I'm not sure I can—"

I was going to finish the sentence, "afford anything in here." But Ilona puts her finger to her lips. "A lunch, good. What field? Banking? Law?" She stops to look me over. "Your hair is adorable. It says 'creative.' Advertising. Publishing. But your clothing. It's not giving me a clear idea of who you are."

"I'm in marketing." I'm surprised. I was prepared for a mean-spirited wisecrack about my outfit, but Ilona has kept her opinion, which can't possibly be positive, to herself. I feel warmer toward her despite her suspiciously friendly relationship with Steve. And who is Jessica?

"You're in marketing?" Steve interjects from across the room, where he's perusing a display of shoes.

The shattering of the silence makes me blush, but having already checked me out once, none of the other shoppers pays me a speck of attention. "Was."

"Huh," says Steve, still over by the shoes. I wonder how he came to be so interested in fashion when the men I know, including Teddy, tend not to notice what a woman is wearing unless it's short, tight, or low-cut. Perhaps his girlfriend Jessica is a model who takes him backstage at all the shows. Or is Ilona his girlfriend? My stomach aches. I shouldn't know about any of this when Vickie doesn't, and yet I can't imagine a way to tell her about it.

He holds up a delicate sandal. "This would be nice on you."

It is a beautiful shoe, but the exchange makes me squirmy. What is keeping every customer in earshot from assuming I'm this man's mistress?

"Marketing." Ilona has tilted her head to one side and is studying me. "So, modern but not outrageous. I'm thinking Zelos Tolma Zoe for suits, and Caroline Blythe or Miss Muffy of Fresno for little dresses." She addresses Steve: "Don't you think?"

"You're the boss, Ilona."

She smiles and turns her attention back to me. "Size four, naturally. Where will you be lunching? The Red Room? Cyclone?"

"Undine's."

"Undine's!" Ilona puts the back of her hand to her forehead and crosses her big, green eyes. The effect is so silly, I can't help but giggle. "I love Undine's! Make sure you order dessert."

"As if you ever eat dessert," Steve calls.

She calls back, "I eat dessert. Any woman who doesn't eat

dessert is guaranteed hopeless in bed." That finally gets a few customers to look back up.

"I agree completely," I say under my breath.

"Iris agrees completely!" Ilona announces.

"Ilona!" I gasp, but I can't be angry with her. She's not the slightest bit snooty.

Ilona leads me to a dressing room with three outfits she's chosen. "I could never get away with that," I protest at the first, a simple, dove-gray sleeveless dress with a daring neckline. I check the price and nearly swoon. "Or pay for it."

"Try it."

So I do, and surprisingly, it looks amazing. The neckline isn't that low once I put it on; it accentuates my collarbone and somehow makes my cheeks look less chipmunky. There's also a charcoal-colored skirt with a blouse of snowy cotton fine as a breeze on my skin, and a lightweight, subtly man-tailored pantsuit Ilona suggests wearing without a shirt underneath.

"That keeps it feminine," she explains when she comes in to check on me. She rolls the pant legs up about a foot and a half, smooths my shoulders, tugs the jacket at the bottom, and steps back to admire me in the mirror.

"Isn't it a little too sexy?"

"Not at all. While we're doing the other alterations we add a hidden button so you're not revealing too much." She demonstrates by holding the jacket shut another half inch above the top button. I stare at myself in amazement. I look like a New Yorker.

"I love everything."

"I knew you would!"

"But I can only buy one thing. I shouldn't even be doing that." I feel bereft already.

"You do get Steve's VIP discount. Half off. See? It pays to be kind to our Steve. He's such a sweetheart."

That can't possibly be right. Half off is almost the wholesale price. What kind of shop sells things at cost? The little voice inside my head has plenty to say, and this is one time it might be smart to listen. Instead I take a breath, preparing myself for a purchase I shouldn't be making but to which I suddenly feel entitled. "Self-denial stifles the soul!" I imagine Joy crooning. For once, her philosophy kind of makes sense.

I tell Ilona I'll take the dress.

"Wonderful!" She hugs me.

"May I ask one thing? Why does Steve get a VIP discount? Because he's with the building?"

Ilona drapes the dress carefully over one arm. "He likes to say it's because he's close with the manager."

"The building manager? Is that you?"

"The store manager, silly. And no, I'm just a shopgirl."

"But I take it the manager is also a she?" It can't be Jessica. Ilona said Steve brought Jessica into the store.

Ilona laughs. "Yes, the store manager is a she. But rest assured there's nothing going on there, if that's what you're wondering. Really, you don't have to worry about any of us here at Rubicon." She openes the door to the dressing room. "You have Steve all to yourself. Well, pretty much."

Steve is waiting in a chair near the register, with Rocky in his lap, when Ilona and I emerge from the dressing room. He puts Rocky on the floor and rises to his feet. He looks so formal, I almost expect him to shake my hand how-do-you-do.

"How did you do?"

"She's beautiful in all of them," Ilona says.

"I have no doubt," he addresses me.

I try not to feel flattered. "I'm taking the dress."

"Why not everything?"

"I wish." I pull the American Express card from my wallet before I can change my mind. The dress costs almost a month's rent. It is the most expensive single item of clothing I have ever purchased, aside from my wedding gown, though I'm counting on getting more wear out of it.

"You come back anytime you like. You're on the list now." Ilona eases the dress into a canvas garment bag, itself nicer than most of the things in my closet. I start to slide my card across the polished-cement counter.

"Wait." Steve lays his hand lightly across mine.

My college friend Evie once told me that she realized her husband was her soul mate the first time their hands brushed together. It happened during a routine chemistry lab. Her entire focus telescoped down to the extraordinary sensation of Doug's skin against hers. In that instant, she said, she knew that this man was someone special.

I never understood what she was talking about until now.

I stare dumbly down at Steve's hand covering mine. I want to turn my palm up and entwine my fingers in his. I want him to wrap his arms around my waist and pull me to him. I want his hands on my body. I want to belong to him, and for him to belong to me.

"You should have everything," he says.

He feels it, too, I think. *He feels the same thing.*

The room is too warm, the rustle of fabric and the hush of shoppers' footsteps too loud. "I can't." My tongue is thick and clumsy inside my mouth. "I can't afford to—"

"It's all right." Steve's voice is kind. "Let me help."

Ilona looks at him, smiles, and slowly, slowly, slides my card back to me.

That breaks the spell.

"Absolutely not. I can't accept your money. Ilona, just the dress." I slide my card back to her.

"Let me do this, Iris." Steve's eyes are deep and hopeful.

"No!"

"Call it a loan."

"But why?" *I don't want you to tell Vickie we went shopping.* Isn't that what he said?

"Consider it an early thank-you for making Vickie's life better. For making *my* life better. It will be another business arrangement. Strictly business, I promise. Every hour we meet, I'll deduct a hundred dollars from what you owe me. If you get a steady job out of this interview, we'll arrange the terms so you pay it off over time."

Ilona finishes putting the dress in its bag. She takes the pantsuit next, marking the jacket with a pin at the spot where she suggested adding a button. She slides the blouse and skirt into a second bag and appraises Steve with a sidelong glance as she slyly curves up one corner of her mouth.

SEVENTEEN

I have to hand it to my conscience. Before unleashing the guilt storm, it lets me enjoy my good fortune for twelve hours. That's twelve hours after I finally agree to let Steve lend me the money; twelve hours after Steve rushes out of Rubicon to the appointment he alluded to earlier, with instructions to Ilona to charge my new clothes, plus alterations, to his account and have everything delivered overnight to whatever address I specify. (To my apartment, only four blocks away? Not decadent, apparently.) It's eleven and a half hours after I use Simon's keys to deposit Rocky safely in his apartment, and eight hours after I drift off to sleep, pushing aside my memory of Steve's hand on mine with fantasies of wearing the gray dress at dinner with Kevin, and the blouse and skirt for lunch with Sandy Christmas. Or should I wear the pantsuit? It's the first happy dilemma I remember having in months.

But by morning the clouds have begun to gather, and by the time the deliveryman from Rubicon drops off the proof of my sins and leaves, tip in hand, I'm awash in shame. What was I thinking, prostituting myself for a few new outfits? Prostituting myself to Vickie's husband? Though I can't put my finger on exactly what the impropriety is, I've clearly crossed the line into it. And Steve—what does he expect to gain from all this? My stomach roils with nausea.

"Kitten!" comes a cry from the hallway, followed by a knock on my door. I get up slowly from my chair to open it. "Good morning, sunshine! Did we do our part for the economy last night?"

I let Simon in, and he rushes for the garment bag. "How very A-list of you!" he says. "Rubicon!"

"How did you know?" The bag isn't marked.

"I know. May I see?"

"If you want."

"Why so gloomy? Don't you like your clothes?" He produces the blouse and skirt and nods approvingly. "Perfect." He extracts the suit. "Zelos Tolma Zoe! How could you possibly not adore this platonic ideal of a pantsuit? Make sure you wear it without a shirt."

"I love it, but I have to return it. The way I got it is just wrong."

"Sweet mother of the Almighty! What did you do? Steal it? Fork over your unborn children? Sell your soul to Satan?" He pulls out the dress and holds it up to me.

"Close."

Simon steps back at arm's length to take in the effect.

"Kitten. Give me your undivided attention. These things will be smashing on you. This is New York City. Thank the Lord you finally ditched that Yankees cap, but you cannot keep schlumping around in sweatpants and sneakers. You may think you're the sweatpants-and-sneakers type, but you're not. Unless you had to kill someone or give up a body part, keep the clothes! They're perfection!"

"You think so?"

"Honey, I am ordering you to keep them. It's an order! If you return anything in this bag, I will call nine-one-one and have the fashion police arrest you." He whips out his cell phone and brandishes it at me. "Don't make me use this!"

I have to smile a little. Of all the people currently trying to run my life, Simon is the only one whose advice has, so far, been pitch perfect.

"Good." He lowers the phone. "Now: Simon says, step away from the garment bag."

I take two steps backward.

"I'm going to put these things in the closet now." He waves the phone at me one last time. "Don't make any false moves."

I've got mail.

There in my e-mail box, hidden among a now astonishing landslide of obscene Matemarket propositions, is a reply from the man I sent an e-mail to:

TO: NewGirl
FROM: BuzzBuzz
SUBJ: Hi

Phone number?

"Now what?" I ask Val that evening, after I've invited myself over to her apartment.

"Give him your phone number." Val steps around me and pulls back a curtain behind the front door to reveal her kitchen: an indentation in the wall with a half-size stove and a sink piled high with dirty dishes. She crouches in front of the mini-fridge and produces a bottle of mouthwash and a bottle of vodka. "Want a Breath Blaster? It's a shot of Grey Goose with a Scope chaser."

"That's okay."

"You spit out the Scope," Val clarifies.

"No, thanks."

"I could make you a Forest Fire in the blender."

The appliance in question is in the sink, with three inches of murky liquid inside it. I pass.

Val slurps a healthy shot from the vodka bottle, swallows,

takes a glug of mouthwash, swishes it around in her mouth, and steps into the bathroom. She emerges wiping her mouth on her wrist and jumps onto the sofa, onto which she's tossed an unopened bag of potato chips. "So." The way she says this and claps her hands together reminds me of Vickie. "You talk to him for three minutes. If he sounds good, go out with him. My computer is right over there. Go send him your phone number."

"I'll do it when I get home."

"Now," Val orders.

It can't hurt, I suppose. I sit down at Val's computer. When I'm finished, I study her memento collage. Running horizontally across the wall above her desk, she has strung half a dozen slender steel cables, to which she's clipped concert and museum tickets, postcards, bar menus scrawled with phone numbers, and dozens of photographs. Most are of people I don't recognize, but there is one of a teenage Val and Vickie in caps and gowns.

"High school graduation. Happiest day of my life," Val says, watching me from her spot on the couch. "Did I look bizarre, or what?"

It's a wonderful snapshot of the twins standing in the sunshine with their arms around each other, their heads thrown back at the same angle, laughing. In the photo, Val wears no makeup, or perhaps a touch of mascara. Her hair is nearly identical to Vickie's, in style and in what must be the twins' natural color: a perfectly attractive sandy brown. Except for the dated perm and fluffed-up bangs, it's the prettiest I've ever seen Val look.

"When did you and Vickie get so different?"

Val comes up next to me. "When I rejected the bourgeois life." She pulls down the photo and studies it, then gives it to me. "Country club weddings, volunteer work, Ivy League husbands—I can't believe she buys into it."

"Being married isn't all bad."

"No doubt. First you trade great first-time sex for tedious sometimes sex. Then you have a man in your house, drinking your beer and expecting you to clean up after him. I bet Vickie makes up all these stories about Steve because she's bored out of her mind." She returns to her spot on the couch, lies on her back, rests her feet on the sofa back, and says from upside down, "I swear, if Steve just let Vickie loose in Saks every day, none of this cheating stuff would ever cross her mind."

I work on rehanging the photo, trying to align it in the absolute center of its allotted length of cable so there's an equal amount of empty space at either end. "Does Vickie know anyone named Jessica?"

"How would I know?"

Let me rephrase that. "You really don't think Steve is capable of cheating on your sister?"

Val sits back up, pulls open the potato-chip bag, and stuffs a chip in her mouth. "Hard to say."

"What do you mean?"

"It's like," *crunch, crunch, crunch,* "if you had a window into his thoughts at any given moment—say walking down the street—he'd be thinking about mortgage rates or golf before he'd be wondering whether the girl in front of him was wearing crotchless underpants. Then again, the guy is a Republican-voting, East Side–living, moneymaking Ken doll. Do I believe he has it in him to cheat? Sure."

I try to concentrate on Val's mementos, but a tingle comes into the hand Steve touched yesterday. I clench both hands into fists and dig my fingernails into my palms. My nails are so short I can barely feel them. I open my hands. "He did tell me once he was trying to get his affairs in order."

"You've spoken to him?"

"It's a long story."

"I'll bet." *Crunch, crunch.* "Will one of his affairs be with you?"

"I can't believe you would even suggest such a thing!"

"I was joking," Val says. "Why is your face so red?"

———————

BuzzBuzz calls the next day. I can barely hear him over the blasting techno/rap on his end of the line, and my first thought is that there's no way this person and I will ever get along, but the conversation gets better once he turns down the volume. He tells me he's a mural artist who lives and works in a formerly abandoned warehouse in a Brooklyn neighborhood called Dumbo—Down Under the Manhattan Bridge Overpass. He asks if I'd like to come see his loft, but when I stammer that it might be better to meet somewhere more public, he apologizes and suggests a friend's gallery opening next Saturday, a week from today, in the Meatpacking District. But aren't Saturday nights for bridge-and-tunnelers? I ask. He laughs. "I *am* a bridge-and-tunneler."

After our conversation I sign on to Matemarket to read his profile. He's never been married and has no children. He has broad shoulders and a noble forehead. He likes Vietnamese food and doesn't own a television. To my surprise, I find I'm looking forward to the date. Maybe it *is* time I got out there.

TO: Iris Hedge
FROM: Steve739271
SUBJ: Wife Coach

Never did give you the pointers I promised yesterday at Rubicon. I'm happy to, if you still want them.

What is this doing in my in-box? I never gave Steve my address. I wouldn't have opened it had the subject line not rung a bell. Having done so, I hate that I feel a shiver of delight.

TO: Steve739271
FROM: Iris Hedge
SUBJ: RE: Wife Coach

Still want them. We also need to set up that payment schedule right
away for the clothes. I'd rather give you the money instead of working
it off. I can give you $100 a week for now and more once I'm working.

It's hopeless. I can't afford $100 a week, and even at that
rate it will be next year before I've paid Steve back. My little
voice hisses, *It's your fault. You let him talk you into buying
those clothes.*
*But they're so beautiful. It's Steve's fault for taking me into
a store with prices he knew I couldn't afford.*
I add another line to my message.

It isn't appropriate for you to be sending me e-mail. Don't do it again.

Click. Now to get back to what I was originally doing: re-
searching Sandy Christmas's company.
An instant-message window appears on my screen.

Steve739271: Ilona gave me your e-mail address. Hope you don't
mind.

Now, this is intrusive. I type in,

Iris Hedge: But since you bought me clothes, now you own me?

and hit the reply button. His answer pops up nearly instan-
taneously.

Steve739271: It's a loan, not a gift.

Iris Hedge: Where are you?

Steve739271: At work.

Iris Hedge: It's Saturday.

Steve739271: People have been known to work on Saturday.

Iris Hedge: What does Steve739271 mean?

Steve739271: Nothing. Got it just now for e-mailing you. You want pointers or not?

The thought of getting bonus information for Vickie assuages somewhat my guilt at accepting expensive clothing from her husband—to say nothing of my guilt at knowing he's taken a special Internet handle just for me.

Iris Hedge: You seemed friendly with Ilona.

Steve739271: Do you want the pointers?

Iris Hedge: Do you go to Rubicon often?

Steve739271: Pointers? Yes or no?

Iris Hedge: How do you know her?

Steve739271: Again, I'd rather you kept our shopping spree to yourself. No need to discuss it with Vickie.

Iris Hedge: Yes, yes, I know.

Now I'm sneaking around like I'm the one having the affair.

Iris Hedge: What did you do to get a VIP discount?

Steve739271: Pointers? Don't have much time.

Iris Hedge: OK, give me the pointers.

I figure it will take him a few minutes to reply, so I go to fix myself a bowl of cereal. I need it to quell the nausea that's crept back. When I return to the computer he still hasn't answered.

Iris Hedge: Hello?

Steve73927 I: Patience.

Iris Hedge: I'm trying.

The man is insufferable.

Steve73927 I: I meant that as a pointer for Vickie. A lot of women lack patience.

Iris Hedge: Maybe because we have to put up with men like you.

So I'm picking a fight. Steve's marital observations have put me in a fighting mood. It's time he got a piece of my mind.

Steve73927 I: Out of time now. Will e-mail you the rest. See you Tuesday.

Darn!

Iris Hedge: Wait!

Steve73927 I: Still here.

Iris Hedge: Who's Jessica?

Iris Hedge: Who's Jessica?

Iris Hedge: Who's Jessica?

EIGHTEEN

M ore patient?" Vickie sounds staticky out of my cell phone. "How? And when did you see him?"

It's late Sunday afternoon, and I needed to escape my apartment, so I'm walking up Amsterdam. "I bumped into him on the street, if you can believe that. Not accidentally-on-purpose, either—really accidentally. We chatted for a minute or two, so consider this bonus material. And I figured out a way to keep crossing his path, so you can keep getting your pointers." It's truthful enough, I suppose; I just hope she doesn't ask how, exactly, I achieved this.

"That's great," she says. "Go on."

I try to steady the inconveniently tiny and slippery phone against my cheek while sliding my right foot out of my mule. This is one of my few still-acceptable pairs of shoes and, at Simon's suggestion—insistence—I'm trying to wear something other than the sneakers. But my instep has already begun to chafe under the leather strap. My shoes were never this hateful when I spent most of my time in them sitting in Los Angeles freeway traffic. "He wanted me to pass along that generally speaking, when he doesn't seem to want to talk to you, it isn't because anything is wrong. He's just in a quiet mood and needs time to himself. He says you could help him get out of it faster by letting him be alone instead of asking him what's wrong." I carefully step over a pair of discarded men's pants splayed across the sidewalk. "He says it's the best way to handle the situation. Personally, I would find it almost impossible."

It's not my place to provide commentary on Steve's advice,

but I can't shake the conviction that I'm leading her down the wrong path. After getting Steve's e-mail last night with his latest pointers, I went into my mail controls and put a block on Steve739271. There. No more surreptitious messages from Vickie's husband.

"It does seem impossible," Vickie says.

I breathe a deep sigh. Maybe it's sinking in. "Vickie, have you ever been to Rubicon?"

"That boutique with the no-name designers? Never been. It's not really my thing. I'd rather buy a label I've heard of. Why? Did you want to get on the list? Maybe Val knows how. But back to the tips. They're hard to follow, but I could at least try."

"Vickie. It's none of my business, but are you sure it's a good idea to follow everything that Steve—ow!"

"You okay?" Vickie sounds concerned. Must be the weak cell phone connection.

"It's my shoes. They're ripping my feet to shreds. I have to stop at Duane Reade and buy Band-Aids." There's a drugstore up on the next block.

"Forget that."

"Vickie, forgive me for inconveniencing you during your oh-so-busy Sunday, but I'm getting goddamn Band-Aids!"

This isn't like me. What would Joy have to say about it? That I'm releasing my pent-up anger as the first step up the "stairway of healing"?

"I didn't mean don't stop at the drugstore," Vickie replies. "I only meant don't bother with the Band-Aids. They're useless. They get wrinkled up in your shoe and make everything worse."

As a matter of fact, I've suffered Band-Aid bunch-up many a time and have thought about going a few steps further and simply binding each foot from toe to ankle with surgical tape. I would, too, if it seemed that it would work.

"What you need is to stop and get yourself some antiperspirant. Get Placid. Not regular Placid, Ultra Placid—the one in the pink can. See, the reason you're having trouble with your shoes is because your feet sweat. Sometimes just the tiniest bit, but it's still there, and then when you walk more than a block or two, the moisture causes friction with your shoe, and you've got a blister. So you spray your feet with Ultra Placid every morning before you put on your shoes. Antiperspirant equals no sweat. No sweat equals no blister."

It's astounding. Here I am getting practical, nonjudgmental help from Vickie, and if that weren't enough, years ago I helped Sandy Christmas/Cassandra Krysakowski recruit a couple of dozen women for Placid, and not one of those women mentioned—what is that medical term? "Going off-label"?—for blister prevention. What a marketing opportunity Placid's brand managers are missing. ("New Ultra Placid for Feet!")

"Does that really work?"

"City girl's secret weapon," Vickie answers.

———

I haven't forgotten about the more important issue: Who's Jessica?

Unfortunately, infuriatingly, predictably, Steve signed off without answering the question and didn't address it in his e-mail. But Vickie seems happy with the information I do pass along; not just the part about allowing Steve some quiet time, but that she should make an effort to pay attention when he does have things he wants to talk about. I tell Vickie, "He says women are always asking men to share their feelings, but when men do, half the time we either don't pay attention or we get mad."

"That's because the only feelings they ever share are the complaining, critical ones."

Something else to bring up with Steve. Even though he won't listen.

"I'll try, anyhow," Vickie continues. "I'm writing everything down."

The woman deserves credit. She seems to be taking this very seriously. And though I want to give Steve a good, swift kick, his advice is hitting home for me, too. When I was first dating Teddy, he used to tell me he loved me ten times a day. After we moved in together, he almost never did. We had fights about this; I'd insist it was proof there was something not right between us. Did I just not pay close enough attention? According to Steve, after the early dating phase men show their love instead of talking about it: "They cook you dinner and come sit next to you on the couch when you're watching TV." Now I remember all the times I'd arrive home late from work, and Teddy would be in the kitchen making me a peanut-butter-and-jelly sandwich. "Thought you'd need *zees*," he'd say in a French-chef accent.

"Iris," Vickie says, "I want to start paying you again. Now, don't argue. You've been so clever with all these accidentally-on-purpose meetings. He clearly has no clue you're working for me. And I know you need the money. How does our old arrangement sound? One hundred dollars an hour, one-hour minimum? Just keep track of how much time you spend with him, and I'll give you the cash. In fact, tell me how much time you've already put in and I'll reimburse that, too."

"You'd really do that?" I reach the Duane Reade and wend my way through the cramped aisles. As usual, the shelves are chaotic and every third item is out of stock. But I find one last can of Ultra Placid.

"Why not? It's his money, anyway."

What if Joy is right and there is such thing as karma? What if my luck really is turning? Money from Vickie will tide me over until I start working for Sandy. My little voice tries to remind me that when I do start working for Sandy, I won't have time anymore to help Vickie; and that I shouldn't be accepting payment from a woman whose husband is buying me clothing. I refuse, absolutely refuse, to listen.

———————

I spend the rest of the day doing chores I've been meaning to get to forever. I sort through a few more boxes in my storage loft, still without finding my corkscrew, but I do locate a single wineglass. I call Evie in Palmdale to wish her and Doug a belated happy thirteenth anniversary. I play exterminator in my e-mail box, gleefully obliterating every last message from Matemarket. I spend some time searching the Internet for names of friends I haven't spoken to in ages. "Jadey Aldebaron" comes up empty. So does "Audrey Vogel." I search for "Valerie Benjamin" and then "Val Benjamin" and find some mentions on a vintage-clothing bulletin board. It appears that four years ago she was trying to track down a specific black Jantzen swimsuit from the seventies and a matching black rubber swim cap with white rubber daisies, but it's unclear if she succeeded.

"Vickie Benjamin Sokolov," in every possible combination, turns up nothing. "Steve Sokolov" gets sixteen pages' worth of mentions, but none seems to be the right Steve Sokolov. I don't think he's the Steve Sokolov who races NASCAR or the Steve Sokolov who heads up the Destin, Florida, Chamber of Commerce or the one in Missouri who keeps a detailed online jour-

nal about morel mushroom hunting. Then, in a moment of in-
spiration, I think to find the Web site for Empire Property
Management. I click on "Our Brokerage Team" and scroll
down the list until I find "Steven Hart Sokolov, Associate Broker." All his biography reveals is that he has been with the
company for ten years, has a bachelor's from Yale and a Whar-
ton MBA, and specializes in industrial and commercial sales
and leasing. No mention of anything personal, not even that
he's married, and there's no photo of him, just an empty
square that says "Unavailable."

Bored by now, I spray my feet with the Ultra Placid, slip into
my shoes, and walk around the corner for a brush for scrub-
bing the tub. I return home and clean the bathroom from top
to bottom. After that, I draw myself a big bubble bath. Tomorrow marks the start of a big week. I have my dinner with
Kevin tomorrow night, a meeting with Steve on Tuesday, a
meeting with Vickie on Wednesday, lunch with Sandy Christmas on Thursday, and the gallery opening with BuzzBuzz on
Saturday. For someone with neither friends nor job, my life
seems remarkably full, and it feels nice that way. I lie back in
the charming-but-chipped footed tub and contemplate a suspicious patch of mold on the ceiling that has probably been
around as long as the building has. I have a good feeling about
Sandy Christmas: She's going to offer me a job.

And not a moment too soon.

NINETEEN

TO: Iris Hedge
FROM: Vickie Benjamin Sokolov
SUBJ: Steve

Dear Iris,

He sent flowers! Three dozen white roses. So sweet! That also hasn't happened since we first got married. He says he chose white so they won't show plaster dust. Isn't that thoughtful?

TO: Iris Hedge
FROM: Kevin Asgard
SUBJ: Agenda

Arrival 7 p.m. tonite for pre-dinner consult, dinner at 8 p.m. (reservation confirmed). KA.

"So how will you answer when he pops the question? My advice is, don't say anything firm until after you've had the ring appraised. I had a client who only found out *after* the wedding that hers was a phony. Four-point-two carats of cushion-cut moissanite. Can you imagine? Everyone else in town had already known for months, too. Needless to say, she used the divorce money to take a gemology course so no man could ever pull a stunt like that on her again." Simon lowers my mascara wand so close to my right pupil, I jerk backward. "Don't pull away. I'm a professional."

I'm in Simon's apartment, where he's preparing me for my dinner with Kevin. I inhale slowly and try to hold my head steady, open my eyes wide, and not blink. "He's not proposing marriage, Simon." I focus on the candles flickering in Simon's fireplace. "This has got to be business-related. His company is transferring him to New York, something like that."

"Will you let him move into your cozy love nest?"

I'd laugh if I weren't terrified of having my eye poked out. "I'm not even divorced yet! And I'm not ready to get serious with anyone. Honestly, I think I may give up on men altogether."

Simon puts the wand down. "That's too bad, kitten. You're a knockout. See for yourself."

He ushers me over to his full-length mirror, a battered antique rotating oval in which some woman much like Great-aunt Zinnia would have admired her cunning new Easter bonnet. Now it's my turn. I look into the glass.

"There she is . . ." Simon sings.

There she is indeed.

My gradual and unplanned metamorphosis from San Fernando Valley yokel into chic, sleek femme fatale is complete. I take in my new haircut, my elegant makeup (Simon has gone with understated eyes but played up my mouth with classic red lipstick), my siren-red fingers and toes, my sexy, expensive new dress. There have been moments when I've felt more swan than duckling—on my wedding day, for one, before the ocean swallowed up my veil. This seems as if it could last.

Simon has been watching me absorb it all. "What do you think?"

"I think I just turned into a different person."

He says, "You did that when you moved here."

"It's the transformational power of divorce." I speak to my own reflection.

"That's not it. It's New York City. It changes everyone. In

your case, for the better. You don't understand that yet, but you will."

At the moment, I am happy to give him the benefit of the doubt. "Thank you." I hug him. "I feel like Cinderella with her fairy godmother."

"That's 'alternative-lifestyle godmother.'" He squeezes my arm. "Now, kitten, I have a little favor to ask."

". . . and he needs me to dog-sit in August, while he's on Fire Island. He rents a house there every summer, but Rocky doesn't 'do' the beach and needs to stay in the city. He'll pay me, though, but I'll feel pretty bad about taking his money when I'm going to be at work all day. You know, after I get that job with Cassandra—Sandy."

Kevin refills my glass. It's hard to tell, but his hand appears to tremble. He arrived here at my apartment with a bottle of twenty-five-year-old Macallan and suggested a drink before dinner. It seems to be for medicinal purposes. I've served his in the newly discovered wineglass.

"The dog-walking lady could have watched him, but guess where she's going? Bridgehampton," I continue. "And Vickie and"—why am I blushing?—"and Steve, they're going to be in Southampton."

Kevin jingles the ice in his glass.

"I am so sick of hearing about the Hamptons. Hamptons, Hamptons, Hamptons. Nobody back home has a summer place. It's such an affectation."

"You've never been in Manhattan in August."

"Yes, yes, yes. Hot, hot, hot. Humid, humid, humid. You know what New York is? A city of whiners. So, in August it's a little sticky. It's sticky out now. I'm not that tough, and I'm handling it."

"Iris . . ."

"These New Yorkers, they're a bunch of pampered poodles."

Even Steve. It disappoints me that Steve would be the name-dropping, social-climbing, Hamptons type. Vickie most certainly is, and Val swears up and down that Steve is exactly like Vickie. But the Steve I've seen shows no insecure, I-must-be-seen-at-this-week's-restaurant-or-people-won't-like-me tendencies. He seems comfortable with himself.

Iris, stop thinking of Steve this instant, before your face bursts into flames. I take four discreet diaphragm breaths and try to pay attention to what's happening now. I should not be pondering Steve's inner life, or the shape of Steve's mouth, or the heat of Steve's hand on mine. . . .

I spring from my seat on the footstool. "Aren't we going to miss our reservation? It must be time to get going."

"We have plenty of time." Kevin stands and steps over to me. He pats my shoulder and guides me to the armchair. When I'm sitting down, he, too, takes a seat—on the bed. He takes another bolt of scotch and clears his throat. Uh-oh, this seems serious. My stomach begins to churn.

"Our alliance has impacted me positively, Iris. We share critical alignment on a number of issues."

What if he really is proposing marriage? I find myself staring at his jacket, searching for the telltale outline of a little box.

"But as this quarter has progressed, I've seen my personal goals evolve. I gathered data, conducted a personal diagnostic, established a strategy, and—"

To what surely will be my undying horror, his eyes start to water.

"Kev!"

He sniffles and again clears his throat.

I set down my drink and take his hand in mine. *Please, let this go smoothly.* "There's something I'd like to say first." No sign of resistance. Good. "Kevin, I've enjoyed our, um, alliance, too. In different circumstances, I might have wanted us to be more serious. You have so much to offer."

"Thanks. You, too." He seems to be taking it well so far.

"It's just that we had an understanding. No commitment, remember? I hope you understand, and that you aren't hurt. I would never want to hurt you. But if you're feeling conflicted, it might be best to take a break from each other for a while."

Kevin looks surprised. He looks astounded. He looks amazed.

He does not look crushed.

"You have no idea what a relief it is to hear you say that." I pull my hand from his. *What?*

"Iris, I've met someone." He slides off the edge of the bed, rises to his feet, and throws an arm around my shoulder. "I wanted you to be the first to know. I'm getting married."

———

There's always somebody somewhere moaning about having been awake all night. Didn't sleep at all. Tossed and turned until daybreak. The California variation on this theme is, "I always wake up right before the earthquake," in which people insist they have a middle-of-the-night sixth sense that rouses them a second before the room starts moving.

It's a myth. The earthquake savant isn't waking up in advance; she simply remembers whatever her mind was processing just before the rude awakening. As for the up-all-nighter, he did so sleep, if only perhaps for minutes at a stretch. It only seems he didn't, for the same reason—he remembers what he was thinking while unconscious. Your brain never stops churning, you know.

I, however, definitely didn't sleep last night. Maybe it's a

first in human history, but I am quite certain I was bitterly conscious the entire eight hours.

"Are you all right?" Steve says when I show up fifteen minutes late for our Tuesday meeting. I'm not offended, because I
look like death warmed over: cadaverous flesh, eye bags, mat-
ted tufts of hair spiking out at odd angles. That's thanks to
Simon's industrial-strength styling goo and the fact that there
was no time even to wet down my hair, since I didn't hear the
alarm go off. Perhaps that contradicts what I just said about
not sleeping.

"Would you like to go for a walk?" he goes on. "It might
make you feel better."

It surely would, but I'm too tired to move.

Steve slides over on his park bench to allow me sufficient
space on which to collapse. I collapse, throwing my left arm
over my eyes. Dramatic, perhaps, but even with my sunglasses
it's too bright. I need something completely opaque there to
block the light. A voice from my memory warns, "You
shouldn't do that, Iris. You need to see what's in front of you."

"Rough night?"

"You could say so," I answer in a monotone. Officially my
evening ended half an hour after Kevin dropped his marriage
bomb. It took only that long for him to explain that he'd decided to "reallocate his attention" to this woman he'd been
seeing in Los Angeles, this Lynn, and to hug me in a brotherly
way and wish me "the best of luck in all future endeavors."

"I'd guess it was husband trouble," Steve says, "except,
you're not married."

Kevin had wanted to take me to dinner as a show of friendship. I declined. Third-party proposal. I should have known.
"Why does everyone assume I'm not married? Do I seem un-
weddable? Is there an 'old maid' sign over my head?"

He uses his thumb and index finger to pluck my left hand

off my forehead. I don't open my eyes but can feel it, a disembodied object dangling limply in his grasp. "No ring," he says, and lets go. My hand falls back heavily onto my forehead. I jump, straighten up, force myself to open my eyes, and fix him with an indignant look.

"So what? You're married, and you don't wear one."

"Not true." He holds up his left hand. A gold band gleams on his ring finger.

He and Vickie really must be getting along better.

Vickie thinks so. Her "He sent flowers" e-mail from yesterday went on about the many ways Steve is responding to her new, more respectful conduct. It wasn't just the white roses. She says she has stopped criticizing him, has stopped badgering him to discuss topics that bore him, and has begun listening to him with no objections. She says he has been nicer, too, making toast for her every morning now, paying more attention when she speaks. She still has no idea Steve is in on the whole thing. She truly believes she and I are the ones fooling him. She thinks he must accept me as a friend—a friend he keeps happening to encounter in Central Park and has never once mentioned to her. She thinks Steve must see her transformation as a coincidence that's in no way related to the things he's telling me. Despite circumstances that are far-fetched to the point of absurdity, Vickie believes what she wants to. If that isn't cognitive dissonance at its purest, I don't know what is.

"My guess is," Steve says, "you're divorced."

All at once I'm too weary to keep my guard up. "Separated. It'll be final in November." I slither back down the bench and study my hands, the classy-sexy red manicure.

"I am sorry, Iris. Divorce is the most traumatic thing."

"It is, I agree. But this had nothing to do with my husband, Teddy."

"Then it's some other guy." He rubs his forehead. "You're in love with him?"

"No. Lord, no. We were just . . ." I feel too exposed. "Never mind."

"You can tell me. You've been helping me; maybe I can help you. And I almost forgot, I brought you this." In his e-mail, along with his Vickie pointers, he instructed me to meet him an hour later than usual, not at the stretching area but at the lower west corner of Central Park, at a spot where the park road is bordered with dark green benches lined up end to end. The benches are mostly empty at this hour of the morning, but on nice days at lunchtime workers come here in uniforms and business suits to eat their deli sandwiches and stare into the park. Now Steve, who's in street clothes and sans Jack Russell, takes two doughnuts from a white bag he's been holding, and presents one to me. I stop wondering about his weird schedule and take a grateful bite. It's a classic Krispy Kreme with exactly the right amount of glaze.

"He's getting married. He told me last night. To a woman he met six weeks ago. He says it wasn't that he was afraid of commitment; he just needed to meet the right girl."

"Ouch," Steve says.

I lay my doughnut on its piece of waxed paper on the curved seat of the bench. "It shouldn't matter. It doesn't. I don't want to marry him. Teddy was enough. If Kevin *had* asked me to marry him, I would have said no."

"But you don't want him to marry someone else."

"Exactly. How petty is that?"

"It's human."

"In any case, I'm through with love. Forever. A date once in a while is fine," I say, thinking about my pending date with BuzzBuzz. "But relationships? I'm done."

Steve scuffs his running shoes in the beige gravel under our bench. When he notices me watching, he plants both feet on the ground. "That's easy to say right after a bad split, but I hope you don't mean it. Somewhere, there's a person who, given the chance, would fall head over heels for you."

I resume the scientific study of the topography of my hands. The faint white circle around my left ring finger, the reverse-shadow memory of the wedding band now retired to my jewelry box, has blended back into the surrounding skin as if I hadn't worn that ring twenty-four hours a day, every day, for three years.

"Nice nails." I've been quiet for so long, Steve must have started looking where I'm looking. "I like your, well, really, your whole look. You looked great before, but the sophisticated hairstyle—and the makeup—they suit you."

I'm blushing again. He thinks I look good right now? With the raccoon rings under my eyes from last night's mascara I didn't bother to remove?

"We should get started." I polish off the rest of the doughnut in three big bites.

"First, what are you doing Monday?"

And did he just say I "looked great *before*"? Would that "before" refer to my magenta- or beige-haired phase?

"Iris?"

And what is he doing commenting on my appearance anyway? The dog.

"Earth to Iris? What are you doing July Fourth?"

July Fourth is three weeks away. I assume I will be spending it as I do every other day—alone in my apartment, eating cereal. I hardly feel like celebrating; July's arrival will mean only that August is right around the corner. August will mark the halfway point of my unemployment benefits. I have got to impress Sandy Christmas at lunch this week.

I crumple the piece of waxed paper. "Let's talk about *your*

July Fourth plans, Steve. Vickie told me—let's see if I've got it straight. That Saturday you and Vickie are going to her parents' house. While she stays for the fireworks on Monday, you'll be catching the train back Sunday night."

"For golf. Right."

What Steve doesn't know, but Vickie also has told me, is that she's not at all pleased about his early departure. But he insists he has an early golf date in Westchester County with an important overseas client he can't ignore, and she's managed not to grill him for details or take him to task for leaving her alone on a national holiday. I admire her self-control. I can only imagine what might really be going on. Is the so-called client a certain blond bombshell? Is there even a golf game at all?

"You're spending the day with your mistress. Jessica. Right?" I already know asking directly won't get me anywhere, that restraint would be the better tactic.

"I've told you I won't answer questions like that. It was part of the terms of our deal."

"I think we should change the terms. Are you spending July Fourth with Jessica?"

He looks at me for a long moment and opens his mouth as if to answer.

I stay perfectly still. He's dead serious. There's no trace of smugness on his face. This could be it: the big confession.

He scuffs his shoe against the ground with extra force. A small cloud of dust rises up from under his feet.

A tickle starts at the back of my nose.

Dust floats higher into the air.

Don't sneeze, Iris. Don't ruin the moment. I'm finally wearing him down . . . down . . . ah . . . ah . . .

"*Achoo!*"

"Bless you," Steve says. I wait for him to go on.

"Did you want to tell me something?"

He looks away.

Behind my sunglasses, I shut my eyes and savor the darkness for a moment, then open them reluctantly. "Right, Steve, golf. A business meeting with a business associate. On July Fourth. Must be one important client, to lure you away from your wife. Or maybe that's your idea of Independence Day."

I'm no longer trying to hide my sarcasm. Even so, he refuses to take the bait. His self-control is as impressive as Vickie's is.

"Forget I even brought it up," he says. "Let's get to work."

Furious at myself as much as at him, I settle back on the bench and prepare for a new round of wife-coaching.

The next day Vickie answers the door of her apartment holding a pair of blue surgical booties in one hand and balancing a bowl of strawberries against her hip with the other. "These are for you," she says. I can't figure out which she means, until I notice she is wearing blue shoe covers over her driving moccasins and that the two workmen in the living room have them on over their heavy boots. "To protect your shoes from the dust," Vickie explains.

"Maybe we should go someplace else." It isn't just an excuse not to wear the booties. Being in Vickie's apartment, even in the vicinity of her building, is making me jumpy. I could almost feel Steve's presence in the lobby, even though Vickie insisted when she summoned me here that he was at his company's Long Island office for the day—she'd even called to check up on him.

In answer, Vickie looks down conspicuously at her midsection. "I'm not really feeling up to it."

So I take the booties and slip them over my backless shoes, thinking on the one hand that at least I don't have to go barefoot, but on the other how ironic it would be if, having finally triumphed over my blister problem, thanks to Vickie, I ended up breaking my neck on the way into her living room, also thanks to Vickie.

I slide-stumble toward my usual chair. The living room is now in full renovation chaos, with plastic draped across the walls, drop cloths covering every piece of furniture; on the floor, the plaster dust is Pompeii-worthy.

Vickie coughs, opens the door to a minuscule terrace, and steps outside into a cacophony of roaring engines and wailing sirens from the street below. "This is my last refuge." She ushers me to one of two wrought-iron café chairs set up at a small matching circular table. We sit, she wearily, as if, despite the supposed improvements in her marriage, she's still up nights worrying. Her undereye circles are even worse than mine were yesterday, and she has a cluster of pimples on her chin. It's a first: blue shoe covers and all, I look better than she does.

The table is laid out with cloth napkins, glasses, and a chilled bottle of Perrier. Vickie sets down the bowl of strawberries and slides it closer to me. "I bought them at Eli's this morning. They're grown upstate in the Hudson Valley. I know most strawberries come from California, but the local ones are really good. Try."

I select a strawberry and take a bite. She's right; it's delicious.

"If you think those are yummy, wait till blueberry season," Vickie says.

Between berries, I fill her in on yesterday's meeting with Steve. The session boiled down to two main points, each so awful in its own way, I don't know which to start with. Vickie looks at me expectantly. I decide to begin with the second point. "He, um, said women should never, ever ask their husbands, 'Honey, do I look fat?' "

I'd been thinking this was the less offensive of Steve's two pieces of advice. As soon as it comes out of my mouth, I wish I could take it back. I look away as Vickie rubs her belly with both hands. "Why would he bring that up now?" She spoons a heap of berries onto her plate. "It's not like I can help it."

I'd thought the same thing when Steve brought up the topic yesterday, and had yelled at him for his shocking insensitivity. "She's pregnant with your child, Steve. Show some respect!" Then, of course, he had looked utterly mortified and hadn't been able to stop apologizing. At one point he even reiterated that he'd like to end our wife-coaching sessions once and for all, but I browbeat him right out of that idea.

I pour some Perrier into Vickie's glass. "We could talk about this some other time. You don't have to follow, or even hear, every last bit of his advice, you know."

"It's all right. I can stand it."

I take an extended drink of my own water. "Okay, he says the problem with the question is that there's no right answer. If he says yes, you'll get mad at him, and if he says no . . ."

Vickie scoops out another heap of fruit. "I'll tell him he's a liar."

"Right. He says, better not to ask at all. Even if you were to have put on weight, he may not have noticed, so why bring it to his attention?"

"I've never thought of that."

"Me neither."

"Though how he could not notice right now is beyond me," Vickie continues.

"Well, I told him if men were smart, they'd all answer that question the same way: 'Of course you're not fat. You're sexy and beautiful.' "

Vickie smiles sweetly at the strawberry she's holding, and says to it, " 'Of course you're not fat, darling, you're the sexiest, most beautiful woman I've ever seen, and I love you.' " She pops it into her mouth.

I take another berry. " 'And even if you were fat, which you aren't in the slightest, I would still thank my lucky stars every day that I married you.' "

Vickie grins. "What's wrong with being fat, anyway?"

"Absolutely nothing." The truth is, I think I'm too thin at the moment.

"Women are supposed to be round. We need to be, to care for our babies."

"Right again. Still," I continue, "if you must ask the question, I suppose it's better to ask a girlfriend."

Vickie laughs conspiratorially and helps herself to more. "I'll spare you having to answer that one."

TWENTY

In the end, I do tell Vickie Steve's other pointer, which is that to accuse one's spouse continually of infidelity creates a self-fulfilling prophecy. In Steve's view, the accused grows resentful and figures, *You already think I'm guilty; I might as well go ahead and do it.* The accuser is then saddled with the permanent task of policing the accused's every move. "A terrible way to live," Steve told me, "no matter which side you're on."

Vickie props a foot across her knee and repositions her blue bootie. "That makes a lot of sense, actually. You know, I'm still starving. Do you want anything else to eat?"

She excuses herself and goes back through the terrace door toward the kitchen. I watch her tiptoe through the plaster dust.

She returns to the terrace with a barbecued chicken in a plastic deli container. "He's right. I should stop assuming he's guilty. You keep saying yourself he's done nothing wrong." She tears off a drumstick.

Tell her, my little voice scolds. *Tell her you have your own suspicions about her husband. Go ahead.* I fidget in my café chair; the iron back is digging into one of my vertebrae. "Perhaps you shouldn't follow his advice to the letter."

"Why not? Our marriage is going great. This year's trip to Southampton might even turn out to be a second honeymoon."

"I don't think so!" I am shocked at how harsh I sound. Vickie notices, too, because her smile fades. Then, incredibly, my moderator persona takes over. "Vickie, I apologize for interrupting," Moderator me begins calmly. "I'm wondering, do you know anyone named Jessica?"

Vickie has just bitten off a huge chunk of chicken leg. She screens her mouth with her hand. "Jessica?" She swallows slowly. A faraway look comes into her eyes. What a relief—she's getting the message.

No, she's only thinking. "When my mother's tennis elbow gets really bad, she sees a physical therapist named Jessica." She shifts in her chair. "Or maybe it's Jana. No, Jana is the receptionist at the country club. What is the name of that physical therapist?"

Never mind, I tell her.

"Oh!" Vickie says. "There's a girl in this building named Jessica."

Goose bumps on my arms. Dry mouth. Momentary vocal paralysis. I watch with detachment as a pigeon flies in for a landing not six inches away on the ledge of Vickie's teeny terrace, fixes me with its beady red eyes, and flies off. Wouldn't it be awful if Steve's mistress has been right here in Vickie's building this entire time?

"Have you ever"—I cough delicately—"seen her with Steve?"

I hold my breath.

Vickie stares at me.

Then she bursts out laughing.

"Oh, my God! A girl named Jessica. A child! I was chatting with her mom in the elevator the other day!" Vickie's eyes are teary-wet in the same way I've now seen a hundred times, except these are tears of mirth. "Take it from a fat, suspicious wife: She's no threat. Oh, Iris," she giggles, "you've been doing this too long."

I've definitely been doing this too long. My idealistic plan to save Vickie and Steve seems to be backfiring badly. There are too many feelings I can't explain: pangs of jealousy when Steve explains how Vickie can improve their marriage and when Vickie talks glowingly of Steve's latest kindnesses. Divided loyalty toward both of them, at different times. And the better I get to know Vickie, the worse I feel about deceiving her. For someone who abhors cheaters, I am feeling more and more like one myself.

By the time Thursday rolls around, I'm thinking it couldn't have come at a better time. Sandy Christmas is going to treat me to lunch and then offer me a job. She virtually told me as much when I called to reconfirm this morning. "I'm so looking forward to catching up with you! I think you're very talented!" Her enthusiasm was heartening.

I splurge on a cab over to Undine's because it simply wouldn't do to perspire in my new shirtless pantsuit and adroitly applied (by me!) eye makeup. On the way I imagine the possibilities: Sandy offers me an apprenticeship, which I parlay into a full partnership in the Christmas Company in eighteen months, and my own shingle in two years. At that point, I could work from anywhere—even move back to Los Angeles. Perhaps somewhere other than the San Fernando Valley. I've always liked Laurel Canyon: those rustic, tree-shaded houses tucked up against the Hollywood Hills. In enough time maybe I could afford one and stock it with books and clothes. The cab driver pulls over exactly seven doors past the spot where I've asked him to, and I accept my receipt and climb out, taking care not to step in a puddle of brackish water at the curb.

Undine's is appealingly decorated with mismatched chandeliers and table settings of odd pieces of old hotel china. "Christmas party? You're the first one here." The hostess leads me to an empty table for two. I sit and continue fantasizing: After Sandy hires me, the very first thing I'll do is pay off Steve's loan, in full, with interest. Five minutes go by in a snap, then five minutes more. I embroider fine details onto my fantasy: I'll replenish my savings and start investing again in my retirement account and, to satisfy that long-ago career columnist from *Cosmopolitan*, put away two months' salary in case a time like this ever happens again. Which it won't, because I am going to be a great moderator.

Another five minutes pass. The hostess seats two businesswomen, each ignoring the other and carrying on her own cell phone conversation, a few tables away. I check my cell for a missed call from Sandy saying she's running late. There isn't one. I set the phone on the table in case it rings.

I flag down the hostess. "Has the other member of my party maybe arrived, but you forgot me?" She promises I'll be the first to know when Sandy shows up.

A waiter comes by praising the gnocchi appetizer. I order it, hoping Sandy won't be offended. By now it's twenty-five minutes past the time we were supposed to meet, and I'm worried about fainting from hunger during the interview.

At thirty-five minutes, the appetizer comes out. I spoon a few gnocchi onto my plate, leaving plenty for Sandy. I know she loves pasta. And Ilona said to save room for dessert.

By forty-five minutes, I've eaten most of the appetizer and duck into the ladies' room to refresh my lipstick. I stand near the sink and call Sandy's office. Her assistant says she's on her way to a meeting. I rush back to the table, sure she'll be there.

She's not.

After an hour, I pay the check and take the subway home. My answering-machine light is on.

"Iris, it's me, Sandy! Listen, I can't make lunch! It's crazy busy around here! Call me soon to reschedule! Does fall work for you?"

Conveniently, Simon is home to listen to me rage. I find him cross-legged on the floor in front of his glass-topped Noguchi coffee table, digging through a grocery bag. The mingled scents of men's cologne and peaches permeate the room. "Half my unemployment check, wasted on a stupid appetizer," I tell him.

"Don't you get it, kitten? It's not meant to be." He pulls a peach out of the bag and carefully peels off the price sticker, then sets the peach on a square green ceramic platter the size of my bathroom floor.

"What's not meant to be? My ever being gainfully employed again for as long as I live?"

"Don't be a drama queen." He pats the empty space next to him on the rug. Rocky appears from behind the half-closed bedroom door and charges over to Simon. "I'm not calling *you*, Mister Piggy," Simon says in a baby voice. "That was for Iris. You think you're going to get some peach, but you're not, are you, you google-eyed food machine? You drooly little glutton." He holds Rocky back with a slippered foot. "You're still taking care of him while I'm on Fire Island, Iris, right? Good. Okay, sit, please, and help me with these stickers."

I take a peach.

"Careful, careful!" Simon directs. "No manhandling!" For a few minutes we peel stickers in companionable silence. Then Simon looks up. " 'Not meant to be,' as in working for this Candy Christmas person. What kind of parents would name a child Candy Christmas? I hope at the same time they wrote the poor girl a check to cover twenty years of psychotherapy."

"*Sandy* Christmas. She made up the name herself. It's called self-branding."

"Then she's even dumber than I thought. Candy Christmas is much cuter. Don't you think?"

"Actually, yes."

"Then it's settled. No working for that one. On to more important topics. How does this look?" He slowly, and with great effort, rotates the platter.

I probably shouldn't tell him I've already left a message for Sandy Christmas that I'm available to reschedule whenever she wishes.

"You must really love peaches." There must be two dozen, stacked artfully in a casual pyramid shape. Several have leaves attached, a straight-from-the-farm effect not easy to achieve with produce from the corner Gristede's. Knowing Simon, he went through three hundred individual peaches, looking for leaves. "How many can you possibly eat?"

He sets the platter in the precise center of the coffee table, turns a few peaches to the right or left, takes one off the top, and sets it on the table just so, as if it had rolled off and landed there. He stands to admire the effect. "They're not to eat, kitten; they're to look pretty."

I keep Simon's concept in mind while I'm dressing for my Saturday-night date with BuzzBuzz: Look but don't touch. It has me in a wardrobe quandary. The skirt and blouse look too uptown for a downtown gallery opening; the dress is far too sexy for someone I've never met. Val should never have insisted I do this. I don't even want to go anymore, if I ever really did.

I start to pull on the pants from my pantsuit and discover something else to be mad at Sandy Christmas about: a dollop of Undine's olive oil on the waistband. I set the pants on the edge of my armchair and retrieve the rest of my dirty dry cleaning off the closet floor, where it's been sitting for weeks, to bring in along with the pants first thing Monday morning. Sorting through the pile, I wonder if, instead of paying to clean all these sad skirts and tops, I really should toss them onto the sidewalk trash heap as Simon suggested.

But this—it just might work for a gallery opening.

I untangle my navy linen shift from the rest of the cleaning. The dress is wrinkled beyond recognition and smells faintly of mildew, but perhaps no one will notice after I steam it out in the shower and give it two dozen or so spritzes of the only fragrance I own: a focus group leftover called Convivial. Ten minutes later, when I pull on the dress, I reek like a perfume factory and look as if I'd just come from a nice eight-hour nap on a park bench. I take the dress back off and slip into the blouse and skirt. Before I walk out the door, I stash fifty dollars and Simon's special lipstick blend in my bag. Then I go to the corner to catch a cab.

The Meatpacking District is yet another of Manhattan's formerly sordid areas that has transmuted into a fashionable neighborhood. The buildings are low and old, the streets are cobblestone, and the effect is of stepping back into old New York—except with bazillion-dollar bankers' apartments. I walk down Little West Twelfth Street to the spot where the gallery should be, and find a windowless brick structure with an unmarked, graffiti-plastered door. My stomach butterflies slam their wings together apprehensively. It's eleven thirty at night. What kind of man makes a date at eleven thirty? What am I doing here? Me, Iris, who thought Steve might chop me up into little pieces and feed me to the ducks.

The butterflies start fluttering again, this time at the thought of Vickie's husband, and as I'm hating myself I understand that Val, in her own way, is right. It is time to get on with my life, to get Teddy and Kevin and, most of all, Steve out of my head. I have to do this and trust it will turn out okay. Who knows?

Maybe I'm too big a cynic; perhaps we do get more than one chance at love.

An artistic-looking couple walks up. The man opens the red metal door, and the two disappear into the building. That settles it. After a final whispered appeal to the dating gods—*please, let this be not so terrible*—I step through the door and climb a clanky metal staircase toward the sound of voices.

The stairs lead to a room with white ceilings and white walls: a big, shiny box populated by gallery goers in outfits so eccentric that my wrinkled, moldy dress would have been right at home. A man in a three-piece orange-mesh suit greets me by holding out a glass canister of small, shiny white squares. He spoons three into my hand and says, "Come back if you need more."

A new art-world drug? Not going to find out. When he's no longer looking, I slip the squares into a trash can near the tired-looking fruit-and-cheese platter set up by the guest book. Now, where is BuzzBuzz?

The sole piece on display is a rubbery, grayish free-form sculpture, whose title, *Chicle Resin No. 4 (White)*, becomes immediately clear. Those little white things weren't drugs but gum; now that I look closely, everyone in the room is chewing. Their jaws pop open and clamp shut in choppy, unconscious unison, like the mouths of an army of robots. Sometimes somebody removes his or her wad and adds it to the sculpture. A man in baggy camouflage pants studies the giant lump, wrinkling his forehead in concentration. Wait, I know that forehead. I step up and touch BuzzBuzz lightly on the sleeve.

My date doesn't turn around. He takes his gum out of his mouth and smashes it onto the sculpture. Then he says, still not facing me, "NewGirl."

"Right, that's me! My name is Iris. What's yours?"

BuzzBuzz leans in toward the sculpture, removes the piece

of gum he just stuck there, squishes it with his fingers some more, and reattaches it. In keeping with the other eccentrically costumed gallery patrons, my date has chosen to wear a thermal shirt with the long sleeves hacked off at the elbows, the better to show off the matched set of dragon tattoos on his forearms. He turns around. "Buzz."

I giggle and blush. "No, your *real* name."

"Buzz." He repeats the word louder and more slowly, as if for someone whose first language isn't English, and looks past me, over my shoulder, for a moment. He wipes his gum-sticking hand down the side of his pants and extends it toward me. I manage to shake it without wincing. Note to self: *Must not use right hand at cheese-and-fruit table.*

Still, Buzz had the right idea asking me here; a gum sculpture is a perfect first-date conversation starter. I study the tiny speck he has contributed. "What do you think of the art?" I emphasize the last word and roll my eyes, Val style, to convey that I'm in on the joke. *Chicle Resin No. 4 (White)* is in no way intended to be art. It's the maker's way of thumbing his nose at the art world.

"A masterpiece." Buzz gestures toward the man in the orange-mesh suit. "Jonas over there spent thirteen years preparing—chewing Chiclets and storing the chewed pieces in refrigerators all over the city. It's pure genius, and an important evolution from his earlier, pink works in Bazooka." Buzz lifts his chin and again looks past me, over my shoulder.

I say, "My thoughts exactly." Not exactly; my thoughts are on what Buzz could possibly be looking at. When he doesn't stop and I can stand it no longer, I turn around to spot a group of Nordic model-types standing near, though not eating, the Brie. And as if I were a superhero, I feel myself transforming yet again into my angry alter ego, Fidelity Girl: making the world unsafe for the unfaithful. "Hey!"

Buzz doesn't seem to hear. I wave my hand in front of his face. "What is it with you? Do you think women don't notice when you leer at other women? Oh, I know what you'll say next: 'It's the male's biological destiny to propagate the species with as many different females as possible.' Right? Well, what are the rest of us supposed to do while you're carrying out your search right in front of our noses? Where's your wallet?"

"What?" I finally have Buzz's full attention.

I look him over. At second glance, his fatigues are so voluminous, they border on rodeo clown pants. I'm not sure I could locate his wallet.

"Where's your wallet, Buzz? It's the female's biological destiny to find the best male to provide for us and our offspring. So perhaps every time a woman catches a man looking, she should take twenty bucks out of his wallet."

Buzz looks at me as if I were crazy, but doesn't move. He seems to be waiting for me to continue my tirade. I can think of nothing further to tell him. So when it turns out to be Buzz who says something to me, I miss it.

"Speak up, Buzz," I snap begrudgingly at his forehead. "I didn't hear you."

Buzz smiles lazily. He tilts his head back and regards me through half-closed eyes. "What I said was, 'How about we go back to Dumbo and fuck?' "

At ten minutes to one on what is now Sunday morning, I should be trying to reach the New York State Department of Labor—surely at this hour there can't be a busy signal. But I had a rare moment of epiphany in the cab on the way home and feel compelled to act on it right away. This is why, instead of calling for my unemployment money, I'm dialing Val and announcing, "Do I have the man for you!" I'd worried briefly that she might be at home asleep, but by the laughter and ruckus on her end of the line, it's clear I need not be concerned. "Where are you?"

"Out," she shouts, "with the Hayes Heeley gang."

"Fun." I try not to sound hurt. Lately the whole world seems to be one big party to which I'm not invited. "I had that date from Matemarket."

Val yells, "How was he?"

I step out of my shoes. "He's *your* perfect man. He's an artist, he's got tattoos over at least twenty percent of his body, and practically the first thing out of his mouth was, 'Come home with me to my loft and let's go to bed.'"

"I missed that. What did he say?"

"'Let's go back to Dumbo and fuck.'" My elocution is so crisp I could be having tea with the queen at Buckingham Palace.

"Cool! Did you?"

"No, I got his number. For you. Want it?"

"Sure, why not? Can you e-mail it to me? I've got to go, Iris." Before she hangs up I could swear she says something that sounds like "namaste." She's gone before I can ask her to repeat it.

I retrieve my bag from the floor and fumble around inside until my fingers connect with something soft: the paper napkin with Buzz's scrawled number on it. I turn on my computer and dash off an e-mail to Val. Afterward, there's nothing left to do but make that dreaded weekly phone call to the Department of Labor. Seconds later I'm pacing across the apartment—six steps, east wall, six steps, south wall—getting a busy signal, hanging up, hitting "Redial," getting the busy signal, hanging up, hitting "Redial," busy signal, hang up, redial; busy signal, hang up, redial; busy signal . . . Repeat twenty-six times; hurl handset against wall in a fit of pique—and watch it clatter in pieces to the floor. Lord have mercy, I've killed it! I leap off the bed and scramble to pick it up. Heart pounding, hands shaking, I fit the batteries back in, snap it all back together and hit "Redial."

I hear a ringing at the other end and want to cheer. Not only has my phone survived, I've gotten through to the unemployment office!

Even more astounding, an actual human being answers. "Namaste!" cries a female voice that sounds, incredibly, like Joy's. It doesn't occur to me that this person might be someone other than an actual live, human customer-service representative from the New York State Department of Labor, nor does it strike me as odd that such a person would sound like my mother as opposed to, say, a frustrated, underpaid government drone. "Gosh," I tell the voice, "I'm calling for my check?"

The customer-service representative who sounds like my mother says, "Iris?"

This spooks me even more: She knows my name?

"Iris, a late bedtime is no good for your qi. Do you have insomnia? Try orienting your bed so your head points east. That should help."

Cognitive dissonance strikes yet again: It *is* my mother. Somehow, my phone has dialed not the unemployment office in New York but self-employed Joy in Scottsdale. "Sorry. I kind of called you by accident."

"It was no accident, Iris. I was summoning you. I've been sending you messages. On your answering machine and through your e-mail. When you didn't answer those, I performed a summoning ceremony."

"I haven't gotten any messages." It's not technically a lie. I am aware that my mother has been calling and e-mailing; I simply haven't been listening or reading.

"Let it in, Iris. Open your heart. You can't close yourself off to what the world is trying to tell you."

"Sure I can, Joy."

I hang up, hang my skirt and blouse back in the closet, and go into the bathroom to get ready for bed. It's only when I walk out, toothbrush in hand, that I notice the flashing light on my answering machine: two new messages. Could one of them be Sandy Christmas? Would she call me on a Saturday night? Simon will kill me, but if it were Sandy and she asked, I'd happily get dressed again and meet her for lunch right now. How much more of an indignity could that be than dyeing my hair Scarlet Sunset or passing along remedial romance pointers?

No, I will not allow myself to hope. No doubt it's Joy and Teddy again. I press the button.

"Hello. It's Ilona at Rubicon. I know it's late Saturday night, and you must be out, but I just got home from the store and remembered you'd had your big interview, and I wanted to see how it went, and how you're enjoying your new clothes. Please remember, if you need anything—alterations, girl talk— let me know." It's not Sandy. But this is a level of service I didn't know existed. I'm beginning to understand the allure of being an "insider" in Manhattan.

Message two. Please let it be Sandy. Pretty please.

"It's Steve."

I drop the toothbrush, toothpaste and all.

"Sorry to bother you at home, but I've been thinking. I can't do this anymore—keep giving you pointers for Vickie, that is. It was a bad idea from the very beginning and now it's best if we stop. I know you'll be upset; it's just the way it has to be. My schedule is going to be brutal through at least the end of the month, so I wouldn't have been able to make our Tuesday meetings, anyway."

No more meetings? Why does this feel worse than being stood up by Sandy Christmas?

". . . need to talk to you about something and it has to be in person. I'd really like to see you July Fourth. The fireworks at South Street Seaport are spectacular, truly, and you shouldn't be sitting home by yourself on Independence Day. It's unpatriotic. So how about we go together?" A pause. "Call me." He ends the message with his cell phone number.

Appalled. Incensed. I should be both. What we have here is a clear case of Vickie's husband asking me on a date. Is that not what just happened? Is that not proof this man is a dog? And yet, my heart jumps. I'm flattered. I want to go.

That makes me appalled and incensed.

And what's this about no more wife-coaching for Vickie? He can't do this to me—I mean, he can't do this to her.

Before I consider what I'm doing—specifically, calling a married man in the middle of the night—I'm dialing Steve's cell phone and listening to it ring. Once, twice, three times, four. This is far too risky. I'm going to wake Vickie.

Just as I come to my senses and am about to disconnect, Steve answers, sounding dazed and weary.

I start right in yelling. "Are you out of your mind? Did I just hear you ask me out on a date? Have you gone insane? And now you've got me telephoning you at this ungodly hour, probably waking up your wife? What were you thinking?" Never mind that *I* chose to return his call. He still deserves to be yelled at. "Where's Vickie? She'd better be asleep or we'll both have hell to pay."

He says nothing for so long that if it weren't for the faint traffic noises on the other end, I'd think we'd been cut off. For a moment I'm happy that I won't be caught by Vickie having a middle-of-the-night tiff with her husband. Then another, even more sickening thought occurs to me. Is it possible he doesn't know who this is?

"I didn't mean to offend you, Iris." So he does know it's me. That's a small relief.

"Didn't mean to? How could you not think asking me out would offend me? If you think I'm going out with you somewhere while you abandon your wife in Greenwich to watch fireworks by herself, you're out of your mind. Unless . . ." *Hang on, Iris; here's an even more appalling possibility.* "Unless you're trying to use me as an alibi. Could that be it? Vickie will be out of town, and you want me to be able to say to her, 'I can assure you, Steve wasn't with another woman. He was with me'? And why can't we meet anymore? Are you so busy with your 'affairs' that you can't make time to help your wife? You're a rotten husband, Steve. Do you know that?"

I imagine him in his and Vickie's dark living room, scuffing his feet in that way he has through the plaster dust, whispering into the phone while Vickie dreams alone in their bedroom. I wonder what he wears to bed. I picture him in lightweight pajama bottoms, the city lights streaming through the window, pale blue and amber on his bare chest.

"I want you to tell me who Jessica is right now," I hiss.

"Iris. You need to believe me. I'm not the man you think I am." He sounds so gloomy and solemn that it only makes me angrier. "There's no ulterior motive. I'm not trying to establish an alibi. I'd simply like to explain some things to you. As friends. It's up to you. I'll be in front of the building, Twelve Seventy-five Lexington, at eight thirty, July Fourth. If you're not there, I'll understand completely, of course, and wish you well. I've enjoyed spending time with you. If you are there, great."

"I won't be there." I carry my fallen toothbrush into the

bathroom and run it under the hottest water the tap will provide.

"I wish you'd reconsider."

"It'll kill Vickie that I won't be passing along any more pointers. That's on *your* conscience. Not that you have one."

"Good-bye, Iris."

I hang up then, and climb into the bed, still in my makeup, and turn out the light.

"Good-bye, Steve," I say into the empty room.

I awake a few hours later, tired, irritable, and unsure what to do next. Call the Department of Labor again? Call Sandy Christmas and leave a second message? Call Vickie and tell her . . . what? That Steve asked me on a date?

None of this seems manageable. Nor does figuring out how to explain to Vickie that her husband and I are no longer speaking. What does is walking over to the deli on Columbus and getting some coffee. ("Good new haircut," the coffee man says to my surprise.) At six thirty on Sunday morning, there is almost nobody on the street, though two blocks ahead of me, a stooped old woman pushes a cart full of newspaper. I take my cup and wander down Columbus past the sidewalk café where, ten days ago, Rocky and I bumped into Steve and Jack/Snooky. The drinking trough is dry, and the windows are painted over, with a notice on the door: "This Space For Lease by Empire Property Management." I'm almost expecting to see Steve listed as the leasing agent, but the contact is someone else, a J. Catherine Armstrong.

Near an overflowing trash basket on the corner, sparrows brawl over a discarded muffin. At the bus stop a woman in her mid-twenties awaits the downtown M7 in a cocktail dress and heels. Is this a walk of shame?

I turn back the other way and walk north, past my corner, where the middle school's bleak concrete-and-asphalt playground is empty of the students who give it life when school is in session. But even in summer, on Sundays it becomes the site of a lavish, city-approved flea market. I sip my coffee and watch the vendors setting up tables of yellowed linens and antique picture frames. Stylish New York couples will begin arriving in a few hours, hand in hand, on their way back from brunch, impulse-buying decorative accent pieces.

What am I doing here? I ask myself for the second time in less than twenty-four hours. Not here at the flea market, but here in New York alone? Did my mother feel this way even once after she went off to Scottsdale? Did she ever, even for a moment, regret what she had done?

Another couple of blocks, and I am standing in front of Rubicon, squinting through steel security bars at windows that would be black-dark even if the store were open for business. I wish I had never left home. Yes, the Valley is a superficial, unsophisticated, plastic place. But it's easy. The sun never stops shining, and the air is predictably brown; cashiers always smile when they give you your grocery bags, and every waiter hopes a TV mogul will sit at his open table. If it's shallow, at least you know what you're getting. In New York, nothing is what it seems and nobody is simple. Steve is an entitled rich kid with compassion for others, a flouter of marital rules with a better understanding of marriage than anyone I know, a cad with a heart of gold. I thought Ilona would be cruel, Simon would be hateful, and Buzz would be soulful. I even misjudged Simon's dog.

At home, I leave a message again on Sandy Christmas's voice mail and try again in vain to get through to the Department of Labor. Then I crawl back into bed and, despite the coffee, fall into a hard, dreamless sleep. When I wake up, groggy and stiff, it's late in the afternoon, and I'm not sure what to do for the rest of the day, let alone the rest of my life. But I have made one small decision. I may not know anything else, but I know what I'll be doing on July Fourth at eight thirty.

TWENTY-ONE

Nothing much happens for the next few weeks. My job hunt remains fruitless; my e-mailbox continues to teem with Matemarket missives until at last I figure out how to take NewGirl's profile out of the running—by claiming to have met someone—and the notes begin to taper off. I phone Val several times, at work and at home, to see if she'd like to have lunch or coffee, but never get through; even when her out-of-office message doesn't have her traveling for focus groups, she doesn't respond. Simon invites me to his apartment a few times, but he, too, is busy; it's high wedding season and he has hair consultations with one overanxious Manhattan bride or another almost every day of the week and, on weekends, wedding-day house calls morning to night. I think of Kevin and his upcoming wedding and miss him, too, or perhaps just the idea of him. I think of what I was doing this time last summer: fighting with Teddy; realizing, painfully, that our marriage just wasn't working.

I leave a message or two for Vickie, hoping to hear from her. I feel obliged to share my suspicions about Steve and this mysterious Jessica person, but she was so angry when I told her there would be no more marriage advice forthcoming that I am sure she plans never to speak to me again. I miss her more than I expected to.

Meanwhile as June progresses it grows ever warmer outside and by July Fourth, it's breathtakingly hot—a wet, woolly heat that I conclude must be what New Yorkers are describing when they complain about summer weather. Despite the most valiant efforts of the air conditioner, my apartment is stagnant and damp at dawn, and by late afternoon, after I've closed the heavy shutters and the curtains on my two curved front windows, the room is stifling. *Should I do this? Is it worth it?* I debate. But I still feel I owe it to Vickie, or at least to myself.

The heat is no better as I cross the park, with its listless picnickers sharing takeout pizza on old bed quilts, hoping for a breeze, and pass the closed shops on Madison and the sleepy, majestic apartments on Park, until I reach Lexington. I stop across the street from Vickie and Steve's building. I have no intention of meeting Steve. I'm here to follow him.

It's eight fifteen, and the sun is still noon hot in the sky. I settle in for my stakeout in the feeble cover of a skinny city tree and watch the traffic on Lexington ebb and flow, and the Merit House denizens come and go. A white-haired couple arrives with a carful of bulk groceries that the doorman loads onto a bellman's cart. (Imagine room to store a dozen rolls of paper towels!) A woman steps out onto the sidewalk carrying a toddler in a backpack-style baby carrier. (Aren't the two of them sweltering?) A few moments later, out comes a trio of middle-aged men in denim shorts and tennis shoes. (Was there ever a time when adults didn't dress like third-graders?) I fan myself with the hat Simon has loaned me for disguise: a straw bowler he said would be cute for Independence Day.

Steve, looking thinner and more tired somehow than he did when I last saw him at our doughnut meeting weeks ago, steps out under the awning. He looks first up Lexington, then down Lexington, and then across Lexington and, finally, diagonally across Lexington, directly into my eyes.

I lower my hat brim and try to fold in on myself, down to a quarter of my width, the better to fit behind the scrawny tree. I hold my breath, as if this will somehow make me thinner. Now, if only there were a way to muffle my telltale heart. Above the street noise, Steve and everyone else in the city must be able to overhear it. Yet, as with every other time before, Steve doesn't seem to notice me. He turns to look back up Lexington one last time, puts his hands in the pockets of his faultlessly broken-in chinos, and crosses to the subway entrance at the corner. For another few moments he stands there, shifting from foot to foot, seemingly waiting. Could he still be wondering if I'll come? He looks around one last time and slowly walks into the station.

That's my cue. As soon as he's down the stairs, I run after him up the street, ignoring the brutal heat, calling, "Sorry! Sorry!" to the pedestrians I dodge past, and charge down the staircase after him. At the bottom, I stop short, duck my head, dig frantically in my purse for my MetroCard, find it, and push through the turnstile. Once on the platform I peek from under the brim of my hat to locate Steve. I'm in the wrong place! This is where the local train stops. To get to South Street Seaport I need to be on the express platform. I hurtle down another set of stairs to the lower tracks. A number 4 train has just arrived, and miraculously, as its doors slide open, I see Steve waiting to board the next car up. Coincidentally, directly behind him is the woman with the baby carrier, to which is now tied a red, white, and blue heart-shaped balloon; and behind her stand the three Merit House gentlemen in their shorts and tennies. Everyone on this platform must be going to the same place. It's too late for me to get into Steve's car; the train doors are already sliding shut, the sweaty crowd behind me pressing me into the car closest to me.

Except that, for once, I've planned ahead, studied my city map, and am betting Steve will get out at Fulton Street. I'll have to trust myself: I'm pinned into the center of my car, with little chance to peek out through the doors to check if he exits somewhere before then.

The train starts with a jolt. I'm thrown off balance and

stumble backward. The woman behind me looks daggers at me. "Sorry," I say, before it occurs to me I'm not at all. As the train lurches its way south, I make another mental note to start using "excuse me" in this kind of circumstance, saving the apologies for times when it's genuinely my fault.

Twenty minutes later the train doors slide open at Fulton Street, and the steaming, glistening human blob drags me out with it and deposits me onto the station platform. I look around wildly for Steve and spot him heading toward the exit turnstile. It's hard to believe how smoothly this has gone so far. How fitting that the first time I have a spying assignment completely under control, I'm working for nobody but myself.

Someone grabs the back of my shirt.

I whip around, fists clenched. I'm not paranoid, but even I know that in this city you have to be on guard.

The tapper turns out to be a woman in her mid-seventies, together with another woman of the same age—sweet, grandmotherly types you'd expect to enjoy guided bus tours, book clubs, and trips to Disney World with their grandkids. "Can you tell us which way to the fireworks, hon?"

I can't locate Steve in the crowd. "Uh . . . it's, um . . ." There he is. Thank goodness.

The woman pats me on the arm. "Never mind, dear, I thought you lived here."

Out on the street it's easy to figure out where I should be heading, since the entire mass of people is going the same way. All I have to do is stay a few paces behind Steve—and his neighbors, still walking nearby, as if they'd all made a date to see the fireworks together. I let the crowd sweep me along, keeping my eyes on Steve's straight back, until we all arrive at the security checkpoint at the pier. The crowd automatically funnels itself into a narrow set of rows, patiently waiting as uniformed police officers pat down pockets, open bags, and wave metal-detecting wands. "The price of freedom," some-one says.

Steve gets through quickly. So do the denim-shorts men, who drift off into the crowd and disappear. The woman with the heart balloon doesn't do as well; the officers motion her off to the side to check over and around her child carrier, like this would be the ideal place to stash explosives. If it weren't two policewomen searching her, I'd think the extra attention had more to do with her tall, slender figure and long, honey-colored hair. The toddler—a boy, it looks like, in blue shorts and tiny red sneakers—is as cute as the woman is pretty, with yellow curls and dimpled pink cheeks. He rubs his eyes as if he's tired, and lays his little head on his mother's shoulder.

In the end, the officers wave her through, and in a few more moments it's my turn. I have no trouble getting past the check-point. I move through and propel my way toward Steve. I've kept my eye on him the entire time.

"Watch it!" someone hollers when I squeeze by too closely.

"Excuse me."

Steve finds a spot for himself down near the end of the wooden pier, and I push forward, trying to get as close as pos-sible, no longer worried about him spotting me. If he hasn't so far, I'm home free. As the sun takes its time going down I look around, at the Brooklyn Bridge looming magnificently above the crowd, at the old pier warehouses renovated, natu-rally, into restaurants and shops.

When I turn my attention back to Steve, I have a moment of fright; he's not standing in the same place. Oh, wait, there he is, a few steps to the left, talking with . . .

The beautiful woman with the heart-shaped balloon.

Talking animatedly, as if he knows this person very, very well. She's laughing at whatever he's saying. I can't hear them over the crowd, but it's evident they haven't just met.

He drapes his arm around her shoulder. The toddler is fast asleep. Steve gently ruffles the boy's hair.

The woman leans in close and says something.

Steve laughs.

All at once I understand who this is.

I duck behind a couple dressed in matching Old Navy flag T-shirts. At the top of my lungs, I yell "Jessica!" Yet again I'm surprised by the strength of my own voice.

The woman turns her head.

Steve turns his head.

The two Old Navy wearers turn their heads. Then, probably thinking they're doing me a favor, they step aside, red, white, and blue human curtains parting to reveal me backstage, exposed, mortified.

———

The next four seconds play out like a time-lapse movie: First Steve's jaw goes slack. His face freezes. Then, slowly, recognition dawns.

For a moment I'm back in a parking lot fifteen years ago, feeling the same expressions blow across my face like storm clouds.

He touches the woman's arm and says something. She smiles and nods. He crosses the eight feet separating us. Then he smiles, a grin of what I could interpret as genuine delight at seeing me, or genuine schadenfreude at catching me. "You made it," he says. "I'm so glad. I'd still like to talk to you."

"I didn't come to see you. I came for the fireworks." My face is aflame. It is clear he knows I'm lying. I pull off my sunglasses and hook them onto the front of the new black form-fitting top I bought last week for six dollars at Rainbow. I squeegee the sweat off my nose as delicately as possible with my right thumb and forefinger. "I was following you, Steve, which you doubtless already know."

He wipes his forehead with the back of his hand. The heat is still unbearable, even with the sun having taken leave of us at last—a guest who's finally understood he's outstayed his welcome.

"I caught you, Steve. It's obvious what's going on here. That woman you're with—she's Jessica."

Steve laughs. "Wrong."

"You're lying."

"She's my sister."

Outrageous! He thinks he can fool me with that? "You don't have a sister! You have two older brothers, Paul and Tommy. Paul is a lobbyist in Washington, and Tommy teaches history at a prep school in Boston. Don't even try to pretend otherwise, because I got it straight from Vickie."

Steve is so calm, it's galling.

"How about I ask her myself? Excuse me." I push past Steve and start over to the spot where he and Jessica were just standing. But Steve's mistress, along with her heart balloon and her towheaded toddler, has vanished: a hallucination, a ghost. I whirl back around so quickly, I almost collide with Steve. "Exactly what is going on here?"

A shrill whistle slices through my question. Then a burst. Then, high above me, the explosion of a thousand pieces of light.

"Oooooh!" shouts the crowd.

The fireworks have started.

"Who was that woman?" I yell. "Steve—"

A shower of diamond glitter floats down over the East River.

He takes the smallest step toward me and gently, so gently, presses his finger to my lips.

My entire body goes liquid. Half a dozen explosions rock the sky. I look at him, then past him, at the blue, green, red, and purple sparkles drifting back to earth. *He's going to kiss me. He really is going to kiss me.*

"I'm so happy to see you," he says.

Who knows if he's shouting or whispering. Who knows where we are. The fireworks, the noise, the city, the heat, have all evaporated, leaving only Steve's touch, the pull of our bodies to each other, and, at long last, the feel of his mouth on mine, his hands in my damp hair, the two of us melting together, heat rising from our embrace like the steam that powers the city and escapes in billows from below the streets. We kiss as fireworks crash across the July sky, as the people whoop and applaud at the spectacle above them, light dancing on their upturned faces. We kiss as "Stars and Stripes Forever" and "God Bless America" swirl around us, the music drowned out by the beat of our hearts. We kiss after the fireworks are over, our arms wrapped tightly around each other, with the crowd pushing past us on the way back to homes and jobs and the responsibilities that await in the morning.

We kiss until I pull away. "No," I say. "No, no."

Steve brushes his lips against my hair. "It's okay. We've both wanted to do this for such a long time."

"We can't."

"We can. I . . . Vickie . . ."

"No!" I cover my ears. I don't want to hear his excuse. I search frantically for Simon's hat, which has fallen near my feet. All I want to do is flee. Down into the sweltering subway, onto a packed train car, back to the lonely safety of my apartment. I take off at a run through the thinning crowd, pushing past anyone in my way. I do not say "excuse me."

And I don't turn around when Steve shouts my name. I keep running, through the twisted, nonsensical streets of downtown

Manhattan, turning corners, running into dead ends, doubling back, and running faster, until somehow I stumble onto the subway station. And once down the stairs and through the turnstile, I lean against the white-tiled station wall and try to will my body to stop shaking. I take deep breaths all the way home on the train, my back pressed against the sliding doors, and at last I'm running up Amsterdam from the Seventy-second Street station to my building, up the front stairs, through the two outer doors, and into my hot apartment, where the phone is ringing.

I unplug it, toss Simon's hat onto my armchair, strip off my sweat-soaked clothes, and lurch into the shower, letting the lukewarm water cool my face. I towel myself off and climb into bed, with nothing on and my hair still wet. I turn the light off and the television on and stare glassy-eyed at infomercials with the sound on mute, wondering what Joy might say about a situation like this, and what on earth I am supposed to do now.

I wake up with a start: *I forgot something!* The thought starts my heart pounding all over again. Surely it can't be good for it to race as much as it has in the past—how many hours? The TV is still playing infomercials, and headlights from cars passing under my window are flashing hypnotically on my ceiling, and I run through some possibilities for what I've forgotten: not Rocky—that starts next week. Not Sandy Christmas—I've given up leaving her phone messages. It's "phone" that finally does it. Right. I still need to call in for my check.

The thought of my weekly tango with the unemployment office busy signal makes me even more miserable than I already am. Then I decide, why not take a whole different approach tonight to this task? I'll assume it will take a hundred tries to get through. I'll put on the speakerphone. After that I'll lie here in the dark, dialing and redialing, until the computer finally picks up. I'm strangely at peace. You need do nothing but stay calm, I coach myself, and for your trouble you'll get paid. I plug in the phone, hit the speaker button, and punch in the number I now know by heart. I wait for the sound of the connection being made, and the busy signal to begin.

It doesn't. The only sound is silence.

I keep waiting.

On the other end, someone clears his throat.

"Who's there?"

"Hello?" he says at the same time.

I'm hoping beyond hope it's anyone but the person I think it is. Teddy's lawyer, a bill collector, some man from my past who's mad that I stole his T-shirt—anyone.

"We have to talk."

It figures. The one time I guess right. "Steve, I'm hanging up."

"First let me—"

"There's nothing to explain! What we did was a mistake that won't happen again. Now, would you hang up? I need to make a phone call."

"Now? Why?" He must think I'm going to call his wife. I should call Vickie, but I just can't face that confrontation right now. Or ever. There's no need to tell her, is there? It's a mistake that will never be repeated, and all we did was . . . I shiver involuntarily as the memory of Steve's kiss plays down my spine.

"I'm calling the stupid unemployment office. It's none of your business anyway."

"Why are you calling the unemployment office now?"

"For my paycheck, and it's going to take fifty tries to get through. So good-bye."

"Don't you know you can do that on the Internet?"

"Good-bye!" I disconnect. Dare I try to use the phone again? What was that he just said about the Internet?

I go to the Department of Labor Web site, and there is a way to claim benefits online. Three minutes later I'm finished. I don't know whether to be jumping up and down with elation or prostrate on the floor, weeping over how much time I've wasted. If one wanted, one could extrapolate this to describe my entire life.

What a mess I've made of everything.

I pick up the phone again. Resolute, I dial Steve's cell number.

He picks up on the first ring. "I'm glad it's you. We do need to talk."

"No. I called to tell you we can never see each other again."

I hear him sigh softly. "Can't we have lunch first? Say, next week?"

"Next week—it couldn't possibly have slipped your mind—you'll be in Southampton. Through Labor Day. *With your wife.* Maybe you'll get lucky and Vickie will be so busy getting pedicures and shopping for designer baby clothes, you'll have time to recruit for your harem." I instantly regret the cheap shot at Vickie. Here we all were thinking she was being pathetic, inventing this cheating-husband nonsense, when, the whole time, she was right.

"Iris, this has all gotten so convoluted—"

"Please, don't call me. Don't try to contact me. Don't just happen to show up where I am. I don't want to bump into you walking down Columbus or at the copy shop."

"What?"

"Forget it. As far as the money I owe you—"

"Don't worry about—"

"—you'll have it by the end of August. I'll leave a check at

Rubicon by Labor Day. You can pick it up when you get back."

"Iris . . ." If I didn't know better, I'd say he sounded despondent.

"Go back to your wife," I tell him before hanging up for the last time.

TWENTY-TWO

Just in case, for the next several days I go out of my way not to cross paths with Steve. I avoid the park in the early mornings (not difficult, really). There's not a chance I'm going near the East Side. On Friday I decide to take a walk uptown, and choose Broadway instead of Columbus so I won't pass Rubicon. While I walk I try Val at the office, and she actually answers the phone.

"How have I been for the past month? Busy busy busy!" she reports. "I've been out every night, and Michelle is being a slave driver. I'm flying out to do more groups tomorrow and then going back for more groups right after those are over and am trying to crash out a report this afternoon. I haven't slept in weeks!"

She doesn't ask how I'm doing. She doesn't recognize that while she complains about being overworked, I can't get a job anywhere. Not anywhere. Last week I stooped to answering a help-wanted ad from a telemarketing firm. When I called the contact to follow up she said she was working through the 312 résumés she'd received. I turn to walk back home.

"Has it ever occurred to you that my life isn't exactly conducive to spiritual renewal?" Val continues.

I realize, suddenly, that the only time Val is ever interested in my life is when she's telling me what to do. Otherwise, she talks about herself. In some ways, Vickie was the better friend. She was a spoiled princess, yes, but she did have a self-awareness her sister doesn't seem to possess. Back in March I would have described Val as a fun-loving free spirit, but now I might as easily call her selfish and unfeeling. As if my ability to judge character weren't already at a lifetime low, I may have gotten the Benjamin twins wrong, too.

"I've got to go back to work. Namaste, Iris," Val says before hanging up. Why is she talking like my mother?

I find myself in front of Fairway, the gourmet grocery store, and wonder if it might cheer me up to eat something other than stale cereal. I go inside, promising myself to spend no more than twenty dollars, but before I know it I'm tossing into my basket every last luxury food I haven't allowed myself for months. I buy estate-grown tea, fresh-baked sourdough bread, imported olives, smoked cheeses, two pounds of organic plums, three boxes of blueberries, baby asparagus, Italian salami, a cheesecake. I ask the cashier to have it delivered. Back out on Broadway I smile at a family passing me in the crosswalk, stop to listen to a saxophone melody drifting down from a brownstone window.

The feeling fades as soon as I get back to my apartment, so empty and small. I've spent days trying not to think about Steve, what the two of us have done. *He was using you, Iris,* chides my little voice. *He was capitalizing on a romantic moment to distract you from the fact that you'd caught him with Jessica, his lover. Above all, he was making sure you won't mention a word of this to Vickie. You must admit, Iris, it's a brilliant strategy.*

"Too bad, kitten, but your little voice is right." Simon's mouth is full of olives, but other than that he is utterly serious. "This guy's a classic married weasel. Believe me, I'm familiar with the type. Don't feel guilty. You were used."

The Fairway deliveryman brought over no fewer than six bags, all at once, three in each hand, without breaking a sweat. Good thing I thought to call Simon, and not just because it kept me from phoning Steve; as it happens, I no longer have much of an appetite.

"Blueberry season. Love it! I'm going to eat a ton of these on Fire Island. Have some, doll face." Simon pulls a few blueberries out of their old-fashioned green cardboard carton. "They're nature's little antioxidants."

"You go ahead."

Simon munches appreciatively. Then he looks up, stops, and waits.

"It's just that he didn't seem to be trying to deceive me," I say, because he seems to want me to say something.

Simon helps himself to more blueberries. "I know, kitten. That's what he wants you to think."

Two days later I'm lying on my bed, searching for hidden messages in the plaster swirls on the ceiling, when the phone rings and, to my surprise, it's Vickie. My heart starts to pound and my stomach starts to hurt, until she tells me she's called to bury the hatchet—which really only makes me feel more awful than I already do.

"I wanted to apologize before I left. We're leaving for the beach in the morning."

Try not to think about it, Iris. "I remember. Have a wonderful time."

"Thank you. We will."

There's nothing left to say. Part of me wants to insist that Vickie confront Steve immediately and demand that he come clean. Another part is pushing to admit my own moment of weakness with her husband. Those parts are being trumped by the part that can't bring itself to say a word.

"You should know something." That's Vickie speaking. "When I first hired you, I was sure I was wasting my money.

You so clearly had no idea what you were doing. Every time you came back insisting Steve was innocent, I wanted to fire you. Actually I wanted to scream at you and then fire you."

"You did scream at me."

"I feel terrible about it, too. You were so helpful, giving me all those tips. I can't believe how much I've learned. Maybe he was cheating before. Who knows. But now I'm becoming the kind of wife he's always wanted. I'd been such a witch."

I stay still and concentrate on my breathing.

"Before you helped open my eyes, I would have just excused my behavior—'Oh, it's hormones,' or whatever—when what it also was, was me being so upset at Steve, wanting him to do everything my way. I'm turning into a better person, though. It's hard to change, but worth it, don't you think?"

How far Vickie seems to have come from the self-absorbed woman I met that first day in Grand Central. I'm more disgusted with Steve than ever, knowing he's now got her right where he wants her. It's *The Taming of the Shrew*, except that in this version Petruchio gets not simply a docile, well-behaved wife, but one he can cheat on with impunity. I hate him. I really do. I look back up at the ceiling and then follow the crown molding around the room, noticing the beauty of the woodwork, carved into oak leaves and acorns.

"Are you all right, Iris? I know you don't have a lot of friends here yet. Will you be okay in the city with everyone gone?"

"I'll be fine." I am not going to cry. I won't.

"Have a good rest of the summer, then. Thanks for being there for me. I'll call you after Labor Day, and we'll go to Bergdorf's again. I have a plan to get you free samples at Bobbi Brown."

"You have a good rest of the summer, too."

"We will. He's promised we'll do a lot of talking and walking on the beach. On the days he has to be in the city, I've got girlfriends I haven't seen all year to catch up with."

Stop! Stop! Danger! "Did you say he's going to be in the city?"

Vickie laughs. "Ever heard of a Hamptons widow? He can't quit working, because somebody has to pay for the beach house. It's fine. He promises he'll be with me a lot more this year than last. There are simply some meetings he can't get out of."

I try to keep the shake out of my voice. "Are you sure it's really business? It seems awfully suspicious."

"I used to think the same way. You said it yourself, though. The more I act as if I don't trust him, the more it'll drive him away."

"Steve said that. I only passed it along."

"I'm glad you did. It's time I put my faith in him."

What would another woman do? Would she break down and confess? Would she insist that Vickie not go on the vacation she sees as a second honeymoon? Would she rob a pregnant woman of the fantasy that her husband will be there for her child?

"There's another thing," Vickie adds quietly. "Promise me if someday you two bump into each other, you'll never tell him the true story."

This is too much to take. "I promise."

"It's a shame, really. He's never, ever mentioned you, but I think you were his first woman friend." She sighs. "I bet he misses you."

"Just please make sure he treats you well."

"Everything will work out for the best. You'll see, Iris."

Memo to all eight million residents of New York City: I apologize. I was wrong to call you a bunch of whining liars.

New York in August really is hell on earth. Compared to now, the Fourth of July heat wave was a gentle breath of spring. This heat, the real heat, begins near the end of the month, after both Vickie and Simon have left town, when I awake early one morning so uncomfortable, I'm convinced my air conditioner has died in the night. On further review I find it's still groaning in my window—it's just no match for the stagnant mass of swampy air that has descended over the city. I find Rocky lying listlessly on the floor of my bathroom, tongue lolling out, head pressed against the base of the toilet, as if recovering from a wild party.

"Come on, Rock." I peel him up off the tile and half-drag him out for his walk. "At least we're wretched together."

He whimpers.

Wretched we are—he because he's stuck wearing a black fur coat, and I because I'm lonely and confused and too lethargic to do much else except take serial cold showers, which still steam up my apartment and further burden my air conditioner. It's even worse when it's time to take Rocky outside; there's no breeze to cool us down or to blow away the stench of three centuries' worth of garbage and urine soaked into the ground. It feels as if I were breathing through a mildewed sponge.

As the days pass with no change, I can do little beyond take Rocky to the curb in front of my brownstone and shuffle to the deli for the daily iced coffees that are now the only thing I'm able to get down. It seems there is an eating plan even more drastic than the divorce diet: the desperately-trying-to-forget-you-kissed-a-married-man diet. By early August I've dropped another five pounds. I look malnourished and skeletal.

One morning when Rocky and I arrive at the deli, a man I've never seen is operating the coffee machine. Where's the other guy? I ask.

The strange man puts a plastic lid on my cup and hands me a straw. "Jersey Shore."

I've been abandoned completely. Art, my mail carrier, has gone back to his home country for a month; Simon calls every few days but is absorbed in the new boyfriend he's met on Fire Island. Val is away, too, though even if she were here, I doubt I'd call her.

And Steve. I try not to imagine him with Vickie, strolling along the shore, the tide soaking the hems of his linen trousers, as they discuss their lives together; or sharing appetizers at a calculatedly quaint outdoor café. I try not to torture myself with thoughts of him gazing into her eyes and kissing her the way he kissed me.

Rocky, stretched out asleep on the worn kitchen linoleum, whines fitfully.

Another day, the phone rings. The lights are off and the shades drawn; the apartment is dark and oppressive. I've long since stopped thinking it might be an offer of work, and let the answering machine pick up. "Checking on you," Vickie says. "If you're not okay, call me." I erase the message as soon as she hangs up.

By the second week of August, week four of my self-imposed exile, I feel so physically and mentally unwell, I make myself go for a walk. It can't be good for Rocky, lying in my apartment day after day. I coax him up and manage to comb my hair. When that wall of sodden, stinking air hits me, I try to disregard it and set out for Central Park, thinking it might not smell as bad there. As we walk over to Central Park West, the wind picks up, blowing a discarded copy of the New York Observer into the street. It's a hot wind, but it's movement.

Too late, I realize the sky has also turned an unearthly shade of green. A streak of lightning tears over the park, accompa-

nied by a cinematic clap of thunder and a drenching hot
shower. Rocky and I stumble back across Central Park West,
but we're soaked through by the time we get to the other side.
There's no use hurrying anymore, so we trudge slowly home
through the storm, the rain plastering my hair and clothes to
my skin.

It figures—the phone is ringing when I arrive, dripping, at
my apartment. I don't pick up, peeling off my sodden clothes
and leaving them in a puddle inside the door. "Rocky, stay," I
command, and step into the bathroom to find an appropriate
dog-rag hidden among the wedding linens. There isn't one.
What does it matter? I step back into the living room to dry
off Rocky with a towel that cost more than a whole day's
worth of unemployment money.

By this time the caller is speaking into the machine. "Iris,
please pick up. It's your husband."

"Husband" gets my attention.

"You need to pick up. It's important. Please."

Teddy isn't speaking in an accent. Despite the heat, an icicle
of fear pricks my heart. I pick up. "What's wrong?"

Teddy's voice is shaking. "I have news."

I start to sweat. Beads of it roll off with the raindrops. Then
I start to shiver. What has happened? His roommate borrowed
his car and used it to rob a bank. The house has burned down.
There's been an earthquake, a flood, a plague of locusts. A me-
teorite is headed for Studio City. Teddy's been arrested. Teddy
has leukemia.

"I got work."

My knees buckle, and I sag onto my bed. A job? That's the
news? Teddy is always getting a job. He's had twenty since I've
known him. "That's good, Teddy. Are the hours okay? I hope
no graveyard shift this time." At least now he can start pay-

ing off my share of our tax refund, one minimum-wage paycheck at a time.

"No, Iris, I got *work*. A commercial. A national commercial, actually. Listen to this: 'Go after it, girl.' " When he
speaks the line his voice is silky-smooth as a lounge singer's.
"My agent just called. I wanted you to be the first to know. It's
a really, really big deal." He takes a breath. "Forty thousand
dollars."

Agent? Teddy has an agent?

"That's not all. Shug's friend is making a student film in
Death Valley. It's called *Death Valley*, and I'm in it. I'm the
crazy drifter who kidnaps the innocent teen hooker at the
truck stop. It's like the third biggest part. There's no pay, and
it's going to be about a hundred and twenty degrees out in the
desert, but he's going to try to get it into some film festivals,
and who knows where that might lead? It could be my ticket
out of voice-over."

Teddy is already looking for a ticket out of voice-over?

"Iris, listen to me. Do you want to come home? Back to
L.A.? We can take it slow, you know. We can have Martin put
the divorce on hold, and you could move back into the house.
I could kick out Miller and Shug. You could stay in the guest
room and we could talk."

I'm stunned and rain-soaked, burning up all over again.

"Are you there?"

Forty thousand dollars?

"Iris? Do you want to come home?"

I could go back to the Valley. I could be with all my friends,
in my old, familiar life. Teddy and I could talk. I squeeze in
front of the air conditioner. Its breeze is none too cool and
smells like wet pug. "But, Teddy, I walked out on you."

"Yes," he says. "Maybe we can make it work this time,
though."

I could leave this city at last and be back in my normal life. It's what I've wished for all along.

"But I can't come home. I don't have a car, or a job, and I've got a dog I'm taking care of," I hear myself say.

The air conditioner churns, and Rocky snores on my towel. I wait for Teddy to say something, and start to shiver again. Will he renege on his offer? Did I hear it right in the first place? Was there ever, anywhere, as pathetic a human being as I?

But I did hear right, and Teddy doesn't renege. "I'm making money now. We'll buy you a car. And you'll find a job. Pat Sweeney would take you back in a heartbeat," he adds, invoking the name of my former boss.

My eyes fill with tears at my husband's sweet naïveté, but my little voice declares, *Vintage Teddy. Yet again he hasn't thought something through. After taxes, and once he pays off his debts, he'll be lucky to have enough left of that forty thousand to get a car* wash, *let alone a car.*

But even before the internal monologue is over, my answer to Teddy is perfectly formed, sparkling-crystal clear. "Teddy." I'm smiling so hard, my cheeks hurt. "I *would* like to come home."

He's never going to change, you know, the voice says.

"Really?" Teddy sounds as if he hasn't been expecting that answer.

"Really. I can't leave here until after Labor Day, though. I'm taking care of my friend's dog until then."

"Actually, that's even better. Work is going to keep me busy. I'll have the commercial to do, and right after that I'm heading out to the desert for the film, and then I'm supposed to leave from there for Baja for a couple of weeks with the guys. I'm not even sure I'll be able to use my cell phone. Why don't we plan to talk the week after Labor Day?"

"That's great, Teddy. And congratulations. It's amazing."

"Bye, Iris. I love you."

I try not to notice that he says the "I love you" in a Russian accent.

That night I dream that Teddy, Steve, and my friend Evie's husband, Doug, are standing with me at a scenic lookout in the Angeles Crest Mountains, on the side of a precarious, twisting road. I'm holding the square plastic container of my father's ashes from the crematorium. Teddy and Doug are joking and laughing. Steve steps forward to help me release my father's remains, beige-colored bits of gravel, over the edge of the cliff. They scatter into the air and become raindrops, and I hold the empty container and sob to Teddy and Doug, "He's gone! He's never coming back!" But Teddy and Doug have vanished. Steve has transformed into my mother, who claps her hands together and says, "Go after it, girl!"

In the morning, something has changed.

Rocky is whining to go out, as usual, and the air conditioner is groaning away in the window. Early light is trickling in through the closed shutters. When I take Rocky outside, it's still as sultry as ever.

Then I realize what's different. For the first time since my trip to Fairway in July, I'm hungry. I consult the fridge: nothing but salami. But the loaf of bread is in my freezer; I take it out and spend ten minutes chipping off chunks with a serrated knife. I eat four frozen slices' worth before moving on, though it's only seven in the morning, to the salami. My stomach doesn't hurt at all.

After breakfast I find myself wanting to go out and do something. It's no good hiding in the apartment, trying to avoid the summer. If the heat has moved in for a while, I should make peace with it. More important, I realize it would be a shame to leave New York without ever having taken advantage of what it has to offer.

I shower and change, set out food and plenty of water for Rocky, leave the bathroom door open so he can sprawl on the tile, and step out into the sweltering city. I walk up the street to the Museum of Natural History and spend three hours in its cool, cavernous halls, admiring dinosaur bones and meteorites. In the planetarium I lose myself in the nebulae and galaxies whirling across the dark dome overhead. I marvel at the life-size whale model in the oceans exhibit and spend a long time standing before the three-million-year-old Lucy skeleton. A sign says those of her species, *Australopithecus afarensis*, were among the first human ancestors who walked on two feet instead of four, allowing them to come down from the trees and venture into uncharted territory. I picture Lucy, alive and whole, a fragile creature so close to human, leaving the safety of her treetop for the wild, windswept savannah.

My walk home takes me past the bench where Kevin and I sat months ago debating Steve's innocence, and I feel a stab of something sharp and painful, but it passes quickly. Back in my apartment I order three dishes from Szechuan Palace and eat most of it, slipping Rocky chicken and water chestnuts. As I'm taking the cartons out to the trash, I think, *I'm going home.*

I spend the next afternoon exploring the Met, its upstairs rooms of Rembrandts and Cézannes and downstairs labyrinths of Greek vases and medieval suits of armor. In the Egyptian hall I find a monolithic black granite sarcophagus and an unscrolled *Book of the Dead;* a mummy lies flat on its back behind a thick wall of glass, yellowed wrapping bound tightly around its small body. Beside me a freckled girl in braces, maybe eleven, whispers to a woman who must be her mother that it was wrong to have dug up the mummy. "Now he'll never get to the afterlife."

Her mother puts her arm around the girl's shoulders. "Sweetie," she says. "Maybe this *is* the afterlife."

In the days that follow I go to the Guggenheim, the J. P. Morgan Library, the Museum of Modern Art, the Whitney. I visit the New York Public Library on Fifth Avenue, with the lion statues crouching at its entrance, and feel transported back to another era. I ride the ferry to Staten Island to see what it's like. As it chugs back toward Manhattan, I take in the jagged skyline, the silent enormity of this place, when approached from the outside in. For a moment staying in New York almost seems worth it. Then I think about my friends, the bougainvillea on the chimney of my house, Teddy's peanut-butter sandwiches. If I try hard, really hard, to be the kind of wife Teddy wants—more supportive, more easygoing—maybe we can make our marriage work.

When I get home I call Teddy to say hello but get only a computer recording that says, "The customer you are trying to reach is out of range."

I begin taking Rocky for longer walks into the park, letting him lead me where he wants to go. One drizzly morning he makes his way over to the reservoir and across to the bottom of the staircase. He starts up the stairs, but I hold tightly to his leash. He strains harder, trembling with the effort.

I drop anchor with my umbrella, planting its point in the earth. "Rocky, no."

He digs in his feet and pulls harder. It takes several more borderline-inhumane yanks on his leash before he lets me lead him away.

We end up back there the next day and the day after that. By the third try the relentless little nuisance has worn me down. I follow him halfway up the stone staircase, and when he stops on the landing, I sit and let him flop onto my feet. The oaks and maples make a canopy over us both. It's peaceful here, as long as I don't think about . . .

"Come on, Rocky. Time to go." I pull his leash, and we walk back toward home.

Even so, we keep returning to the reservoir, and as the days go on, I dwell less and less on what happened. On the staircase early on the last Thursday in August, I linger on a step with a cup of coffee and a collapsible bowl of water for Rocky—bought at Gracious Home and to be bequeathed to Simon once I leave. I'm surprised to discover that the thought of Steve has become a faded bruise, only painful if I press down on it deliberately. Someday soon this all will be in the past. I'll be back home, with a job and another chance at my marriage, and I won't focus on my failures.

Teddy will never change, my little voice insists. *He is who he is. You'll end up in exactly the same relationship, with exactly the same problems.*

I think back to the sounds of my old street: the eucalyptus trees rustling, cars rushing past on the freeway above, my neighbors having a pool party, bursts of laughter and soft splashes drifting up from their side of the fence into the ozone-scented Valley air.

That life you're so homesick for—it isn't your life anymore, the voice says.

"*Woowoowoowoowoo! Woowoowoowoowoo!*" Rocky leaps up from his spot at my feet. "*Woowoowoowoowoo!*"

"Shush!" I give his leash a quick jerk. Dogs aren't allowed at the reservoir, I remember, and though it's not against the rules to have Rocky down here on the staircase, I still get harsh looks from the disciples who run the track even in this weather.

Rocky can't get his mind off the squirrel, or the butterfly, or the leaf, or whatever it is that's bugging him. He barks and howls frantically.

On the path below us, a dog barks back with equal frenzy.

So that's what it is. Perhaps its owner will have the sense to avoid confrontation, to lead his or her scrappy mutt off in the opposite direction.

It's too late. The dog, an energetic, tan-and-white dog, bouncing and straining at the end of its leash, comes rushing up to us. The dog is followed by a brown-haired, brown-eyed man about six feet tall, wearing shorts and a T-shirt, about to go for a run.

I freeze. Rocky howls. Jack—because it is Jack—leaps vertically into the air.

Steve strides toward me. "Hey!"

I'm already up and running.

"Wait!"

I don't wait. I pick up the pace instead. Heat or no, I'm in far better shape now than I was in May—all that walking and Rollerblading and mad-dashing—and feel almost no pain racing back toward my side of the park. The only thing slowing me down is Rocky, so I stop to pick him up and continue my sprint, at the same pace, with his fifteen-pound deadweight in my arms. Behind me Steve is still calling after me, and Jack is still barking. That, too, eventually fades away, until the last sounds left are my feet against the ground, and the clink of Rocky's heart-shaped name tag as I bounce him along.

I run until I reach the west wall of the park, and only then allow myself a peek behind me. Steve is nowhere to be found. Just in case, I continue jogging until I reach the steps of my brownstone, and set Rocky down on the sidewalk. The minute I stop, I'm overcome with dizziness and nausea. Feeling about to faint, or throw up, or worse, I hunch helplessly against the banister, hoping the sensation will pass.

It does, after a minute or two of deep breathing. When it seems possible, I straighten halfway up and start up the stairs. I'm soaked in sweat, exhausted, and desperate for water. So focused am I on my goal of getting into my apartment, so intent, that I nearly trip over someone sitting at the top of the stair-case.

"Oh! Sorry! Pardon me!" I manage to eke out before re-membering my vow to stop apologizing automatically.

"Only you can pardon you."

The voice is all too familiar. I jerk my head up. When I do, I'm sick and dizzy all over again.

This time it's got nothing to do with the heat.

My mother rises from her spot on my stoop. She dusts off her skirt and spreads her arms open in welcome.

"Look who's here!" she says.

TWENTY-THREE

Is it possible to die of shock? I jump about a foot into the air and shriek. Three passing construction workers stop. One calls, "Need help?"

I wave at him. No, everything's peachy, thanks.

Only it's not. It's not because here is Joy, in full goddess mode, teleported somehow from the Arizona desert, standing on my stoop. She's blonder than I remember, and tanner, too. She's wearing an ankle-length broomstick skirt, a watermelon-colored short-sleeved cotton sweater and espadrilles, and sunglasses attached to a beaded chain around her neck. As she steps toward me, her chime ankle bracelet gives a delicate ping, and a crystal prism around her neck sends a piercing shaft of light into my eyes.

She envelops me in a patchouli-scented embrace. "It's been too long!" I pry myself free. It's far too hot for a hug, even if I wanted one. She stands back to take me in—my red face, wet hair, and bedraggled clothing. "I was looking for a sacred space in which to rebalance my energy, and I thought, if there's a sacred space anywhere in this city, it will be in the park. I stopped over to see if you'd like to accompany me."

It's like the nightmare where you're rooted to the spot and can't run, fight, or call for help. "What are you doing here?"

"Darling, I came for the New Age Expo." Joy makes a clucking noise with her tongue. "You didn't open your heart to the communication, Iris. I suspected as much. That's why I assumed it would be better to drop by. It's a good thing I did. You look very, very unbalanced."

Naturally I'm unbalanced. It's six hundred degrees out here;

I've just finished a quarter-mile sprint wearing sandals and carrying a dog, to escape from the cheating husband of an identical twin; only to find my estranged mother on my doorstep.

"I don't want to rebalance my energy. I want to go inside and lie down."

"I understand. We each seek our own peace. Here." She takes from her tooled leather tote bag a card that says "Guest Pass." "For you. The Expo is at the Javits Center, and I've written my booth number on the back. You can always stop by my hotel, too. I'm on Central Park South at the Intercontinental, Room Ten-twenty, though I may be changing. The feng shui is a little"—she lowers her voice—"off."

I take the pass numbly.

"Namaste." Joy goes twinkling down the stairs.

I rouse Rocky and, zombielike, unlock my building's outer and inner doors and then the door to my own apartment. I unhook Rocky's leash from his collar and drop it onto the floor. Then, though it's barely eight in the morning, I do the only thing I can think of to do. I find the last bottle of alcohol in the apartment, the 1998 Cheval Blanc Bordeaux that was a wedding present from my coworkers. "To celebrate a milestone," someone wrote on the card.

If this were a movie the audience would be shouting, "No, Iris, no! Not the 1998 Cheval Blanc! You and Teddy will want that for your tenth anniversary! Go to the wine store on Columbus and buy some of that cheap Spanish red with the charging bull on the label!" Sorry, this is an emergency. I am simply incapable of processing the idea of my mother in Manhattan without an attitude-adjusting beverage.

I run down to Simon's for a corkscrew, then come back upstairs and uncork the Bordeaux. I am about to guzzle recklessly from the bottle when my conscience gets the better of me. I set the bottle on my fireplace mantel. Then I get my one wineglass, pour a bit of wine into it, swirl it around, inhale, and take a delicate sip.

Delicious. Sublime. Nectar of the gods, with a flawlessly balanced concupiscence that . . . oh, enough with the wine review. Three healthy gulps, and the muscles in my neck and shoulders relax. One glass, and I'm feeling much more myself again. Two, and the room is starting to spin. I stand shakily and pour myself a third glass.

BZZZZZ!

The front door buzzer sends me through the roof. This time I shriek even louder than I did at Joy, lurch backward, and fall against my armchair. This is it; I'm having a nervous breakdown, for real.

BZZZZZZZ! the buzzer sounds again. *BZZZZZZZ! BZZZZZ! BZZZZZ!*

I fling myself at my intercom, intending to hit the Talk button—to scream at whoever it is to get me an ambulance. Instead of "Talk," though, I accidentally push "Enter," and before I can stop it the front doors are opening and slamming shut and someone is knocking insistently on my door. That sets Rocky barking again. By now my nerves are so shot and I'm so drunk that without thinking, I yank open the door. Without even putting on the chain.

In runs Jack.

Steve storms in behind him.

"Iris . . ." Steve begins just as Jack rushes at Rocky, and the two dogs start jumping excitedly all over each other and us, and I lose my balance completely, tumbling backward, this time over my footstool, which overturns, sending my wineglass shattering into a thousand pieces, wine splattering everywhere, and me crashing to the floor hard, 1998 Cheval Blanc Bordeaux, arguably one of the greatest vintages of recent memory, streaming down my face.

Steve lunges toward me, his mouth contorted with what looks like fear. He drops to his knees and puts his arms around me. "Iris!"

I burst into tears.

Steve holds me at arms' length, checking me for signs of injury. "Shh," he says at last, folding me into his arms again, as I sob harder and harder. "You're okay. You're okay. You're fine." He uses his hands to wipe wine and tears from my cheeks. "Your place is a mess, but you're fine."

"I'm not f-f-fine!"

"You are. I'm here now," he murmurs. I sob into his running shirt. It's slightly damp, but mostly it's soft and warm and more comforting than anything I can remember, and he keeps rubbing my back until I start to calm down ever so slightly. The dogs have stopped jumping and barking and are now quietly eating Jack's leash.

"I'm drunk," I tell Steve. "I'm a wreck. Joy is here." Joy! I'd forgotten for a moment. I start sobbing all over again.

"Shh." He stands up. "Why don't you get in the shower?"

I look at him cagily.

"I'll go. I'll take these two outside. Would half an hour be long enough?"

"I g-g-guess."

"Good. I'll get you something to eat, and when I come back I'll work on putting your apartment back together." He hooks Rocky's leash onto his collar and clicks his tongue. Both dogs stand obediently. "Mind the broken glass," Steve reminds me. He opens my door and steps out into the hallway, closing it with a gentle click.

I listen until both front doors close. Then I scrape myself off the floor and totter into the bathroom. When I see myself in the mirror I almost start crying all over again. My face and clothes are streaked with wine and tears and dust and sweat.

Steve must feel pretty sorry for me. *I* feel sorry for me. I try to put it all out of my mind and step into the shower, hoping the water will drown out my little voice warning me not to let my guard down. *Don't let Steve fool you. He's just like everybody else.*

I squeeze my eyes shut and stand under the spray.

Thirty minutes later, when the buzzer sounds again, I manage not to jump. When I open the door in a clean top and my old sweatpants, Steve looks relieved. He brings the dogs inside, where they go straight for the food bowl in the kitchen. I take him up on his invitation to sit and rest, and spend the next fifteen minutes eating the scrambled-egg-on-a-bagel he's brought me and watching him sweep up broken glass, mop the floor, and sponge wine stains off my furniture. Then he notices my face and straightens up.

It's embarrassing, but watching him has me all teary. I bug my eyes out to keep them at bay, blinking a few times for good measure.

"What is it? You can tell me."

It sounds so much more genuine than Joy's typical "I'm here for you" that it nearly takes my breath away. "I was just thinking"—the words come out in a half-sob—"I've never seen a man use a sponge mop."

He looks at me quizzically for a moment, then chuckles.

"It's almost a miracle." I'm crying again.

Steve rearranges his expression into something more serious. "That's what you were thinking?"

I giggle, first a little bit, and then a little bit harder and a little bit louder, until I'm laughing helplessly. That makes him laugh again, and then I laugh harder because he's laughing, and soon I'm nearly hysterical. How could anyone not see the humor in Steve rescuing me from yet another mess of my own making?

I start to sob. The deep, shuddery kind of sobbing where your mouth gets all twisted up and your nose starts to run uncontrollably and you gulp for air and no matter what you do, you can't make it stop. I hide my face and hope fervently that Steve will have the decency to put down the sponge mop and leave. He doesn't. That is, he does set aside the mop, but only so he can crouch down and gently pull my hands back from my face.

"Tell me," he says softly as I whimper and gulp for air. "Tell me."

I manage to eke out, "Joy just showed up. Right on my doorstep."

"What?"

"No, who. Joy killed my father and ruined my life and now she's h-h-here and I should have checked my e-mail and I'm still drunk and I'm making no sense! Why are you in New York? Why aren't you in Southampton?"

"Why were *you* at the reservoir?"

"I was walking the d-dog," I answer between sobs. "How do you know my address, anyway? Does no one think to c-c-call first anymore?"

Steve gets up, and in an instant I've gone from praying he'll leave to fearing he'll leave. But he's not leaving. He's pulling up my wine-spattered footstool alongside the armchair. He balances on it, not looking the slightest bit comfortable, and leans toward me. "Ilona gave me your address. It was forward of me to ask for it. Why don't you tell me about this Joy person? From the beginning."

Just like that, I'm done sobbing. And then I'm talking. Maybe it's the wine. Maybe it's more than that. For reasons I will never fully understand, I choose Steve to confide in, to share the story I've never told anyone, not from the beginning. The story begins with my father taking me for an eye examination during my senior year in high school.

"Where was your mother?" Steve asks from below me on my footstool.

"Joy? At one of her classes—Qigong or Taoist yoga or one of the self-actualization workshops she was always taking. I didn't resent that she was rarely around, not then. I loved her for wanting to make herself a better person. What a joke."

It's time to bug out my eyes again. Steve produces a tissue out of thin air and passes it over. The thought *I must look awful* runs through my mind before I forcibly eject it. I am entirely over what happened between us on July Fourth, and couldn't care less about looking attractive for him. I blow my nose noisily.

Steve hands me another tissue. I clutch it. He pats my arm. "I'm still listening if you want to talk about it."

I guess I do want to. It makes no sense, but Steve, to me, in this matter, is trustworthy. I clear my throat. "Anyway, this day—it was February seventh, I remember exactly—my dad took me to Dr. Lieberman and waited for me in the waiting room, and when it was over we were joking around because the doctor had given me some of those hideous disposable sunglasses, and I was saying, 'Do these work with my outfit?' But when we got outside, I tossed them in the garbage. There was no way I was putting them on. The doctor's office was in a busy strip mall, and what if someone from school saw me in them? Is this boring you?"

"Not at all."

"Are you sure?"

"Go on."

In the kitchen, Rocky picks himself off the floor. He wanders over to me and leans with a grunt against my ankles. It seems okay to keep going. "I wasn't wearing the ugly doctor sunglasses and didn't have my own, because I'd accidentally left them in my locker. So while my dad was searching around for the car, there I was behind him like this." I hold my arm over my eyes. "Basically walking across a busy strip mall parking lot, off busy Ventura Boulevard, which is sort of like the Broadway of the San Fernando Valley, with my eyes shut."

"This sounds like something you would do."

"It was moronic. When my dad turned around and noticed, he told me to stop it. He insisted I open my eyes, which was just the height of irony, considering what happened next."

"Which was?"

"I kind of pulled my head up and squinted in what I thought was my father's direction, practically blind from the sun, and I saw . . ." The details of the scene are still vivid: I can remember how the spring haze had turned the sky white and diffused the sun's light into a generalized glare that made everything stark and surreal. The painted lines on the parking lot had nearly worn away, so that the cars were all parked slightly off-center, some straddling two spaces. "I saw my mother. In this parking lot, on this random Monday afternoon. She was with a man I'd never seen in my life, standing very close to him, but not seeing me."

"She wasn't expecting you to be there," Steve says. "If you're not looking for something or expecting something, it can be there in front of you, and your mind glosses right over it. It's as if your brain can't process the information so it ignores it."

"Did I ever tell you that?"

"It's a theory of mine. Go on."

I tell him about forcing myself not to shut my eyes again, watching my mother reach up and put her arms around this man, unfamiliar to me but clearly not to her, a tall man with a graying ponytail, in shorts and sandals; my eyes burning in pain as I watched him reach around her waist and pull her toward him, and waiting in dumb horror for the kiss I knew would come next, as sloppy and passionate as anything I'd beheld in the halls of Valley High. Then, with my insides twisting up into a tortured knot that would eventually come to be my constant companion, rushing over to see how my father was taking this—my kind, dutiful father in his studio-accountant suit, with his bad heart.

"Oh, no," Steve says quietly. "Did he have—"

"Not right then." My voice sounds cold. "The heart attack came eight months later. They'd split up. It was my first semester in college. He was gone before he reached the hospital."

"I'm so sorry."

"Thanks, me, too." It's brusque, but Steve can't possibly expect all my self-protective detachment to melt away instantly just because the story has finally been told.

"What did he do in the parking lot, when he saw your mother?"

My armchair is soft and enveloping. My apartment is surprisingly cool. Yet I can't seem to get comfortable. I try crossing my legs, lying sideways and throwing them both over the arm of the chair. I finally turn toward the wall and drape myself over the chair back. "He didn't see her," I say into the upholstery.

He didn't, I go on, because he wasn't looking for her. He was focused on finding the car and making sure he got me safely into it before I walked blindly into traffic. He was already there, unlocking the doors, holding the passenger side open and reaching in for his own sunglasses on the dashboard, holding them out to me and calling to me to watch where I was going and get into the car.

I put on his dark glasses and got in. Dad asked if I was feeling all right. He said I looked strange. "Like you've seen a ghost," he said. "Dr. Lieberman didn't put something in your eyedrops, did he?"

I didn't know what to do. I sat stupefied as he put the key in the ignition and the car came to life. I made myself turn and see what my mother was doing, but she and the ponytail man had disappeared. The entire incident had taken maybe five or six seconds, and I was already wondering if I'd seen it wrong, even knowing I hadn't.

I asked him, "Dad? Do you and Mom . . . Is there anything going on with you two?"

Dad eased the car onto Ventura and accelerated north. At the stoplight, he slowed down to let another car into the left-turn lane ahead of him. "Do you mean, are we having problems?"

I allowed myself to hope. Maybe he already knew. "Yes. You know, like, with your marriage."

All he did was smile at me. He said, "The only problem we're dealing with is, how soon after Iris goes off to college can we rent out her room?"

And I knew he had no idea.

"I spent the rest of the evening in my room, listening to the Smiths on my Walkman and staring out at the backyard. I told my dad I wasn't feeling well, which wasn't a lie, and when my mother got home much later, I didn't come out to say hello."

Steve still seems to be listening, and I tell him about how the next morning I tiptoed out of the house early. I sat in my car in the school parking lot until it was time to go in, and then after classes I drove up to Mulholland Drive, parked on the side of the road and looked out over the Valley until it got dark, and went home and straight into my room. I did that for two weeks until one night my father knocked on my door and asked, "Is there anything you need to tell me?"

I told him I was busy studying for midterms.

As it turns out, it was a lucky thing I'd gotten into college early-decision, because I pretty much bombed every test and term paper through the end of the year. My final report card was so dismal, I ended up being the only one of my friends who didn't graduate with honors. All this time my father was trying as hard as he could to get me to open up. He even took me out for breakfast and asked if I was having love troubles. It was horrible. I wasn't the one having love troubles; he was.

"Where was your mom during all this?" Steve asks.

"Going about her business. Acting exactly the same as always—oblivious and benevolent. Her behavior was so normal, I started doubting myself again. If it all had happened now, I would have followed her to catch her in the act." It's been months since I've done this much talking, and my throat is sandpapery. "With my spying talent, I probably would have accidentally run her over with my car."

Steve grins. "I wasn't going to say anything."

I manage a smile. "It is pretty pathetic. I'm the world's most inept private eye."

"You're not the best."

"Not the best? I'm the *worst*."

"But you're plucky. Like a grown-up Nancy Drew. I like that about you, Iris. I liked it the first time I met you. Nobody else does things quite the way you do." He picks up my water glass and hands it to me.

"Um, thanks."

"I didn't mean to interrupt you, if you feel like finishing your story."

I still do.

It went on like that the entire summer, I continue, me hiding out in my room with the curtains drawn (good grief, much as I did this summer) and not taking calls from any of my friends. I was a high-school graduate with three whole months of freedom I couldn't enjoy. All I could think about was my mother and that man with the stupid ponytail, and that my father was being made a fool of and I knew it and was too big a coward to do a thing about it.

"Then finally, the night before my parents drove me to college, I couldn't stand it anymore. My dad had gone out to get me toothpaste or something, and I was in my room packing the remainder of my clothes into boxes, and something came over me. I stomped into the kitchen. My mother was making herself coffee—this was before her macrobiotic diet—and I stormed in and blurted out, 'I know what you're up to!'

"Joy was holding a coffee mug. I remember exactly which one, an old one of my dad's, white with black letters that said 'Accountants do it by the book.' I thought she'd be afraid of me, but she looked emotionless, the way she always looked when I did something inappropriate. It was all those parenting books she'd read, where parents are never supposed to appear shocked or upset. That got me even madder, so I yelled, 'You're having an affair!' "

I demonstrate for Steve how Joy arranged her face into the special concerned look she used when I'd get really angry. "Then she started talking. I had assumed she would deny it and had an answer ready. It was an ultimatum: Either you tell Dad or I will. She surprised me. Instead of pretending she didn't know what I was talking about, she said as plain as can be, 'I've fallen in love with someone.' " My voice cracks a little but Steve either doesn't notice or doesn't mind.

"I wanted to grab my dad's coffee mug and throw it at her. My teeth started chattering. I sat at the kitchen table and put my head down. Joy kept talking. She went on and on: She didn't plan it to happen, and it had nothing to do with how much she loved me, as if I were a first-grader who thought this was my fault. She said she'd been a good wife to my father for nineteen years, and 'now, it's my time to be selfish.' She said she still cared for my dad but wasn't in love with him anymore. Just when I was about to start crying, my dad's car came up the driveway. I couldn't face him and got up to run into my room. Before leaving the kitchen, I told Joy I never wanted to speak to her again. To this day, I never really have. The next day, all the way to Pomona, I didn't say more than ten words to either of them, and when my dad went to hug me good-bye, I just—"

I'm about to lose the battle with the tears.

"—I pulled away. A month later, Joy finally broke the news to him, and he moved into an awful condo in Woodland Hills, and then a few months after that, he was gone."

I start crying again, but Steve looks neither horrified nor disgusted; living with Vickie must be good practice in dealing with unchecked female emotion. The thought of Vickie makes me cry harder. But I'm so far into my story now that I might as well finish the last little bit.

"The worst of it," I sob, "the worst thing of all was, I never did tell him the whole story. I kept planning to but never found the courage. He died not even knowing I was as big a liar as she was."

Steve says quietly, "It wasn't your place to do that. It was their problem, between the two of them."

A fresh burst of hot tears courses down my cheeks.

"They needed to find their own way," Steve goes on. "I've learned that from this . . ." he gropes for the word. ". . . From this adventure we've all been having, you and me and Vickie. Husbands and wives have problems. They all do. In the end each has to take responsibility for his or her contribution to those problems and to decide together, like adults, whether to keep trying or to move on."

The Elixir I put on after my shower runs into my eyes and stings them. Steve gives up handing me individual Kleenexes and just forks over the box.

"You and I have some things to talk about," he says. "Maybe now isn't the right time, but there's a lot I need to tell you. Very soon, because the longer things go on like this the less I'll be able to forgive myself." He looks very odd. His eyes are intent and his mouth is turned down at the corners, as if he has finally understood that infidelity isn't a victimless crime. "That was quite a story, Iris," he adds.

There's no excuse for what happens next.

My mother had a dozen for what she did to my dad and me. That partnerships are meant to dissolve when the partners' work together is complete. That change, though painful, is part of becoming whole. That it is our spirit, not our rational mind, that chooses whom to love—to name a few. Even if I could make myself believe these things, I know I'll only be hurt, badly, when what's done is done and Steve finally says what's on his mind: He's committed to working things out with Vickie and owes it to his marriage, or however he'll choose to phrase it. It also violates every rule I have ever set for myself and is so counter to my "sense of Irisness" that never, ever would I have thought myself capable. It will hurt a friend who doesn't deserve to be hurt. It will hurt my husband. It will forever change the way I view myself. It's the most despicable act I can think of, made even worse because it binds me, in its selfishness and dishonesty, to the one person whose actions I find unforgivable. Yet for the first time in my life I can't hear my little voice saying *shouldn't, mustn't, don't*. I feel utterly incapable of doing the right thing.

For the first time in my life I don't want to.

I slide to the edge of my armchair, lean forward, and kiss Vickie Benjamin Sokolov's husband on the mouth.

There's nothing tentative about it. My lips part with his, my tongue finds his, and I crush myself to him as if he belonged only to me.

He doesn't back away.

But he doesn't surrender. Not entirely. He holds his arms at his sides and keeps his back straight—a response that, at any other time and from any other man, would send me crawling away in shame. With Steve, I am emboldened, slipping my hands under his shirt and grazing his back and chest with my fingertips and kissing him fearlessly, ravenously, until his breathing quickens and his skin burns and at last he lets me pull the shirt up and over his head. I take his hands in mine and pull him from the footstool onto the armchair, on top of me. When I move my lips down the side of his neck, he tastes of salt and smells of sweat and sunlight and cut grass.

"Please," I whisper.

He kisses me back then, pressing his mouth against mine and covering my body with his, and I know he wants the same thing I do and wants it now, here, whether it's right or not, if only for this moment.

"We shouldn't," he breathes.

"I don't care."

"You've been drinking."

"I'm fine now." I tug at the elastic waist of his running shorts.

"This isn't right."

"Shh." The talk will come all too soon, but for this moment he is mine. I slip down farther underneath him, my lips moving down his chest and torso.

He stops talking.

He also stands up.

My heart constricts.

But he isn't leaving me this time, either. Instead he takes my hands in his and helps me to my feet. "Watch that footstool," he whispers. "It's a killer."

I laugh.

He does, too, curling his arms around me. Then he leads me to the bed—two steps—and in an instant we're lying together, face to face, pulling off each other's clothes, touching and tasting each other, slippery with sweat from the hot August day and from desire.

"Wait." I reach behind me frantically, feeling for my nightstand drawer and groping inside for a condom. "Could you?"

He takes it, kisses me again, unwraps it, and puts it on.

And then we're entwined, wrapped around each other, my fingers pressing into the muscles in his back, pulling him in closer, deeper. I realize my eyes are open and I'm watching his face, in a way I've never been able to do with any man, not even my own husband. It surprises me, as does the intensity with which Steve returns my gaze. It feels intimate. *Soul mates,* I think, and giggle before I can stop myself.

"What?" Steve asks, tracing my lips.

"I'm just not used to this."

"Me neither," he answers quietly, moving his hands down, caressing and exploring my body until I no longer care what he meant, which part of this he's not used to; until the light begins to radiate outward, gathering and gaining strength and heat and then, at last, exploding high above us, fireworks sparking and flaring and drifting back down like stardust.

Afterward, he stays on top of me, his heart against mine, our breathing slowly returning to normal.

"Am I crushing you?" he murmurs into my neck.

"No. Don't ever move." I hold him tight, sliding my hands

along the length of his spine, until it occurs to me that he actually is crushing me. "Maybe you should move," I gasp, this
time because I can't breathe.

He rolls himself off me and then pulls me on top of him.
"That better?"

"Perfect." There's a stray piece of goose down, escaped
from one of my pillows, stuck to his damp cheek. I pick it off
and kiss him on the spot where it had been.

"It was," he says. "You are."

"Do you want anything? Water?"

"Stay here." He untangles himself and steps into the bathroom, where I hear water running. He comes out with a damp
towel and then goes into the kitchen for a glass of water. "It's
our tradition." He shares the glass with me and uses the towel
to wipe my hot face. "Good?"

I nod. He climbs back onto the bed and puts his arms
around me. "It wasn't your husband who was cheating? I
thought maybe he'd walked out on you."

"I left him. But he wasn't cheating. Not as far as I know."
I'm feeling intensely sleepy—the wine, the confession, our
lovemaking, all of it. I close my eyes and let myself enjoy the
feeling of this man so close to me. "I left because I didn't know
how to make a marriage work."

———————

Steve is speaking quietly. Slowly I turn over, but the bed is
empty. Fading afternoon light filters in through the closed window shutters. I must have fallen asleep. I search the dim room
for signs of motion until my eye stops on a strip of brighter
light on the floor. My door is half open, and through the opening I see Steve, dressed now, in the hallway with Rocky and
Jack, talking on his cell phone. I slip out of bed and tiptoe

closer to the door. "The day got away from me," he is saying in a voice that's achingly cozy. "I'll be there soon."

I leap back into bed and under the covers, leaving a minute space to see out of. A moment later, Steve steps back inside and quietly closes the door. He unclips Rocky's leash and tiptoes to the kitchen. I hear him fill Rocky's food bowl and murmur a few words. I shut my eyes as he steps to the bed and sits down carefully next to me. He caresses my back and whispers, "I need to go now."

I don't say anything. If he knows I'm awake, he'll tell me now that this can never happen again, we've made a terrible mistake, and he's going to step up his efforts to work things out with Vickie. I turn, as if in sleep, and bury my face in the pillow.

There's the sound of a leash jingling—it must be Jack's. Steve whispers loudly, "Shh, boy, wait."

He stands up from the bed. Then I feel him lean down close. "Whatever happens, don't ever regret this," he says in a low voice. His nearness is intoxicating. And then, so quietly it almost gets lost under the hum of the air conditioner, he whispers, "It was real."

TWENTY-FOUR

I'm walking Rocky the next morning when the familiar chirp of "La Cucaracha" starts coming from my pocket. *Don't answer that phone, Iris, whatever you do.* I'm in for a lifetime of crushing depression and soul-sucking guilt. For now I should try, though I suspect it will be impossible, to get on with my day. Nope, not going to answer. Not going to do it.

I answer.

"Yesterday was wonderful." The sound of Steve's voice weakens my knees to the point that I forget to be furious at myself. "You there? Doing okay?"

"Doing okay." This is not entirely untrue. It must be that I've finally told someone about my mother, gotten that off my chest. It's lifted me somehow, even as misery seethes and shifts just below the surface, preparing to burst through.

"I borrowed a shirt," Steve says. "I couldn't find mine last night and didn't want to wake you, so I pulled one out of your drawer. It's the Bellagio or something from Vegas. I'll get it back to you."

"Just throw it away. You'll need to get rid of the evidence."

Silence. Then he says, "We do still need to talk."

Look, it's my old friends Mr. Guilt and Mrs. Depression. Here they come now.

He lowers his voice. "Especially now that we've . . ."

Yes, by all means, especially now that we've. "You're going to tell me I've got you all wrong." My throat has begun to constrict, and my voice is squawky.

"That *is* what I want to tell you. May we have dinner later? I'd say lunch but I have to be somewhere this afternoon."

Just the idea of food has my stomach doing cartwheels. I need to sit down. Luckily there are plenty of benches nearby, mostly unoccupied at that, since any even marginally sane person is either inside an air-conditioned office building or vacationing someplace civilized, like Antarctica. I choose a bench under a tree. The shade makes little difference. Rocky whines and rears up on his hind legs. I haul him up, and he puts his hot, round head in my lap. "You know what?" I say into the phone. "I can't have dinner with you tonight. Maybe some other time. Like never. And shouldn't you be getting back to the beach?"

"Never is not an option. Really, this is important."

"I'm busy tonight." To be exact, busy in front of the television, flipping channels. I'll call all my old California friends, too, and tell them I'm coming home. I'll call Teddy, if I can get through, and see how his movie is going.

At the thought of Teddy, my stomach contorts in shame.

Even with the bad cell phone connection I can hear Steve trying not to sound irritated. "If you can't make it, you can't make it. We don't have to do it tonight, but we do next week. So, lunch, Monday, one o'clock, at the Lakeside Restaurant. That's at the boathouse in Central Park. Reservation under Steve. You'd better be there, because I know where you live."

A memory: Steve shivering as I kiss his neck and shoulders, Steve caressing my back, Steve's hands on my body. *Meet me at my apartment in fifteen minutes,* I want to tell him. *Make love to me again.* I resist with every last shred of willpower. I can't do this again. I can't. Life is a disaster already.

"See you Monday." He hangs up before I can argue.

I replace my phone in my pocket. "What do we do now, gargoyle?" I stand Rocky up on my lap and hold his front paws. He wags his stumpy tail and sticks out his tongue. He's still ugly but, after all we've been through together, endearing, too.

"Want to know something, Rocky? I didn't much like you at first. It's okay to say so now, because I don't feel that way anymore. My first impression was wrong. I think you're a good guy." It's clear that Rocky is not only listening but also knows I'm talking as much about Steve as about him. "Hey, don't get me wrong. Even if Steve weren't married to Vickie, and I weren't going back to Teddy, I still wouldn't get involved with him. I'm not going to meet him for lunch, Rock."

Rocky whines. It occurs to me that my biggest fear has finally come to pass. It's bad enough that I've followed in my mother's footsteps; now I'm having a conversation with a dog. And worse, I don't think he believes what I'm saying.

I lower Rocky to the pavement and set him down squarely on all four paws. He performs the wiggly body shake of a dog who's been idle too long and wants to move. I do not allow myself to say, "Come on, let's go," or "Want to take a walk?" Instead I lead him wordlessly to Central Park South.

It sounds as though there's a fraternity kegger going on on the tenth floor of the Intercontinental. You can hear the party noises all the way from the elevator. I make my way down the hall to one closed door and stand for a few moments, too confused to knock. This can't be the right room, can it? I turn to go back to the elevator. At the same moment, the door opens and a barefoot woman a few years older than I am emerges and nearly collides with me. Rocky, on his leash, barks sharply.

"Oops!" the woman and I exclaim at the same time. Then, "Excuse me!" Then we both laugh—though I can't say whether her laugh stems, as mine does, from nerves.

"You must be here for the meet-and-greet!" The woman wears a bindi on her forehead. She takes my arm. "Come in. Don't worry, you didn't miss it. And she's amazing."

It's not a frat party; it's a Joy party. There have got to be fifty junior Joys stuffed into the room, which isn't a room at all but a suite. There's a catered spread of twigs and leaves, uniformed waiters dispensing a green, grassy juice, a woman in the corner playing a sitar (or is it a zither?) and patchouli incense burning everywhere. Presiding over the scene is my mother, twinkling and jingling all over the room as her disciples crowd around asking questions and hanging on her every word.

"We are each other. The energy of the universe flows within us. With quiet minds we feel the oneness of the life force," she's saying to three women clutching shot glasses of liquid turf. The listener on the right puts her arm around the listener in the middle. "Don't you see, Anne, that's what we've been trying to tell you all along!" Anne smiles through her tears. They all hug, my mother included.

Walking over here to confront her, I imagined my mother would finally apologize for everything, all of it—for putting me in the most awkward position of my life, for showing me that those we love are never who they seem to be, for burdening me with emotions and assumptions I ended up bringing to my own marriage. And most of all, for leaving my father to die of a broken heart. I want to run out of the room. She hasn't seen me yet; nobody would be the wiser. I'm shaky, though, and feeling a bit sick. I have to rest for a moment. At the far end of the room a small hallway leads to a half-open door. My mother's bedroom? Surely no one would notice if I went in for a moment to compose myself before the ugly scene. I tiptoe over to the door and slip inside, seeking the same thing everyone here is seeking: peace.

The room is packed. Crowded with two dozen women admiring what, it dawns on me, must be my mother's new line of products—the products she's here to introduce. The women dab each other with essential oils with names like "Harmony" and "Gaia," pick up and inspect yoga props, candles, desktop waterfalls, smudge pots, wind chimes, earrings, anklets, amulets, prayer shawls, caftans, head wraps, sandals, soaps, dream journals, refrigerator magnets, and wall plaques, all with the logo "Bliss Bits from Joy!" In the center of the king-size bed, two women sit together cross-legged in an empty pink plastic kiddie pool. "My rebirthing ceremony made me whole again!" says the one with her back to me.

Her voice makes me pause. Her sandy-brown bob makes her look, from the back, almost like Vickie. "Ever since then, my spirit has been cleansed," she says, sounding like Vickie.

Remarkably like Vickie. So much like Vickie, she could be Vickie. Or Vickie's identical twin.

She turns and spots me, and her mouth widens into a virtuous, rosy-cheeked smile. It lights up her gray eyes and wrinkles her freckled nose adorably.

"Iris! Namaste! I was wondering if you might show up!" She scrambles out of the pool, vaults off the bed, and wraps her arms around me. "You won't believe this!"

She's right. I don't believe this.

"Val," I say weakly, "what are you doing at my mother's meet-and-greet?"

And it is Val—the undyed, conservatively made-up Val, who up until right now existed only in the high school graduation-day snapshot on her apartment wall. She unhands me, hugs herself, and sways slightly back and forth so that her white silk knee-length djellaba, with long, flowing sleeves that cover the tips of her fingers, rustles softly against her loose white silk pants. She looks enlightened enough to be levitating, but her jeweled sandals are planted firmly on the hotel carpet. My brain feels much the way my laptop must when I make it open too many programs at once. Val beams. "None of this would have happened without you, Iris. You and your e-mails!"

Most of my questions center on why Valerie Benjamin looks like a pampered suburban housewife. This conundrum has become even more primary in my mind than the riddle of why she is here.

"It had never occurred to me that the way I was living went so against my sense of Val-ness. Then in, oh, June I guess it was, I'm doing another series of groups for Michelle, and my flight is delayed. I'm sitting in O'Hare going out of my skull with boredom, so I get on my laptop and start reading some of those 'Bliss Blitz' newsletters you've kept sending to me. Was it a message, Iris? Were you trying to tell me I needed to change my life?"

A woman elbows past carrying a Bliss Bits from Joy! Tibetan singing bowl. Her waist-length braid whomps my arm.

"I just thought you'd think they were funny, Val."

"I couldn't stop reading. I was riveted. All the way to Indianapolis I reflected on the choices I'd made, and came to understand I wasn't being true to myself. I wasn't respecting my spark of inner divinity. I spent a good couple of weeks pondering this deeply and decided there was more to life than running around and having pointless sex. I needed to be true to myself. I needed to focus on Val."

The green juice must be spiked. That's the only answer for what's going on here.

She presses her hands to her chest. "I've never been happier. I owe it all to Joy. When I realized she was coming to town this week, I even cut my vacation short to see her. Cut my vacation short! Humidity be damned! The old Val never would have done that!" She flings her arms around me again and kisses me on both cheeks, stumbling over Rocky, who's been sitting quietly on my feet this entire time. He yelps in surprise.

"Sorry, doggie. Iris, you've got to come downstairs. I have something amazing to show you!" With her right hand she drags me by the left wrist back through the main room of the suite, where my mother is still surrounded by admirers. Val pulls me toward the door. "Did you get to pay your respects?" she asks. "I already did. You never told me Joy was so accessible!"

As usual, she doesn't wait for me to answer, so there's no need to tell her I've chickened out.

Val whisks Rocky and me into an elevator. I try not to stare at her as we descend, and think back to our last couple of phone conversations, her ending them with Joy's trademark "namaste." Val must be just trying on this goddess stuff temporarily, the way she tries on haircolor and men. I give her three weeks before she's back to her old self.

"You're going to be so amazed!" She hugs herself again. "You and your e-mails!"

At the lobby, Val makes a beeline for the hotel bar; apparently, there's one thing about her that has remained constant. Pulling me with her, she sweeps across the room as if she were skipping through a field of daisies.

"Pookie!" She drops my hand and flings herself into the arms of a vaguely familiar-looking man in khakis and a polo shirt. From within the embrace, she says breathlessly, "Iris, you did this! Remember, you sent me that phone number? Of that guy you said would be perfect for me?" She smooches him.

I twist Rocky's leash like a noose around my finger and rack my brain.

"You e-mailed her the number of some guy you met on the

Internet," the man interjects. "You told her you'd found her Mr. Right." Val smooches him again.

Now I remember what she is talking about. "But you've got it all wrong. I sent you Buzz's number, Val. This isn't Buzz."

"Of course it isn't Buzz," she says mid-smooch. She pulls back and looks at him. "Pookie, this is Iris."

The man smiles with white-white teeth. "And so it is! You're not a redhead anymore, Iris. Great to see you again!" He extends both arms as if to hug me. I dodge him. "You don't remember. She doesn't remember," he says to Val. Then, to me, "Joe. The endodontist. From the Hotel Royal. Remember?"

Val plops into an upholstered love seat and tugs Joe down next to her. She crosses her legs lotus-style. She looks at me looking down at her and Joe. "Can you believe it, Iris?"

As a matter of fact, I'm totally mystified.

Val leans against Joe's shoulder. "I called the number you gave me, but the person who answered wasn't named Buzz; he was named Joe. *This* Joe. This wonderful, wonderful man. I didn't know that yet, of course. I just thought I'd dialed wrong."

"She read me the number, but it was my number," Joe says. "She sounded so cute I didn't want her to hang up. I told her, 'Instead of Buzz, why don't you go out with me?' "

How could I have sent Val Joe's number? I think back to the night at the gallery, of Buzz standing at the fruit-and-cheese table, writing on a napkin. I remember putting the napkin into the inside pocket of my handbag. Then I picture the night at the Hotel Royal with Joe, he also writing down a phone number on a napkin. That explains it. When I get home and look in my handbag, I'll find a crumpled-up napkin with "Buzz" and a phone number scribbled on it.

"God works in mysterious ways, doesn't She?" Val kisses Joe again. "Iris, did you know Joe grew up in Darien? We're pretty sure we met once at a tennis tournament. Anyway, our first date was two and a half months ago, and we've been inseparable ever since. It's my longest relationship!"

Joe kisses her on her nose. "Have you told her the best part yet?" Val shakes her head. "Go ahead, tell her."

"Ta-daa!" Val raises her left hand and shakes down her caftan sleeve to reveal a diamond as big as the Ritz. "We're getting married! I told you it was amazing! Who would have believed I, of all people, would find my soul mate?"

TWENTY-FIVE

More?" Ilona leans over the black leather lounger I'm occupying and gracefully refills my glass of iced tea. I drink it down. "Better?" Ilona asks. "Honestly, I was shocked when you walked in here."

I blush. The cutoffs and kitten-heeled slides I threw on this morning don't remotely go together. I am also wearing a twenty-year-old Hansen Surfboards T-shirt that Kyle Trilbee, a San Diegan with whom I, at twenty-three, had an intense three-week relationship, wore in junior high school. Aside from being faded almost beyond recognition, it's much too tight. "I look awful. Believe me, Ilona, all I was going to do was walk Rocky in the park. I hadn't planned to drop in on Joy's party, or to come here." I did stop home between the hotel and Rubicon to drop off Rocky, though. I might have thought to put on something nicer to wear.

"I only meant that you looked upset. Your outfit is fabulous. Fabulous."

I was upset. Am upset. Because of her connection to Steve, Ilona is probably the last person from whom I should be seeking comfort. But I couldn't think of anywhere else to go.

"Whose top is that? Jack Jerusalem? Adler?"

"Kyle Trilbee."

She pauses. "Kyle Trilbee? From where?"

"Cardiff-by-the-Sea. Near San Diego."

"Well, he's fabulous. Maybe we should get him for the shop. The best part, though, is the way your shoes give it all a tarty little twist. An inspired choice."

I let myself put the guilt aside, just for a moment. Me, inspired?

"I can't believe you're not in the Hamptons," I tell Ilona. "I expected to come up here and see one of those 'We're closed the entire month of August' signs."

"You know, usually we do lock up for a couple of weeks. This summer my bosses have had some legal things to take care of, so neither of them could get away. I felt bad and offered to take my vacation in September, after all the chaos is hopefully over." She sighs. "Divorce."

"Who's getting a divorce?"

"My boss."

"I wouldn't wish divorce on anyone."

"Especially with a child involved, and a terrible custody battle." Ilona's sadness is genuine, and yet she's as beautiful unhappy as she is happy.

"I can't even imagine. If my husband and I had had a child, I would have never left, no matter what."

"You mean your ex-husband, yes?"

"My husband. I'm moving back home."

"To California?" Ilona frowns. "You're sure that's what you want?"

"I'm sure." (*Is that why you just cheated on Teddy?* my little voice interjects out of nowhere, and I feel ill all over again.) "I knew we had almost nothing in common when we got married, but I still should have tried harder to—why are you looking at me like that?"

The store phone rings. Ilona walks over to the counter, leans across, and picks up. "Rubicon. Thank goodness! I've been on pins and needles all day. Are you in court now? Tell me some good news." She sweeps a curtain of hair behind one ear and listens intently. Her expression grows grave. "You sure? Okay,

then, concentrate on that. You'll get custody. You have to."
She hangs up quietly and walks over to me.

"Do you need to get back to work?" Something tells me
she's moved on to other concerns besides Teddy and me.

"It's okay. I'm worried, that's all."

"About your boss? That's so remarkably sympathetic." I
liked my old boss in Brentwood fine, and Michelle seemed
okay until she fired me, but I can't imagine getting too upset
over either of their personal lives.

"We're talking about a dear, dear friend." Ilona massages
her temples for a moment, then opens her green eyes wide.
"But just so you understand, Iris, I don't think couples should
force themselves to stay together if deep down they know they
shouldn't. No matter how hard you try, if the marriage isn't
right, it won't work. Not really."

The doorman opens the door, and three women rush over
with squeals and hugs.

Ilona looks at me apologetically. "I've probably said too
much anyhow." She stands up to greet her customers. "Come
back anytime, Iris. Think about what I said."

After that, I decide to spend the rest of the afternoon being
quiet. But sitting in my armchair with Rocky on my feet, trying to reread *The Custom of the Country*, I keep drifting
between self-hatred and thoughts of last night. Was it only
eighteen hours ago that we were together?

I step over Rocky to the bed, laying my cheek on the pillow
Steve used and breathing in the faint scent of him I find there.
I'm woozy and exhilarated and heartbroken all at once.

"Iris," I say. "This is over. You can't have this man. You
never could, and you still can't now, even though you . . ."

This is the problem with talking to yourself. When you
speak words out loud, even into a room where only a dog is
listening, they become real. If I say what I was about to say,

then I can't go home to Teddy. Once those words leave my mouth, I can never take them back.

So I say this instead: "You're going to end this once and for all. You're going to call Vickie in the Hamptons and tell her . . ."

Perhaps I should tell her she should most definitely reconsider staying married to Steve, because now I've slept with him and can therefore say without hesitation that he's cheated on her. Unfortunately, I don't think this through until I've already picked up the receiver and dialed Vickie's cell phone number and am waiting for the line to connect. Fortunately, when I realize I have no good idea what to tell her, the call hasn't gone through yet. "Lucky break," I say into the emptiness, and hang up.

But five minutes later the phone rings.

"Hello, Iris," says Vickie, and although I was just about to call her myself, my stomach flip-flops. Vickie doesn't sound good. Her voice has a steely edge I've never heard before. "You can probably guess what this is about."

I can hear, in the background on her end of the phone, the low roar of traffic. Trucks, sirens, the whole bit. Everyone says summer traffic in the Hamptons is apocalyptic, but it can't be this noisy, can it?

"Vickie, where are you right now?"

"I came back early. I'm in the apartment. My apartment. He's going to go back to Southampton tonight and wonder where I am, and I don't care. I don't want to speak to him."

Fear harpoons me in the chest. "Vickie, before you jump to any conclusions, we should talk this through."

"He's cheating. For real, Iris. I suspected something was going on, so I followed him to his so-called meeting in the city and saw the whole thing."

Each word is a punch in the gut. Not to say I don't deserve

to be caught and punished; I do. Vickie helped keep me in cereal and introduced me to The Elixir and Ultra Placid. I would give anything not to have betrayed her in this way. I would give anything to take it all back. "Please. I can't even begin to explain. I feel terrible." Beyond terrible. There's no word for how terrible I feel.

"It's not your fault."

"It *is* my fault!" It comes out a howl. I don't know who feels worse. She's the victim, but she will be able to look at herself in the mirror and know she wasn't the one who went against every last personal more and, in doing so, wrecked three people's lives. Hers, mine, and Teddy's. And the baby's life, too. My eyes brim with tears.

"It isn't. You did exactly what I asked you to do. I asked you to find out whether he was cheating. Then I asked you to keep getting tips from him, which you did for as long as you could. I thought he'd changed." Vickie laughs, bright and brittle. "My only regret is not being quicker to put it all together. I truly believe some part of my brain didn't want to know."

Nobody's watching. So this time I don't bother to bug out my eyes. The tears fall silently, streaming down my cheeks.

I've just lost my only two friends in New York. Vickie and Steve.

"If you can believe this, Iris, I'm pretty sure he wanted me to find out. There he was, right in front of my eyes, kissing this woman. Not even a beautiful woman. An entirely ordinary woman, like every other woman out there. Not special at all. Not chic, not beautiful. A big nothing."

For the first time I feel a spasm of anger. I am not ordinary. I am not like every other woman out there. I never was. Then, through this miasma of sorrow and fear and offense, a question fights its way into the light: How could Vickie possibly have seen us kissing unless she was watching through my window? "Vickie, when did you see this? Did you talk to him?"

"I drove in this morning and saw him, twenty minutes ago. And no, I didn't talk to him. He didn't even see me. I ran home and called a locksmith to change the locks, and then called you."

Anger at Vickie gives way to anger at Steve. Twenty minutes ago I was in Rubicon with Ilona. So who was he kissing?

Jessica. It can only be Jessica. After being with me last night.

"There they were at La Goulue. Right in front at a sidewalk table. Can you believe it? If it hadn't been August, with everyone out at the beach, the whole Upper East Side would have seen him drinking wine with this shabby, dumpy, mousy nobody."

Anger at Steve gives way to utter disbelief. With her model's figure and honey hair, Jessica is anything but mousy and shabby. It can only mean that besides Vickie, Jessica, and me, there is at least one more woman in Steve's life. Can I believe it? That the man who less than twenty-four hours ago told me, "It was real" would in fact have not just one but at least two other mistresses to whom he's been whispering exactly the same thing? "What a dog," I hiss. "What a worthless, amoral dog."

Vickie laughs, and surprisingly, there's a genuine note of humor in it. "I'll say he's a dog. He could have taken the poor thing somewhere fancier."

I actually start laughing myself. What else is there to do?

"Iris, I need your help, just one more time. Would you do one last thing for me?"

"It's not a good idea." Given the circumstances I'm the last person who should be involved.

"Pretty please. He doesn't know I know any of this. Eventually I'll have to tell him I know he's cheating, and when I do, he'll have some perfectly reasoned excuse and make it seem like I'm imagining the whole thing, and if that happens, I'll take him back like always. I need you there to make sure I don't fall for it this time. I'll pay you if you want. Please say you'll help. Please, Iris."

What I have to do becomes plain as day. I'll come clean with Vickie and ask for her forgiveness, though I don't expect she'll give it to me. Steve doesn't know it yet, but he's going to come clean, too. I'll have to find some way to tell Teddy, but not before I've dealt with Vickie and Steve. "Can you wait until after the weekend to confront him?"

"Easily. I'm so furious right now, I'm afraid I'll push him out a window. I'm sure he'll call here looking for me when he gets back to the beach and I'm not there. But I'm not answering the phone."

"Then I'll help you, but you should know this in advance: You may learn a few things you'll end up wishing you hadn't. I want to make sure you understand that, and that you can live with it." My hands are actually shaking.

"I understand. I'm going to get an earful. The thing is, I already know what he's capable of. Hearing it once and for all won't make it any worse. It already is true, and it's time for me to figure out my next step."

I know now what's different about Vickie. She isn't crying. She doesn't sound sad at all. Angry, yes. Resigned, yes. Self-possessed, though, also, and strong. As ready as she may ever be to hear the truth. I'm ready, too, ready to own up to my sins. I will not be like my mother, tossing out hollow excuses and not taking responsibility for my part in this disaster.

"All right, then," I tell her. "Meet me for lunch on Monday. One o'clock, at the boathouse in Central Park. I'll make sure your husband is there, too."

TWENTY-SIX

If I said, "Monday morning dawned hot and muggy," it wouldn't be entirely accurate. The day of my big confrontation is unbearably warm and damp, as every day has been for weeks. But I can't say for sure that it has dawned that way, since I truly believe this time I *have* been up the entire night, listening to Rocky's labored breathing and worrying about what the day has in store for me. So it's impossible for me to separate Monday morning from Sunday night, except that when the sun finally does come up, I take Rocky out to the curb, hurry back inside, lie back down on the bed to rest for a moment, and instantly fall into a deep sleep. I even have a nightmare I can't remember the details of, but it's bad enough that at some point I say to myself in the dream, "This is awful. Wake up, for heaven's sake, and go after it, girl!"

So I wake up to find that it's past noon. This is not good. I must get to the restaurant early. I take a five-second shower, promise myself to beg Simon for a haircut the second he gets back from Fire Island, slip into my Rubicon blouse and skirt, touch Rocky's head for luck, and head out the door. Hustling through the park, I regret not having had a few moments to get my thoughts together. I have obsessed over this meeting for the past forty-eight hours but am still at a loss for what to say, or even where to start. Perhaps Steve will be a good husband, for once, and explain it to Vickie himself. This is, after all, between the two of them and really has very little to do with me. *You keep telling yourself that,* says my little voice.

By the time I get to the boathouse, on the east side of the park, my stomach hurts so acutely, I want to turn around and go home. Instead, I breathe and step up to the host at the door. He sizes me up and smiles, a low-energy, toothless grimace. I return it in kind and tell him I have a one o'clock reservation. I scan the large, airy room and wish I'd thought to have Vickie come at ten minutes past one. I'm counting on the surprise factor to get Steve to tell all, and it won't work if the two of them arrive at the same time.

"The name?"

"Steve." *The Dog,* I add silently.

The host leans over his enormous black-leather book and uses a thick marker to slash a line through a name on the list. He leads me to a table at the far end of the room, set back from the doors that open onto the lakeside patio, but still with a view of the water. It's a table for four, an unexpected blessing. I'd been fretting over having enough room at a table for two after Vickie arrived.

Once the host leaves, the busboy doesn't remove the two extra place settings, and even fills up all four water glasses. It's a service gaffe that might come in handy. Even if it weren't sweltering, I'm feverish with fear. It's a two-glasses-of-water kind of afternoon.

Vickie walks into the restaurant.

Everyone has heard the expression "her blood turned to ice." This is what it feels like: Your entire body goes hot, then cold. So cold you get goose bumps, even on the Monday of the last week in August in New York City. So cold the little hairs on your arms stand up and you imagine that if you jumped into the lake, sparkling picturesquely before you and your fellow diners, your body would turn the surrounding water into a solid slab of ice: Central Park swans frozen in place, rowboat oars fixed into the water at odd angles.

This jumping-into-the-lake thought is not an idle one. As the host escorts Vickie over—all moonfaced, tree-trunk–legged, thirty extra pounds of her—throwing myself into the lake seems the only way to escape this mess.

She looks down at me, her brow damp with fatigue. "Thank you for getting this table. There's no way I'd fit at one of those tables for two."

"Vickie, you're . . ." I can't even say it. I just gesture at Vickie's enormous middle. She's still standing and I'm rooted helplessly to my chair, so it's right at my eye level. "You're . . ."

Vickie laughs ruefully. "A whale? No kidding. Do you know how many more weeks I have to go? *Ten.* Can you imagine? How could I get any bigger? Iris, what on earth is wrong? You look about to cry."

"You're carrying Steve's baby!" I *am* about to cry.

The host guides Vickie into a chair, a tugboat nudging a cruise liner into its berth. He unfolds her napkin and drapes it over the place where her lap used to be. Vickie stares at me. "Are you okay?"

I take a long, deep breath and try to compose myself. Seeing her again has finally brought home the seriousness of what I have done. How could I have slept with her husband? How could I have been so selfish?

Vickie picks up her sweaty glass of icewater and presses it against her equally sweaty cheek. "I definitely could have planned this better, don't you think? What woman in her right mind plans a pregnancy so she hits her third trimester in August?" She takes a camel sip of water. Then she slowly shakes her head. "What woman in her right mind decides to have a child with a man she's known all along is untrustworthy?"

"Vickie, you . . . I have to tell—"

"Do you know I cried like a crazy person right before my wedding?"

"I didn't, no," I choke out. She's carrying her baby the way Carmen Riggio, from Hayes Heeley, once said women do if they're having a girl: low down and spread around her hips. She's hollow-eyed and sallow, too. Carmen said baby girls steal your beauty, while baby boys make you glow.

"I was with Val, getting into my dress," she continues, "and Val let it slip that about a year earlier, she'd had a little . . . What did she call it? She'd had a little *encounter* with Steve at my parents' New Year's Eve party. 'Encounter,' that's what she said. Val swore she didn't sleep with him, they kissed for all of three seconds, and that they were both drunk and the whole thing was meaningless. That kind of thing is never meaningless. Not when it's your sister and your fiancé, and you find out on your wedding day."

I shake my head mindlessly.

"I was beside myself. I started crying, and screaming at Val, and decided to call off the wedding, then and there. It seemed like an impossible obstacle to me, starting a marriage hearing that." She rubs her hand across her belly, caressing the child inside her. "But in Greenwich, Connecticut, you don't cancel a three-hundred-person wedding, with your hair already up and the guests on the way. It simply isn't done."

I have the same feeling I did the first day I met Vickie, in Grand Central, and thought she was Val playing a trick on me: This has got to be a colossal practical joke. Any moment now, Vickie will pull the pillow out from under her dress. Just kidding! I was never really pregnant! April fool!

"No matter," she says. "What's done is done, and I'm ready to hear what you have to say. Where is Steve, anyway? I told him not two hours ago that if he was late, I'd kill him."

"You told Steve?" My heart sinks. I wanted Vickie's presence here to be a surprise. Now that he knows she's coming, he'll never show up. "But I thought you weren't speaking to him."

"I'm not. He came back from Southampton Saturday morning looking for me but I wouldn't let him in. I have no idea where he slept. Probably at *her* house. Anyway I called his secretary today and left a message."

The waiter comes by with menus.

"We need a few minutes, please." Vickie folds her hands and sets them on the shelf of her belly. He steps away. She says to me softly, "Go ahead and start without him. I can handle it."

I guess I'll have to break the news to her myself.

I reach under the table for my handbag and pull from it something I've brought especially for the meeting. I set it on my lap under the white tablecloth. "Please know, Vickie, that I've come to think of you as a friend, one of my only friends here, and that's all going to end in about two seconds. I regret that more than you'll ever believe." I slowly pull the object out from under the tablecloth. It's a soft bundle of navy blue cotton fabric, and my hands tremble as I unfold it and hold it out to Vickie. "I think you can guess how I came to have this."

She takes it: a man's T-shirt, laundered and laundered to gossamer softness, with a small, worn "New York Athletic Club" logo near the left shoulder.

Vickie studies it. Her face tells me nothing. The busboy silently sets down a basket of bread. I turn away and watch the host at the front of the restaurant, talking on the phone, adding an entry to his reservations list. When Vickie raises her eyes, she has a confused look. She sets the shirt on the table.

My eyes fill with tears. Vickie used to be the crier. Now I'm the one on the verge of sobbing at all times. I suspect that Vickie hasn't cried once since she called two days ago—her eyes are certainly dry now. But that won't last for long.

Vickie asks, "What is this?"

Steve walks into the restaurant.

He looks agitated and nervous, in a way I've never seen him look before.

My heart pounds as the host leads him over. I can't believe he's here after Vickie let it drop that she was coming, too.

Steve takes in me, his pregnant wife, and his T-shirt—the shirt he left in my apartment, the one I couldn't help but steal and never planned to use as evidence. The shirt Vickie now holds in her swollen hands.

"Surprise," I say coldly. "Yes, I brought Vickie along, too. I thought she'd like to join us."

He is pale and seems caught off-guard. Unable to speak.

Vickie looks from me to him and back to me again. "What's this about?"

But now I can't answer. I'm too busy taking in the woman behind Steve.

The tall, willowy, honey-haired woman from the night of the fireworks. Jessica. Steve's mistress. Holding hands with her blond toddler.

I want to kill him.

"How could you?" I say to Steve, low, furious, murderous.

Vickie doesn't yet understand the significance of this. She looks at Jessica, bewildered. "You?" she asks. "From the elevator?"

Steve cuts Vickie off, quietly but firmly. "I'm so sorry, Vickie, and I wish you didn't have to be here for this, but if you can bear with me I promise to explain everything in a moment," he says to her. "But first, Iris, there's someone I'd like you to meet."

It's impossible to tell what Vickie is thinking. "I guess I can wait," she says. She scoots herself, in her chair, to the side, not taking her eyes off Steve and me, as the host pulls out both remaining chairs. Steve holds on to the back of a chair and calls, "Sweetheart, come sit next to me," in the direction of Jessica, who has scooped the little girl up onto her hip. For the child is a girl after all; she's wearing a pink dress, and a flower barrette in her blond curls.

"Here?" Jessica moves the chair aside to make a new space at the table. She asks a passing busboy, "A high chair, please?" and he nods and scurries to the kitchen.

The five of us—Vickie and I in our chairs (should we get up?), and standing above us Jessica, the little girl, who looks to be about eighteen months old, and Steve—watch one another to see who will speak next. It isn't going to be me. My brain can't make sense of any of this. This is certainly not the scene I was expecting.

"Wed!" the child announces. "Wed!"

Steve's eyes soften. "You're hungry for some bread, sweetheart?" He removes a roll from the basket on the table, tears off a piece, and offers it to her. She holds it in her chubby fist and gnaws on it happily. Steve reaches out his hands and takes her into his arms, kissing the top of her head.

"Dada," the child coos.

That ends the silence.

"Iris, this is the woman I was telling you about, from the elevator." Vickie indicates Jessica, then asks her, "What are you doing here?"

Jessica doesn't have time to answer, because as Vickie begins speaking, so does everyone else.

"You'd like the high chair here?" the busboy inquires, moving it into position.

"What did the baby just call you?" I say to Steve.

"Who dis?" the toddler asks Steve, pointing at me.

It's unclear what Emily Post would say about who gets the first introduction in such a situation, but this time the toddler wins out.

"This, sweetheart, is my friend Iris," Steve tells her gently. "Iris, this is my daughter."

My hand flies to my mouth. I whip my head around toward Vickie. How will she take this—that her husband doesn't just have a mistress; he has a child with his mistress? A mistress who lives in their building, no less?

Steve doesn't seem to be worried whether dropping this bombshell may send his wife into premature labor. He puts his arm around Jessica. "This is Clare," he continues. "Clare, this is Iris."

I stare at Clare. "Your name is Jessica." I check Steve's face for confirmation. "Her name isn't Clare; it's Jessica."

Of all people, Vickie shakes her head. "No, no. You're mixed up, Iris." She leans over clumsily to retrieve the child's sippy cup, which has fallen to the floor, braces one hand on the edge of the table to lever herself back to a sitting position, and hands the cup to the toddler. "*This*," she says, "is Jessica. The little girl from our building. Remember I told you?"

"Dessa!" the toddler announces.

"You say your name is Clare?" Vickie asks the woman.

"It is." The woman smiles. Oh, God. Vickie doesn't deserve this. She really doesn't.

Vickie extends her hand. "I'm Vickie Benjamin Sokolov in Twelve-C. It's nice to meet you, formally."

I'm in awe of Vickie. She's handling this amazingly well.

"It's nice to meet you, too, Vickie," Clare—tall, blond, willowy Clare—answers. Then she extends her hand to me. "And you, Iris. I've heard so much about you."

"Clare's my sister," Steve says.

I'm not thinking clearly enough to remember that Vickie has told me Steve only has brothers. I'm too busy being horrified by the conclusion to which I've already jumped. "You're sleep—" I can't bring myself to say that. "You're having se—" Definitely not that, not in front of a baby. "You're having an aff—" Nothing sounds right. There's no good way to say it. "You're having whatever you want to call it, with your *sister*?"

Steve's eyes crinkle. "I may be having whatever you want to call it, Iris." He puts his hands on my shoulders. "But not with my sister."

There it is. Right out in the open. I'm stunned that he's let it drop like that. Doesn't he have any regard at all for Vickie, having to find out, in a crowded restaurant, that her husband has fathered a daughter with—all right, if not his sister, *somebody*?

I want to punch him. I would punch him, but not in front of an innocent child. What I wouldn't give to be sitting at any other table than this one, to be with anyone else in the restaurant—with that arrogant-looking business-suited man rushing up to the host's desk, barking something impatient. I close my eyes, then open them. I'm still in exactly the same place. I scan Vickie's face to see how she's taking it, waiting for the tears or the anger that I know will be her reaction, and that I am dreading beyond words because I deserve it all. Why hasn't she said anything yet?

Except that Vickie no longer seems to be paying the slightest bit of attention to Steve, Clare, Jessica, or even me. She's become distracted watching the businessman striding over to our table. The man pushes Clare aside, none too gently, to claim one of the chairs. "What the hell is this?" he addresses all assembled.

Vickie draws her mouth into a tight line and finally, at long last, speaks. "Would someone," she says slowly, "would someone please tell me what this is about? I don't seem to be in on the joke."

I glare fiercely at Steve. My face burns. Not with embarrassment but with unchecked fury. When I speak, it frightens me. "You know what? You do it. You tell her what this is all about. In fact, while you're at it, tell everybody. I'd like to know, myself. Go on." My hands are clenched into fists. "Explain yourself. You're her husband."

Vickie stares at Steve.

Steve stares at Vickie.

"Iris, what are you talking about?" Vickie says. "This isn't my husband."

TWENTY-SEVEN

People in New York make scenes every day. They get into screaming matches on the bus. They expose themselves on street corners and pass out drunk across the sidewalk in broad daylight. The rest of the city keeps right on going, changing seats, walking around, stepping over. Little wonder, then, that not a soul in this restaurant is watching this scene unfold. To me, though, it appears as if everything stops. The white-aproned waiters carrying their trays, the clink of silverware, the faint lapping of the lake outside, little Jessica with soggy breadcrumbs on her chin. The whole world seems to hold its breath.

"*This* is my husband," Vickie says, gesturing at the businessman.

He's a little under six feet tall, with brown hair and brown eyes. He looks to be in his mid-thirties, a man who owns a Jack Russell terrier, who went to an Ivy League college, and whose driver's license, were I to check it, would show that his name is Steve.

In short, a man fitting the description of every other man in New York.

"Would one of you people tell me what in Christ's name is going on?" demands Vickie's husband, checking his watch and then crossing his arms over his chest. "I don't have time for this."

I don't say a thing. Instead I look at the other man. The stranger I've been tracking for three months.

Vickie looks at him, too. So does Vickie's husband. So does

Clare. So does the little girl in his arms. *His* little girl. Jessica.
Jessica the blond bombshell.

"Who are you?" I ask him.

"I told you," he says. "My name is Steve."

You'd think pandemonium would break out after that, but it's
more as if the police had raided our little French farce—everyone simply scatters. Clare says something about Jessica needing a nap and confers with Steve in a voice too soft to
overhear. Steve hugs and kisses the toddler, and Clare disappears with her, back out into the afternoon.

Vickie faces Steve—Steve her husband—with sparks shoot-
ing out of her eyes.

"What the hell did *I* do?" he protests.

She gives him the most furious, piercing look I've ever seen
a person give anyone. And then, pinning him with her stare,
she reaches carefully down for the extra glass of water the busboy left on our table. She brings it to her lips for a dainty sip.

And she throws the rest in his face.

"We'll discuss all this at a later date, in private," she says,
places the empty glass delicately back on the table, and turns
on her heel and waddles out of the restaurant. Her husband
stands openmouthed, stiff as the statue of Daniel Webster in
Central Park, as the water drips from his expensive silk tie,
down the perfectly creased legs of his suit, and pools under his
immaculately shined loafers.

He flips open his cell phone and stomps away in the opposite direction.

Steve and I, that is, not-Vickie's-husband Steve and I, are left
standing by ourselves in the middle of the restaurant. The
waiter and busboy begin to clear the table, removing the un-

touched plates and napkins, stripping the linens, straightening the un–sat-in chairs, mopping the wet floor.

I wait for Steve to speak first.

He appears to be waiting for me.

I adopt moderator body language: eyes soft but gaze steady, hands loosely at sides, palms curled forward in a gesture of approachability, mouth somewhere between nonpartisan and party hostess. "I'm open to whatever you feel like sharing," the stance is meant to convey. Inside I'm about to boil over.

"This must come as a shock," he begins.

I keep the artificial smile going.

"I hope you can forgive me," he adds.

The host leads a party of four to our abandoned table: two teenage girls and their parents. He begs our pardon as everyone gingerly steps around Steve and me.

"We should talk outside. I'm sure you have a lot of questions." Steve strides manfully toward the door. After a few feet he looks back to see if I'm behind him. I am, but only because I feel foolish loitering next to a family eating lunch. Once outside, I march directly out to the park road and start to turn right, intending to walk home the way I came—only this time perhaps stopping at Bethesda Fountain, the famous one with the angel on top, to help myself calm down. Ahead of me, Steve seems to be going in the same direction. He stops again and looks back.

"Yes. There are a few things I need answered." My tone is not a moderator tone. It is the tone of a woman who feels . . . what? "Betrayed" comes to mind, but that doesn't make sense. Steve never promised me anything, and I never expected anything. I don't want anything. I'm going back to Teddy. "Why did you tell me you were Vickie's husband?"

Steve removes his sunglass case from his shirt pocket. He pulls out his glasses and rubs them with a cloth. Though the day has turned overcast and we are already standing in the shade, he puts them on. I recognize the gesture. This is a person who wants to melt into the ground and disappear. Well, let him feel that way. He should.

"I didn't tell you I was Vickie's husband. *You* told *me* I was Vickie's husband."

"You *told* me you were Vickie's husband!"

Steve sticks his hands in his pockets.

"That day in the park, remember? The day I admitted to following you. Only I wasn't following you. Okay, I was following you, but only because I thought you were Steve. The real Steve. You did nothing to persuade me otherwise. You were the one who had a fit when you heard Vickie had hired me. You were furious and yelling, 'Vickie is crazy! Vickie is crazy!' Remember?"

"I said *my wife* is crazy. And you didn't say *Vickie* had hired you; you said *my wife* had hired you. It didn't seem farfetched. I'm in the middle of a miserable divorce, Iris, and Stephanie, my ex, is suing me for custody of Jessica. I wouldn't have put it past her to hire a private eye to follow me, to concoct some reason why I'm unfit to care for my child." He looks surprisingly fierce. "Funny, isn't it, considering she walked out on us when Jessica was two weeks old."

I do not allow myself to feel bad for him. "None of that explains why you've been pretending to be someone you aren't. You went to so much trouble, too. You played me like a fool for three months! All the phony appointments, taking off across the park—'Golly gee, got to be somewhere,' running off with Jack Russell. Next you're going to tell me that's not your dog."

"That's not my dog."

I turn my back on him and march up the road, in the opposite direction from where I'd planned on going. I'll cross over somewhere by the reservoir. It's well out of my way, but I'd walk home via New Hampshire if I thought it would help me escape.

"Where are you going?"

"Wherever you're not!" I quicken my pace.

Steve matches me step for step. Considering his legs are longer and he's not in a skirt and heels, he's able to keep up with no trouble, and talk, too. "The appointments weren't phony. I've had meeting after meeting with lawyers, child psychologists, social workers, you name it. It's incredibly difficult for fathers to get full custody, and you have to jump through endless hoops. I've had court dates. And I've needed to be at work first thing in the mornings so I can finish everything I need to do and get back home to my daughter. As for Jack, he belongs to Clare."

"Oh, yes. Your *sister.*"

"Clare *is* my sister, Iris. She happens to live in Merit House, the same building as Vickie. Most mornings I get up early, head uptown from my place, and drop off Jessica with Clare, so I can get some exercise. The trade-off is, I take Jack with me if he wants to go out. I do my run, go back to Clare's, shower, and rush off to work. I pick up Jessica at three, and then Clare goes in to work."

I focus on the scenery as I continue, with Steve at my side, up what, I've remembered too late, is one of the steepest hills in Central Park. Above my head, a bronze statue of a mountain lion crouches on a granite ridge. If real, its next move would be to leap onto me and rip my heart out.

I trudge north, past the Met, and consider his explanation. All right, it's plausible. Let's assume for a moment it's true. That means everything that has happened is a result of two simple mistakes I made the very first morning of my first day. The first mistake was arriving five minutes late. I must have missed Vickie's Steve, who probably really was slipping out for an early-morning tryst. The second mistake was jumping to conclusions about the man I did see. I could blame Vickie— showing me that stupid little postage-stamp–size photograph, giving me only the most perfunctory description of her husband. But the final mistake, the one I made four days ago and the only one that really counts, was all mine.

Steve says beside me, "Do you have other things you want to ask?" He sounds vulnerable. I fight back another twinge of sympathy as I quicken my steps, hoping to discover a secret path back to the Upper West Side.

"I do. The first morning I followed you, why did you act so suspiciously?"

He wrinkles his forehead: *I don't understand.*

"That first morning at the reservoir. You were there with Jack. You were running, and you looked right at me and then took off down the embankment and vanished. If you're so innocent, why were you trying to lose me?"

"I have no idea what you're talking about."

"You do so. I know you do."

"No," he insists. "I don't."

"Well, then," I say, "it's a good thing we've walked this far."

———

It feels strange to be climbing the reservoir staircase not in sweatpants and sneakers. Dust settles between my exposed toes; the seams of my skirt strain as I take the steps two at a time. Being here with Steve makes me wistful, too, for the anticipation I felt before our meetings, back when he was still Vickie's husband and I was looking forward to learning another new thing about him, even if it was only to report back to Vickie. How odd to think of that as a more innocent time.

"Now," I say once I've marched him to the upper track.

"The first day, this is what you did. You ran up here. I was following behind you. You and Jack took off full bore, and then when you rounded that bend up there—see it?—you glanced back at me and then ran down the embankment. Don't tell me you didn't know I was following you."

He's grinning again.

"It's not funny."

Steve allows the smallest chuckle.

"It's not funny!"

"It is funny," he says. "When was that? Must have been May or June, right?"

"It was in May."

"I do remember that day. Glorious weather, I recall. I don't remember anyone following me, though. You're a better detective than you think, Iris. What color hair did you have back then?"

"Answer the question."

"It was the first day I'd brought Jack to the reservoir. I'd run there alone a lot, but not with him. Come with me."

He leads me toward the curve where he disappeared. My heels sink into the track as I walk. It's a good quarter mile to the spot in question.

When we get there, he points to the fence. "Read."

There's a green Parks Department sign attached to the fence: "No Dogs, Carriages, Skates, Skateboards, Tricycles, Bicycles."

"I ran past the sign, looked back when the 'No Dogs' caught my attention, and realized why so many people had been giving me dirty looks."

"You sprinted down a . . ." I glance over the edge of the track. ". . . a forty-five-degree slope that's probably covered in poison ivy because you didn't like people giving you dirty looks?"

He grins. "You know how these runners are."

I'm holding my breath, pressing my lips together, the way I used to do to keep myself from yelling at Teddy.

Teddy!

How on earth will I explain all this to him?

Steve continues, "That's the last time I brought Jack up here. After that, we stayed down there." He points to the lower track.

I push the worry to the back of my mind for now.

"It's entirely true. You know it is, too."

All right, maybe he didn't deliberately set out to deceive me. He is not part of a conspiracy among the residents of Manhattan to humiliate the new girl from the San Fernando Valley. That doesn't change the fact that he kept up this charade for an entire summer. And for what? So he could put another notch on his bedpost? As a distraction during his ugly divorce?

"You could have told me." I speak carefully because otherwise I really will start screaming. "Four little words. One simple sentence: 'I'm the wrong man.' Just once this entire summer. You could have found the right moment. You could have made me listen. Four words, and this whole mess would have been over. Why didn't you?"

"I did say that. I kept telling you I wasn't the person you thought I was."

He's right, you know, my little voice chimes in. No. He's not right. "You wore a wedding ring, Steve! If you weren't trying to trick me, why would you do that?"

Steve drags his shoe against the gravel of the track. I can at least have the satisfaction of knowing he's nervous. "All I can say is, I haven't been myself since Stephanie left me. The divorce has made me a little crazy. This isn't the kind of thing I would ever have done under normal circumstances. And I'm slowly getting my sanity back. I want you to know that."

"Goody for you."

He holds up his hand. "I was trying to trick you with the ring. By then I did want you to believe I was Vickie's husband. But I took it off again weeks ago, and you didn't even notice. I wasn't wearing it when we made love."

Still, the zap buzzes through me. It's not fair. "Well, then. I guess that gets you off the hook."

"Iris, I wanted to tell you. I tried plenty of times, too, but you wouldn't let me. You'd run away or make a big speech about how it was my duty to save Vickie's marriage."

"I thought it was *your* marriage! I didn't mean you should interfere in a total stranger's marriage! Here's a vulnerable woman, a woman you don't even know, whose husband is cheating on her while she's pregnant, and you're manipulating her behavior, playing around with her life? What kind of a person does that?"

"Isn't it exactly what you were doing? Interfering in a stranger's marriage?"

Right again, Iris, says my little voice.

"I know you had Vickie's best interests in mind. Believe it or not, I really began to think I could help." Steve reaches out to put his hand on my arm. I swat it away and jump out of his reach. "And I didn't think it would go on this long. You have to believe me. I'm sick about it."

"Good. You should be." I want to cry again, thinking of Vickie. I had just as much a part in this charade as Steve did. He didn't force me to pass along his stupid pointers. I pushed him into it. "I think I've heard enough. You know, Steve, I'm leaving New York and I'm going back to my husband. We're going to start over. And I'm glad I never have to see you again. You're a liar and a cheat and a user."

I must get away from here. Not by mincing, dainty and ladylike, a quarter mile back to the staircase. I need to leave immediately. I slip off my shoes and, with them in one hand and my purse in the other, run down the reservoir embankment, over sharp stones and past suspicious-looking bushes, wincing with each step. *To hell with you, Steve,* I fume as I skid to a stop on the lower track. Without looking back, I slip my shoes back onto my filthy feet and limp out into the city. *To hell with you, too, New York. I can't wait to leave. Moving here was the worst mistake I've ever made in my life.*

Waiting on Fifth Avenue, hand in the air to flag down a taxi, trying to calm myself, I feel something brush the top of my head.

I jump back and flick it away. Then I spin around to see what it was. I find it on the brick sidewalk behind me: an early autumn leaf, big as my hand, its blood-red points curled toward me as if waving good-bye.

TWENTY-EIGHT

Tuesday after Labor Day. The day life starts up again in New York.

The middle school across my street swarms with students, shouting to one another across the playground, playing basketball at recess, sweating in their too-warm new clothes. The owners of the tiny specialty stores—the olive oil boutique on Amsterdam, the sock shop on Seventy-fifth—take down their handwritten "On Vacation" signs and reopen their doors. A banner goes up on the front of the former sidewalk café with the doggie drinking trough, now reopening, without the trough, as a tapas bar. I leave a message on Teddy's answering machine asking him to call me the minute he returns from Mexico. As I ponder how to tell him about what I've done, my neighbors, one by one, return home.

One day at the deli, I find that my favorite coffee man is back. A few days after that, Rina the dog lady waves to me as she climbs the steps to my building. Later, when I go out to the mailbox to collect my unemployment check, Art is jangling his mammoth key ring.

"You still here?" He raises his blue USPS cap in a salute. "I thought you must move on to bigger things by this time."

"I *am* moving," I tell him.

I've never noticed how broad Art's grin is. It lights up his whole face. "Good for you!" he shouts. "Jersey? SoHo?"

"Studio City, the San Fernando Valley, California."

His grin fades slightly. "You give up on living here so soon?"

"I'm not giving up. It's just that California is my home. Everything is too hard here. Nothing makes any sense."

"It's New York. Supposed to be hard. But you work hard enough, your dream comes true." He unlocks the mailboxes and pulls out the letters waiting to be sent.

I try to clear my throat of the small lump that seems to have materialized there. "Don't you miss your home? Don't you miss Guyana?"

"I miss Guyana." He pulls a bundle of incoming mail from a plastic bin on the floor next to him and begins to sort it into the mailboxes. "New York is my home."

———

I call Vickie and am relieved to hear she's not angry at me for my terrible detective work.

"How are you doing?" I ask. "I'm worried about you."

"I'm doing well," she says simply. "Surprisingly well." I offer to repay, over time, the money she paid me, but she tells me it isn't necessary. "I got a lot out of it. All that advice from Steve—the other Steve—it changed my life."

"It didn't stop your husband from treating you like dirt. In the end, what changed?"

"I stopped treating everyone else like dirt," she says. "Iris, who was that other Steve, anyway? He looked familiar, like maybe I'd seen him in the pages of *Kitty*. I keep meaning to ask his sister the next time I bump into her."

I think of Vickie and Clare chatting in the elevator. At some point, Clare must have realized who Vickie was and shared their conversations with Steve. How else would he have known how Vickie and her husband were spending their Fourth of July weekend?

"If you do happen to see him, please thank him for me."

"I won't be seeing him again."

"That's too bad. He seemed like a nice person." She sighs softly. "Iris, I miss you. I hope we can see each other soon. In a few weeks, when things settle down, let's please have lunch."

"I'd like that." I don't tell her I won't be here in a few weeks.

A few afternoons later I'm on the phone to PKS Associates, leaving a message for Pat Sweeney, my former boss, when there's a commotion in my hall.

The outer door slams. The inner door slams. Heavy footsteps stamp into the foyer. There's a crash, then the thud of a large object hitting the floor.

"Damn!" someone shouts.

"*Woowoowoowooo!*" Rocky leaps from his spot on the bathroom floor, rushes into the living room, stands on his hind legs and waves his front paws in the air, and then runs into the kitchen. I hear him in there pushing his food bowl around with his nose.

"Anyway, Pat, I'll be back in town soon. I'd love to talk with you about coming back to work as a recruiter," I tell his voice mail in a rush, and hang up. I slide on the safety chain and open the door, peering out into the dim hall. There is Simon, suntanned, sleek—and sprawled on the threadbare rug, surrounded by luggage, trying to extricate himself from the bicycle locked to the staircase.

"Welcome back!" I pull off the chain and rush out to meet him, just now realizing how much I'd missed him. I'd forgotten: Vickie and Steve weren't my only friends here. I couldn't have stuck it out as long as I did without Simon.

"And what a welcome." He makes a tragic face and sticks out his grease-smudged calf. "Who is responsible for this godforsaken rust heap, anyhow? Tonight let's saw off the lock and throw the thing out onto the sidewalk."

"Simon, you have no idea how lonely it was around here

without you." I extend a hand to help him up, then realign his dog tags, peace sign, and cross and inspect the grease stain. "Don't worry, it comes off with rubbing alcohol. How was your summer?"

"I'm in love!" He dusts himself off and gives me a hug. "I'm in love! His name is Shane and he's beautiful. Like Michelangelo's *David*, except circumcised." He holds me out at arm's length. "Kitten, you need a haircut, stat! Give me a few minutes and meet me down in the OR. Just let me get The Elixir in the fridge before it goes bad. Where's the little pudgeball?"

I make a kissing sound. Rocky emerges from the kitchen, tongue lolling. Simon scoops him up and squeezes him. Rocky nibbles on Simon's chin. "I'll write you a check downstairs. You did a good job with him."

"Thank you. It was nice taking care of him. He was the only thing that kept me from throwing myself under a bus."

"You had a bad summer? Why didn't you come stay with me? Rocky would have learned to deal with the beach. What are you doing, competing for the Miss Martyr crown?"

The idea of visiting Simon on Fire Island had never occurred to me. "I assumed you wanted to be alone."

"Oh, brother." Simon pretends to slap himself. "Well, you get free hair and makeup. Downstairs. Deal?"

A half hour later I'm sitting on one of Simon's dining chairs as he alternates between wetting down my hair with a spray bottle and interrogating me.

"Let me get this straight. You did the Porthault tango with Vickie's husband, but you thought he was someone else."

"Wrong. He wasn't Vickie's husband, but I thought he was."

"Vickie's husband who is cheating, or is not cheating?"

"Is." I turn my cheek to avoid getting water in my eyes. "Not with me, with a mousy woman he took to La Goulue."

"Then your Steve: He is cheating or isn't cheating?"

"Isn't. And don't call him 'my' Steve."

"I don't get something. That day Vickie called, when you were hungover, and told you her husband had a meeting on Columbus. When you went up there you saw your Steve, not her Steve. If your Steve isn't Vickie's husband, what was he doing there?"

"Don't call him 'my' Steve. I don't know. The girls at Rubicon make it sound like he's in there all the time buying clothes for women. Or it was a coincidence. New York is one big small town. People cross each other's paths all the time."

"True," Simon agrees. "But you do realize you're the worst detective who ever lived."

"So I've been told. But it's over. I'll never spy on anyone again. And I'm never going to see not-Vickie's-Steve again."

"You mean your Steve."

"Stop calling him that! I hate him."

"On the positive side," Simon says, "you never have to tell Vickie you did the deed with her husband. Since it wasn't her husband after all." He aims his spray bottle at the top of my head and fires. "Have you talked to her?"

"A little." Since our brief phone conversation we've exchanged e-mails, but Vickie has her hands full right now. She and Steve are in couples counseling. She's preparing for the baby and helping organize a benefit she committed to last year. "I'm going to tell her eventually, Simon. Once her life calms down, I'll explain my part in all this mess. Otherwise I'll never be able to live with myself."

Simon stops spritzing. "*Excusez-moi?* No *comprende.*"

"What I did was wrong. I *thought* I was sleeping with her husband. The fact that it wasn't her husband is irrelevant."

"Honey, you are crazy. You didn't sleep with her husband; you slept with someone she had never seen before and didn't

know from Adam. No harm, no foul. Keep it to yourself. I
know of what I speak, kitten. I listen to women all day long.
If Vickie is someone you care about, then spare her the weepy
confession. That's you wanting to clear your conscience.
Didn't you say she's about to have a baby?"

"Yes."

"So she's pregnant for the first time, about to go into labor,
she caught her real husband at a bistro having a real tryst with
a real woman, she has to deal with all of that unpleasantness,
and in the middle of this you want to tell her, 'Sweetie, by the
way, I, too, stabbed you in the back'? Sorry, but you need to
get past this one on your own."

"I owe it to her."

Simon combs a section of my hair between his fingers,
stretches it straight, and trims off a quarter inch. "If you truly
want to do the right thing, you'll carry this one to your grave.
Semper Fi. That's the Marine Corps motto. 'Always Faith-
ful.'"

I don't say anything for a long time, concentrating instead
on the snip-snip of Simon's scissors and the drift of my hair
cuttings falling onto his hardwood floor. As I listen and consider things quietly, I'm surprised to realize Simon is right. It
would be self-indulgent to apologize to Vickie for anything beyond following the wrong man in the first place. It would do
no good to tell her about my affair. Nor does Teddy need to
know, not right away. I made a mistake I won't ever make
again. This I know for certain.

Besides, in a few weeks none of this will matter anymore.
Other things will happen, life will continue, and I'll have the
strength to keep moving forward. The worst is over, and I've
made it through.

"You told me you were in the Army, not the Marines," I
say.

"I was in the Army." Simon takes a step back. "I dated a marine." He considers my hair and snips one final snip over my left ear. "Done." He hands me a mirror. "We should go somewhere. You are absolutely perfect."

I look at my reflection.

For once, I'm not blushing at a compliment.

Simon was speaking the truth when he insisted New York had changed me for the better. I'm not the same person I was when I arrived. I'm stronger and more confident. I don't know what life has in store for me, but I'm not afraid to face it. I've made it here. I've survived New York. *This is who I am*, I think. *I'm going to be okay.*

And then I make a decision that surprises me, even as I know it's right.

"Thank you, Simon, and I would be honored to go somewhere with you another time. Right now I need to make a phone call."

———

"You're positive? It's a big step, and we both should be sure." Teddy sounds more mature than he ever has before. I'm pleasantly surprised at the transformation and hope, for both our sakes, that it will last.

"I've thought it through, and to me it makes sense. I'm hoping you feel the same way." As for myself, I'm trying to sound measured and rational, even though my heart feels about to burst.

"I do," he says. "Yeah. I really do. I did a lot of thinking down in Mexico. I was going to talk to you but was ready to go with whatever you wanted. But that's kind of what I've always done with you, Iris—let you run everything. It's better that we both came to our own conclusions, and even better that it was the same one."

"I agree, Ted."

"This is what you want? You're okay with it?"

"I think we're doing the right thing."

"All right. In a few weeks you should get the documents. You just have to sign in a few places and get it all notarized, and then the healing can begin, or however you say it. I'll repay the tax money I owe you, too. With interest." He pauses. "Why are you laughing? Was it 'The healing can begin?' I knew I was sliding into sappy with that one."

"No . . ." I giggle. I am laughing from happiness and nervousness and sorrow and delight because, in this final decision to separate for good, Teddy and I have just shared the best moment we've ever had together.

I spend the next thirty-six hours in my storage loft, sorting through the last of my moving boxes, making room for mementos I want to keep, by letting go of the things I no longer need to keep. I put my stolen T-shirt collection into boxes, along with shoes and jackets and dresses and shorts and tank tops that suited the old me better than the new. When the boxes are full, I drag them one by one onto the sidewalk. I check from my window a few hours later; everything is gone.

I find my corkscrew at long last, in the bottom corner of the very last box I unpack.

One afternoon I spot a "Help Wanted" sign in the window of the newly opened tapas bar. After a talk with the manager I get a job on the lunch shift. I find that waiting tables is more satisfying than I remember. So far I haven't spilled a single plate on anyone.

I get a call from my college friend Evie, who says she read in the *Los Angeles Times* the wedding announcement of a

Kevin Asgard and a Lynn somebody, in San Marino. Was this my Kevin Asgard?

He was never mine, I tell her.

"That's so terrible. I thought you two were soul mates. You must be crushed."

"I'm not, though. Not at all. Look at it this way, Evie. Kevin found a woman who shares his end-state vision."

The first week of October, the phone rings. I've got a rare day off from work and am intently focused on *The Bold and the Beautiful*, so when the caller says, "It's Sandy!" the name doesn't mean anything.

"Hi." I'm curt, assuming this is Visa or MasterCard saying I'm late again on my minimum payment.

"Sandy Christmas! Remember? I'm wondering if you'd like to do some freelance moderating for me! For the next three months I've got more projects than I can handle! We could start off with you taking over one or two, and if we like working with each other, you can feel free to take as many as you would like! The more the merrier, as far as I'm concerned!"

The pay is two hundred dollars an hour.

"Let me think it over and get back to you." I'm not sure I'm ready to return to marketing. I don't know if I believe in it anymore. Waiting tables may not pay much, but it's simple and straightforward and honest.

"Make that two hundred fifty an hour!"

"When do I start?"

The last week of October I visit Vickie at New York Hospital, where she's given birth two weeks early to a healthy nine-and-a-half-pound baby. I bring white roses and avert my eyes when it's time for her to breast-feed. She tells me not to worry, she's already gotten over all pretensions of modesty, thanks to twenty hours of screaming "back labor." Her face, as she describes the ordeal, glows with happiness.

"And you and Steve. How is the couples counseling going? What are you going to do?" I ask.

"Leave him." Vickie turns an expression close to ecstasy on her newborn—a son, after all, whom she's named William, after her grandfather. The baby has fallen asleep while nursing, his fist curled around a corner of a pink-and-blue striped flannel blanket. "Actually, I'm going to leave him *and* take him for everything he's worth, including the dog. Have you ever heard of Donny 'the Hammer' Rosen, the divorce lawyer? He's ruthless. He, not our therapist, finally got Steve to admit to having affairs—that woman I caught him with was hardly the first—and get himself a blood test for . . . you know."

"He's clean?"

"Thank God. He's fine, so that means I am, and most important, the baby is. I would have killed him if he'd done anything to harm this child. Donny's going to go for way beyond the maximum child support and alimony, and I'll keep the apartment. Between us, Iris, I'd have made do with much less. My life was bourgeois and meaningless, anyway. Naturally I'd still need a huge closet." She laughs. "Which reminds me. I bought you a present."

"You did?"

"A whole lot of presents. Val put up her entire wardrobe of vintage clothing for sale on eBay, and I bought it. She felt those black things were all wrong for an endodontist's wife, but I thought you might enjoy having them. If nothing else, we can have fun watching Val's face when you show up at the wedding in her backless Helmut Lang dress with the peekaboo zippers, and then you can sell the pieces yourself. The collection's worth a small fortune." A shadow crosses her face. "Please tell me you don't think I'm being patronizing."

I hope my expression makes clear how I do feel. "I have only one thing to say."

She looks worried.

"Isn't Val's wedding at the Greenwich Country Club? Wouldn't the zipper dress be inappropriate?"

Her face relaxes back into a smile. "Terribly! But you'll be with me, and I'll be wearing the Courreges minidress. That is, if you'll let me borrow it."

In the end, of course, Vickie is her sister's postpartum maid of honor and wears a perfectly presentable pink silk suit, with absorbent pads in her nursing bra underneath, to Val's wedding. Val floats among her 350 guests in a custom-made, hand-beaded Reem Acra gown. For our dates, Vickie brings William, and I bring Simon. As we pay our respects in the receiving line, Simon studies Val's makeup, leans over to me, and whispers, "Bobbi Brown Number Four."

I wear my dress from Rubicon, though it makes me sad to put it on. I've been coming to terms slowly with Steve's no longer being part of my life, and the idea that it will, eventually, stop hurting to think about him. I've had his phone number blocked so that even if he does call me, I won't be tempted to pick up. Still, I need to pay back the debt I owe him, the debt that every day weighs heavy on my conscience.

———

In November I return home from two moderating sessions in New Jersey to find a FedEx envelope on the table in the foyer. It's to me, return address Teddy's lawyer.

It's final.

It's official.

I'm divorced.

I feel fine.

When I pull out the paperwork, another, smaller envelope falls out. I go into my apartment, settle into my armchair, and open it. Inside are two pieces of paper. One is a handwritten note. "Thank you for everything," it says. "Here's the money I owe you, with interest."

The second piece of paper is a check from Teddy: two thousand dollars. I'm touched at the gift, and I turn the check over in my hands, looking at the blank lines on the reverse waiting for my signature. I turn to the front again and read my former husband's name, Ted Killingwirth, and the address of the house that used to be ours but is his now to take care of.

And then I see I've made a mistake.

The check isn't for two thousand dollars.

It's for twenty thousand dollars.

TWENTY-NINE

Miraculously, it doesn't bounce. Even more miraculously, when I fall to the floor in shock, I manage not to give myself a concussion.

Okay, I don't fall to the floor. I do turn right around, shut the door behind me without bothering to lock the dead bolt, and sprint three blocks to the bank, where I squeak in just under closing. I could deposit the check through the ATM, but I want to see that thing go directly into human hands. I endorse it and slip it to the teller through the little space in the Plexiglas barrier, and consider asking her to pinch me.

It isn't a dream. The money clears ten days later, and after I put half of it in savings for future "times like this," I spend one satisfying evening paying off my credit card balances in full, in front of the television. Then I open a bottle of wine, pour some into my lone wineglass, and, all by myself, make a toast.

"To survival." I raise my glass. "Survival," I echo, and take a sip. It tastes wonderful. Even all by myself.

On TV a commercial is playing. In it, a smiling career woman applies New Ultra Placid Extra to her underarms, grabs her briefcase, and steps confidently out of her house, tossing her hair as she goes.

"Go after it, girl!" my former husband says.

———————

After that, there are only two items left on my emotional to-do list, and one of them, I admit, I haven't worked up the nerve for. That's to speak with my mother. Since the day of the ill-fated meet-and-greet I've picked up the phone a dozen times but have always backed out at the last minute. I finally conclude that I'm not quite ready for a full conversation, and give myself permission to start smaller.

TO: Joy
FROM: Iris Hedge
SUBJ: Long time

True to form, I start and discard this one about a dozen times, too. I want to tell her I finally understand that life isn't black-and-white, that people can do bad things and maybe learn from them and change, and that I've spent too long blaming her for the problems in my life without understanding the problems she might have had in hers. For now, such a sweeping declaration is more than I can handle. A short note, however, is not.

TO: Joy
FROM: Iris Hedge
SUBJ: Long time

Dear Joy:

I'm sorry I didn't get to see you while you were here. I tried to stop by your hotel room but I'm not sure you saw me, and then I got overwhelmed and left.

I just want you to know that everything is fine.

Your daughter,
Iris

I hit "Send," and then call Rubicon and ask for Ilona. She seems thrilled to hear from me. "I thought you moved back to California!"

I changed my mind, I tell her. And I wanted to make sure she was working today, because I have a favor to ask.

"Iris, it's just wonderful you decided to stay in New York. Name your favor. I'm happy to help."

"I'd like you to pass something along to Steve. I'm sure he's told you he and I . . . I mean, you see him every once in a while. Don't you? He still comes in occasionally?"

Ilona laughs. "Occasionally. You could say so."

I hate that my breath catches at the thought of Steve bringing other women to the shop and loaning them money, too.

"You should know, my dear, that he was taken by you the first day he met you. He talked about you—a cute, peculiar girl who ran over him in the park. He said he'd felt an instant connection and wished he had asked for your phone number. When he kept on crossing paths with you after that, he said it was as if fate were bringing you together. I don't think he would have done any of this if he hadn't thought you were the one he couldn't let get away. And of course he didn't realize you had engineered everything."

My turn to laugh, or at least try to.

"I'm sorry, Iris. Excuse me for one moment." I hear her cup her hand over the receiver and say to a customer, "The black, definitely. You do know black is the new black?" Then, to me, "Please forgive me. You were saying?"

"I won't keep you. I'll come by quickly and drop this off. Would half an hour from now be all right?"

"Hmm. Better make it an hour."

"All right. And thanks."

"Anything I can do to help," Ilona answers.

I dress up for Rubicon. Partly it's vanity, not wanting to feel dowdy yet again next to the beautiful Ilona. But it's also that I've become accustomed to looking the part. I may not have been born and raised in New York City, but that doesn't mean I have to broadcast it.

I love my new fall wardrobe. Yes, fall. It's official, with the leaves in Central Park "at peak"—in full autumn color. I've long since put away my summer-weight Rubicon dress, skirt, and blouse, and though I am wearing the pants from my pantsuit, I've dipped into my treasure trove of vintage Val-wear for a nubby tweed Chanel jacket—over which, after pulling it out of the carton, I nearly fainted—and a scarf of an unidentified fur just moth-eaten enough to drive home the point that I'm not trying too hard. I know this because when I ran the outfit past Simon, he's the one who suggested the scarf.

Then he added, "Hang in there, lambie. Any day now, this'll all be second nature to you."

I find an envelope and slip into it a check for payment in full of Steve's loan—the entire sum, not just the "balance" left over after I supposedly worked part of it off. I also include interest, at the same rate my Visa card charges. My little inner voice, sounding suspiciously like my dear great-aunt Zinnia, chides me that a proper lady would also include a brief note thanking Steve for his generosity and apologizing for the delay in repayment. I plead extenuating circumstances and seal the envelope with just the money. Just before I'm about to leave I check my e-mail.

TO: Iris Hedge
FROM: Joy
SUBJ: RE: Long time

Dearest Daughter:

I did see you at my meet-and-greet. I went to find you and was disappointed that you'd left.

I am glad you are on the path to wellness after your split from Teddy. Leaving your father was an important step in my spiritual awakening, but it was the hardest thing I've ever done. It took me a long time to feel whole. Remember, Iris, that life is a journey. Keep your heart open and you will love again.

Please keep in touch.

Love,
Joy

P.S. To help light your way I am sending you an awareness candle.

It's a start.

I step out onto the street. The sky has gone black, and a chilly gray wind spins dead leaves into sidewalk cyclones. Maybe when I get back home I'll light a Presto Log and re-inaugurate my fireplace. I pick up the pace to Rubicon's front door, where the doorman, seeing my face, nods and lets me in. Two wealthy-looking women on the sidewalk give me what seem to be envious glances. "She's on the list," one of them says before the heavy barrier shuts behind me.

Ilona, busy with a customer at the register, gives me a small smile and mouths, *Wait.* No problem; I'm content to browse. I am so relieved to be putting this debt behind me—the last thing keeping me from closing the door on my former life—I almost feel like rewarding myself with new clothes. Simon did say I'd need a heavy coat. I admire a stylishly cut parka, which the store is showing accessorized with suede boots and a cloche. I'm not really going to spend money today. But Sandy Christmas seems pleased with my work and has scheduled me to help her on two more projects. Meanwhile, Carmen Riggio, happy on maternity leave, called last week to say she's considering not returning to Hayes Heeley, and that if she doesn't, Michelle will be looking for someone to take her place. "If nothing else," Carmen said, "you can bet Val won't want to commute from Darien for much longer." My chances of being fully employed again, in the near future even, seem to be looking up.

Ilona sends her customer out of the shop with a hug and a promise to have her purchases delivered by this evening. She waves me over to the register.

I walk over and lean against the counter. "I have a question for you, Ilona. Something has been bothering me about this place."

"Ask me anything."

"Why does Rubicon have a list? It seems so elitist and snobby that only certain people are allowed in."

Ilona leans close and whispers. "Want to know a secret? It's not that hard to get on the list. See Hugo over there?" She indicates the doorman. "Hugo has a photographic memory. The first time you come to the store and knock on the door, he won't let you in. But if you come back a day, week, or even months later, Hugo will recognize you and happily open the door. See? It just takes a little persistence."

"Then why not just let anyone in? What's the point?"

Ilona laughs. "It's the world's greatest marketing gimmick. If we let anyone in, we'd be just another boutique in New York. Haven't you ever noticed that the more you can't have something, the more you want it?"

"I've noticed," I admit, blushing.

"Now," she says. "What can I do for you? I saw you loving that parka."

"I promise someday soon to come back here and clean the place out. For now, would you mind please passing this along?" I pull the envelope from my purse.

Ilona doesn't take it. She claps her hands to her cheeks cartoonishly. "Silly me! I have something for you in the back. Let me go get it, and then I'll take that."

She vanishes into the back room. As she steps in, Chantal, the salesgirl who took care of Rocky, emerges. She's holding a tray with a glass of champagne. "Nice to have you back." Chantal holds out the tray. "For you. Management insists."

"That's sweet, but I'm only here for a moment."

The door swings open, and Ilona steps back through. Her eyes are sparkling. In her hand is a glass of champagne.

"Weren't you listening, Iris? Management insists."

The voice doesn't belong to Ilona. It belongs to Clare, who follows behind her, also holding a glass.

"Have some, Iris. Management refuses to take no for an answer."

That voice doesn't belong to Clare. It belongs to Steve, who follows behind her, also holding a glass. Finally, from behind Steve, steps Jessica, with a sippy cup of juice. She doesn't say anything, just looks at me with guileless, curious eyes.

My heart is pounding as hard as if I were running the Central Park Reservoir.

"This is management." Steve puts one arm over Clare's shoulder. "My little sister Clare, manager of Rubicon and Rubicon Annex."

"Welcome to our humble shop," Clare says, and smiles.

Steve reaches down and touches Jessica on the head. "Miss Jessica, Rubicon mascot."

Jessica hides behind Steve's legs.

"And I'm kind of—"

"The money man," Clare interrupts. "Former Wall Street banking whiz turned Rubicon principal investor and fashion arbiter. You probably recognize him from the party pictures in the *Times*."

Steve looks embarrassed. "That was years ago, Clare. I don't go out anymore."

Ilona says, "These days he keeps to himself, comes in here,

or to Rubicon Downtown, to handle all the billing and book-keeping, and then goes straight home to be with Jessica. She's the only woman in his life."

"You two are the ones . . ." I look at Ilona. "Of course. Steve and Clare are the ones you were telling me about, your bosses, going through the custody trial. But why was Clare involved?"

Steve says, "It was just me going through the trial. Clare was there for support. And she must have done something right, because the trial's finally over, and I won." He picks up Jessica and hugs her. "You're all mine, now and forever, little one."

"Dada." Jessica snuggles into his neck.

"He's absolutely devoted to that little girl," Ilona tells me. "He's raised her from birth."

"We're all so relieved," Clare says. She lowers her voice. "Stephanie, she walked out on them, you know. Now she's shacked up in Palm Beach with an eighty-year-old hotel mogul. She finally just gave up and signed away her daughter."

"The witch," whispers Ilona.

"It's the only decent thing she's ever done in her life," whispers Clare.

"Not now, you two," Steve says, indicating Jessica.

Clare says, "He won't let us say one bad thing about S-T-E-P-H-A-N-I-E in front of the baby."

Jessica says, "Bops?"

Ilona laughs. "Somebody was back there playing with a big cardboard box." She kisses the top of Jessica's head. "Would you like me to take you back to the box?"

Jessica holds out her hands. Ilona reaches out to take her from Steve. "Go ahead, everyone. Keep talking. I'll watch her. Steve, did you bring the photos of her in the little pink dress?"

"They're in back, in the Photo/Copy Express bag."

Ilona winks at him as she carries the little girl into the back room, leaving me, Steve, and Clare.

"Look, that's Deeda Mendenhoffer over there. Isn't the Eastside Children's Home Autumn Gala this weekend? She looks as if she'd like some help." Clare glides over toward the shoes.

And then there were two.

Steve hands me the glass of champagne. He steps around from behind the register, joining me on the customer side of the counter. He looks into my eyes and smiles, sweet and hopeful, and though I fight it, when he touches my arm my anger and resolve start to crumble.

"I'm doing fine without you," I tell him.

"But Iris . . ." He sets down his glass and reaches for my hand. His skin feels cool against mine. "I'm not fine at all without you." And before I can answer, I'm in his arms again, our faces inches away, breathing each other in, wanting to make the connection complete. "Come outside for a minute," he says. "Will you, please?"

Outside, the sky has grown darker and the wind stronger. The sidewalks are nearly deserted, as people scurry back to their warm apartments.

Steve doesn't seem to notice. "I've been wanting to tell you a few things." He raises his voice against the wind. "The first is that I'm sincerely sorry for what I did. I wanted to ask you out on a real date every time we bumped into each other, but I never could work up the nerve. I should have done it that day by the Daniel Webster statue, when I realized you weren't working for my ex and had me confused with someone else. I was trying to get up the nerve when you came up with the idea to keep meeting. That speech you made! It hit home for me. Part of me really believed that I could do this good deed, help save someone from divorce, and be with you at the same time. In my insane state I thought I'd see you once or twice more, pass along some generic advice, and finally tell you the truth and ask you out."

I can't help but be touched. "You were too scared to ask me out? Why?"

"I don't know. What I felt for you, I hadn't felt for any woman since Stephanie. It was overwhelming. I wasn't ready for that again. Then, just as I was getting comfortable with the feeling, I realized if I did confess, you would be gone from my life. Do you remember that day in front of Rubicon? You said the only reason you had anything to do with me was because I was Vickie's husband. After that I consciously decided to keep playing along, just to have you in my life. I can't believe I even put my old wedding ring back on." He shakes his head. "What an idiot."

"It's true, though. I wouldn't have ever seen you again."

"I suppose that's a small consolation." The wind blows my fur scarf up against my cheek and rumples Steve's hair. "It was when you said Vickie was pregnant that I finally realized things had gone too far, and that's when I left that message saying I wouldn't meet anymore. Still, every time I visit Clare I want to knock on Vickie's door to apologize for what I've done. Do you think it would do any good? Is she all right?"

"She's doing quite well. She wants to thank you. She says your advice changed her life."

A momentary look of relief crosses Steve's face. "And you, Iris. I hope someday you'll be able to forgive me."

An empty paper coffee cup rattles across our path. Steve raises his voice against the wind. "The other thing is, in case I've left you with this impression, that I don't believe wives should bow down to their husbands. No more than I believe husbands should bow down to their wives. When I gave you those pointers, I was just trying to think of what a woman might do to improve her own behavior. I picked behaviors a lot of men seem to complain about, but that isn't to say there aren't plenty of things men do that women deserve to complain about. In no way did I mean to imply that women are the only ones responsible in a marriage."

"You didn't?" I shout back.

Steve takes my arm and leads me into the doorway of ACME Cleaning Supply, a lotion and bubble bath shop a few doors away. It's shielded from the elements and a bit warmer. I glance across and down the street at the storefront church whose doorway I stood in to spy on him six months ago. The steel doors are now painted green instead of orange, and there's a freshly lettered sign over the door with a picture of a dove holding an olive branch in its mouth.

In a more normal voice, Steve continues, "I wanted to do what I could for this unfortunate woman I didn't know. I knew she had no control over how her husband chose to behave—I learned from my own marriage that none of us has control over anyone else. In my own backward way, I thought maybe I could help her be the best person she could be, so that if the marriage failed, she'd know she'd done all she could. That's what I wish I could say about my marriage."

"You said your wife was crazy."

"She's a very troubled person. Still, I can't blame her for everything that went wrong. Nothing is ever that simple."

I take his hand. He's not wearing a coat, and his fingers are freezing. I lace my fingers with his and try to transfer any remaining warmth to him. "No, Steve. It never is."

He's going to kiss me.

He's really going to kiss me.

"I'm not ready to get serious with someone, Steve. Not yet."

"Then let's go slowly," he says.

He leans in and kisses me softly. All it takes is that one kiss, and nothing that's gone wrong between us matters anymore. He presses his lips to mine harder, his hands on either side of my face, clutching me to him as if he never wants to let me go. I let him hold me, let myself imagine a life with him in it, let myself admit I want that more than I've wanted anything in a long time. When he finally does pull away, he brings his lips to my ear and whispers, "I love you, Iris Hedge."

"I love you, too, Steve . . ." I stop then and pull back.

"What is it?"

"What's your last name, anyway?"

He laughs. "Turner."

"Steve Turner." I try it out, testing the feel of it. "You're sure?"

"Positive," he murmurs. "Any other questions?"

I have hundreds of them. I want to know if he feels Jessica is ready to accept me in his life, even as just a friend of her father's. I want to ask him what I can do to help her feel more comfortable with me. I want to know if he puts his socks in the hamper. I want to know what exactly went bad between him and his ex, why she walked out, what he feels he did wrong, whether he's over her. I want to know where he grew up, what books he reads, what he eats for breakfast, whether he prefers white wine or red.

Before I can think of where to begin, a woman comes up to us. She's about my age, wearing sweatpants and sneakers and a bewildered expression. I wonder if maybe she isn't from around here, and wait for her to approach Steve for directions.

She turns to me instead. "I'm lost. Can you help?"

I tell her I'll do my best.

"I'm trying to get to the Museum of the City of New York and have no idea which way to go."

"You're on the wrong side of town, but don't worry. Just

walk over a block to Central Park West and then four blocks up to the subway stop at Eighty-sixth Street. Take the train uptown—make sure you're going uptown—one stop to Ninety-sixth. Then you transfer to the M106 bus, take it across the park, and get off as close as you can to One-hundred-and-third Street. You'll be on Madison, so you'll walk back one block . . ."

It's clear this woman won't remember a thing as soon as she walks away. It's too much.

"You know what? It's cold and late. You might want to go to the New-York Historical Society instead. It's a block over and two blocks down, and they have a great exhibit of photos of New York immigrants. That is, unless you have to get to the other museum today."

"I don't." She pulls her denim jacket more tightly around her. "I've got time. I just moved here."

"For what it's worth, it gets easier."

She heads off into the wind, in the direction I've pointed her. Steve and I watch to make sure she doesn't make a wrong turn.

When she's out of sight, he looks at me with love and admiration shining in his eyes. "How do you know so much about New York?"

"I live here," I say, and pull him in for a kiss.

About the Author

I wrote this novel because I was tired of being constrained by the facts.

For almost half my life I've been a journalist, for the most part a newspaper reporter. And, a few bad apples aside, newspaper reporters take facts very seriously. Facts are not things to be invented, distorted, ignored, or otherwise messed with.

After college I went to journalism school at the University of Southern California. One of my very first assignments was to sit for a day in a courtroom, any courtroom, and report on whatever happened to transpire. Out of sheer indolence, and because it was such an ordeal to find parking downtown near the really exciting courts, I chose to observe traffic court— where people fight speeding tickets. For hours I sat, reporter's notebook in hand, glazing over as people came before the judge with their petty, unnewsworthy complaints. One man successfully contested a ticket he'd gotten for rolling through a stop sign by arguing that an untrimmed city shrub had blocked the sign from view. This was about as good as it got. My assignment was due the next day.

Back at my apartment I called my parents, dismayed. "I have nothing to write about," I told them. "Nothing happened. I'm going to flunk out."

"So make something up," joked my dad. "Who would know?"

By then it had been drilled into my head that this was the absolute worst, number-one no-no of my chosen profession: You Can't Write About Something Unless It Really Happened. "Would you go to a doctor who'd cheated her way through medical school?" I answered in a minor self-righteous huff.

Still, I can't say Dad's idea hasn't whispered itself in my ear at many frustrating moments in the years since. When an editor, looking over my article about people with shoe-free homes, would say, "Cute story. You know what would make it a cover story? Go find some guest who went to somebody's shoe-free house and ended up breaking a toe," I'd for a moment wish it *were* okay to make things up. Do you know what it takes to track down an anecdote that specific? Well, now I do: You have to cold-call the entire United States of America, one home at a time.

But if, halfway through writing a novel, you find yourself wishing your main character's name were Iris instead of Ivy or wishing daffodils were still in bloom in May, thinking, *It would be so much more interesting if she were in the middle of a divorce, rather than already divorced,* or wanting to change any other aspect of the who, what, when, where, or why, you may do so. In novel-writing, this sort of thing is encouraged. I have to say, the vacation from reality has been a joy.

As for that journalism-school assignment, let the record reflect that in the end, I turned in a brilliant—and entirely accurate—retelling of the stop-sign story.

Visit my Web site at www.laurenlipton.com.

Lauren Lipton

 **5** SPOT ⬛ •••• SEND OFF

Five more New York City–girl remedies for Iris's little crises:

1. Blisters. There's no such product as Ultra Placid. But the antiperspirant trick really does work—and any brand will do—especially with sandals. Under closed shoes Iris could have used a second line of defense: toe covers. These weird little protective triangles, which look like the toe ends snipped off a pair of pantyhose, are available at drugstores and department stores, and probably two out of three Manhattan socialites are secretly wearing them inside their Manolo pumps.

2. Home hair-dye disaster. If she could tell her hair color was too intense after she rinsed it out, Iris could have gotten right back into that shower while her hair was still wet and washed it again. (Ideally she'd have a clarifying shampoo, like Neutrogena Anti-Residue Shampoo, just kind of lying around the house.) She'd have gotten a bit more of the dye out, and in desperate times we take help in whatever increments we can get.

3. Humidity hair. Iris would need to forgo groceries for six months to afford one, but the Japanese straightening treatment at Salon Ishi is genius for keeping blown-out hair from going awry during New York summers.

4. Makeup phobia. Benetint, by BeneFit, is a liquid lip stain that's scary-pink in the bottle but goes on to look like your lips, only rosier. Had Iris worn some under her ChapStick, she would have looked not like a woman wearing no makeup, but like a naturally perfect woman wearing no makeup. (Oh—and, because I know you're wondering, Bobbi Brown Number Four is a real lipstick shade, also known as Bobbi Brown "Brown.")

5. Olive oil on her pantsuit. Someone who'd lived in New York longer would have heard of the Professional Stain Remover Kit from Upper East Side dry cleaner Madame Paulette. Each travel-sized kit contains three separate chemical formulas. You choose which to use depending on the stain (oil = solution number three) then play mad scientist, dabbing on the top-secret ingredients in sequence. Ten minutes later you're stain-free and feeling inordinately pleased with yourself.